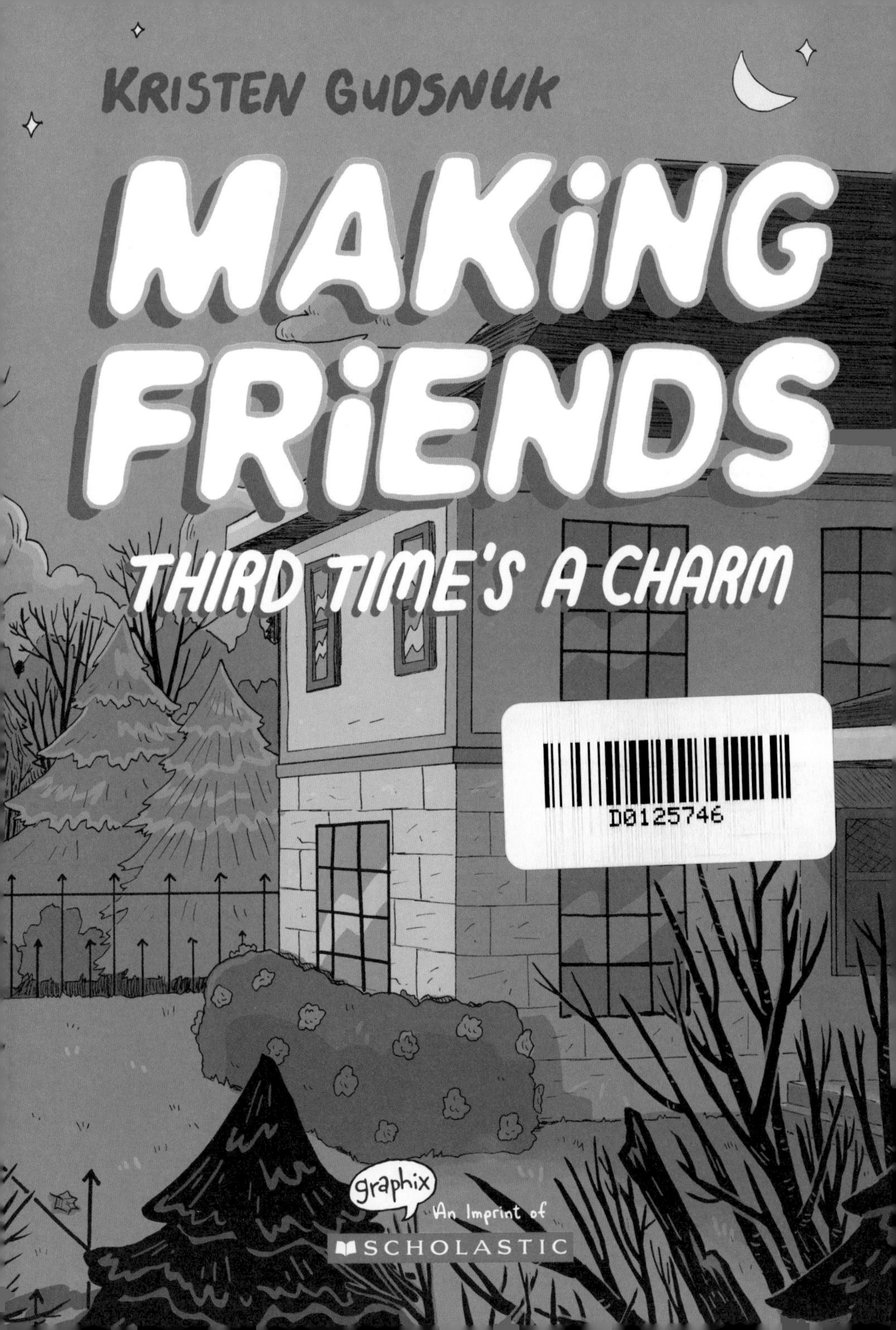
KRISTEN GUDSNUK
MAKiNG FRiENDS
THIRD TIME'S A CHARM
graphix
An Imprint of
SCHOLASTIC

Library of Congress Control Number: 2020946621

ISBN 978-1-338-63080-0 (hardcover)
ISBN 978-1-338-63079-4 (paperback)

10 9 8 7 6 5 4 3 2 1   21 22 23 24 25

Printed in China 62
First edition, August 2021
Edited by Megan Peace
Creative Director: Phil Falco
Publisher: David Saylor

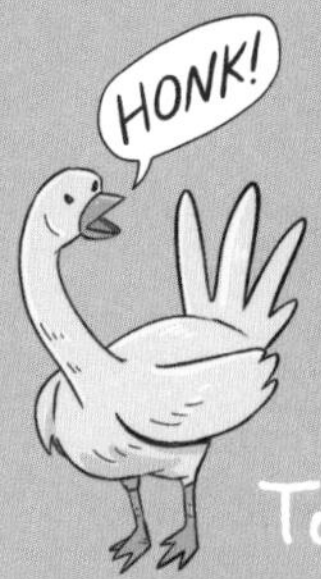
HONK!

To Jordan

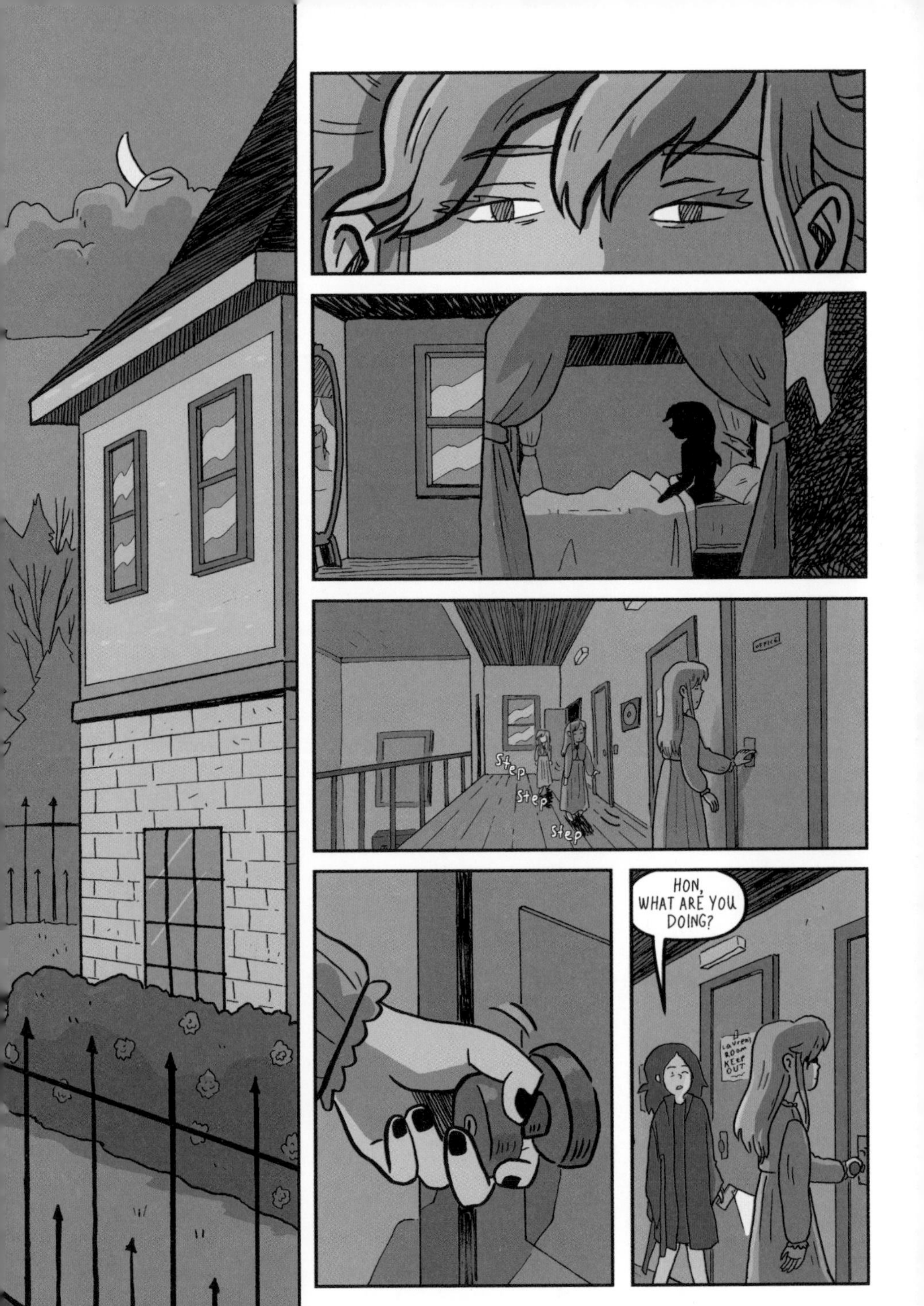

step
step
step
HON, WHAT ARE YOU DOING?
LAUREN'S ROOM KEEP OUT

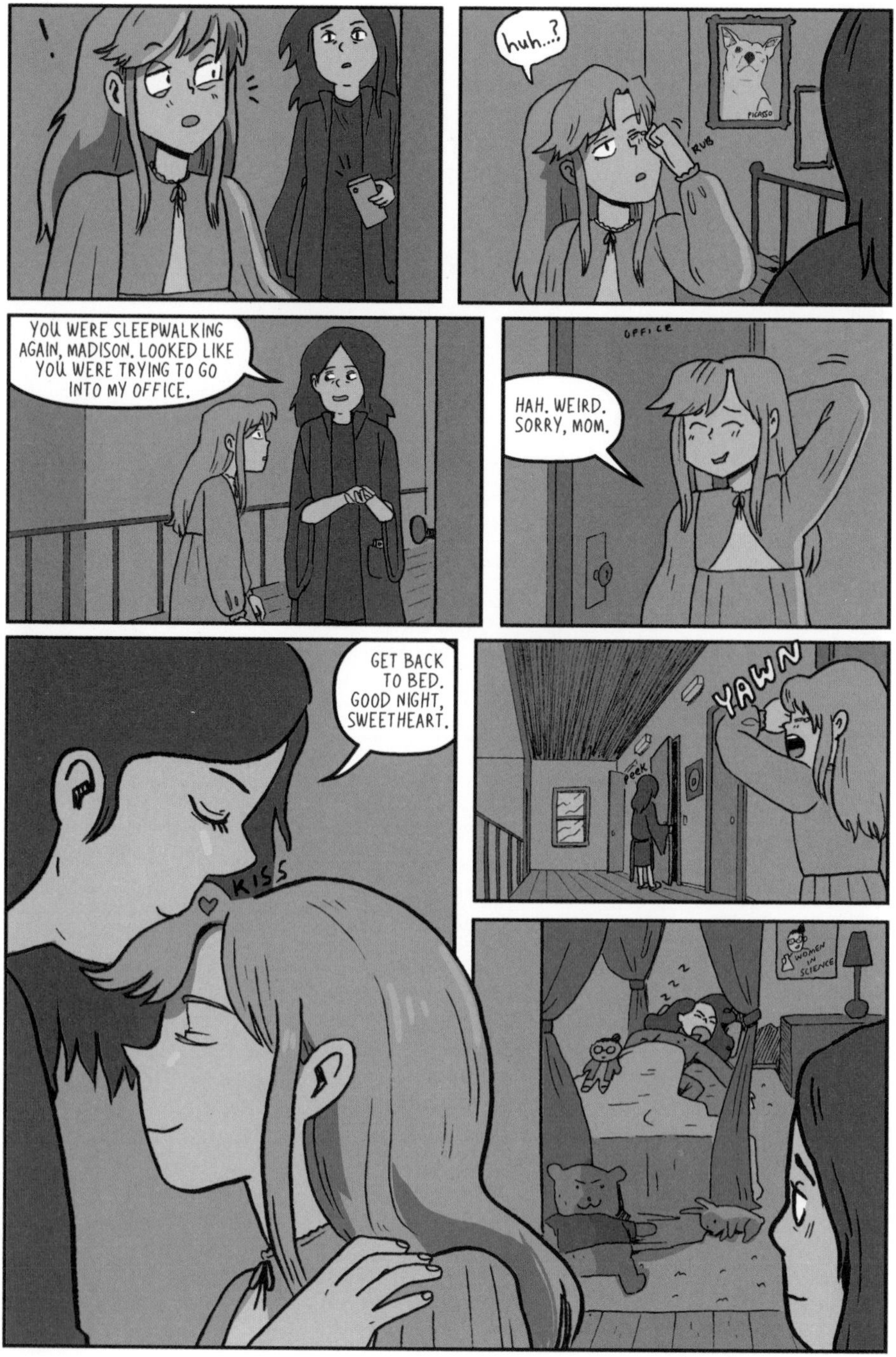
!
huh...?
PICASSO
RUB
YOU WERE SLEEPWALKING AGAIN, MADISON. LOOKED LIKE YOU WERE TRYING TO GO INTO MY OFFICE.
OFFICE
HAH. WEIRD. SORRY, MOM.
GET BACK TO BED. GOOD NIGHT, SWEETHEART.
KISS
YAWN
PEEK
WOMEN IN SCIENCE

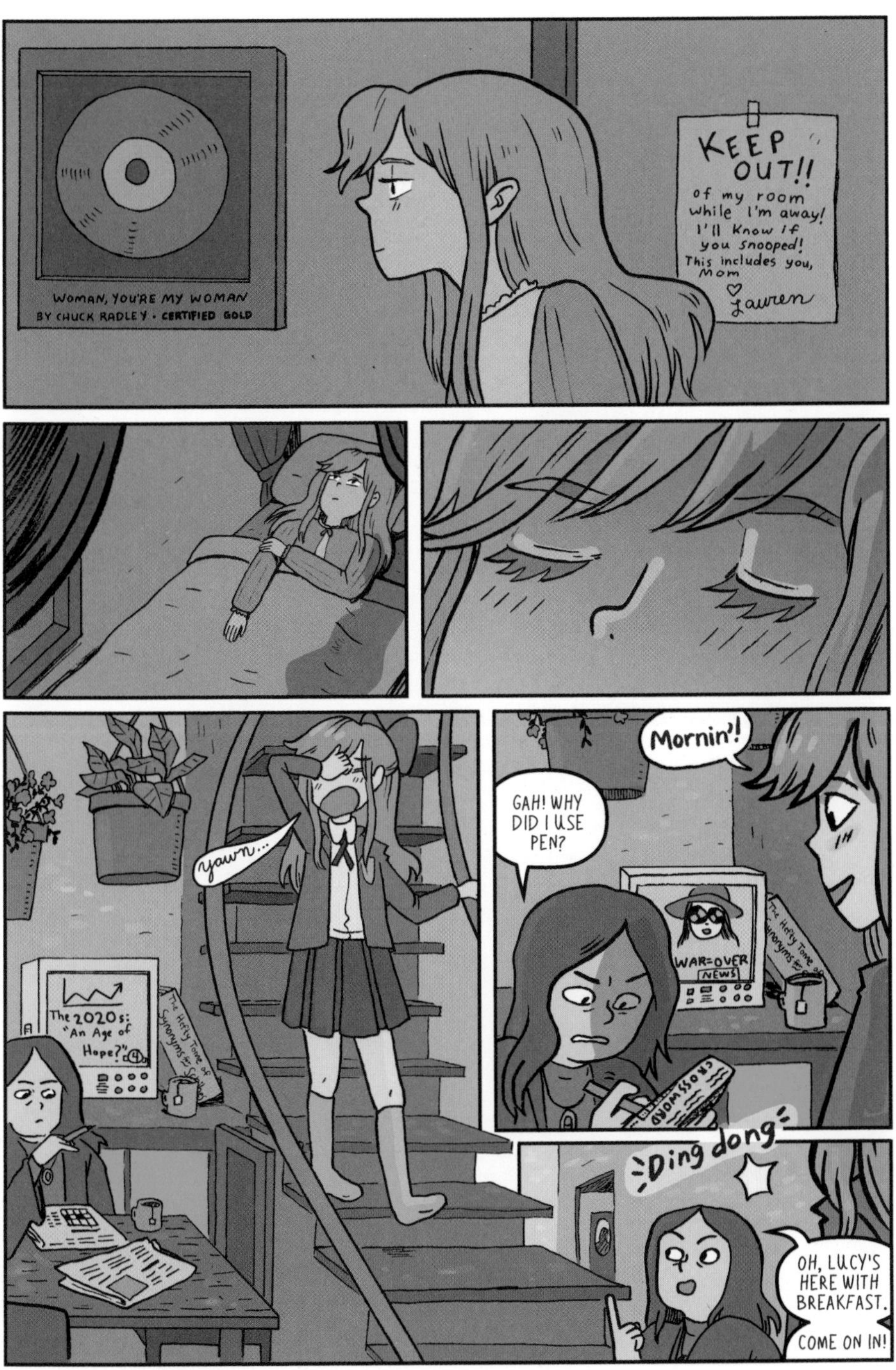
WOMAN, YOU'RE MY WOMAN
BY CHUCK RADLEY • CERTIFIED GOLD
KEEP OUT!!
of my room while I'm away! I'll Know if you snooped! This includes you, Mom
Lauren
yawn...
The 2020s: "An Age of Hope?"
The Hefty Tome of Synonyms
Mornin'!
GAH! WHY DID I USE PEN?
WAR=OVER
NEWS
CROSSWORD
Ding dong
OH, LUCY'S HERE WITH BREAKFAST.
COME ON IN!

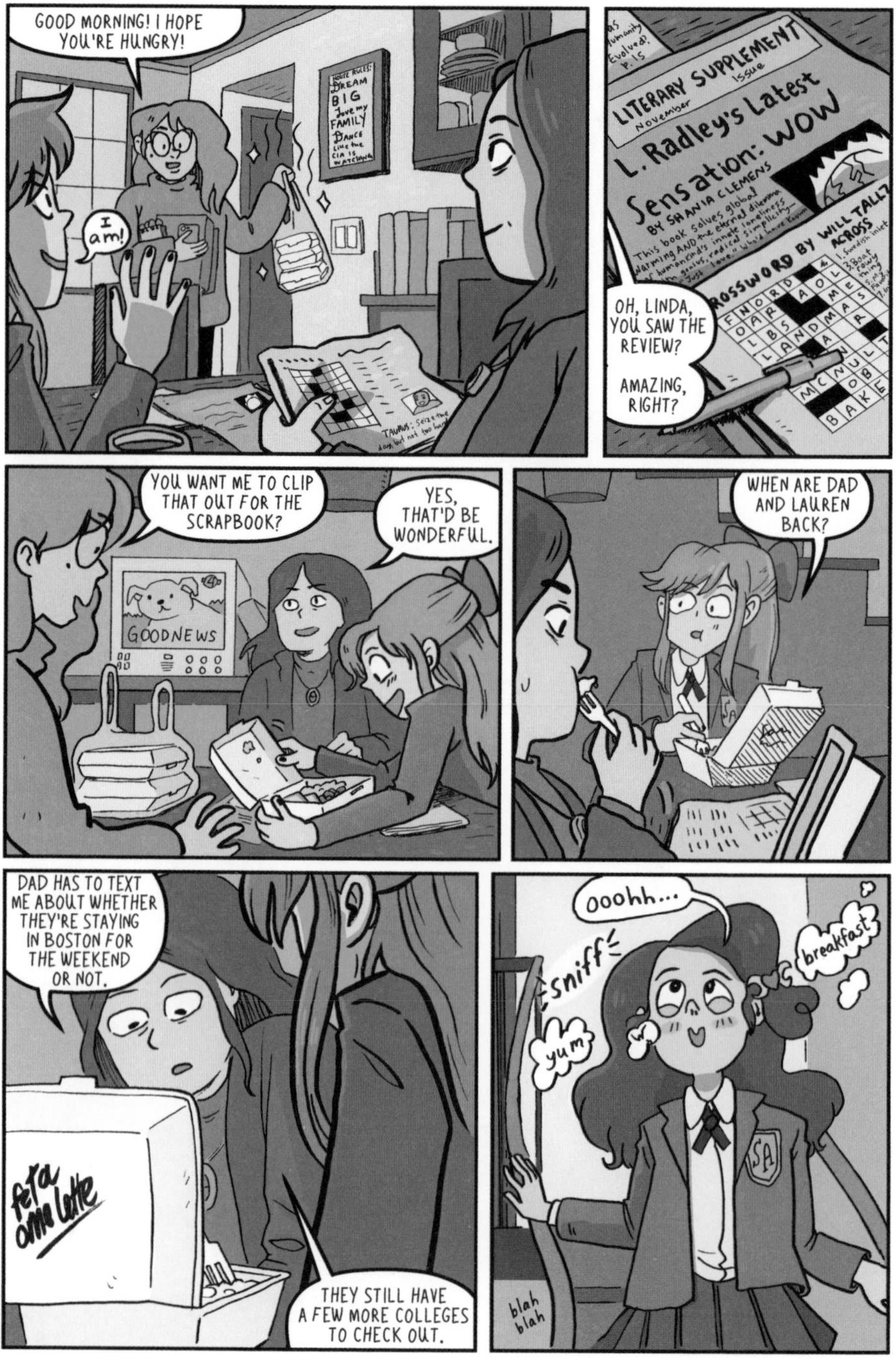
GOOD MORNING! I HOPE YOU'RE HUNGRY!
I am!
HOUSE RULES: DREAM BIG Love my FAMILY DANCE like the CIA is WATCHING
LITERARY SUPPLEMENT
November Issue
L. Radley's Latest Sensation: WOW
BY SHANIA CLEMENS
CROSSWORD BY WILL TALLZ
ACROSS
OH, LINDA, YOU SAW THE REVIEW?
AMAZING, RIGHT?
YOU WANT ME TO CLIP THAT OUT FOR THE SCRAPBOOK?
YES, THAT'D BE WONDERFUL.
GOODNEWS
WHEN ARE DAD AND LAUREN BACK?
DAD HAS TO TEXT ME ABOUT WHETHER THEY'RE STAYING IN BOSTON FOR THE WEEKEND OR NOT.
feta omelette
THEY STILL HAVE A FEW MORE COLLEGES TO CHECK OUT.
ooohh...
sniff
breakfast
yum
blah blah

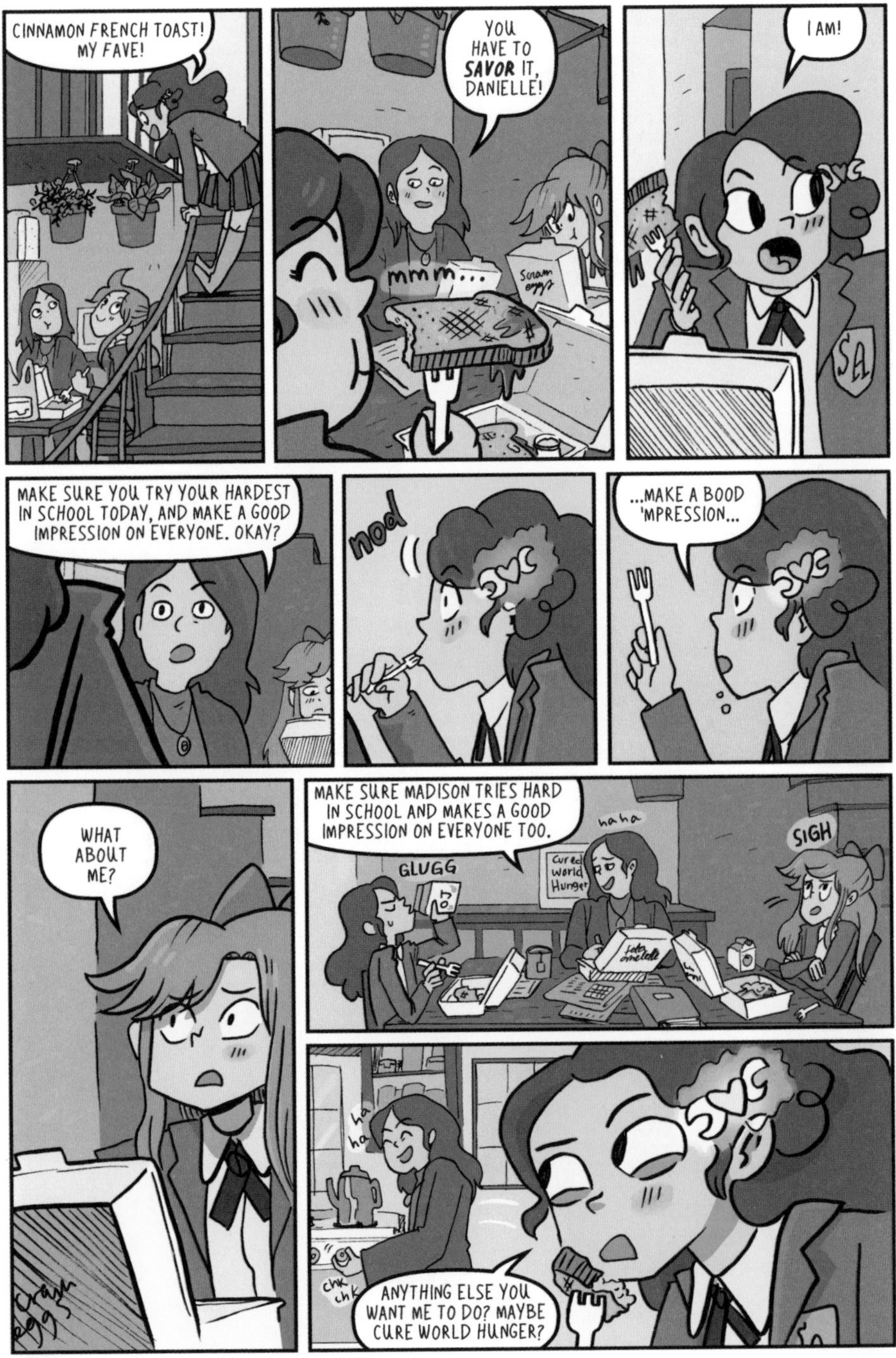
CINNAMON FRENCH TOAST! MY FAVE!
YOU HAVE TO **SAVOR** IT, DANIELLE!
mmm....
I AM!
MAKE SURE YOU TRY YOUR HARDEST IN SCHOOL TODAY, AND MAKE A GOOD IMPRESSION ON EVERYONE. OKAY?
nod
...MAKE A BOOD 'MPRESSION...
WHAT ABOUT ME?
MAKE SURE MADISON TRIES HARD IN SCHOOL AND MAKES A GOOD IMPRESSION ON EVERYONE TOO.
haha
GLUGG
Cured World Hunger
SIGH
ha ha
chk chk
ANYTHING ELSE YOU WANT ME TO DO? MAYBE CURE WORLD HUNGER?

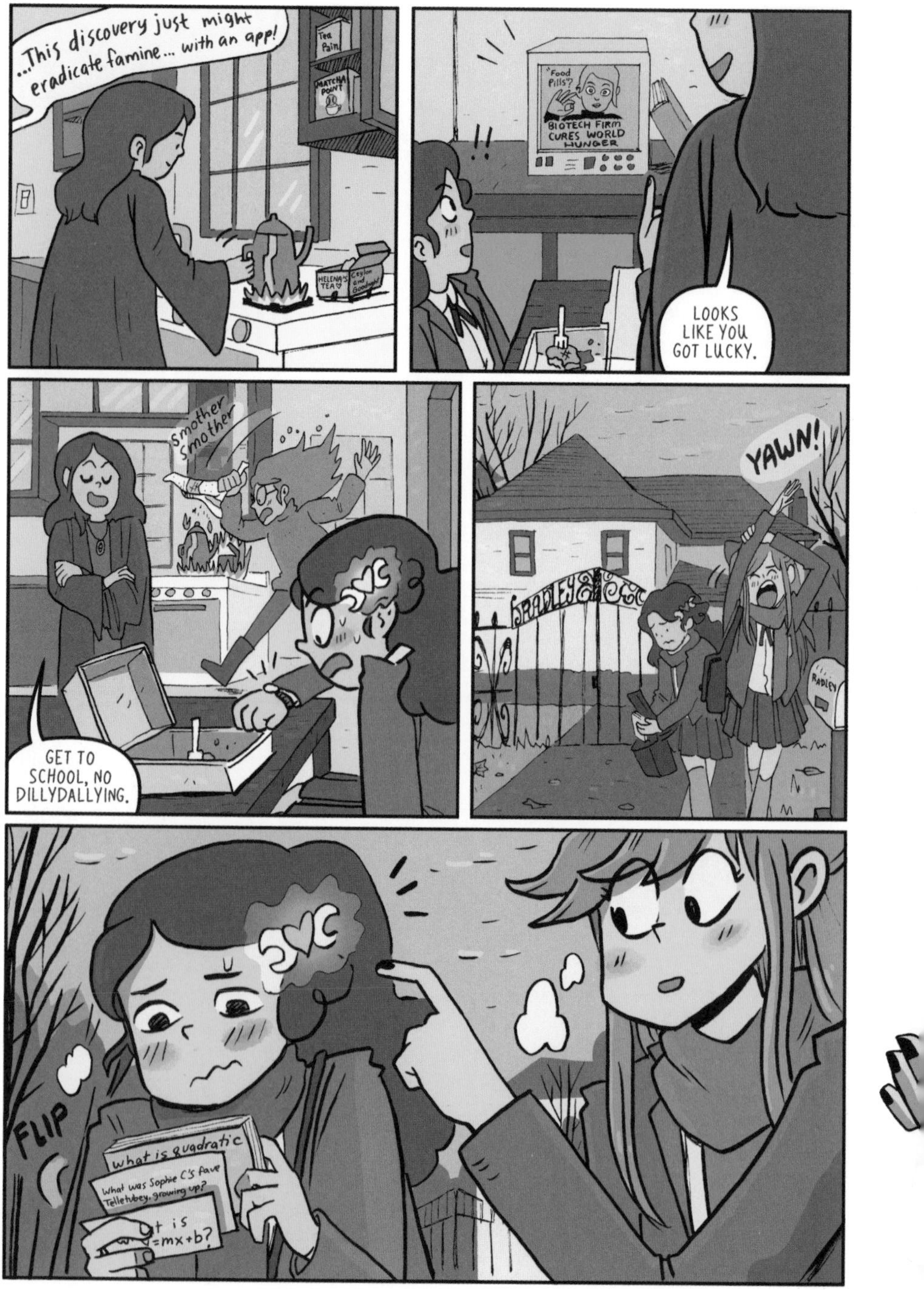

...This discovery just might eradicate famine... with an app!
Tea Pain
MATCHA POINT
HELENA'S TEA
Ceylon and Goodnight
"Food Pills"?
BIOTECH FIRM CURES WORLD HUNGER
!!
LOOKS LIKE YOU GOT LUCKY.
smother smother
GET TO SCHOOL, NO DILLYDALLYING.
YAWN!
RADLEY
RADLEY
FLIP
what is quadratic
What was Sophie C's fave Telletubey, growing up?
=mx+b?

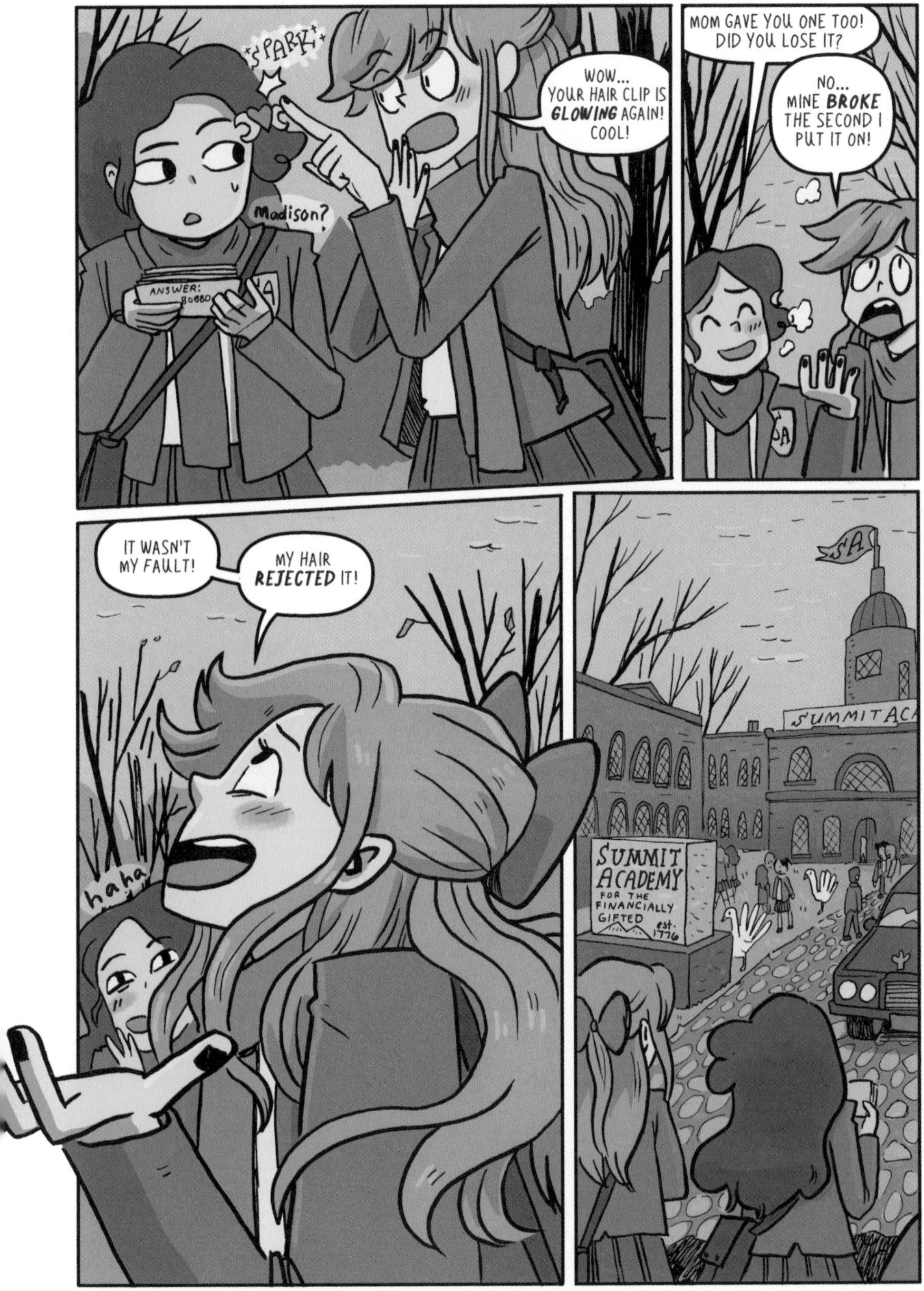
SPARK
WOW... YOUR HAIR CLIP IS **GLOWING** AGAIN! COOL!
Madison?
ANSWER: BOBBO
MOM GAVE YOU ONE TOO! DID YOU LOSE IT?
NO... MINE **BROKE** THE SECOND I PUT IT ON!
IT WASN'T MY FAULT!
MY HAIR **REJECTED** IT!
haha
SUMMIT ACA
SUMMIT ACADEMY FOR THE FINANCIALLY GIFTED est. 1776

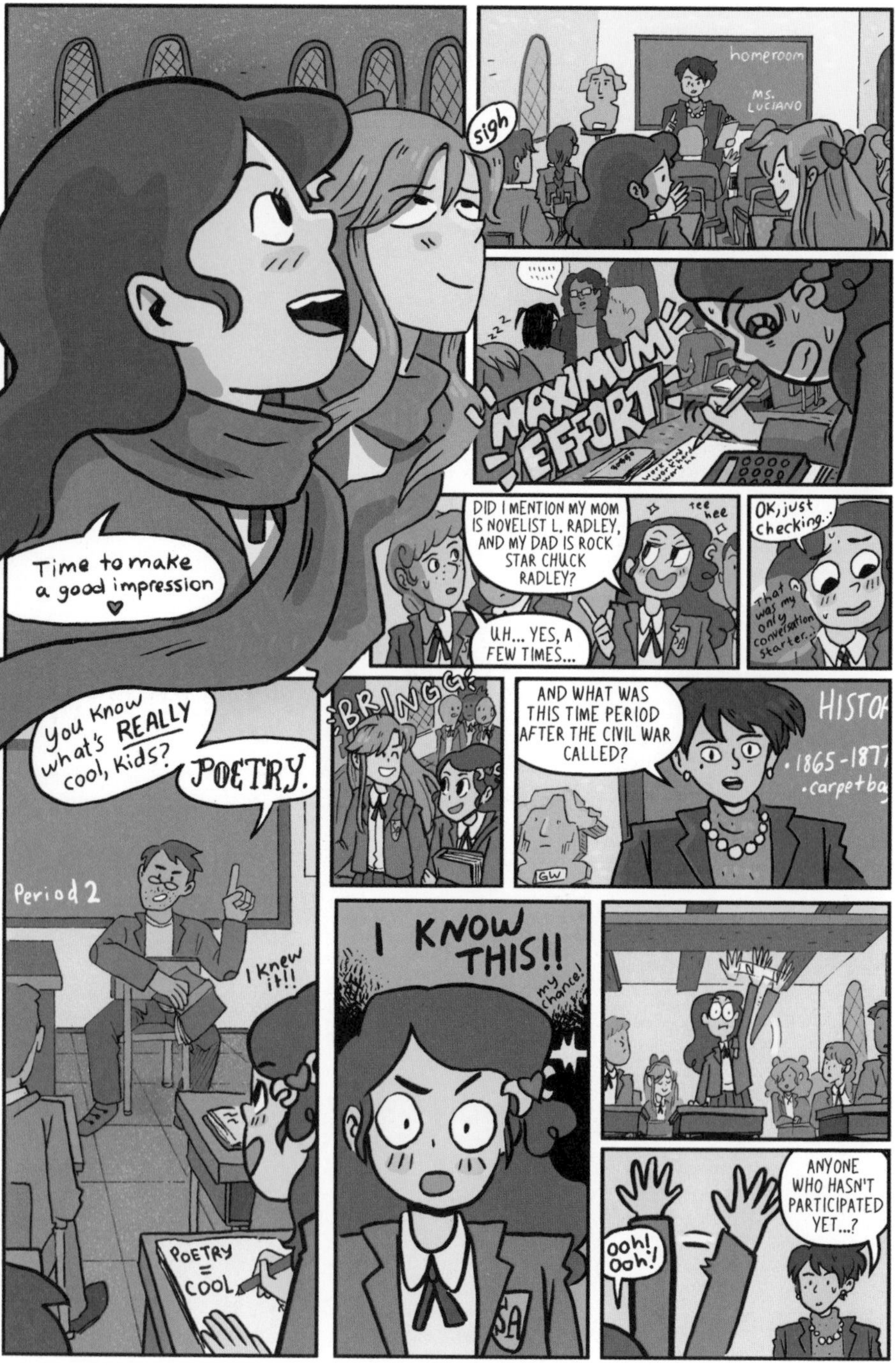
Time to make a good impression ♥
sigh
homeroom
Ms. Luciano
MAXIMUM EFFORT
DID I MENTION MY MOM IS NOVELIST L. RADLEY, AND MY DAD IS ROCK STAR CHUCK RADLEY?
tee hee
UH... YES, A FEW TIMES...
OK, just checking...
That was my only conversation starter...
You know what's REALLY cool, kids?
POETRY.
Period 2
I knew it!!
POETRY = COOL
BRINGG
AND WHAT WAS THIS TIME PERIOD AFTER THE CIVIL WAR CALLED?
GW
I KNOW THIS!!
my chance!
ANYONE WHO HASN'T PARTICIPATED YET...?
ooh! ooh!

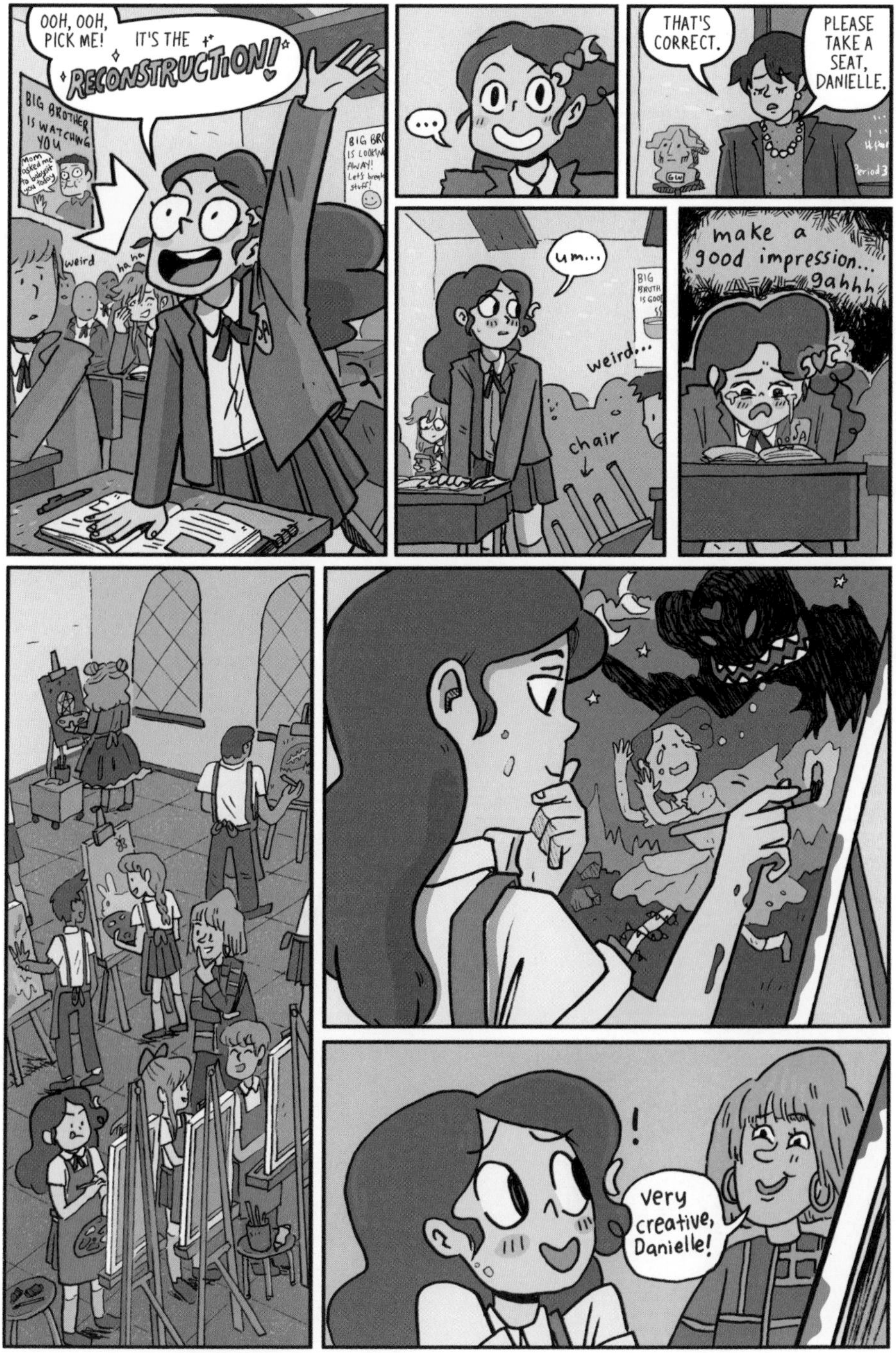
OOH, OOH, PICK ME! IT'S THE RECONSTRUCTION!
BIG BROTHER IS WATCHING YOU
Mom asked me to babysit you today
BIG BRO IS LOOKING AWAY! Let's break stuff!
weird
ha ha
...
THAT'S CORRECT.
PLEASE TAKE A SEAT, DANIELLE.
Period 3
um...
BIG BROTH IS GOOD
weird...
chair
make a good impression... gahhh
!
very creative, Danielle!

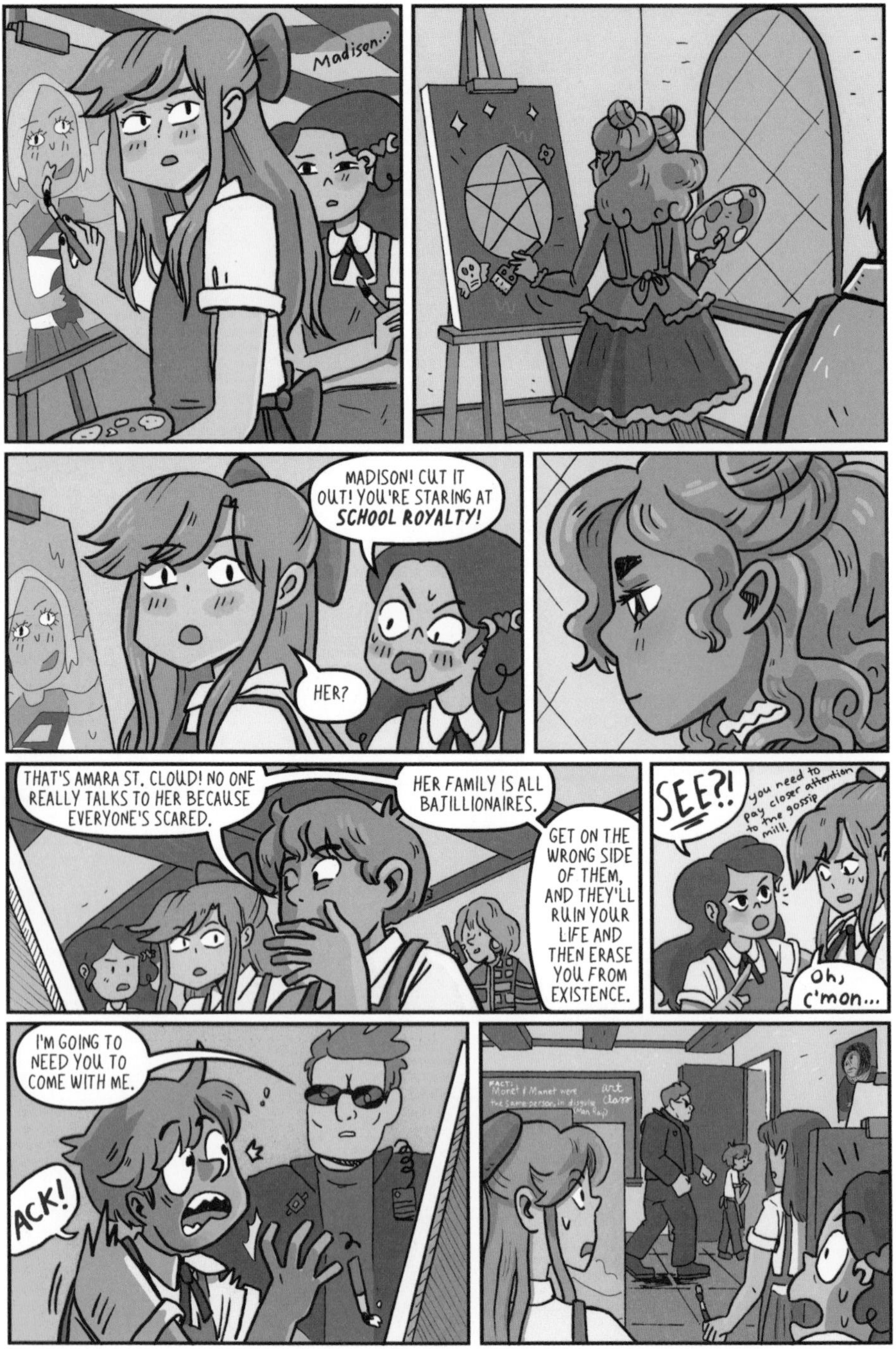
Madison...
MADISON! CUT IT OUT! YOU'RE STARING AT SCHOOL ROYALTY!
HER?
THAT'S AMARA ST. CLOUD! NO ONE REALLY TALKS TO HER BECAUSE EVERYONE'S SCARED.
HER FAMILY IS ALL BAJILLIONAIRES.
GET ON THE WRONG SIDE OF THEM, AND THEY'LL RUIN YOUR LIFE AND THEN ERASE YOU FROM EXISTENCE.
SEE?!
you need to pay closer attention to the gossip mill!
Oh, c'mon...
I'M GOING TO NEED YOU TO COME WITH ME.
ACK!
FACT: Monet & Manet were the same person, in disguise (Man Ray)
art class

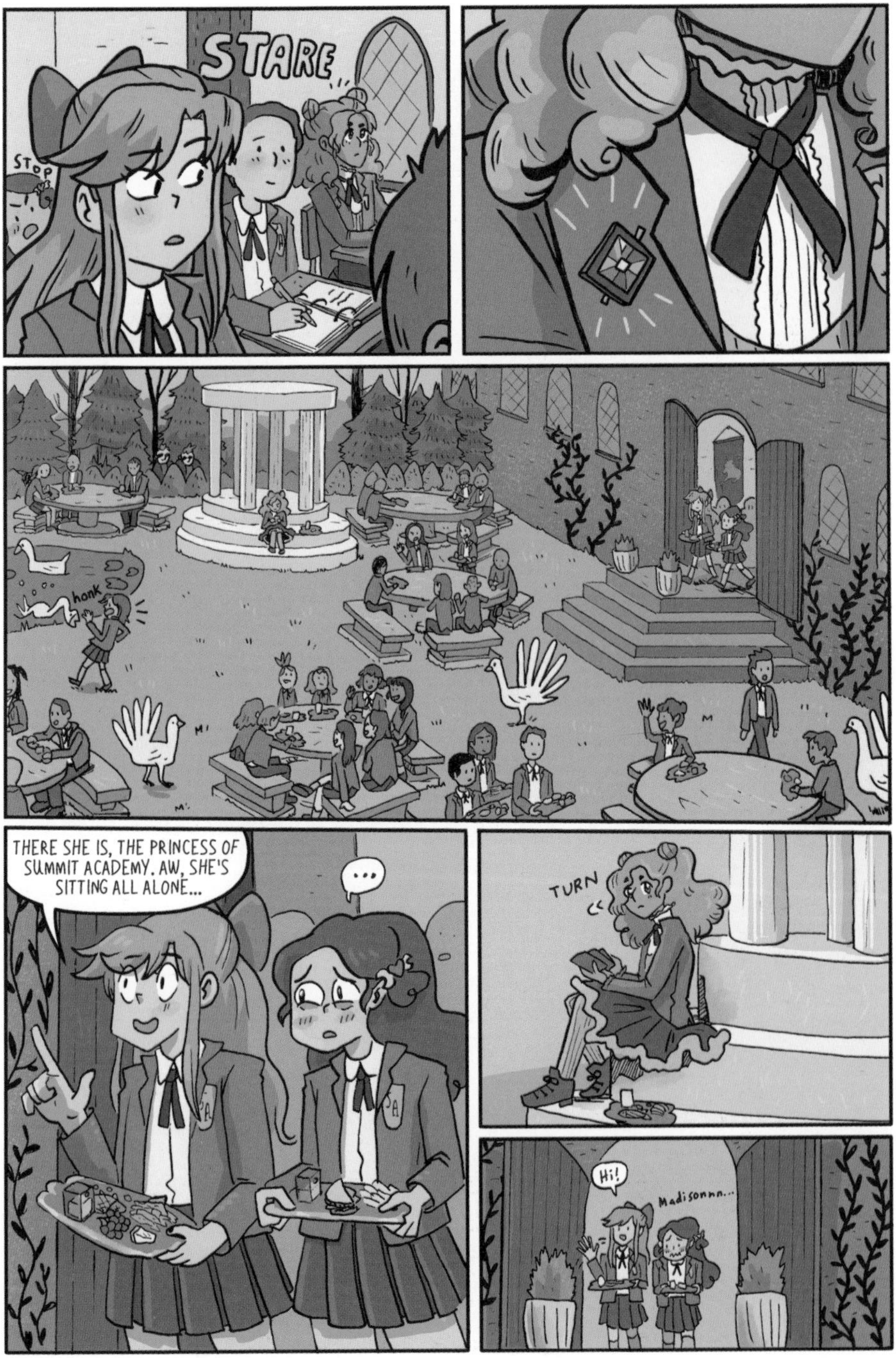
STARE
STOP
honk
THERE SHE IS, THE PRINCESS OF SUMMIT ACADEMY. AW, SHE'S SITTING ALL ALONE...
...
TURN
Hi!
Madisonnn...

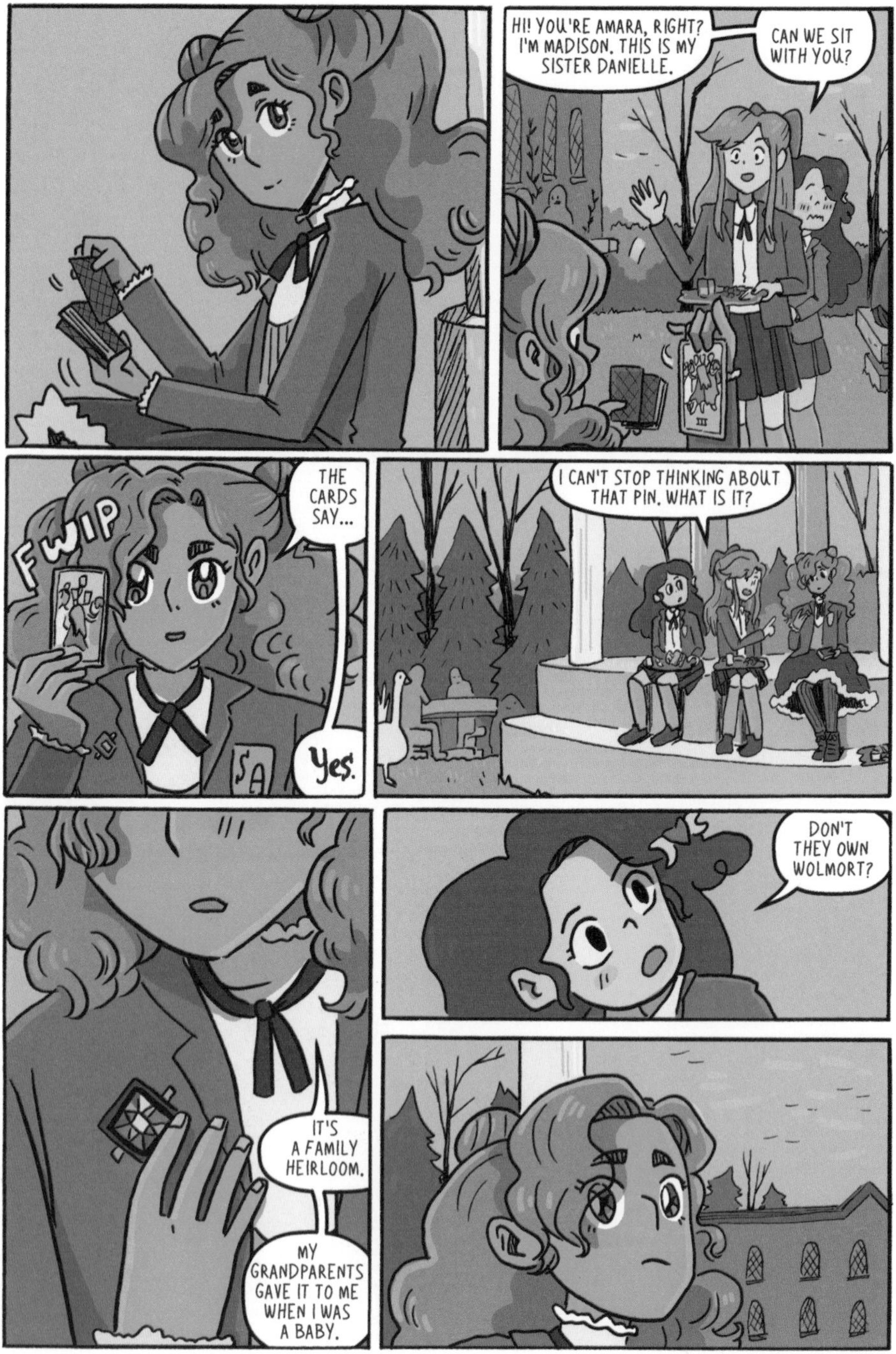
HI! YOU'RE AMARA, RIGHT? I'M MADISON. THIS IS MY SISTER DANIELLE.
CAN WE SIT WITH YOU?
FWIP
THE CARDS SAY...
Yes.
I CAN'T STOP THINKING ABOUT THAT PIN. WHAT IS IT?
IT'S A FAMILY HEIRLOOM.
MY GRANDPARENTS GAVE IT TO ME WHEN I WAS A BABY.
DON'T THEY OWN WOLMORT?

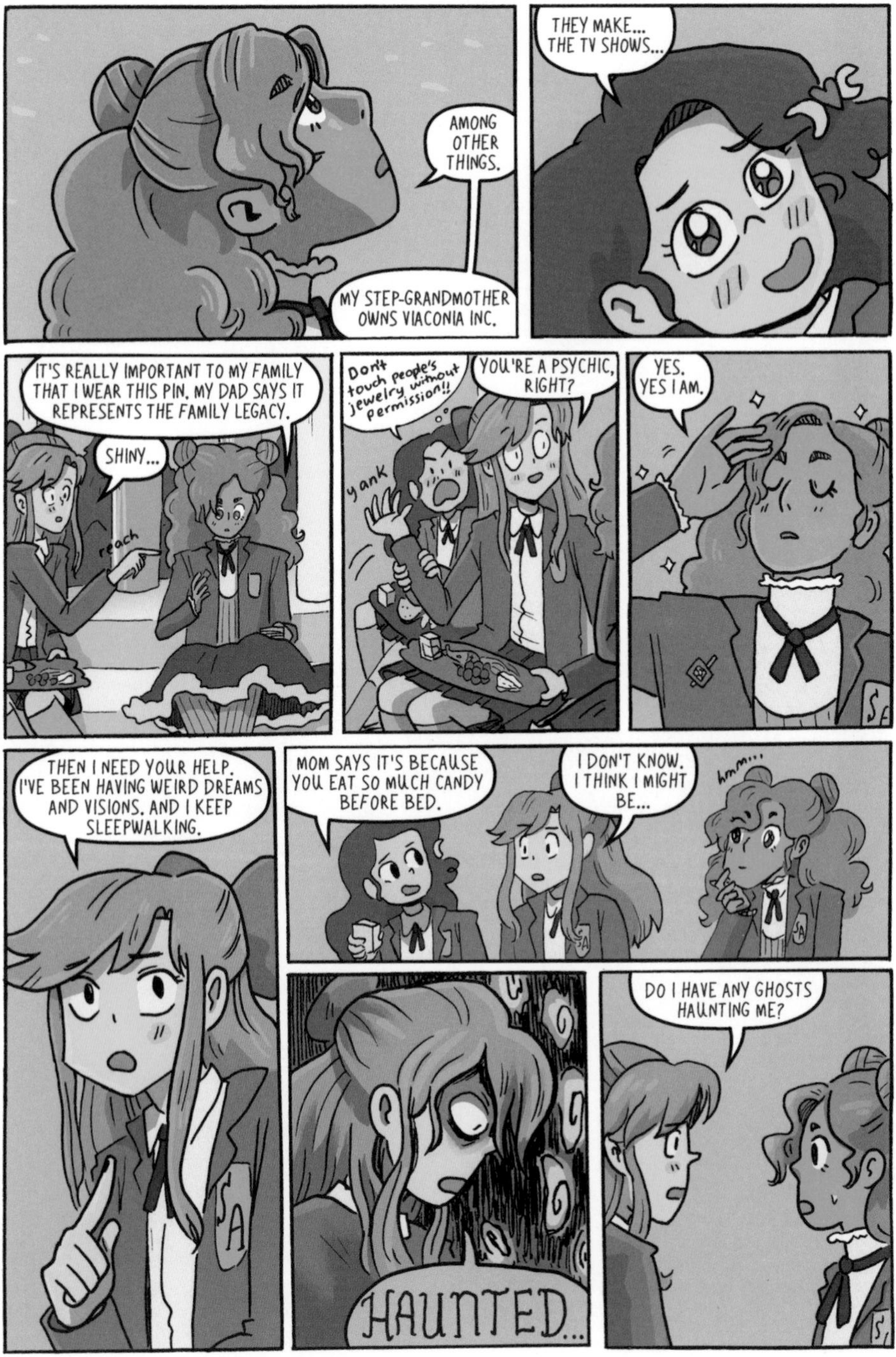
AMONG OTHER THINGS.
MY STEP-GRANDMOTHER OWNS VIACONIA INC.
THEY MAKE... THE TV SHOWS...
IT'S REALLY IMPORTANT TO MY FAMILY THAT I WEAR THIS PIN. MY DAD SAYS IT REPRESENTS THE FAMILY LEGACY.
SHINY...
reach
Don't touch people's jewelry without permission!!
yank
YOU'RE A PSYCHIC, RIGHT?
YES. YES I AM.
THEN I NEED YOUR HELP. I'VE BEEN HAVING WEIRD DREAMS AND VISIONS. AND I KEEP SLEEPWALKING.
MOM SAYS IT'S BECAUSE YOU EAT SO MUCH CANDY BEFORE BED.
I DON'T KNOW. I THINK I MIGHT BE...
hmm...
HAUNTED...
DO I HAVE ANY GHOSTS HAUNTING ME?

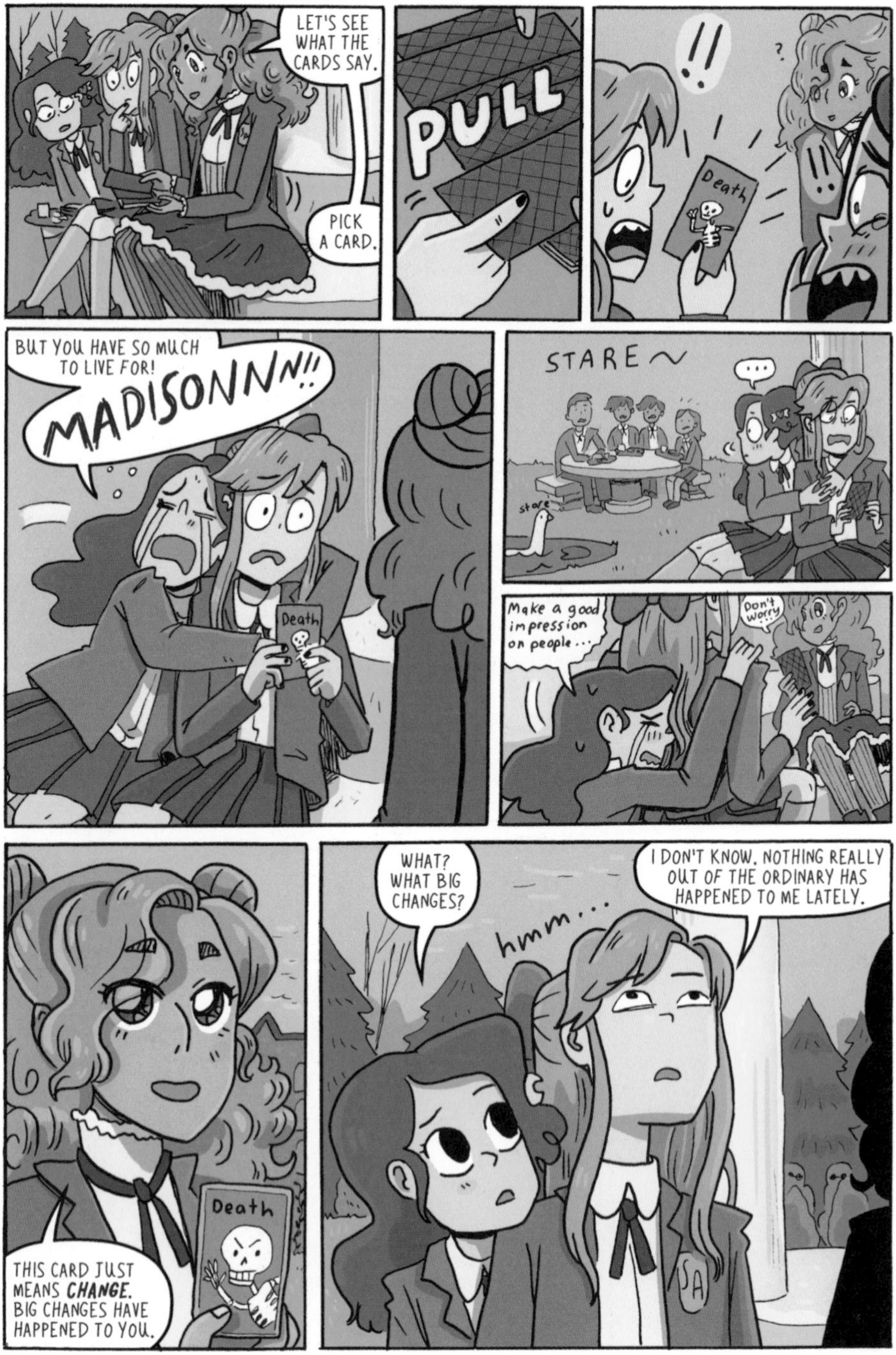
LET'S SEE WHAT THE CARDS SAY.
PICK A CARD.
PULL
!!
?
Death
BUT YOU HAVE SO MUCH TO LIVE FOR!
MADISONNN!!
Death
STARE~
...
stare
Make a good impression on people...
Don't worry...
THIS CARD JUST MEANS CHANGE. BIG CHANGES HAVE HAPPENED TO YOU.
Death
WHAT? WHAT BIG CHANGES?
hmm...
I DON'T KNOW. NOTHING REALLY OUT OF THE ORDINARY HAS HAPPENED TO ME LATELY.
SA

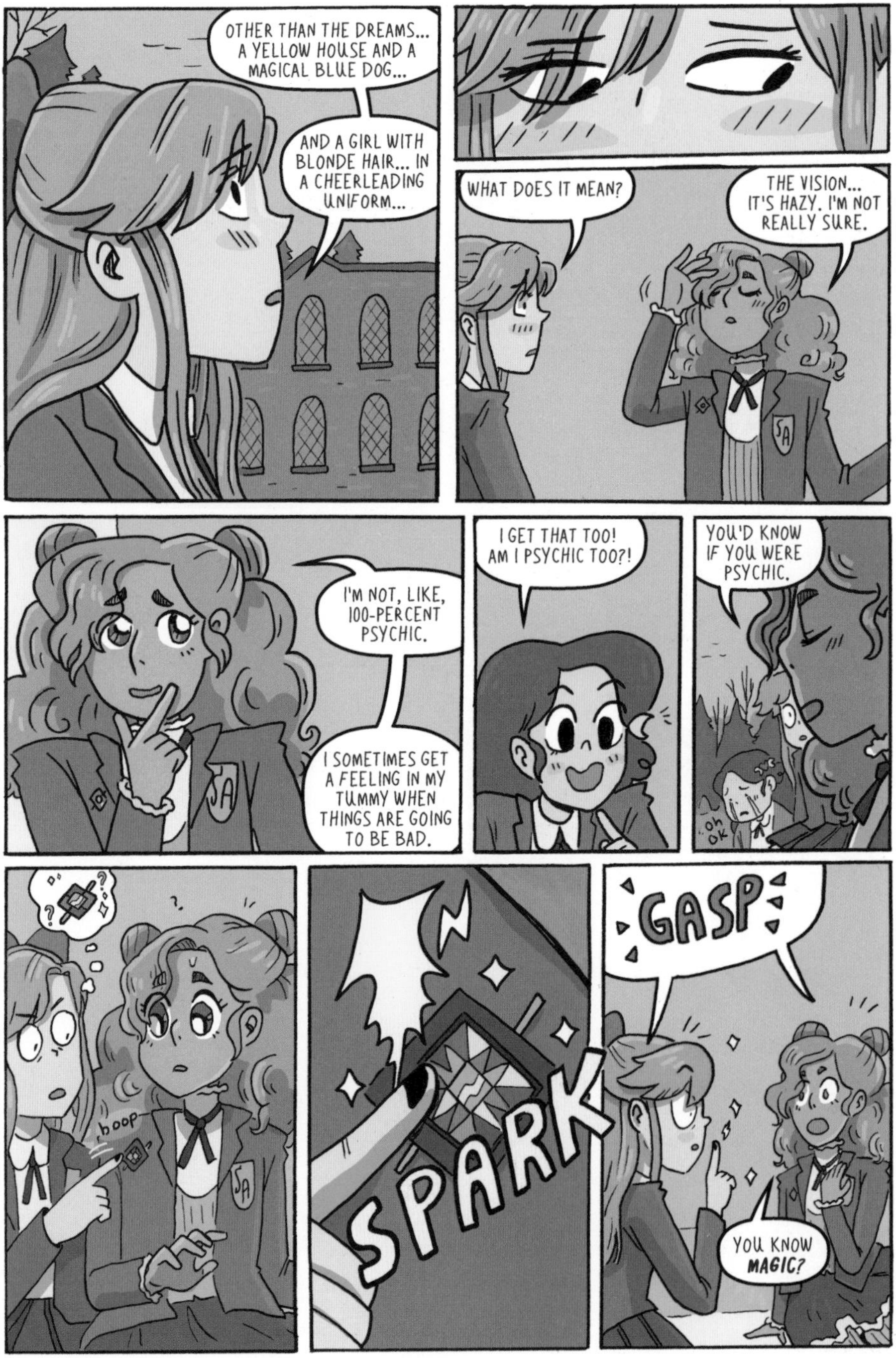
OTHER THAN THE DREAMS... A YELLOW HOUSE AND A MAGICAL BLUE DOG...
AND A GIRL WITH BLONDE HAIR... IN A CHEERLEADING UNIFORM...
WHAT DOES IT MEAN?
THE VISION... IT'S HAZY. I'M NOT REALLY SURE.
I'M NOT, LIKE, 100-PERCENT PSYCHIC.
I SOMETIMES GET A FEELING IN MY TUMMY WHEN THINGS ARE GOING TO BE BAD.
I GET THAT TOO! AM I PSYCHIC TOO?!
YOU'D KNOW IF YOU WERE PSYCHIC.
oh ok
boop
SPARK
GASP
YOU KNOW **MAGIC?**

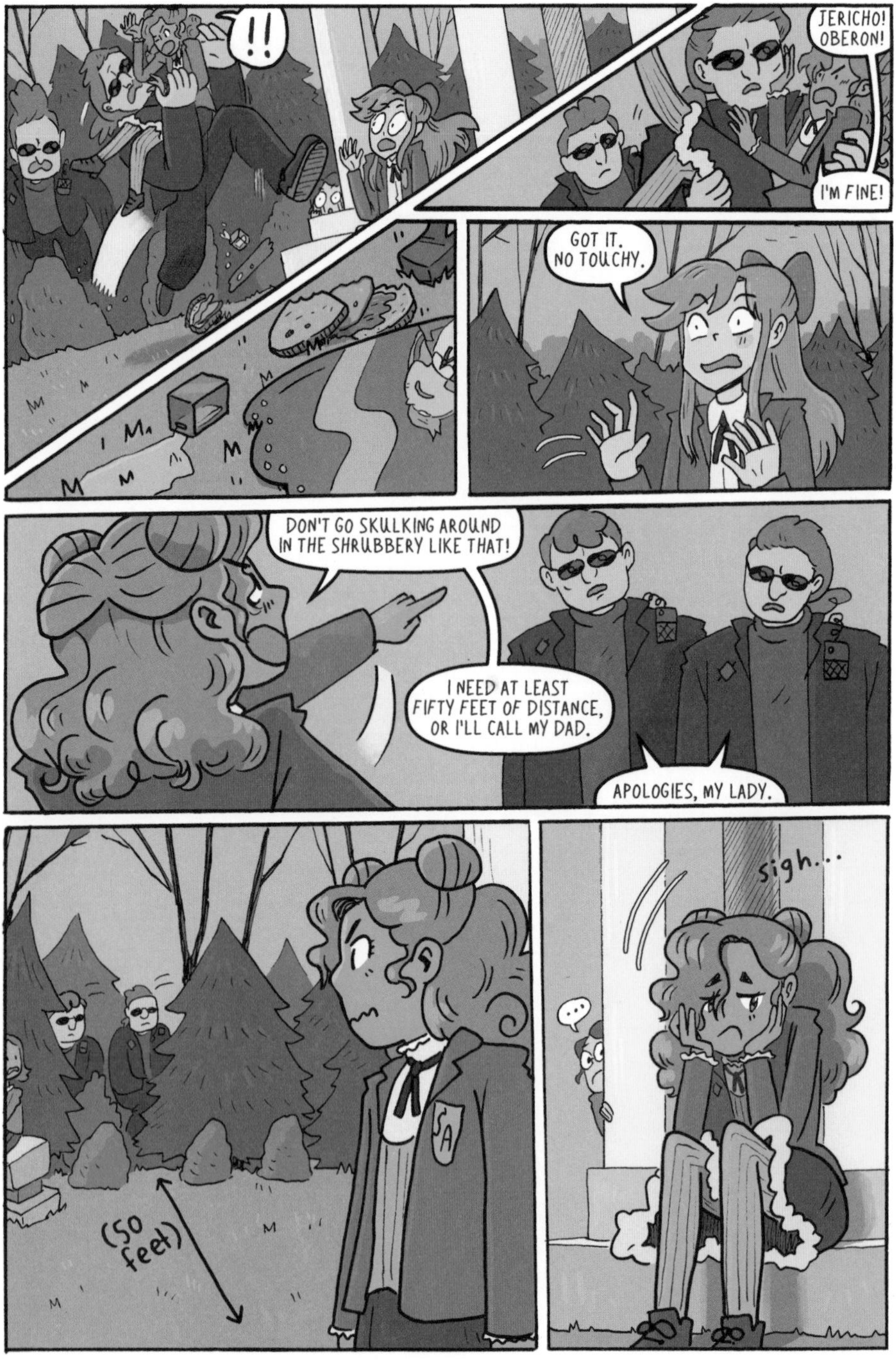
!!
JERICHO! OBERON!
I'M FINE!
GOT IT. NO TOUCHY.
DON'T GO SKULKING AROUND IN THE SHRUBBERY LIKE THAT!
I NEED AT LEAST FIFTY FEET OF DISTANCE, OR I'LL CALL MY DAD.
APOLOGIES, MY LADY.
(50 feet)
sigh...

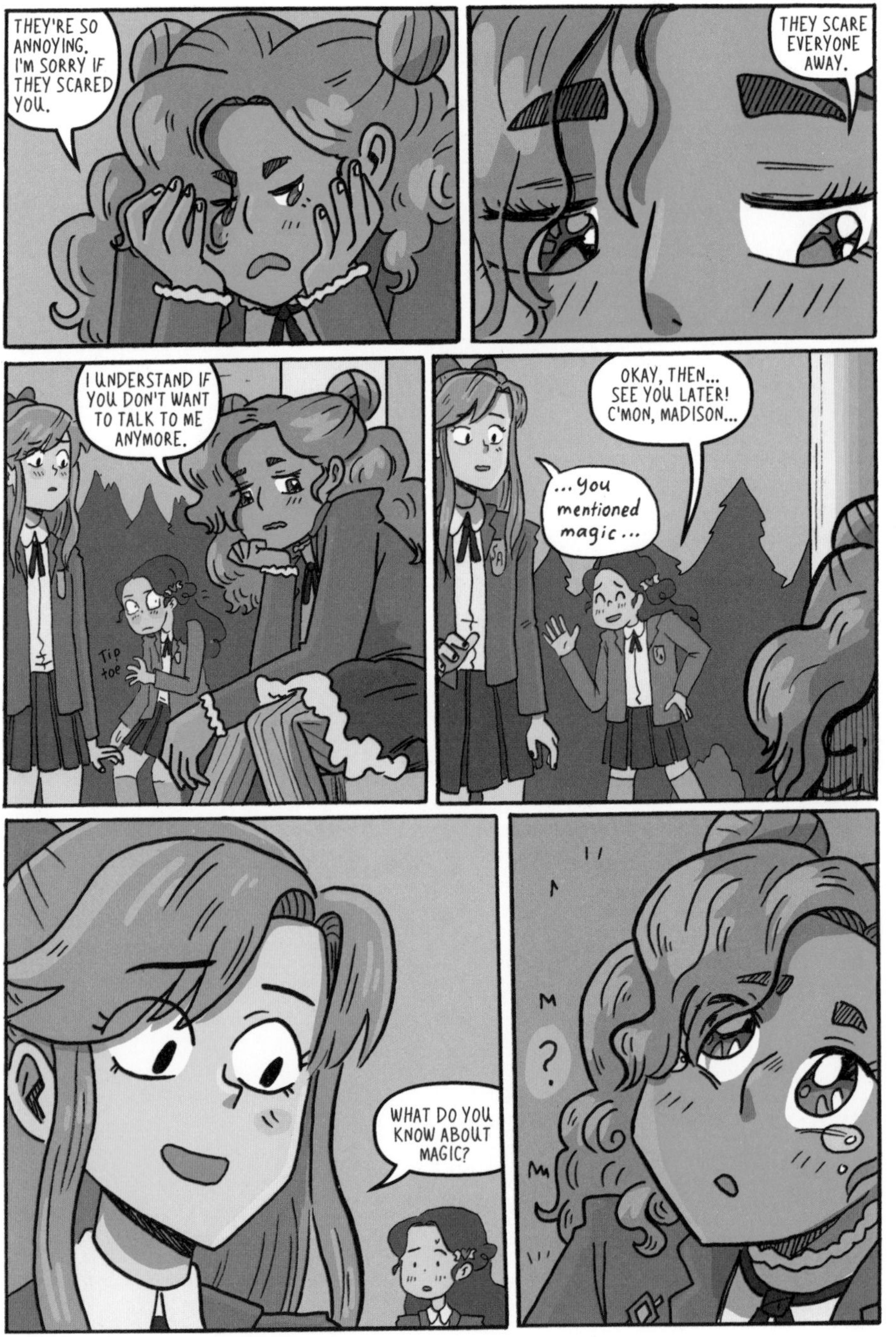
THEY'RE SO ANNOYING. I'M SORRY IF THEY SCARED YOU.
THEY SCARE EVERYONE AWAY.
I UNDERSTAND IF YOU DON'T WANT TO TALK TO ME ANYMORE.
Tip toe
OKAY, THEN... SEE YOU LATER! C'MON, MADISON...
...you mentioned magic...
WHAT DO YOU KNOW ABOUT MAGIC?
?

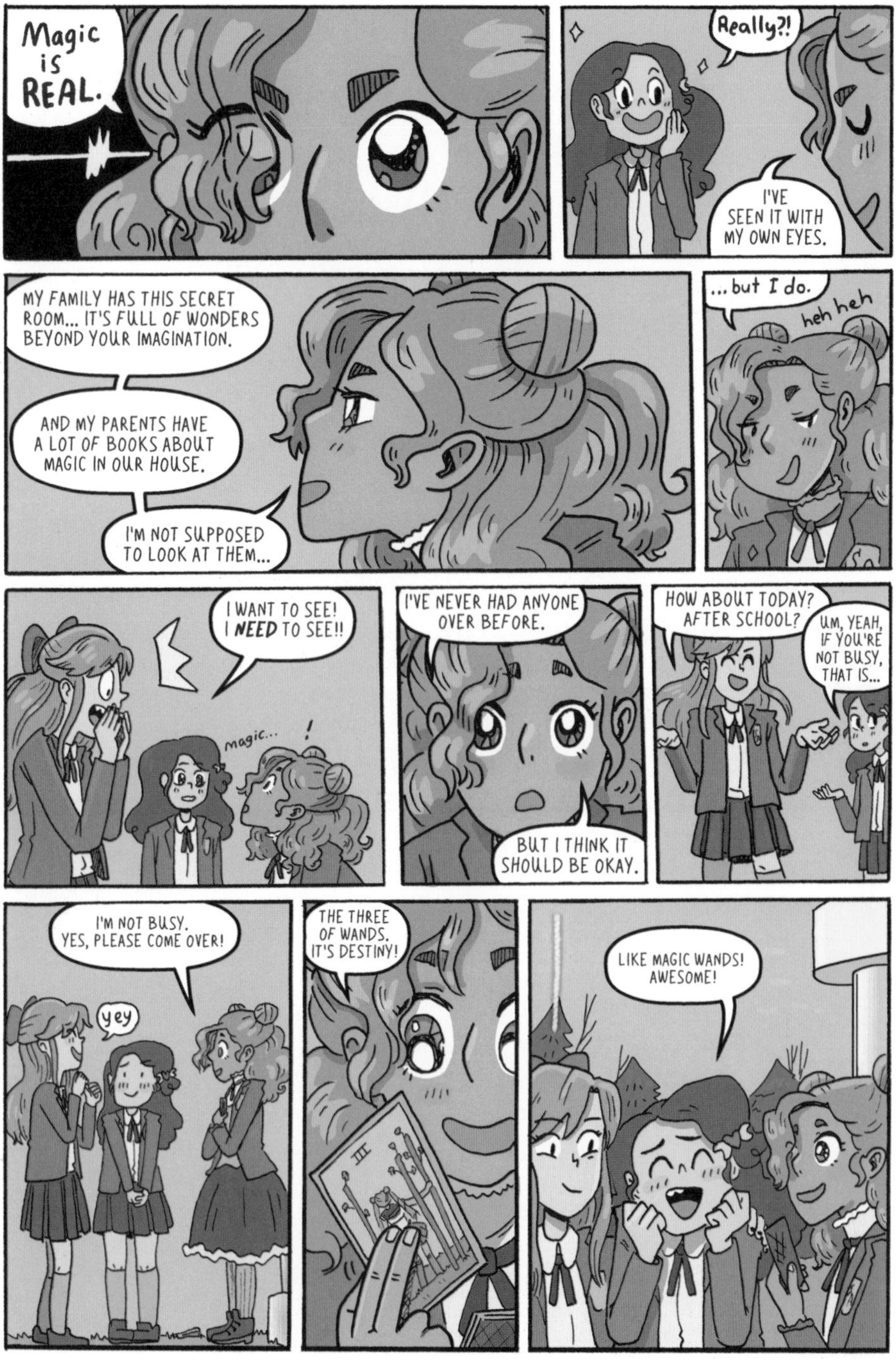
Magic is REAL.
Really?!
I'VE SEEN IT WITH MY OWN EYES.
MY FAMILY HAS THIS SECRET ROOM... IT'S FULL OF WONDERS BEYOND YOUR IMAGINATION.
AND MY PARENTS HAVE A LOT OF BOOKS ABOUT MAGIC IN OUR HOUSE.
I'M NOT SUPPOSED TO LOOK AT THEM...
...but I do.
heh heh
I WANT TO SEE! I NEED TO SEE!!
magic...
!
I'VE NEVER HAD ANYONE OVER BEFORE.
BUT I THINK IT SHOULD BE OKAY.
HOW ABOUT TODAY? AFTER SCHOOL?
UM, YEAH, IF YOU'RE NOT BUSY, THAT IS...
I'M NOT BUSY. YES, PLEASE COME OVER!
yey
THE THREE OF WANDS. IT'S DESTINY!
LIKE MAGIC WANDS! AWESOME!

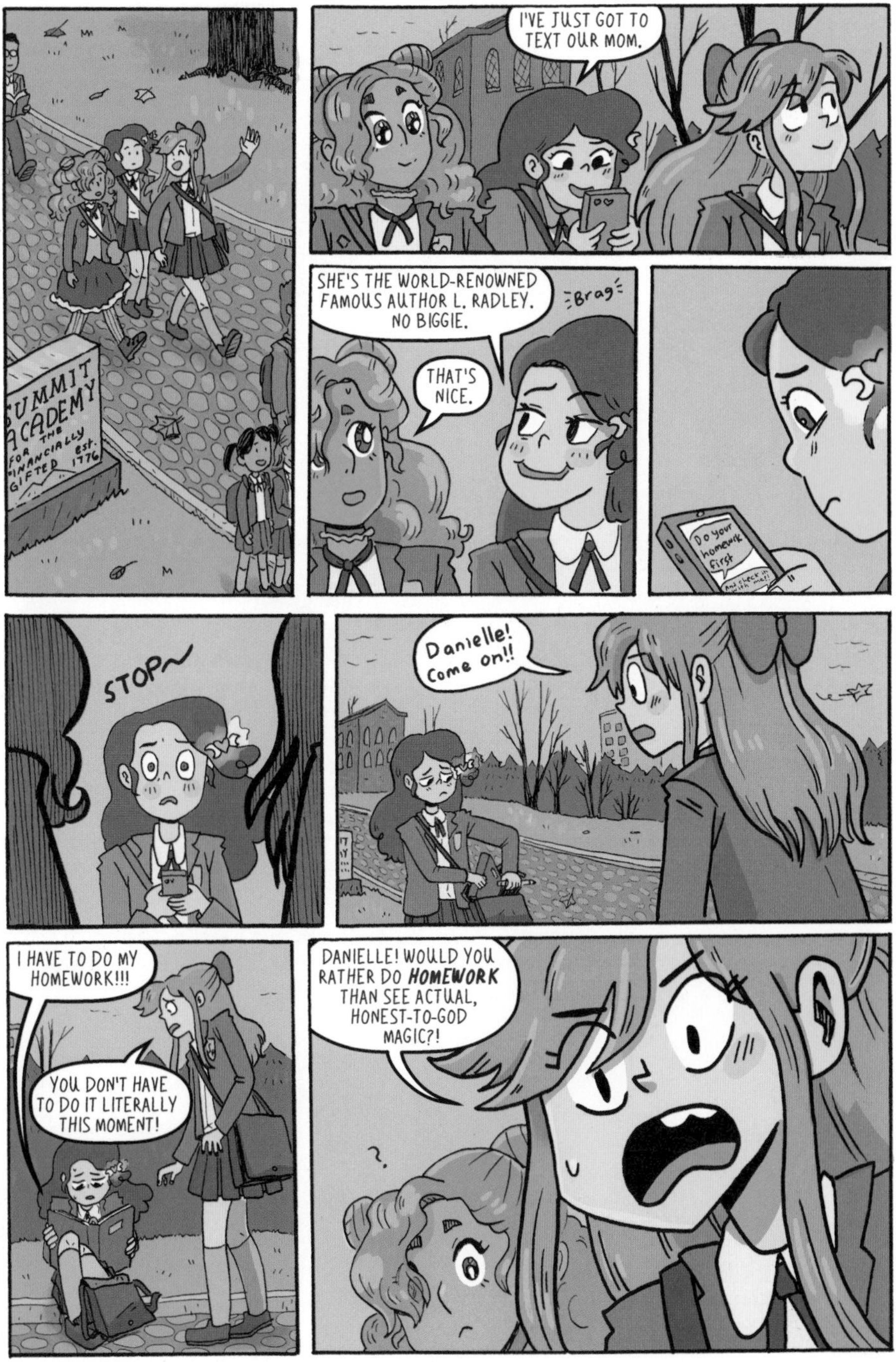
SUMMIT ACADEMY FOR THE FINANCIALLY GIFTED est. 1776
I'VE JUST GOT TO TEXT OUR MOM.
SHE'S THE WORLD-RENOWNED FAMOUS AUTHOR L. RADLEY. NO BIGGIE.
Brag
THAT'S NICE.
Do your homework first
And check in with me!!
STOP~
Danielle! Come on!!
I HAVE TO DO MY HOMEWORK!!!
YOU DON'T HAVE TO DO IT LITERALLY THIS MOMENT!
DANIELLE! WOULD YOU RATHER DO **HOMEWORK** THAN SEE ACTUAL, HONEST-TO-GOD MAGIC?!
?

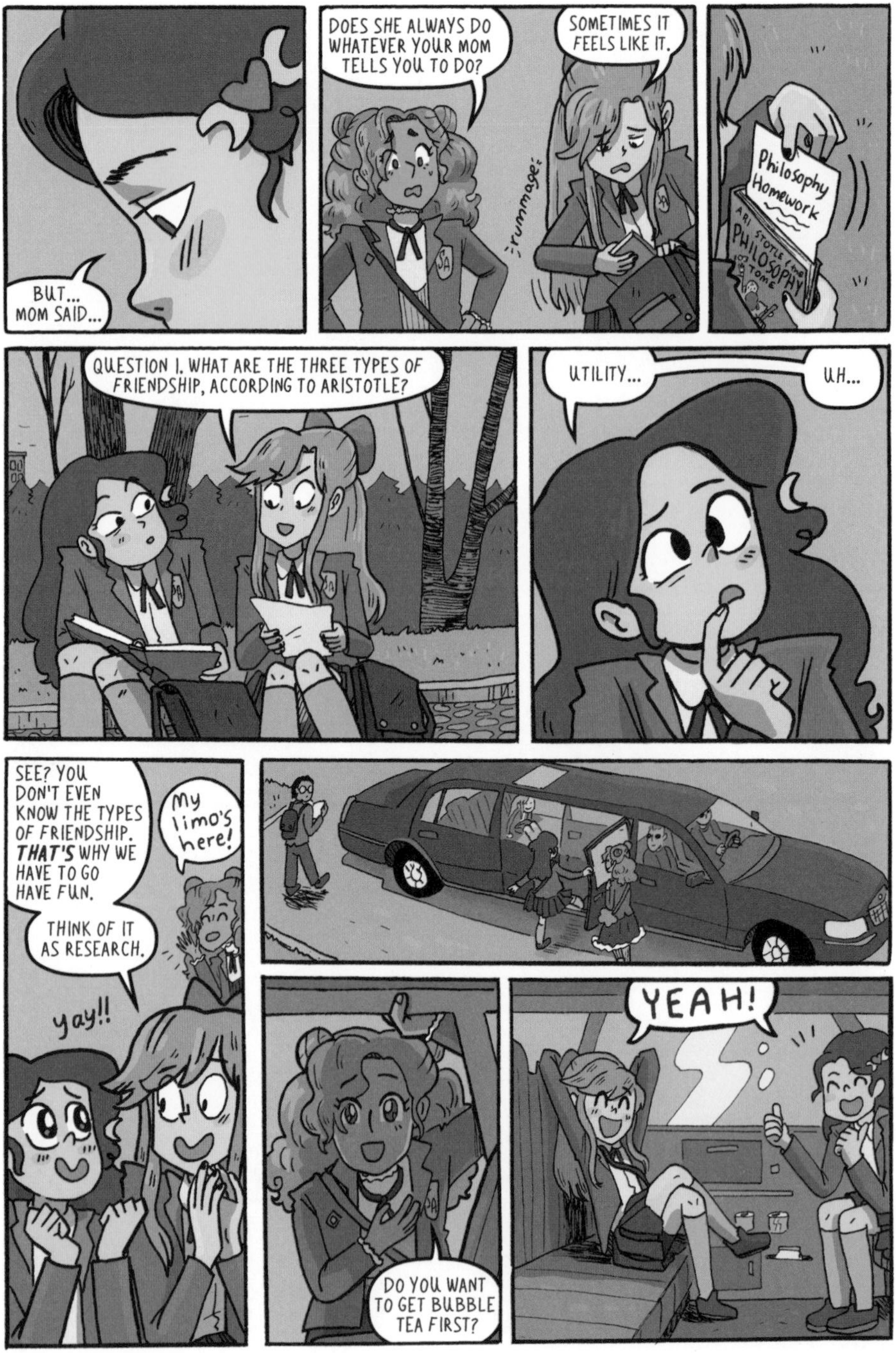
BUT... MOM SAID...
DOES SHE ALWAYS DO WHATEVER YOUR MOM TELLS YOU TO DO?
SOMETIMES IT FEELS LIKE IT.
rummage
Philosophy Homework
ARI STOTLE'S (the) PHILOSOPHY TOME
QUESTION 1. WHAT ARE THE THREE TYPES OF FRIENDSHIP, ACCORDING TO ARISTOTLE?
UTILITY...
UH...
SEE? YOU DON'T EVEN KNOW THE TYPES OF FRIENDSHIP. **THAT'S** WHY WE HAVE TO GO HAVE FUN.
THINK OF IT AS RESEARCH.
My limo's here!
yay!!
DO YOU WANT TO GET BUBBLE TEA FIRST?
YEAH!

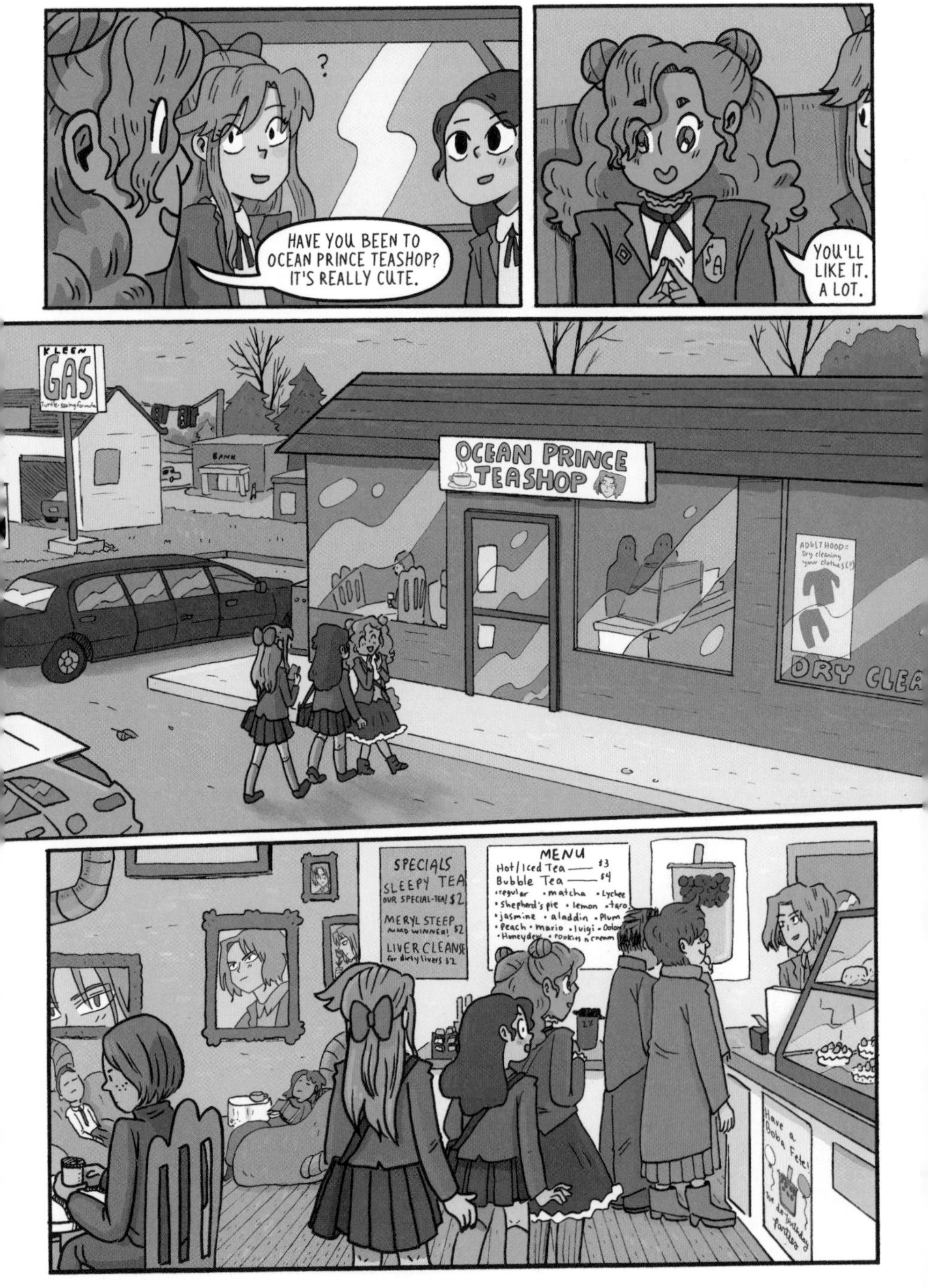
?
HAVE YOU BEEN TO OCEAN PRINCE TEASHOP? IT'S REALLY CUTE.
YOU'LL LIKE IT. A LOT.
KLEEN
GAS
BANK
OCEAN PRINCE TEASHOP
ADULTHOOD= Dry cleaning your clothes(?)
DRY CLEA
SPECIALS
SLEEPY TEA
OUR SPECIAL-TEA! $2
MERYL STEEP
$2
LIVER CLEANSE
for dirty livers $2
MENU
Hot/Iced Tea —— $3
Bubble Tea —— $4
•regular •matcha •Lychee
•Shepherd's pie •lemon •taro
•jasmine •aladdin •Plum
•Peach •mario •luigi
Have a Boba Fete!
we do birthday Parties

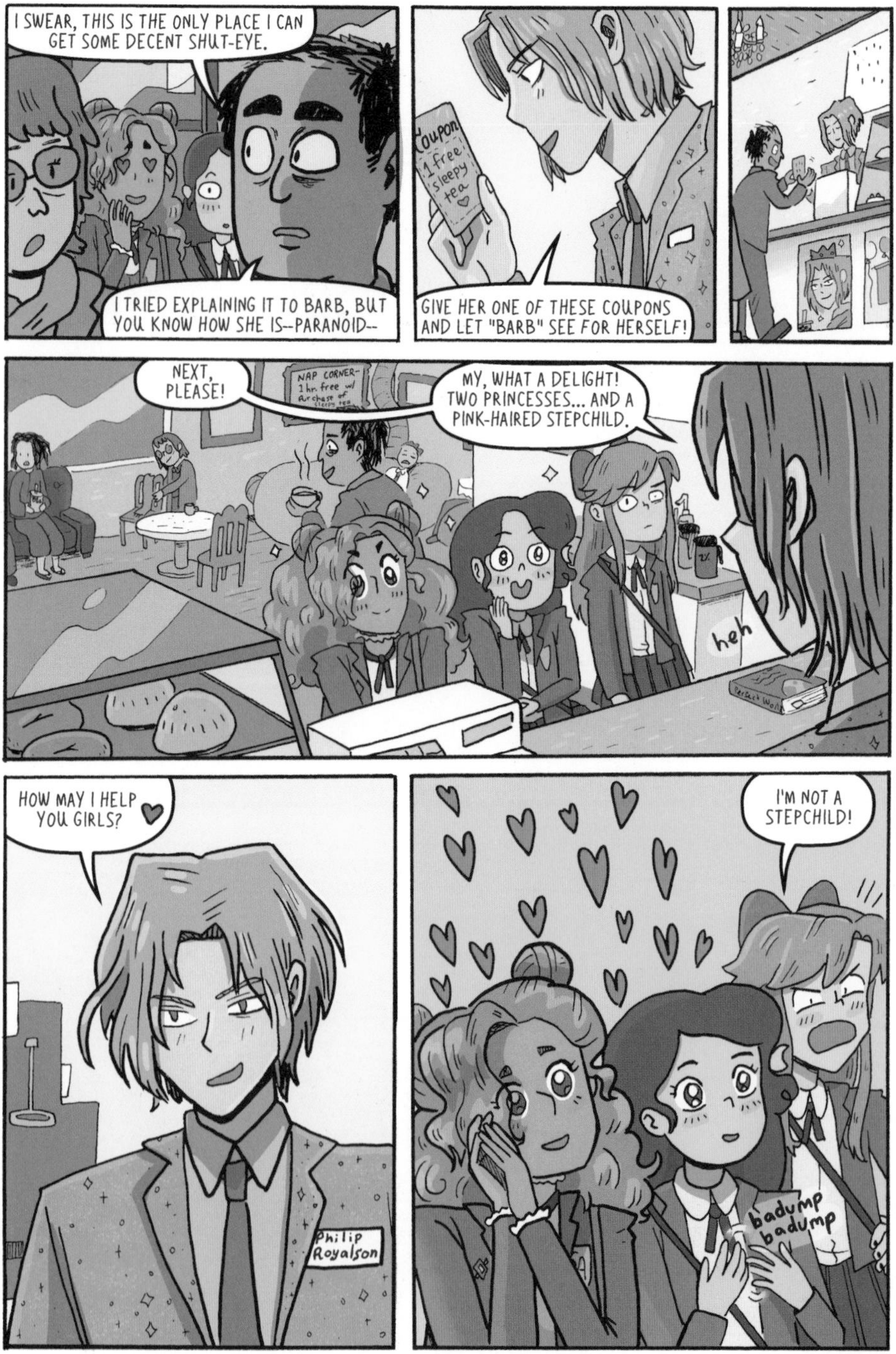
I SWEAR, THIS IS THE ONLY PLACE I CAN GET SOME DECENT SHUT-EYE.
I TRIED EXPLAINING IT TO BARB, BUT YOU KNOW HOW SHE IS--PARANOID--
Coupon
1 free sleepy tea
GIVE HER ONE OF THESE COUPONS AND LET "BARB" SEE FOR HERSELF!
NEXT, PLEASE!
NAP CORNER- 1 hr. free w/ purchase of sleepy tea
MY, WHAT A DELIGHT! TWO PRINCESSES... AND A PINK-HAIRED STEPCHILD.
heh
HOW MAY I HELP YOU GIRLS?
Philip Royalson
I'M NOT A STEPCHILD!
badump badump

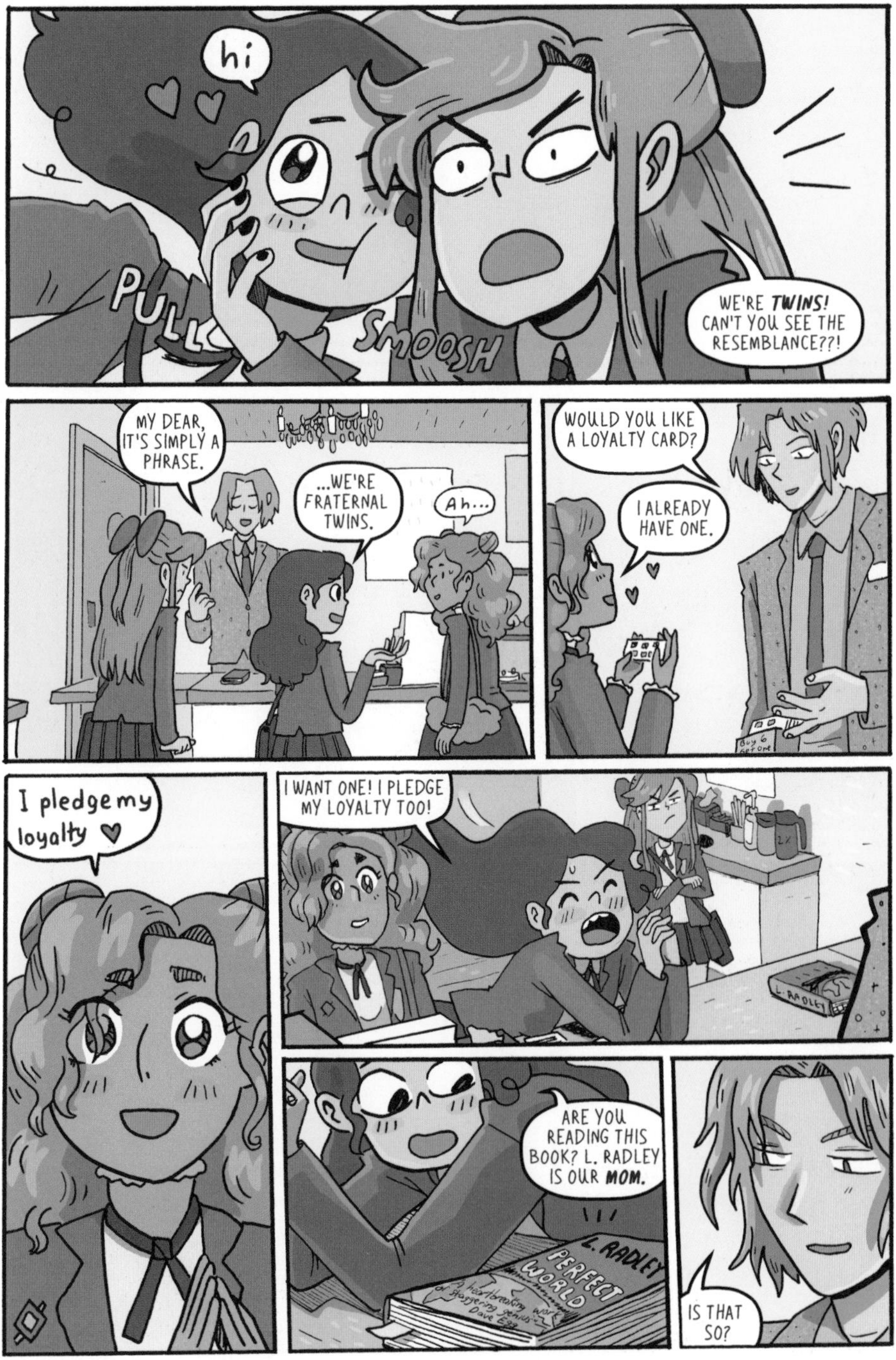
hi
PULL
SMOOSH
WE'RE **TWINS!** CAN'T YOU SEE THE RESEMBLANCE??!
MY DEAR, IT'S SIMPLY A PHRASE.
...WE'RE FRATERNAL TWINS.
Ah...
WOULD YOU LIKE A LOYALTY CARD?
I ALREADY HAVE ONE.
I pledge my loyalty ♥
I WANT ONE! I PLEDGE MY LOYALTY TOO!
L. RADLEY
ARE YOU READING THIS BOOK? L. RADLEY IS OUR **MOM.**
L. RADLEY
PERFECT WORLD
A heartbreaking work of staggering genius
Dave Egg
IS THAT SO?

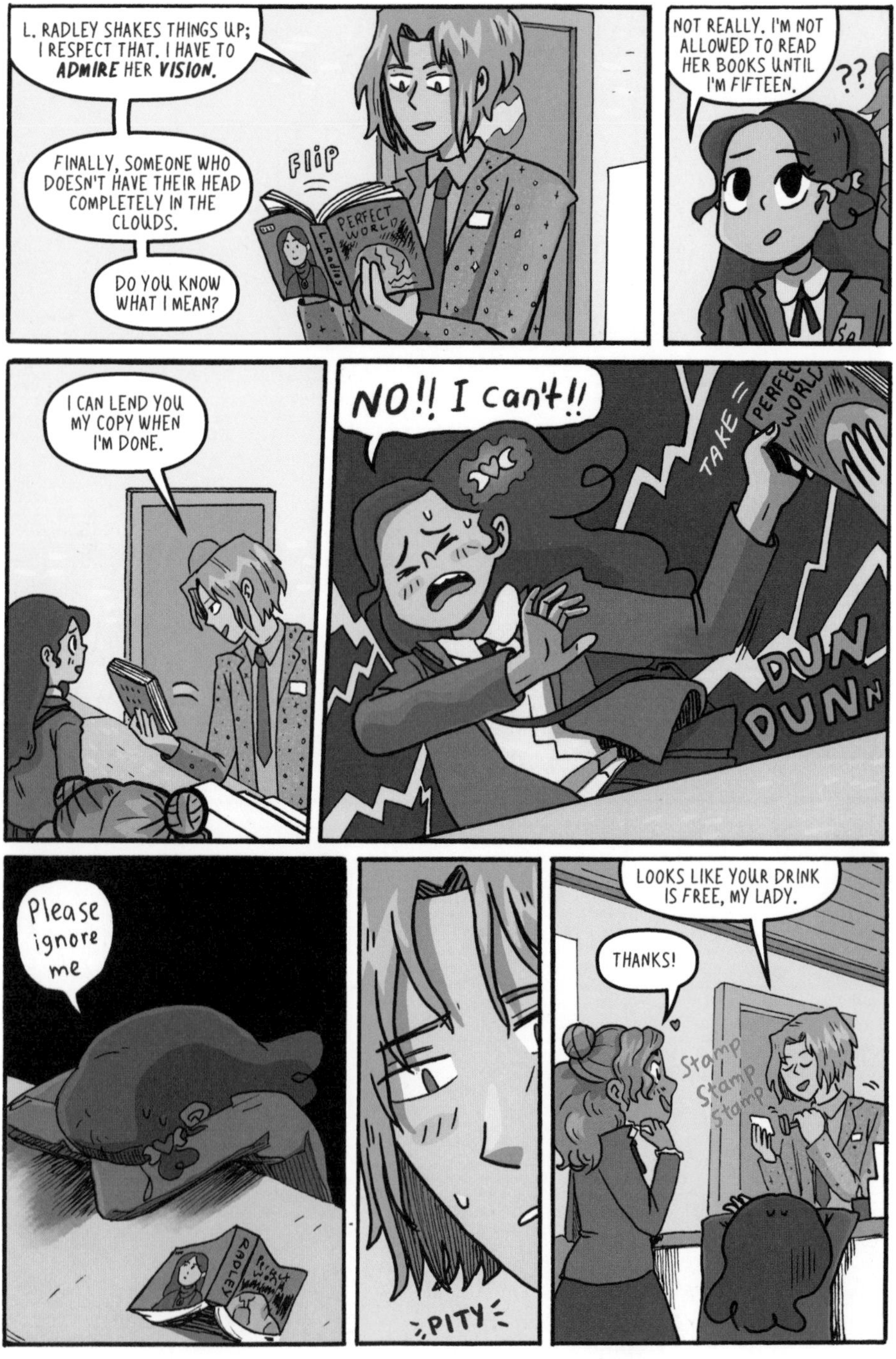
L. RADLEY SHAKES THINGS UP; I RESPECT THAT. I HAVE TO **ADMIRE** HER **VISION.**
FINALLY, SOMEONE WHO DOESN'T HAVE THEIR HEAD COMPLETELY IN THE CLOUDS.
DO YOU KNOW WHAT I MEAN?
FLIP
PERFECT WORLD
L. Radley
NOT REALLY. I'M NOT ALLOWED TO READ HER BOOKS UNTIL I'M *FIFTEEN.*
??
I CAN LEND YOU MY COPY WHEN I'M DONE.
NO!! I can't!!
TAKE
PERFECT WORLD
DUN DUNN
Please ignore me
RADLEY
PITY
LOOKS LIKE YOUR DRINK IS FREE, MY LADY.
THANKS!
Stamp Stamp Stamp

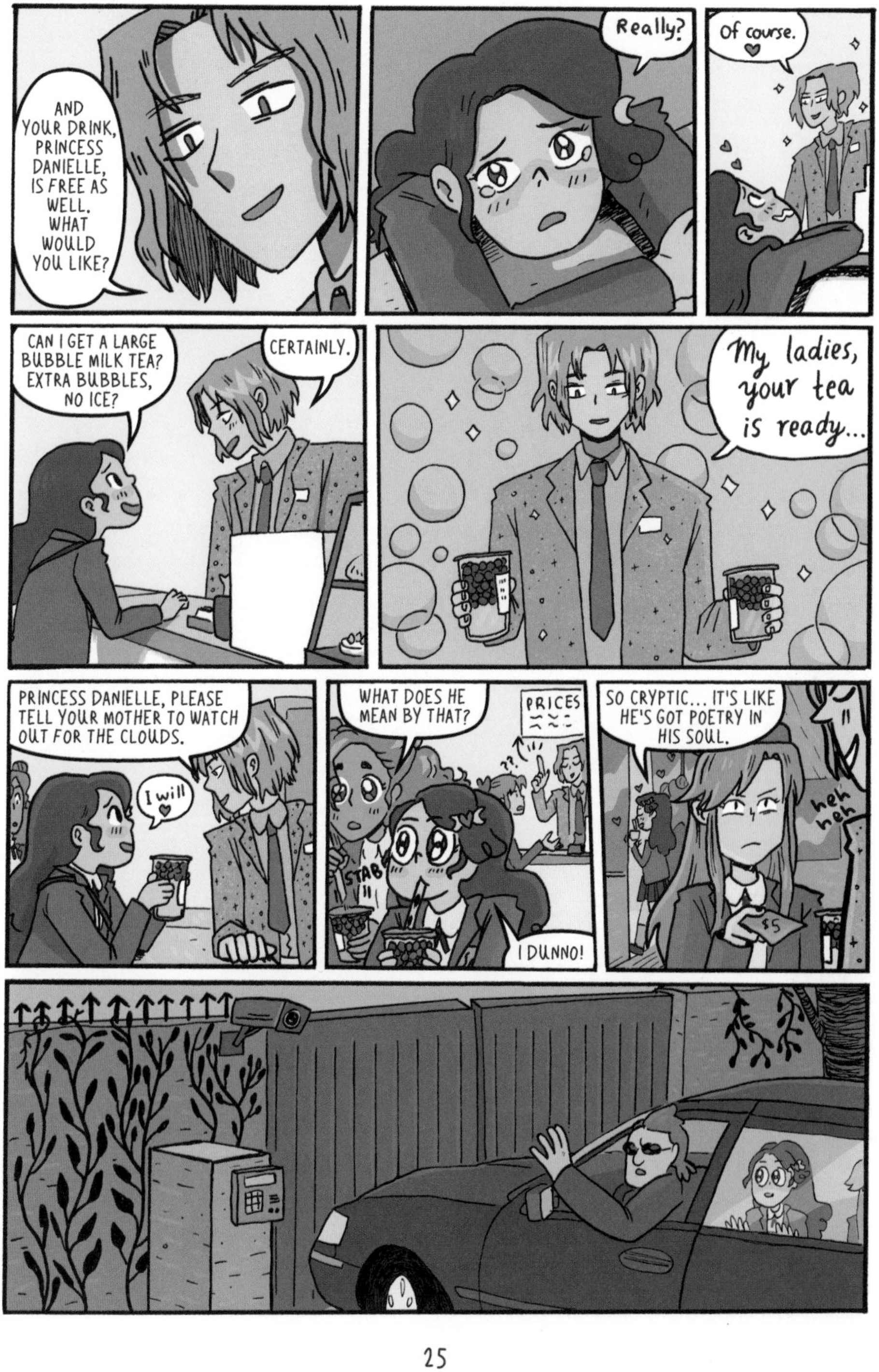
AND YOUR DRINK, PRINCESS DANIELLE, IS FREE AS WELL. WHAT WOULD YOU LIKE?
Really?
Of course. ♥
CAN I GET A LARGE BUBBLE MILK TEA? EXTRA BUBBLES, NO ICE?
CERTAINLY.
My ladies, your tea is ready...
PRINCESS DANIELLE, PLEASE TELL YOUR MOTHER TO WATCH OUT FOR THE CLOUDS.
I will ♥
WHAT DOES HE MEAN BY THAT?
PRICES
STAB
I DUNNO!
SO CRYPTIC... IT'S LIKE HE'S GOT POETRY IN HIS SOUL.
heh heh
$5

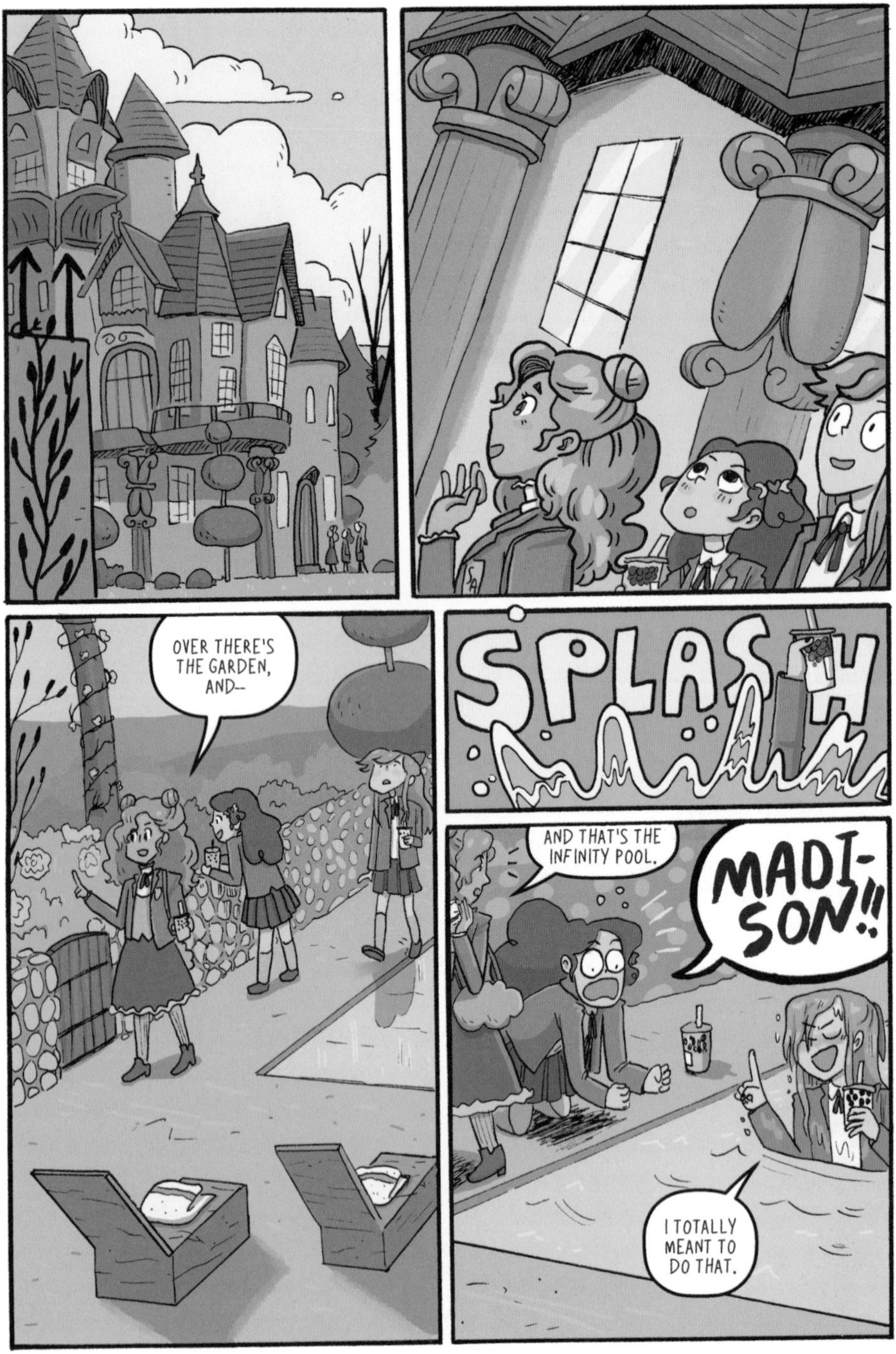
OVER THERE'S THE GARDEN, AND--
SPLASH
AND THAT'S THE INFINITY POOL.
MADI-SON!!
I TOTALLY MEANT TO DO THAT.

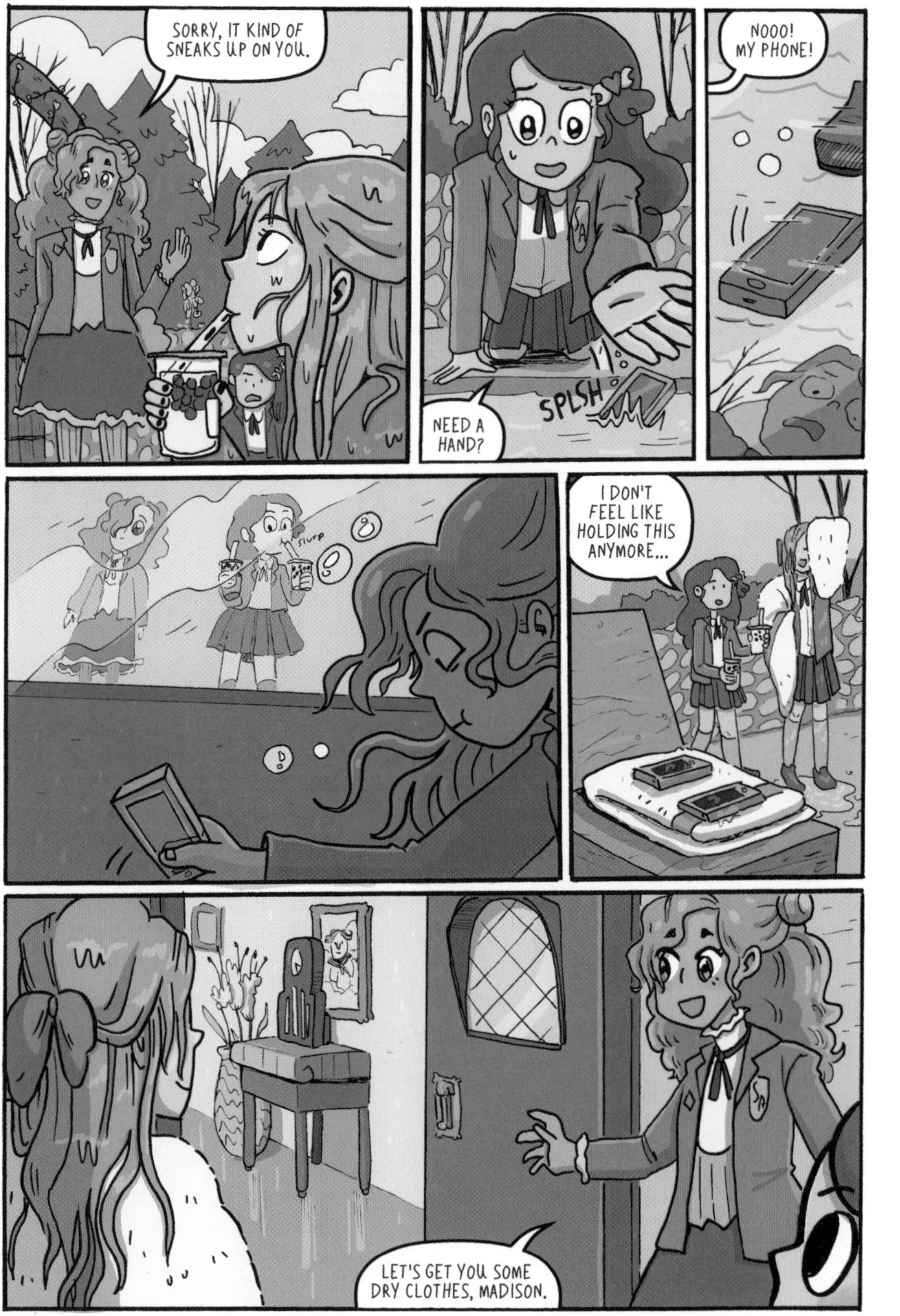
SORRY, IT KIND OF SNEAKS UP ON YOU.
NEED A HAND?
SPLSH
NOOO! MY PHONE!
slurp
I DON'T FEEL LIKE HOLDING THIS ANYMORE...
LET'S GET YOU SOME DRY CLOTHES, MADISON.

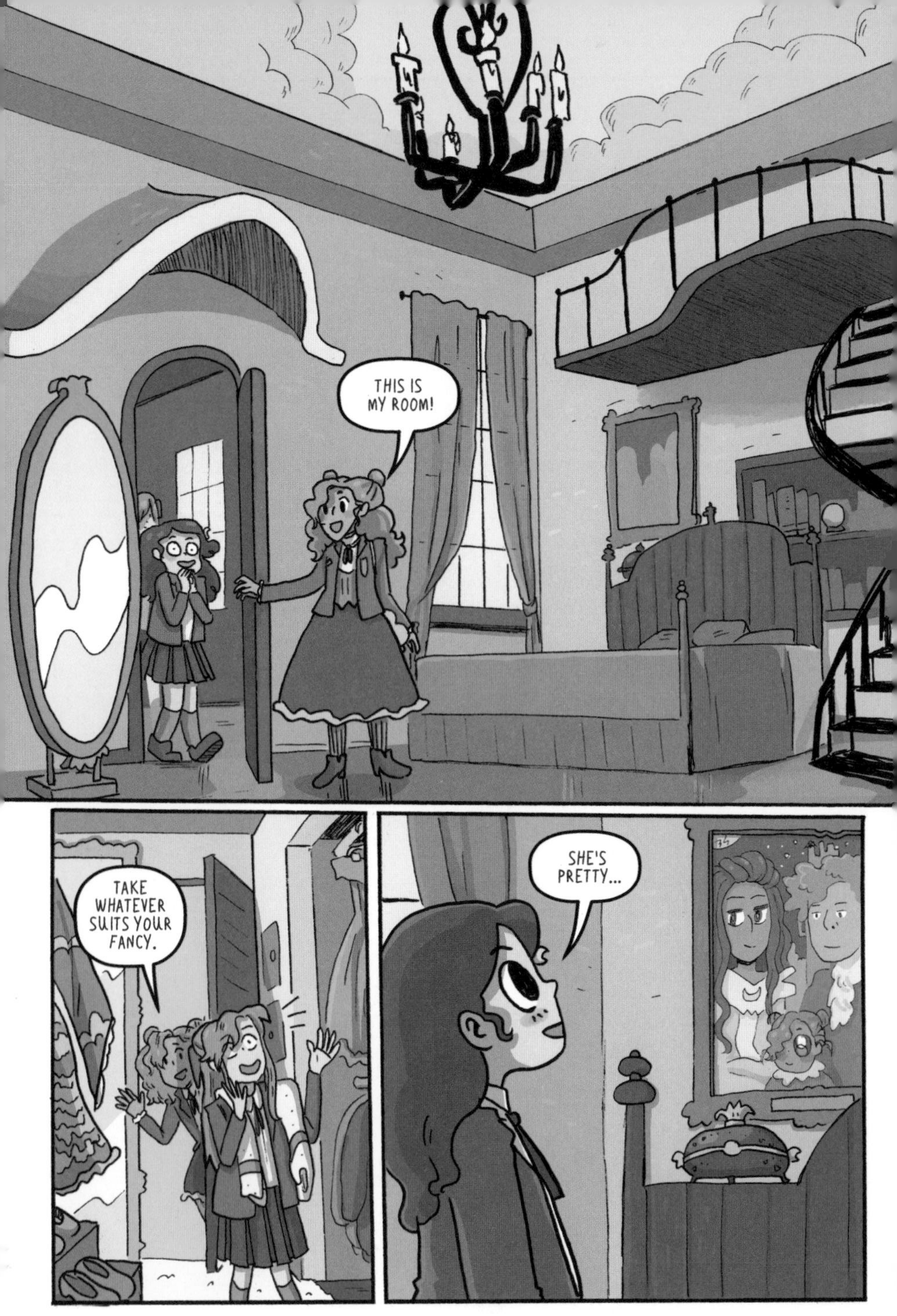
THIS IS
MY ROOM!
TAKE
WHATEVER
SUITS YOUR
FANCY.
SHE'S
PRETTY...

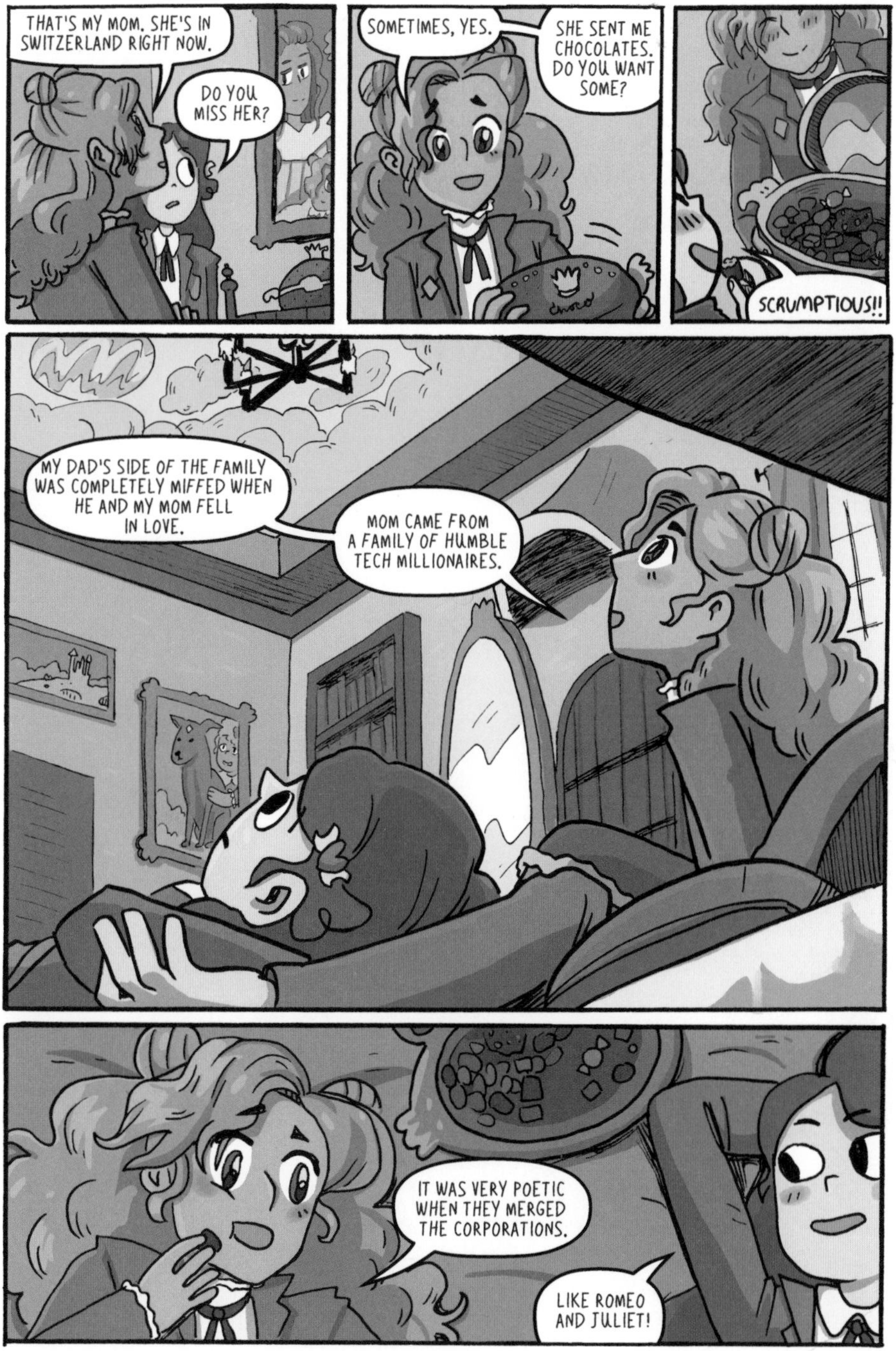
THAT'S MY MOM. SHE'S IN SWITZERLAND RIGHT NOW.
DO YOU MISS HER?
SOMETIMES, YES.
SHE SENT ME CHOCOLATES. DO YOU WANT SOME?
SCRUMPTIOUS!!
MY DAD'S SIDE OF THE FAMILY WAS COMPLETELY MIFFED WHEN HE AND MY MOM FELL IN LOVE.
MOM CAME FROM A FAMILY OF HUMBLE TECH MILLIONAIRES.
IT WAS VERY POETIC WHEN THEY MERGED THE CORPORATIONS.
LIKE ROMEO AND JULIET!

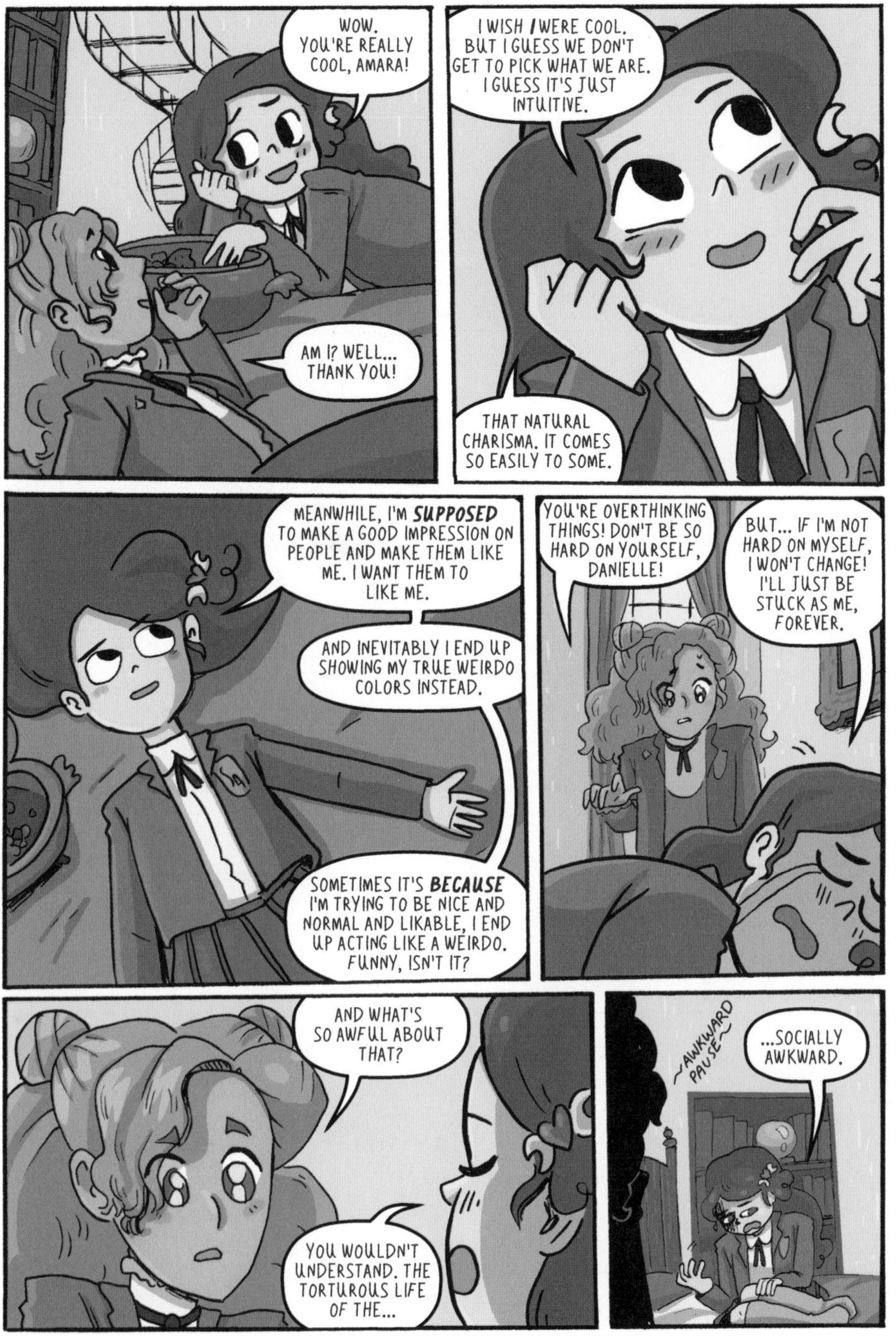
WOW. YOU'RE REALLY COOL, AMARA!
AM I? WELL... THANK YOU!
I WISH I WERE COOL. BUT I GUESS WE DON'T GET TO PICK WHAT WE ARE. I GUESS IT'S JUST INTUITIVE.
THAT NATURAL CHARISMA. IT COMES SO EASILY TO SOME.
MEANWHILE, I'M **SUPPOSED** TO MAKE A GOOD IMPRESSION ON PEOPLE AND MAKE THEM LIKE ME. I WANT THEM TO LIKE ME.
AND INEVITABLY I END UP SHOWING MY TRUE WEIRDO COLORS INSTEAD.
SOMETIMES IT'S **BECAUSE** I'M TRYING TO BE NICE AND NORMAL AND LIKABLE, I END UP ACTING LIKE A WEIRDO. FUNNY, ISN'T IT?
YOU'RE OVERTHINKING THINGS! DON'T BE SO HARD ON YOURSELF, DANIELLE!
BUT... IF I'M NOT HARD ON MYSELF, I WON'T CHANGE! I'LL JUST BE STUCK AS ME, FOREVER.
AND WHAT'S SO AWFUL ABOUT THAT?
YOU WOULDN'T UNDERSTAND. THE TORTUROUS LIFE OF THE...
~AWKWARD PAUSE~
...SOCIALLY AWKWARD.

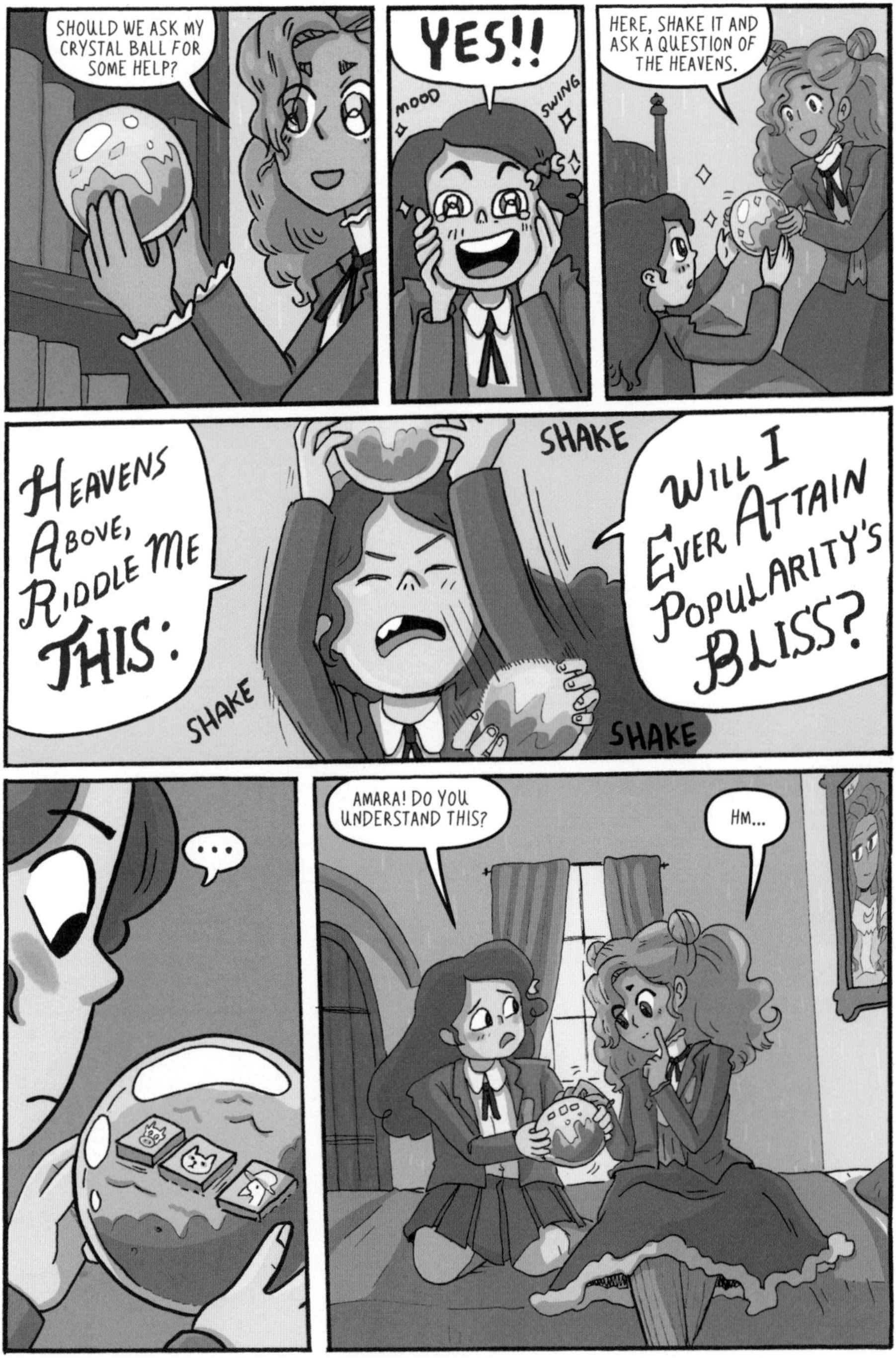

SHOULD WE ASK MY CRYSTAL BALL FOR SOME HELP?
YES!!
MOOD
SWING
HERE, SHAKE IT AND ASK A QUESTION OF THE HEAVENS.
HEAVENS ABOVE, RIDDLE ME THIS:
SHAKE
WILL I EVER ATTAIN POPULARITY'S BLISS?
SHAKE
SHAKE
...
AMARA! DO YOU UNDERSTAND THIS?
HM...

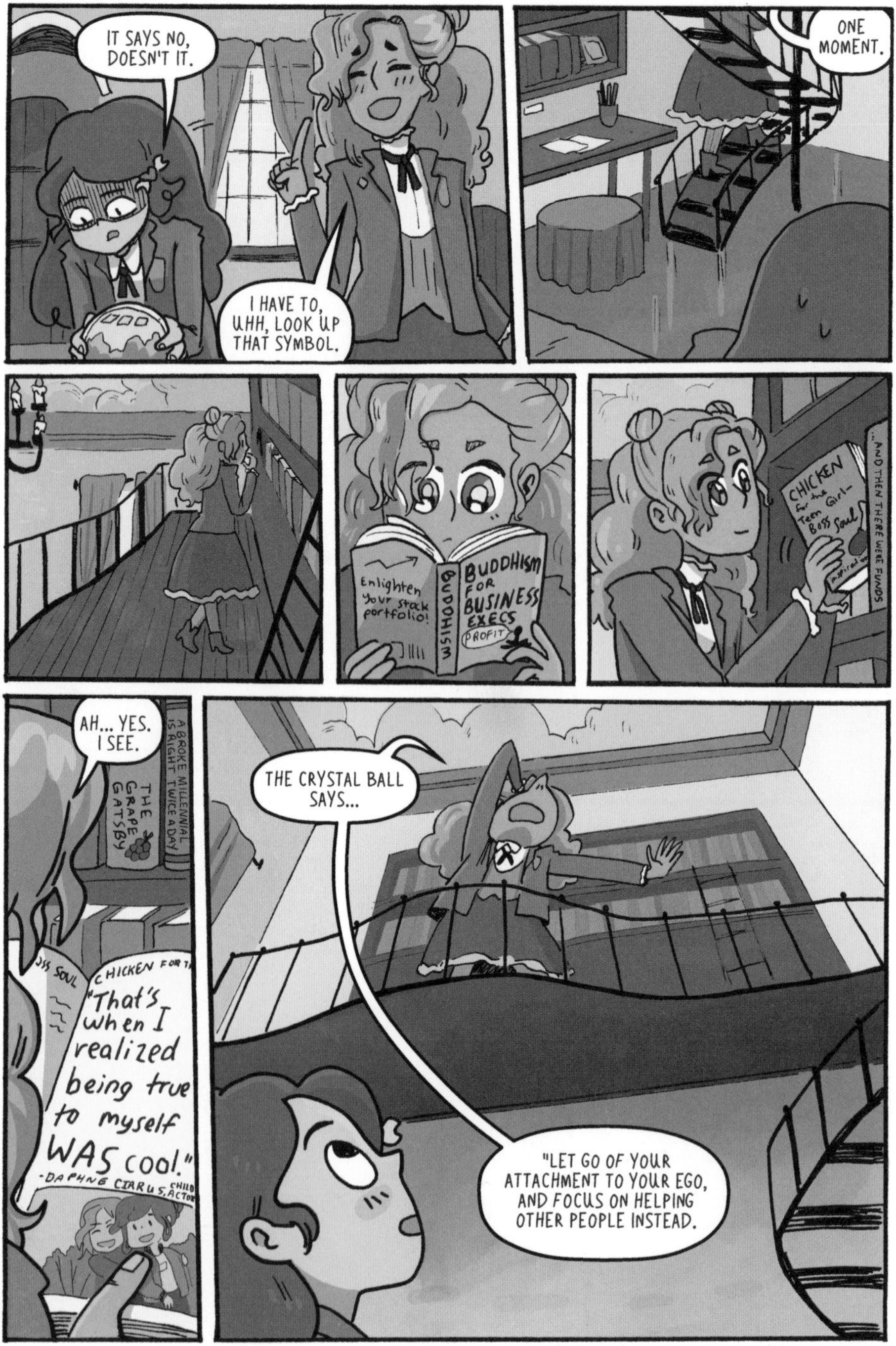
IT SAYS NO, DOESN'T IT.
I HAVE TO, UHH, LOOK UP THAT SYMBOL.
ONE MOMENT.
Enlighten your stock portfolio!
BUDDHISM
BUDDHISM FOR BUSINESS EXECS
PROFIT
CHICKEN for the Teen Girl-Boss Soul
...AND THEN THERE WERE FUNDS
AH... YES. I SEE.
A BROKE MILLENNIAL IS RIGHT TWICE A DAY
THE GRAPE GATSBY
CHICKEN FOR TH
SS SOUL
"That's when I realized being true to myself WAS cool."
-DAPHNE CIRRUS, CHILD ACTOR
THE CRYSTAL BALL SAYS...
"LET GO OF YOUR ATTACHMENT TO YOUR EGO, AND FOCUS ON HELPING OTHER PEOPLE INSTEAD.

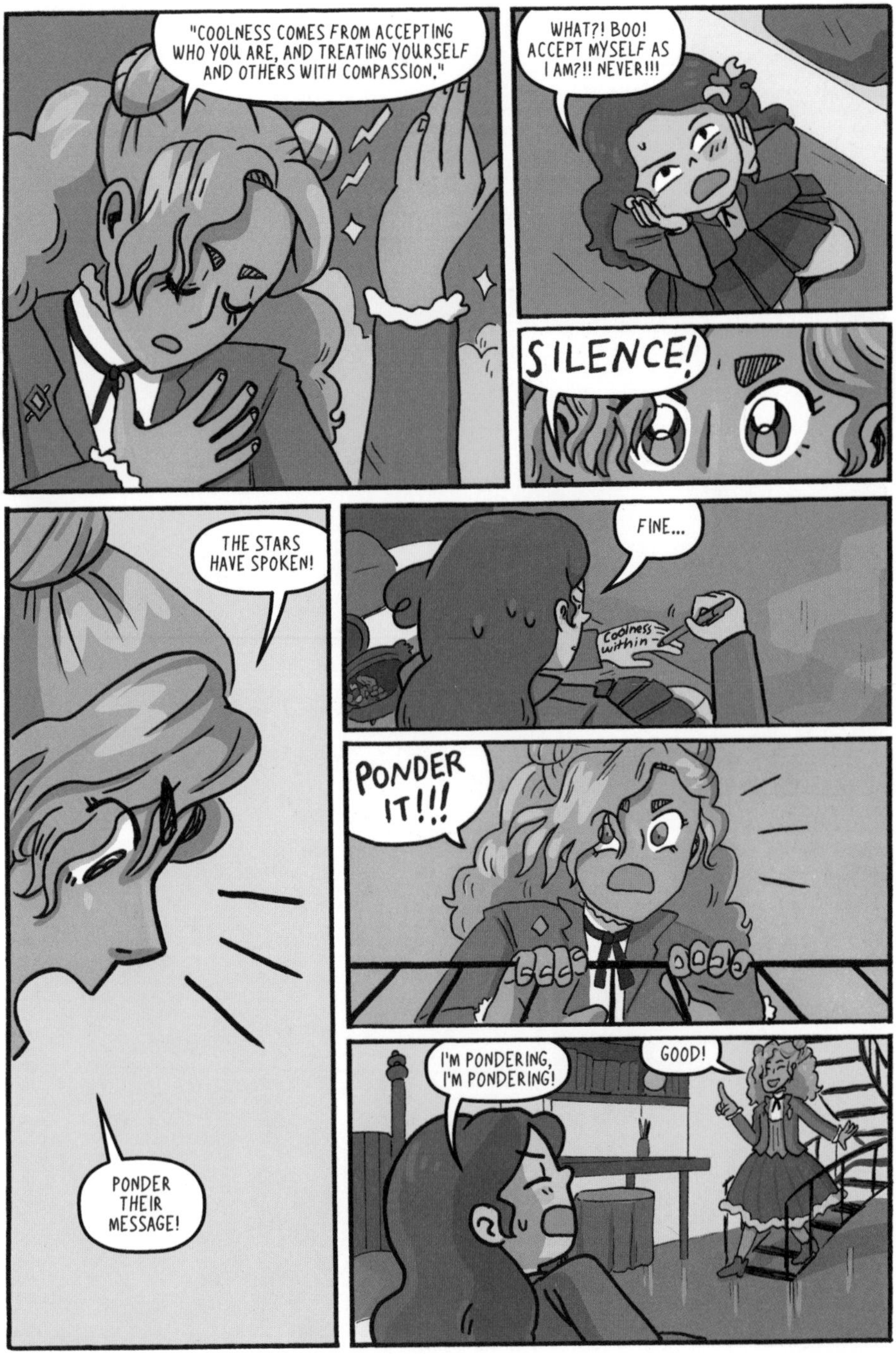
"COOLNESS COMES FROM ACCEPTING WHO YOU ARE, AND TREATING YOURSELF AND OTHERS WITH COMPASSION."
WHAT?! BOO! ACCEPT MYSELF AS I AM?!! NEVER!!!
SILENCE!
THE STARS HAVE SPOKEN!
PONDER THEIR MESSAGE!
FINE...
Coolness within
PONDER IT!!!
I'M PONDERING, I'M PONDERING!
GOOD!

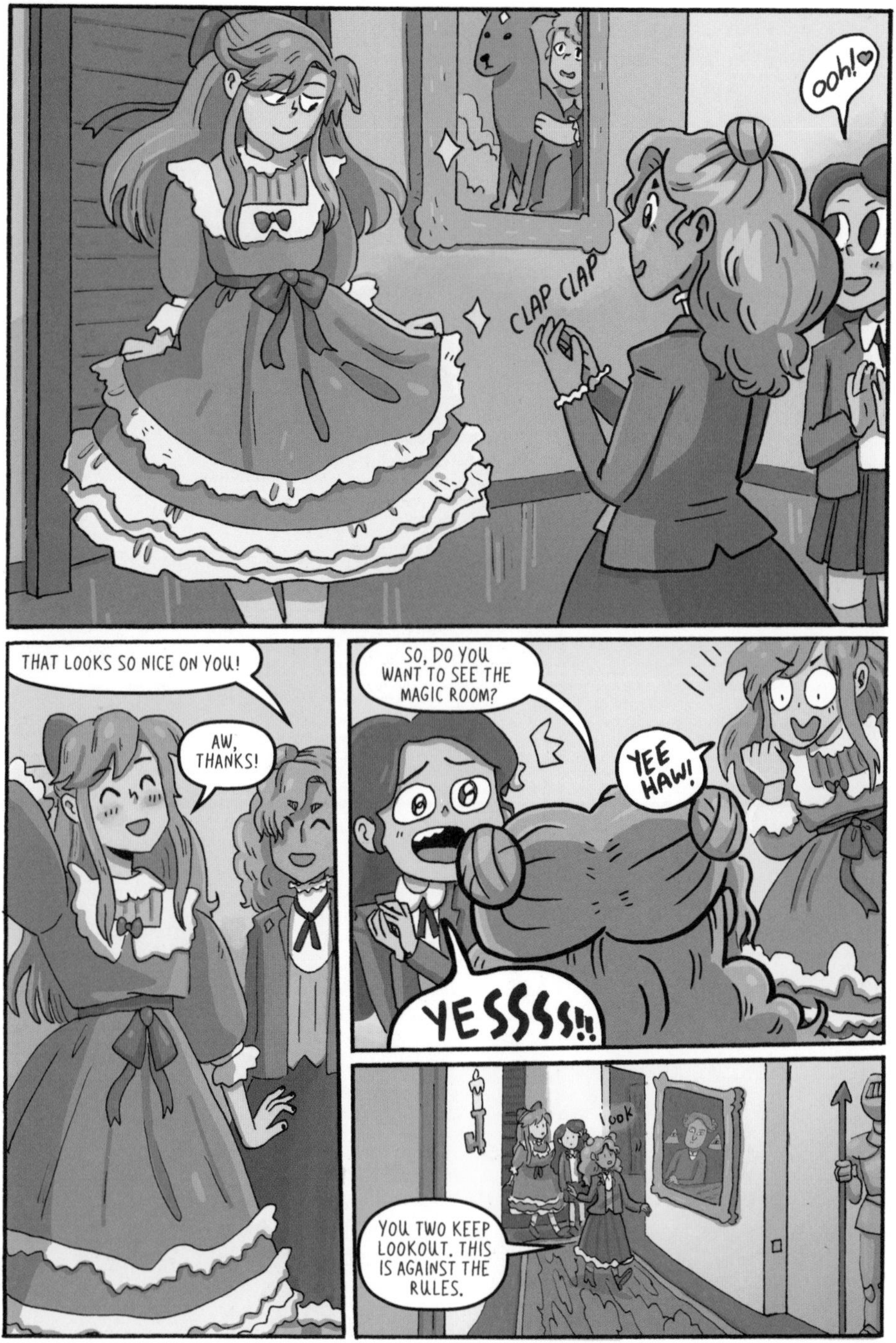
ooh!♡
CLAP CLAP
THAT LOOKS SO NICE ON YOU!
AW, THANKS!
SO, DO YOU WANT TO SEE THE MAGIC ROOM?
YEE HAW!
YESSSSS!!
look
YOU TWO KEEP LOOKOUT. THIS IS AGAINST THE RULES.

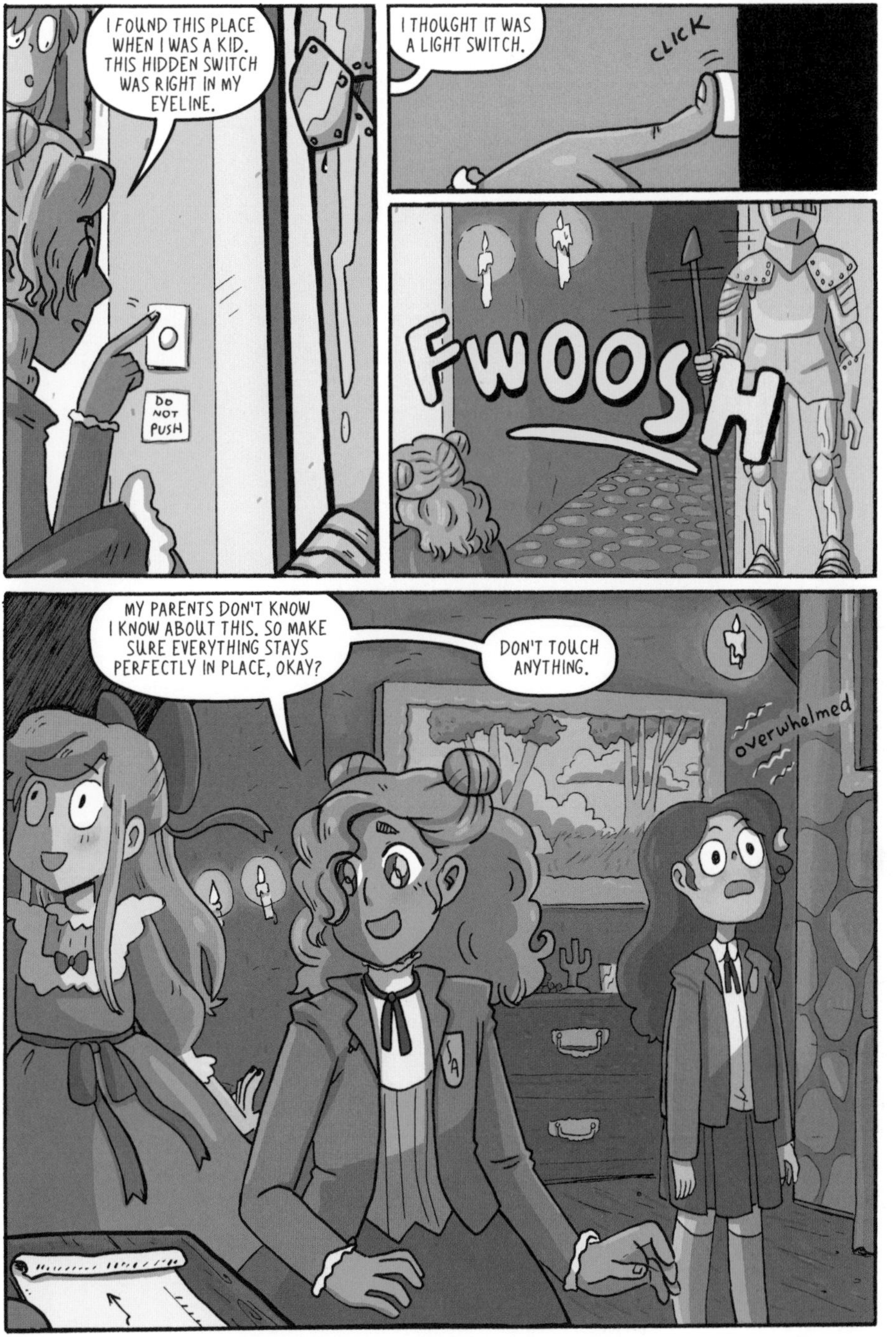
I FOUND THIS PLACE WHEN I WAS A KID. THIS HIDDEN SWITCH WAS RIGHT IN MY EYELINE.
DO NOT PUSH
I THOUGHT IT WAS A LIGHT SWITCH.
CLICK
FWOOSH
MY PARENTS DON'T KNOW I KNOW ABOUT THIS. SO MAKE SURE EVERYTHING STAYS PERFECTLY IN PLACE, OKAY?
DON'T TOUCH ANYTHING.
overwhelmed

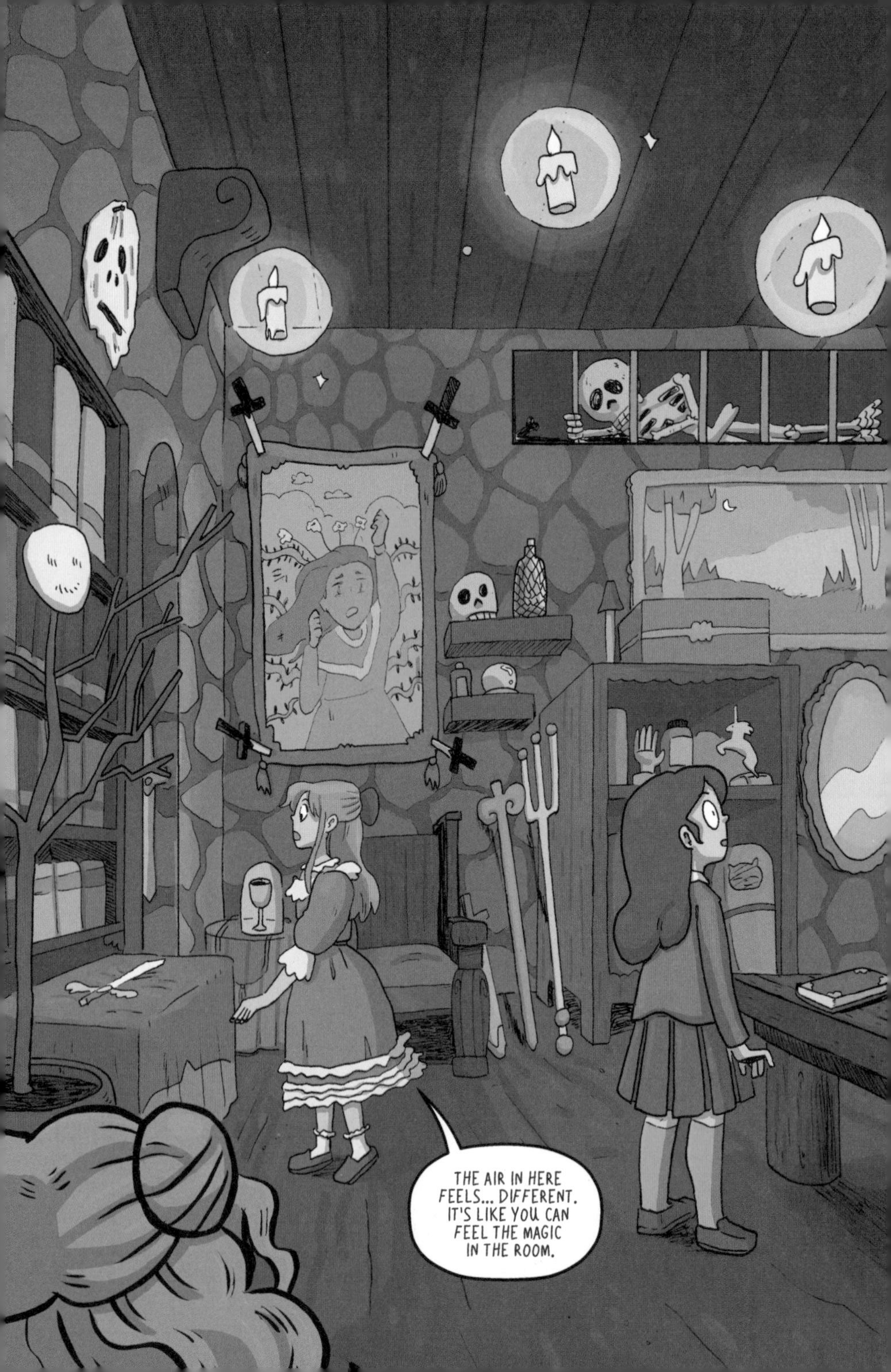
THE AIR IN HERE FEELS... DIFFERENT. IT'S LIKE YOU CAN FEEL THE MAGIC IN THE ROOM.

EVERYTHING IN THIS ROOM FEELS LIKE IT'S CALLING TO ME.

GLOW

TOUCH

BZZRT

!!

Chicken &the Warlock's Soul

MADISON! I SAID--

MY BAD.

Thank youu

WHAT WAS THAT?

THUMP THUMP

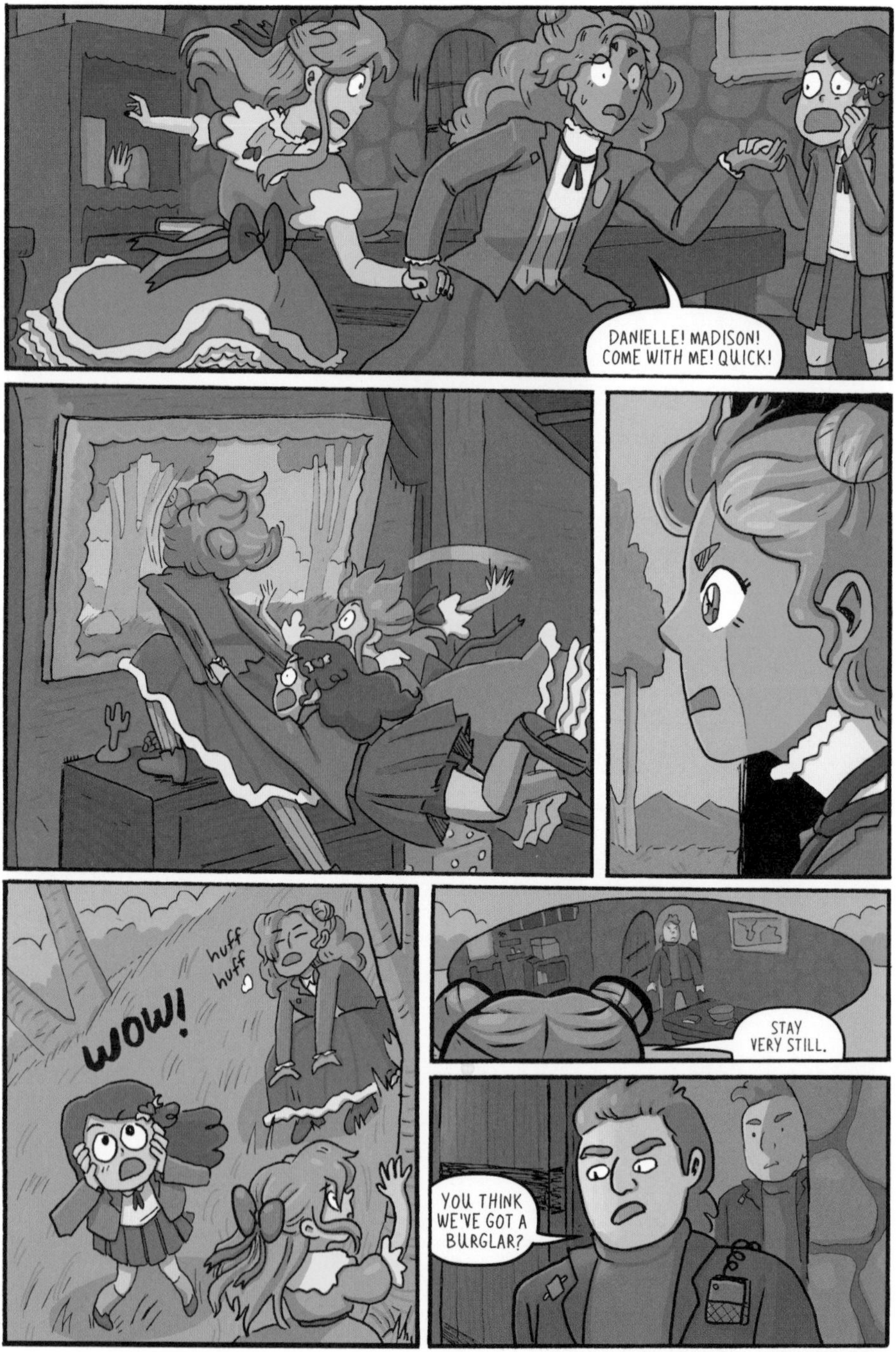
DANIELLE! MADISON! COME WITH ME! QUICK!
huff huff
WOW!
STAY VERY STILL.
YOU THINK WE'VE GOT A BURGLAR?

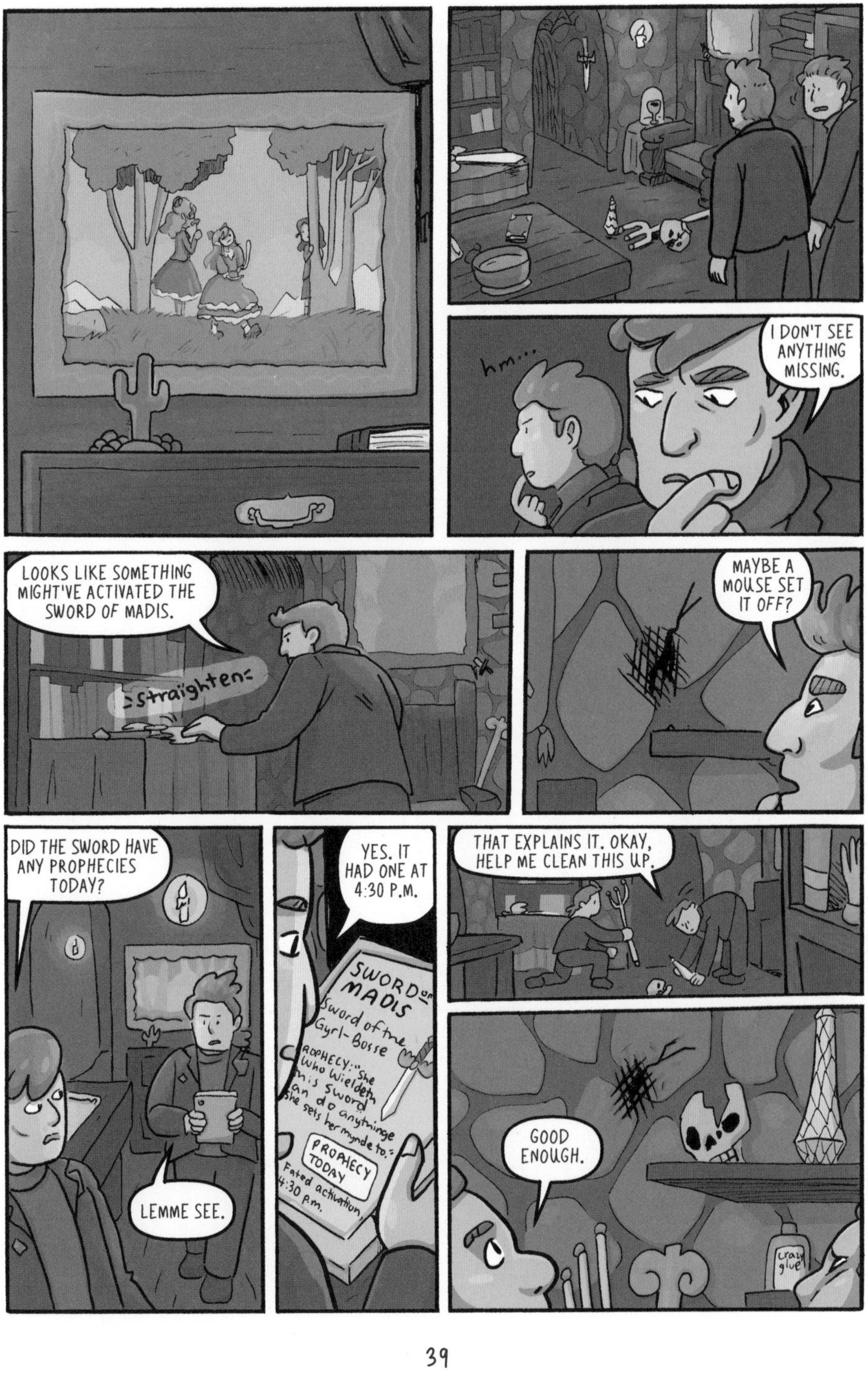

hm...
I DON'T SEE ANYTHING MISSING.
LOOKS LIKE SOMETHING MIGHT'VE ACTIVATED THE SWORD OF MADIS.
:straighten:
MAYBE A MOUSE SET IT OFF?
DID THE SWORD HAVE ANY PROPHECIES TODAY?
LEMME SEE.
YES. IT HAD ONE AT 4:30 P.M.
SWORD of MADIS
Sword of the Gyrl-Bosse
ROPHECY: "She Who Wieldeth his Sword an do anythinge she sets her mynde to."
PROPHECY TODAY
Fated activation, 4:30 p.m.
THAT EXPLAINS IT. OKAY, HELP ME CLEAN THIS UP.
GOOD ENOUGH.
crazy glue!

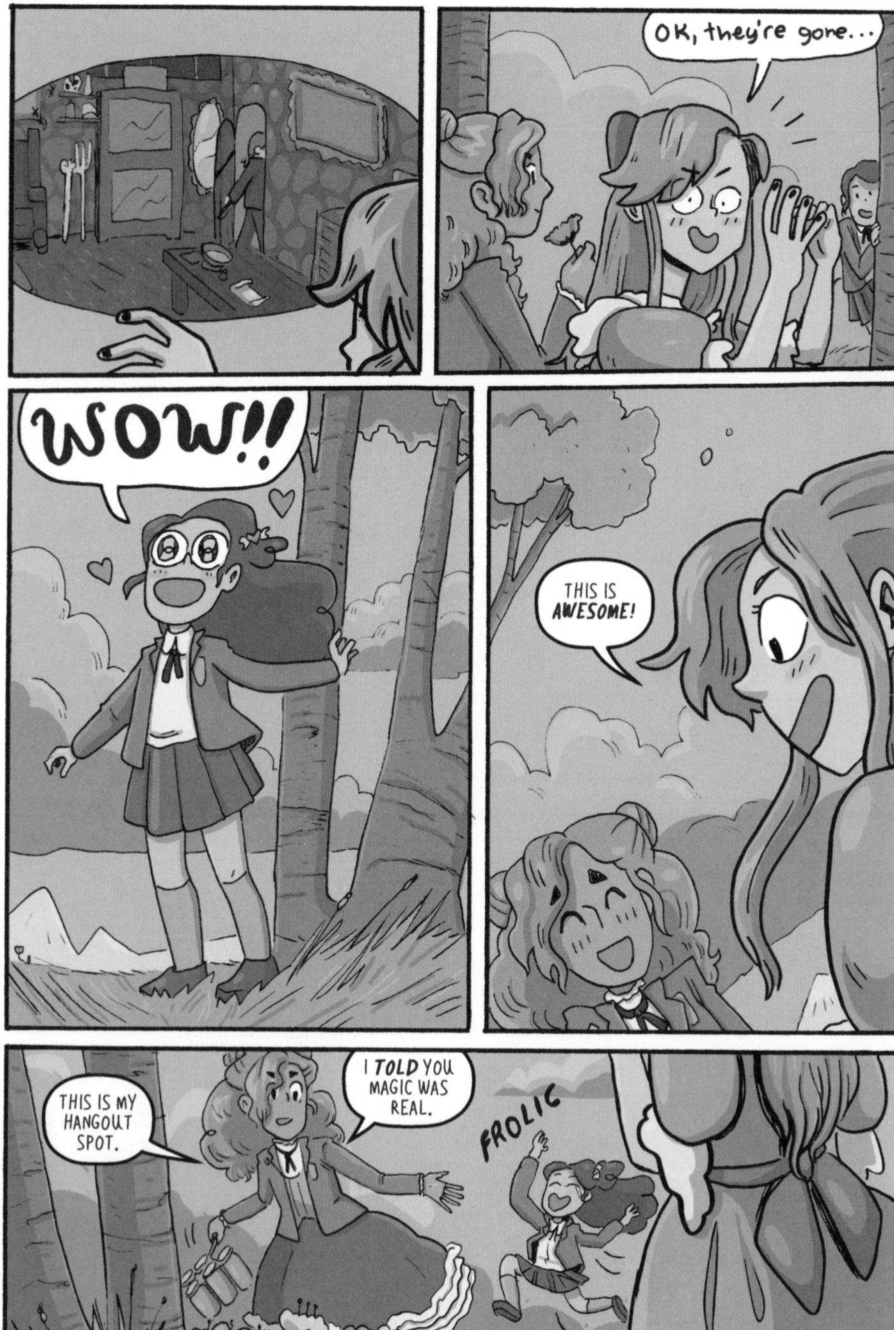
OK, they're gone...
WOW!!
THIS IS AWESOME!
THIS IS MY HANGOUT SPOT.
I TOLD YOU MAGIC WAS REAL.
FROLIC

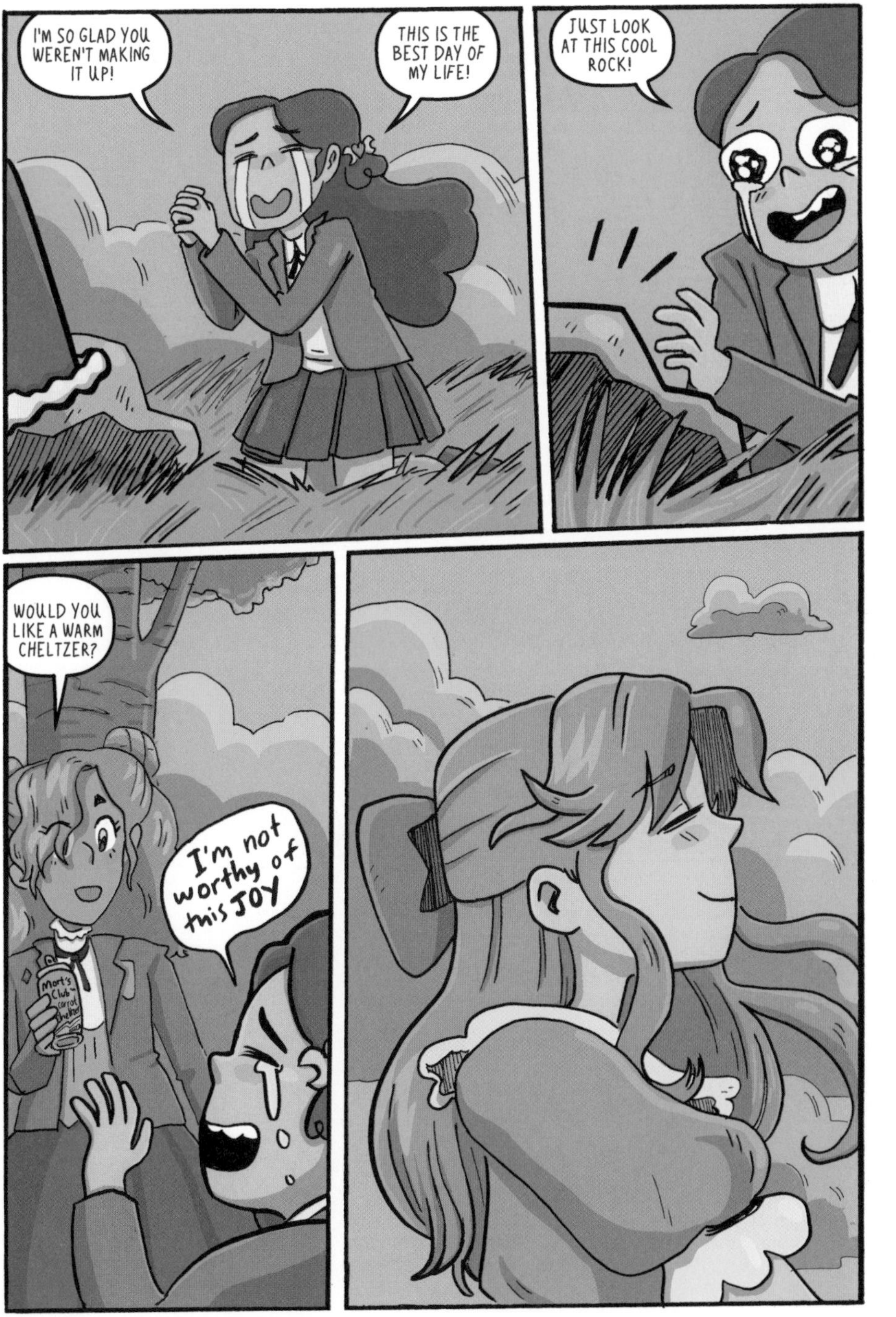

I'M SO GLAD YOU WEREN'T MAKING IT UP!
THIS IS THE BEST DAY OF MY LIFE!
JUST LOOK AT THIS COOL ROCK!
WOULD YOU LIKE A WARM CHELTZER?
I'm not worthy of this JOY

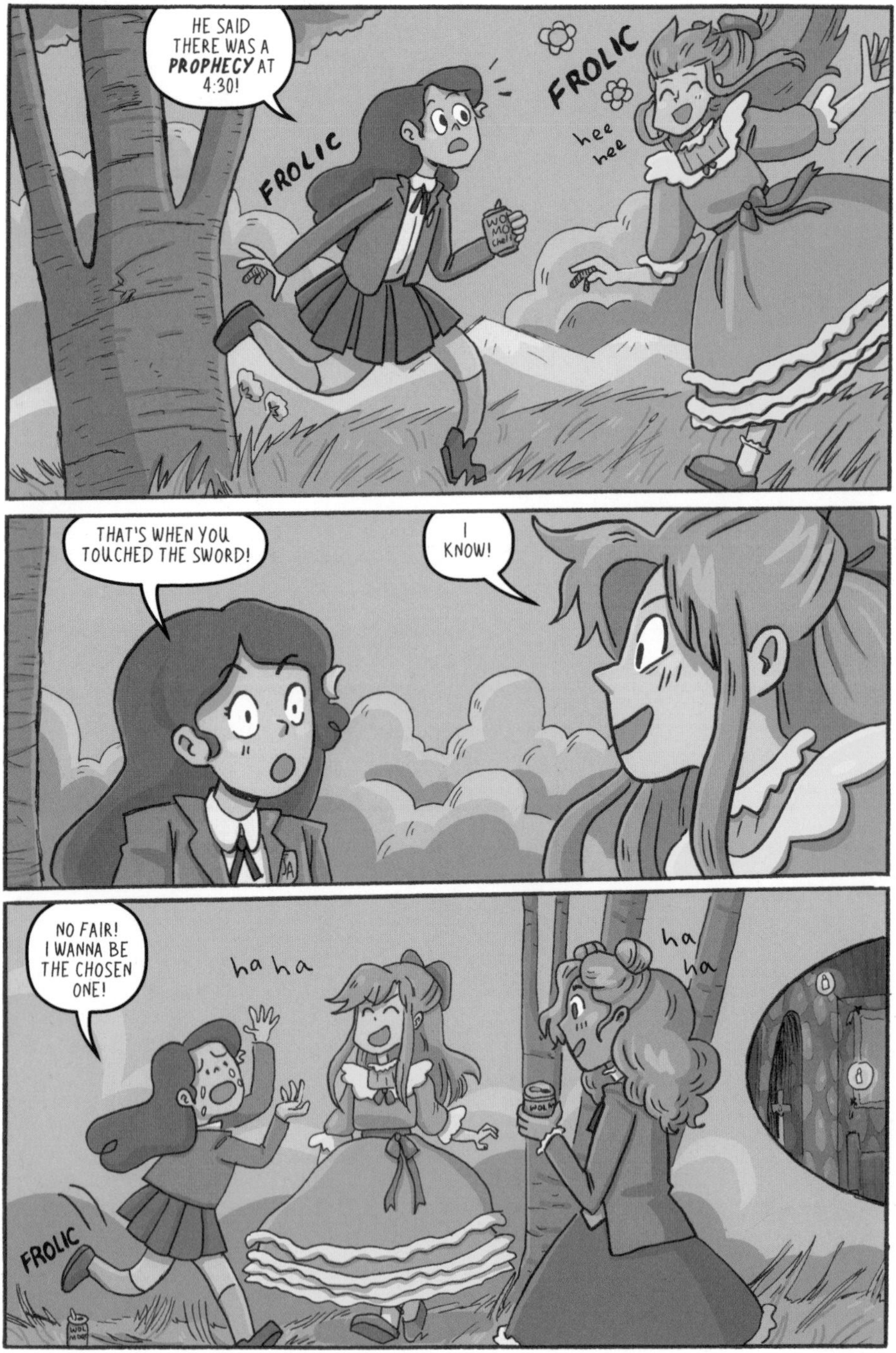
HE SAID THERE WAS A **PROPHECY** AT 4:30!
FROLIC
FROLIC
hee hee
THAT'S WHEN YOU TOUCHED THE SWORD!
I KNOW!
NO FAIR! I WANNA BE THE CHOSEN ONE!
ha ha
ha ha
FROLIC

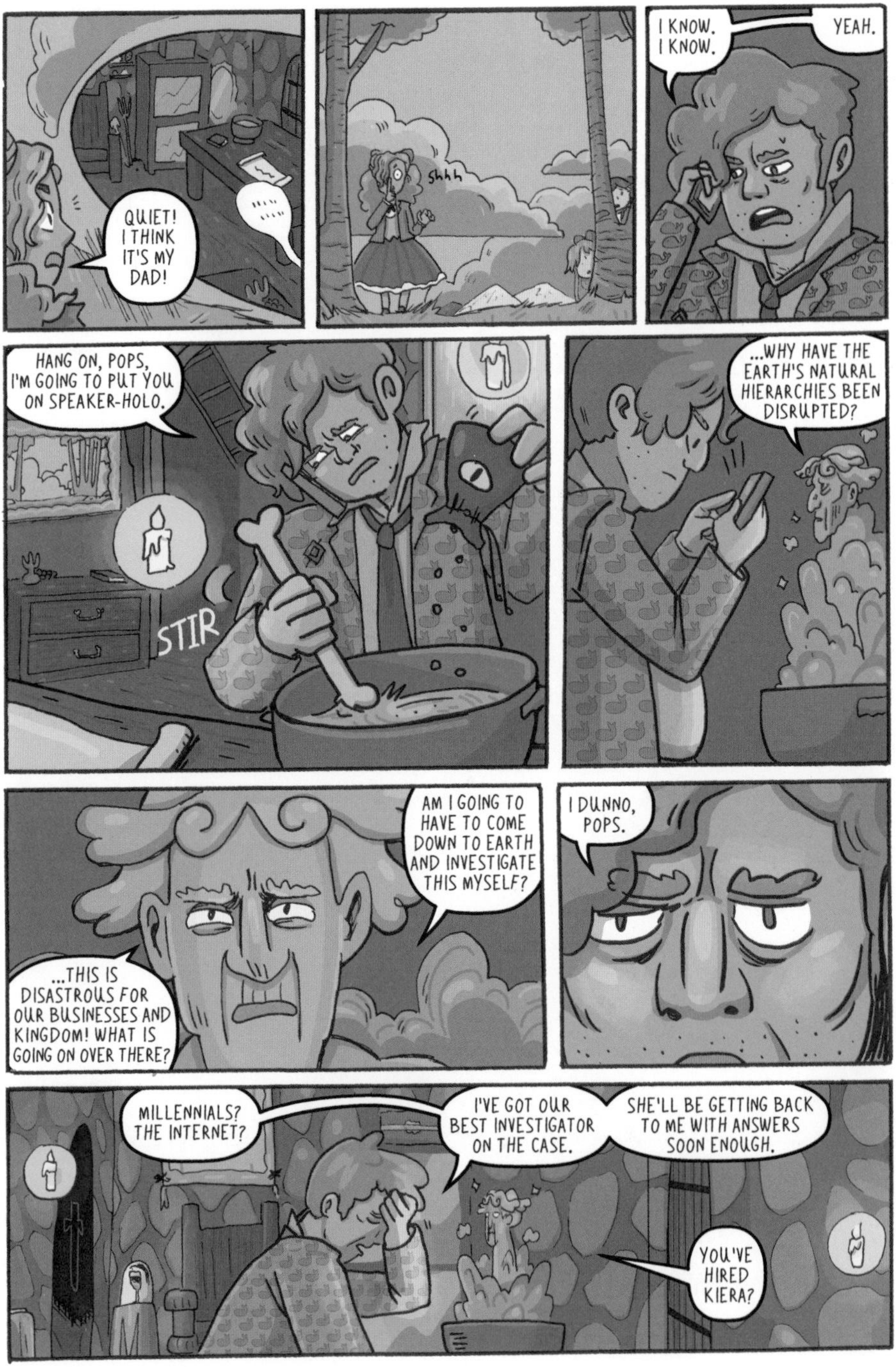
QUIET! I THINK IT'S MY DAD!
Shhh
I KNOW. I KNOW.
YEAH.
HANG ON, POPS, I'M GOING TO PUT YOU ON SPEAKER-HOLO.
STIR
...WHY HAVE THE EARTH'S NATURAL HIERARCHIES BEEN DISRUPTED?
AM I GOING TO HAVE TO COME DOWN TO EARTH AND INVESTIGATE THIS MYSELF?
...THIS IS DISASTROUS FOR OUR BUSINESSES AND KINGDOM! WHAT IS GOING ON OVER THERE?
I DUNNO, POPS.
MILLENNIALS? THE INTERNET?
I'VE GOT OUR BEST INVESTIGATOR ON THE CASE.
SHE'LL BE GETTING BACK TO ME WITH ANSWERS SOON ENOUGH.
YOU'VE HIRED KIERA?

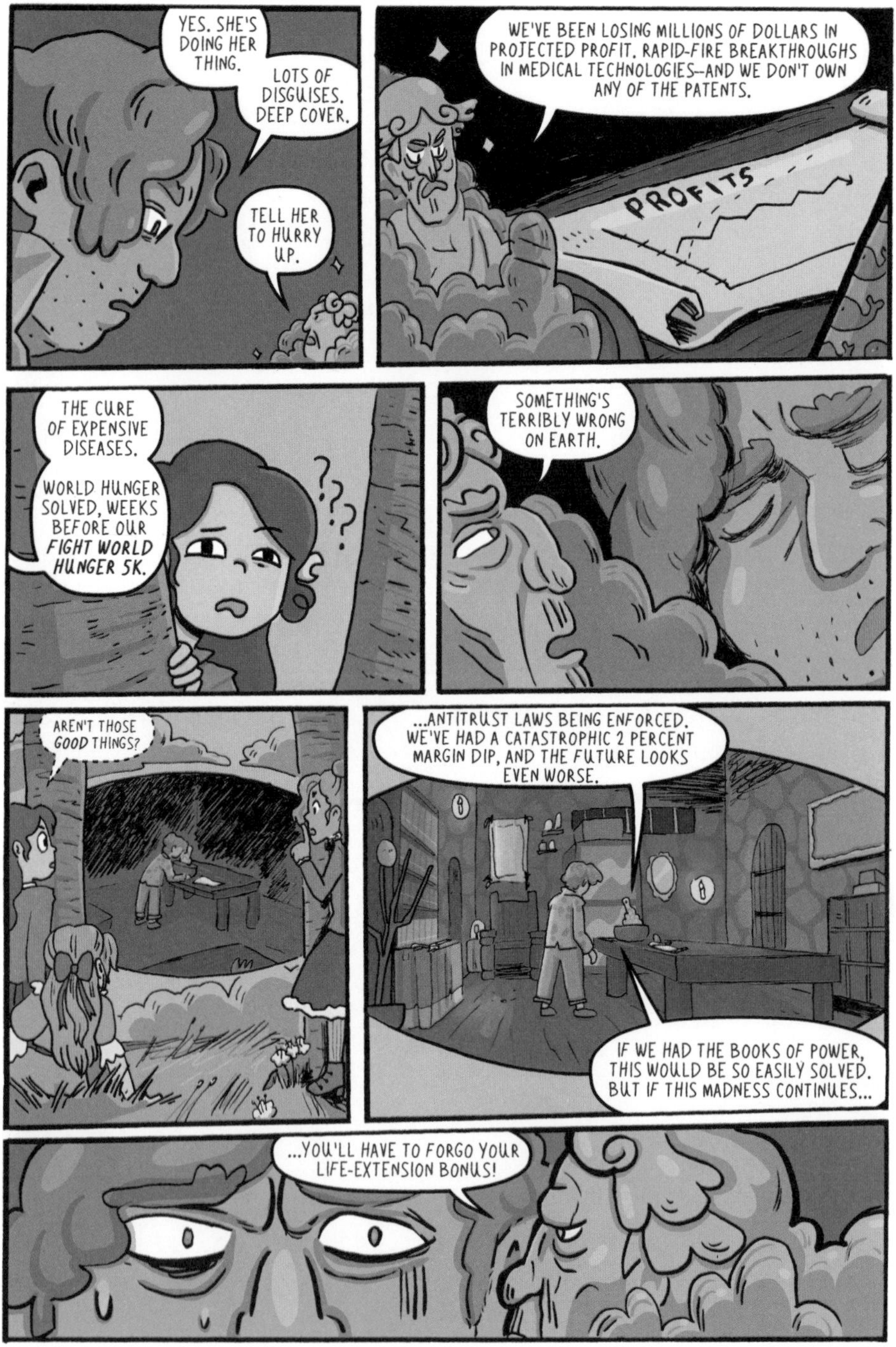

YES. SHE'S DOING HER THING.
LOTS OF DISGUISES. DEEP COVER.
TELL HER TO HURRY UP.
WE'VE BEEN LOSING MILLIONS OF DOLLARS IN PROJECTED PROFIT. RAPID-FIRE BREAKTHROUGHS IN MEDICAL TECHNOLOGIES--AND WE DON'T OWN ANY OF THE PATENTS.
PROFITS
THE CURE OF EXPENSIVE DISEASES.
WORLD HUNGER SOLVED, WEEKS BEFORE OUR *FIGHT WORLD HUNGER 5K.*
???
SOMETHING'S TERRIBLY WRONG ON EARTH.
AREN'T THOSE *GOOD* THINGS?
...ANTITRUST LAWS BEING ENFORCED. WE'VE HAD A CATASTROPHIC 2 PERCENT MARGIN DIP, AND THE *FUTURE* LOOKS EVEN WORSE.
IF WE HAD THE BOOKS OF POWER, THIS WOULD BE SO EASILY SOLVED. BUT IF THIS MADNESS CONTINUES...
...YOU'LL HAVE TO *FORGO* YOUR LIFE-EXTENSION BONUS!

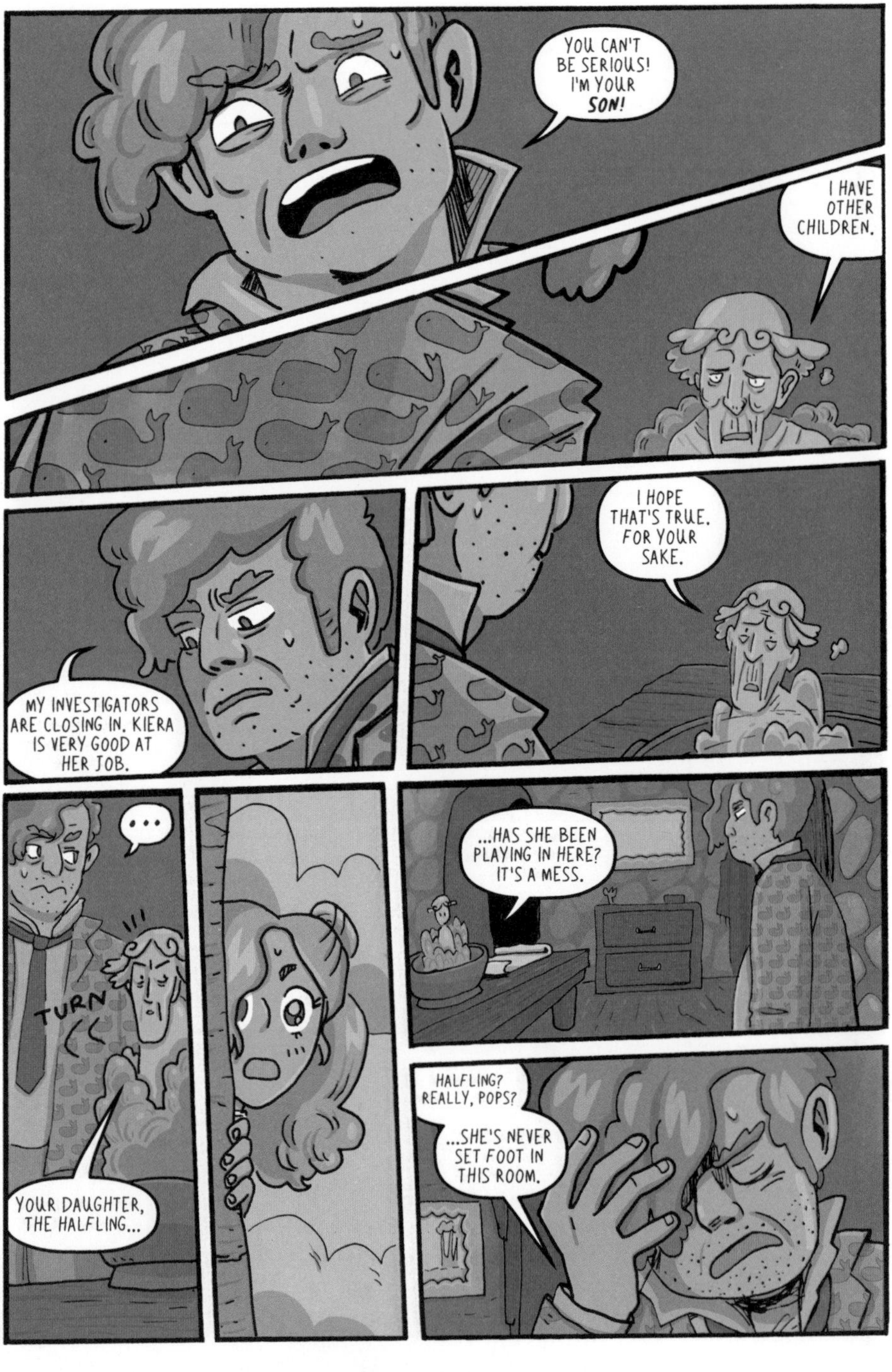
YOU CAN'T BE SERIOUS! I'M YOUR SON!
I HAVE OTHER CHILDREN.
MY INVESTIGATORS ARE CLOSING IN. KIERA IS VERY GOOD AT HER JOB.
I HOPE THAT'S TRUE. FOR YOUR SAKE.
...
TURN
YOUR DAUGHTER, THE HALFLING...
...HAS SHE BEEN PLAYING IN HERE? IT'S A MESS.
HALFLING? REALLY, POPS?
...SHE'S NEVER SET FOOT IN THIS ROOM.

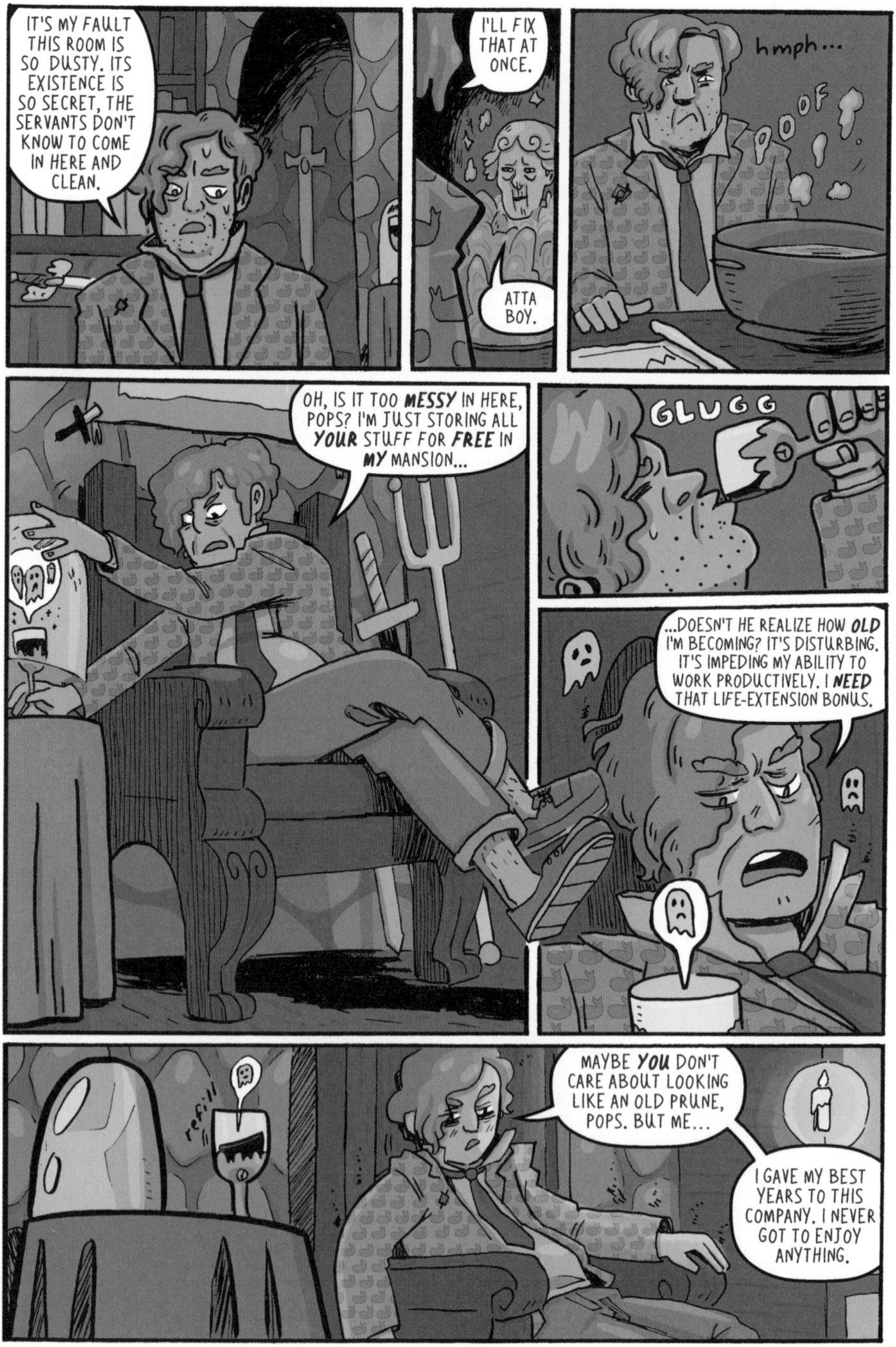
IT'S MY FAULT THIS ROOM IS SO DUSTY. ITS EXISTENCE IS SO SECRET, THE SERVANTS DON'T KNOW TO COME IN HERE AND CLEAN.
I'LL FIX THAT AT ONCE.
ATTA BOY.
hmph...
POOF
OH, IS IT TOO MESSY IN HERE, POPS? I'M JUST STORING ALL YOUR STUFF FOR FREE IN MY MANSION...
GLUGG
...DOESN'T HE REALIZE HOW OLD I'M BECOMING? IT'S DISTURBING. IT'S IMPEDING MY ABILITY TO WORK PRODUCTIVELY. I NEED THAT LIFE-EXTENSION BONUS.
refill
MAYBE YOU DON'T CARE ABOUT LOOKING LIKE AN OLD PRUNE, POPS. BUT ME...
I GAVE MY BEST YEARS TO THIS COMPANY. I NEVER GOT TO ENJOY ANYTHING.

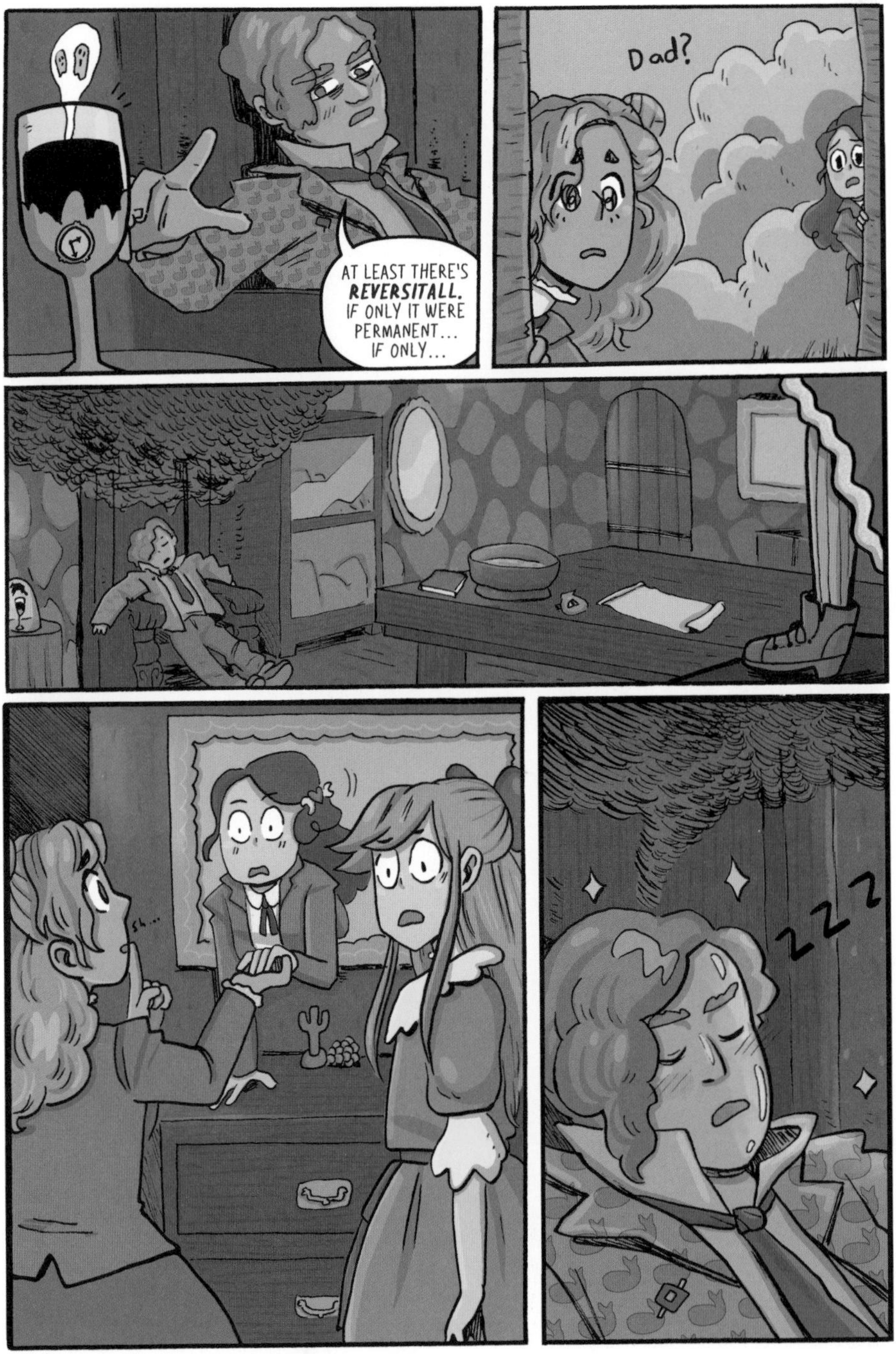
AT LEAST THERE'S **REVERSITALL.** IF ONLY IT WERE PERMANENT... IF ONLY...
Dad?
sh...
Z Z Z

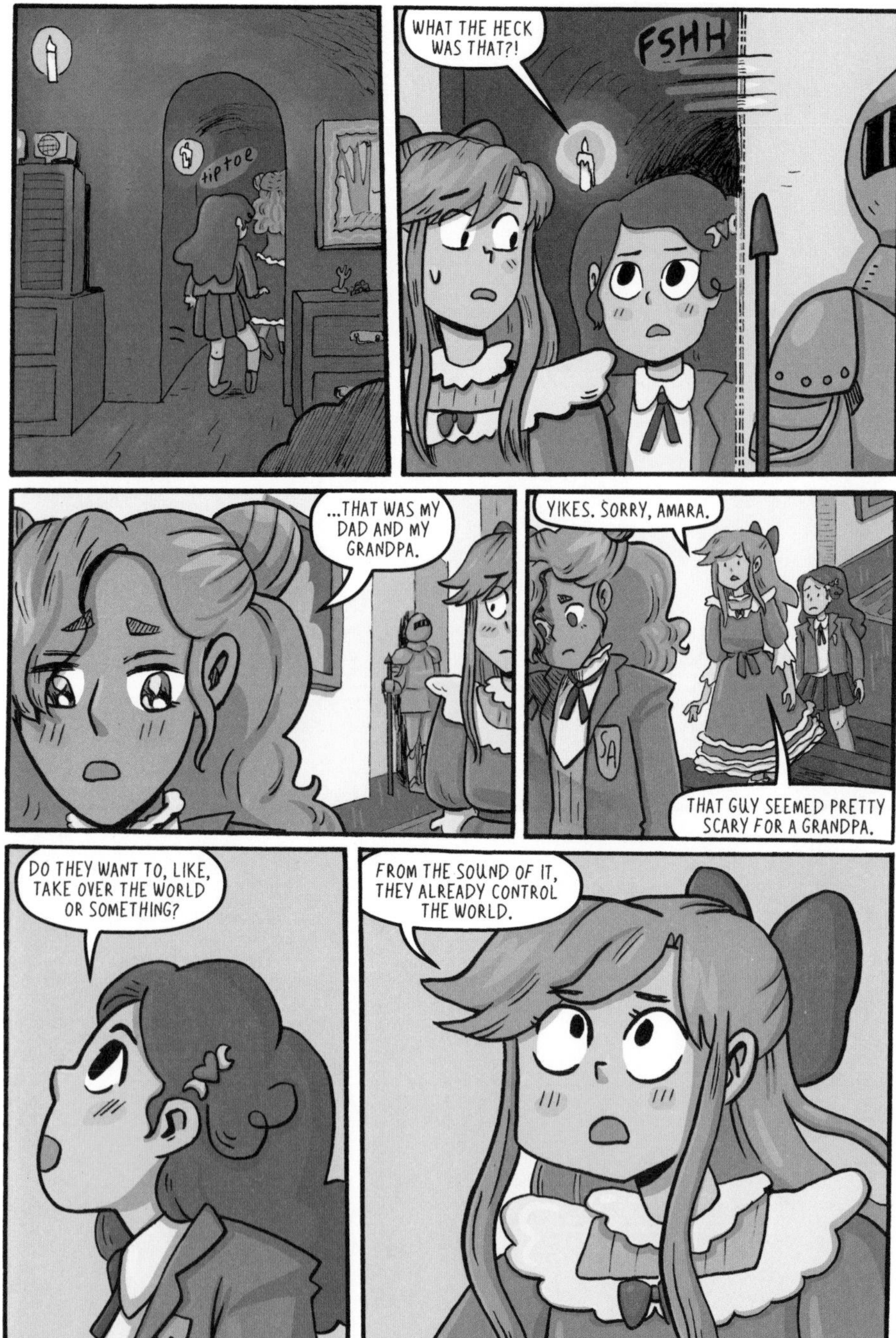

tiptoe
WHAT THE HECK WAS THAT?!
FSHH
...THAT WAS MY DAD AND MY GRANDPA.
YIKES. SORRY, AMARA.
THAT GUY SEEMED PRETTY SCARY FOR A GRANDPA.
DO THEY WANT TO, LIKE, TAKE OVER THE WORLD OR SOMETHING?
FROM THE SOUND OF IT, THEY ALREADY CONTROL THE WORLD.

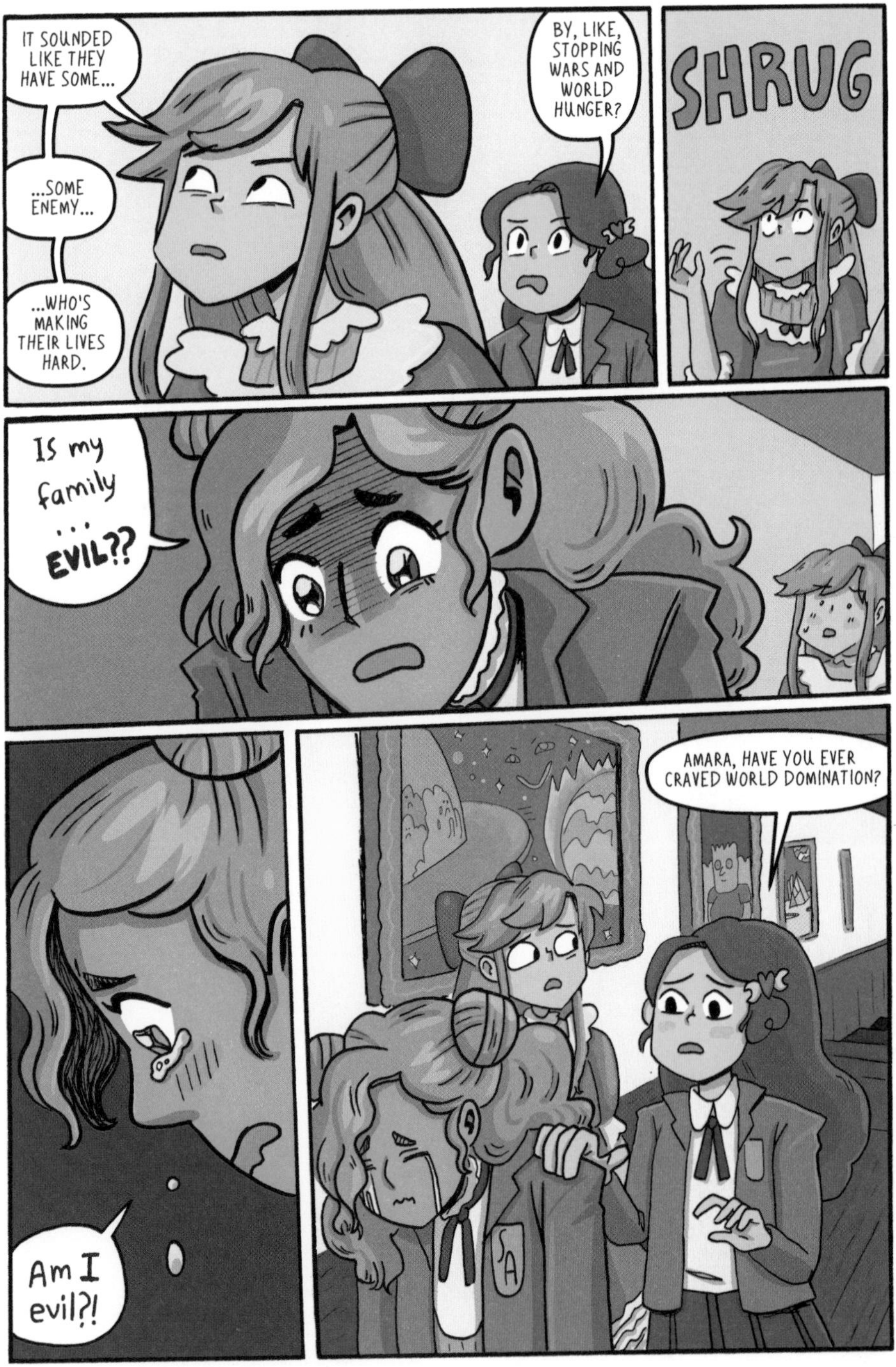
IT SOUNDED LIKE THEY HAVE SOME...
...SOME ENEMY...
...WHO'S MAKING THEIR LIVES HARD.
BY, LIKE, STOPPING WARS AND WORLD HUNGER?
SHRUG
Is my family . . . EVIL??
Am I evil?!
AMARA, HAVE YOU EVER CRAVED WORLD DOMINATION?

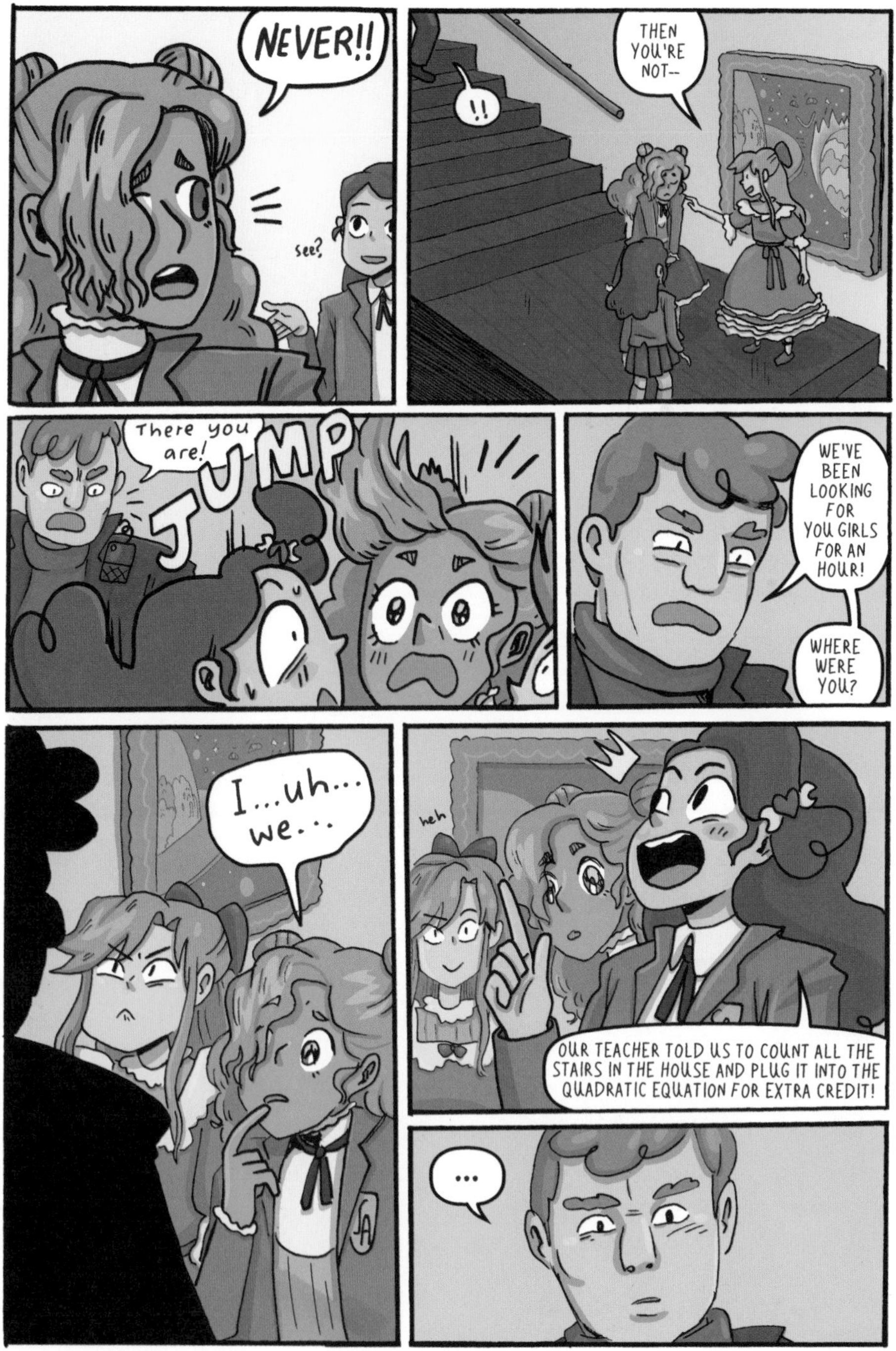
NEVER!!
see?
!!
THEN YOU'RE NOT--
There you are!
JUMP
WE'VE BEEN LOOKING FOR YOU GIRLS FOR AN HOUR!
WHERE WERE YOU?
I...uh... we...
heh
OUR TEACHER TOLD US TO COUNT ALL THE STAIRS IN THE HOUSE AND PLUG IT INTO THE QUADRATIC EQUATION FOR EXTRA CREDIT!
...

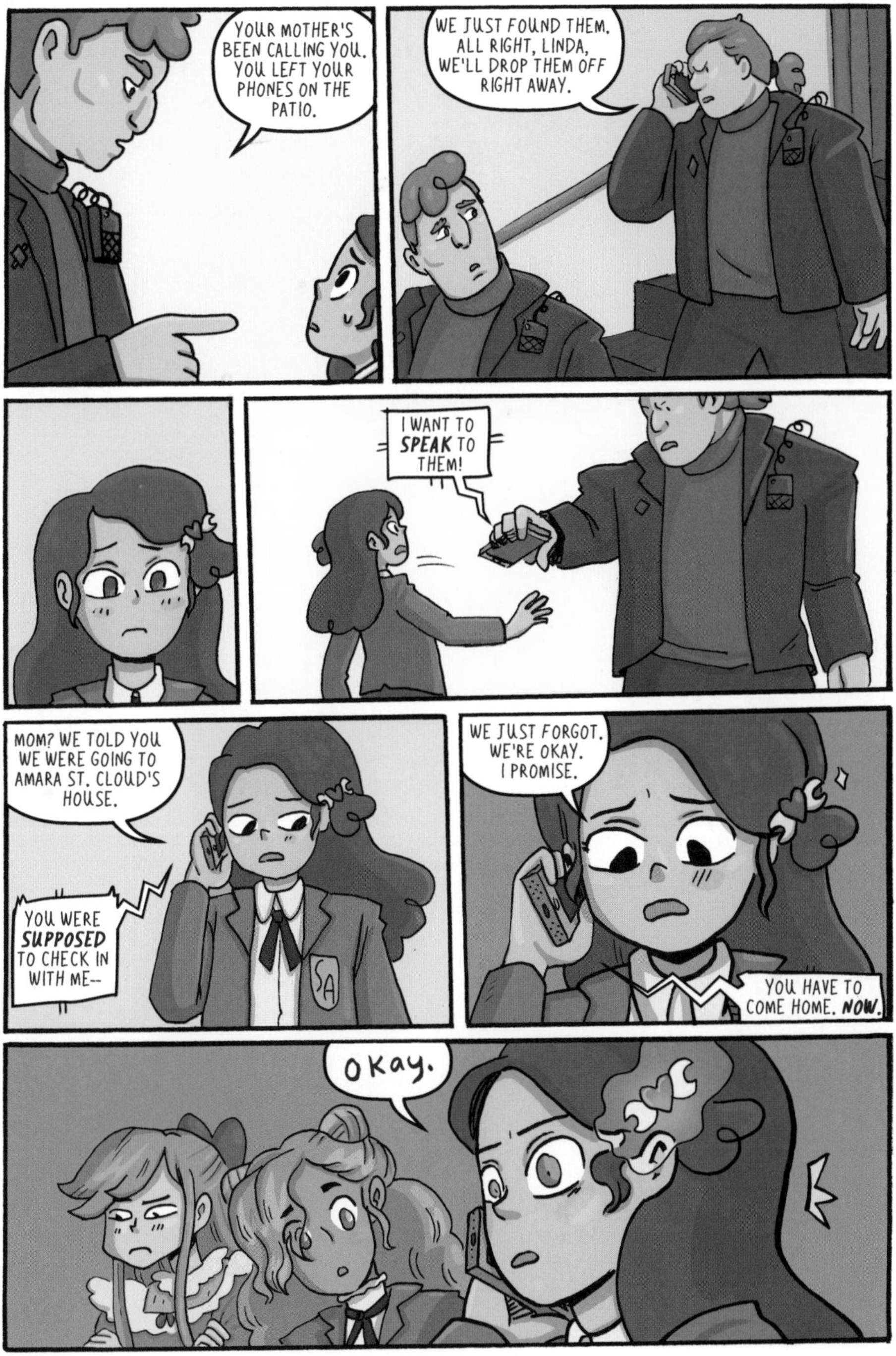
YOUR MOTHER'S BEEN CALLING YOU. YOU LEFT YOUR PHONES ON THE PATIO.
WE JUST FOUND THEM. ALL RIGHT, LINDA, WE'LL DROP THEM OFF RIGHT AWAY.
I WANT TO **SPEAK** TO THEM!
MOM? WE TOLD YOU WE WERE GOING TO AMARA ST. CLOUD'S HOUSE.
YOU WERE **SUPPOSED** TO CHECK IN WITH ME--
WE JUST FORGOT. WE'RE OKAY. I PROMISE.
YOU HAVE TO COME HOME. **NOW.**
okay.

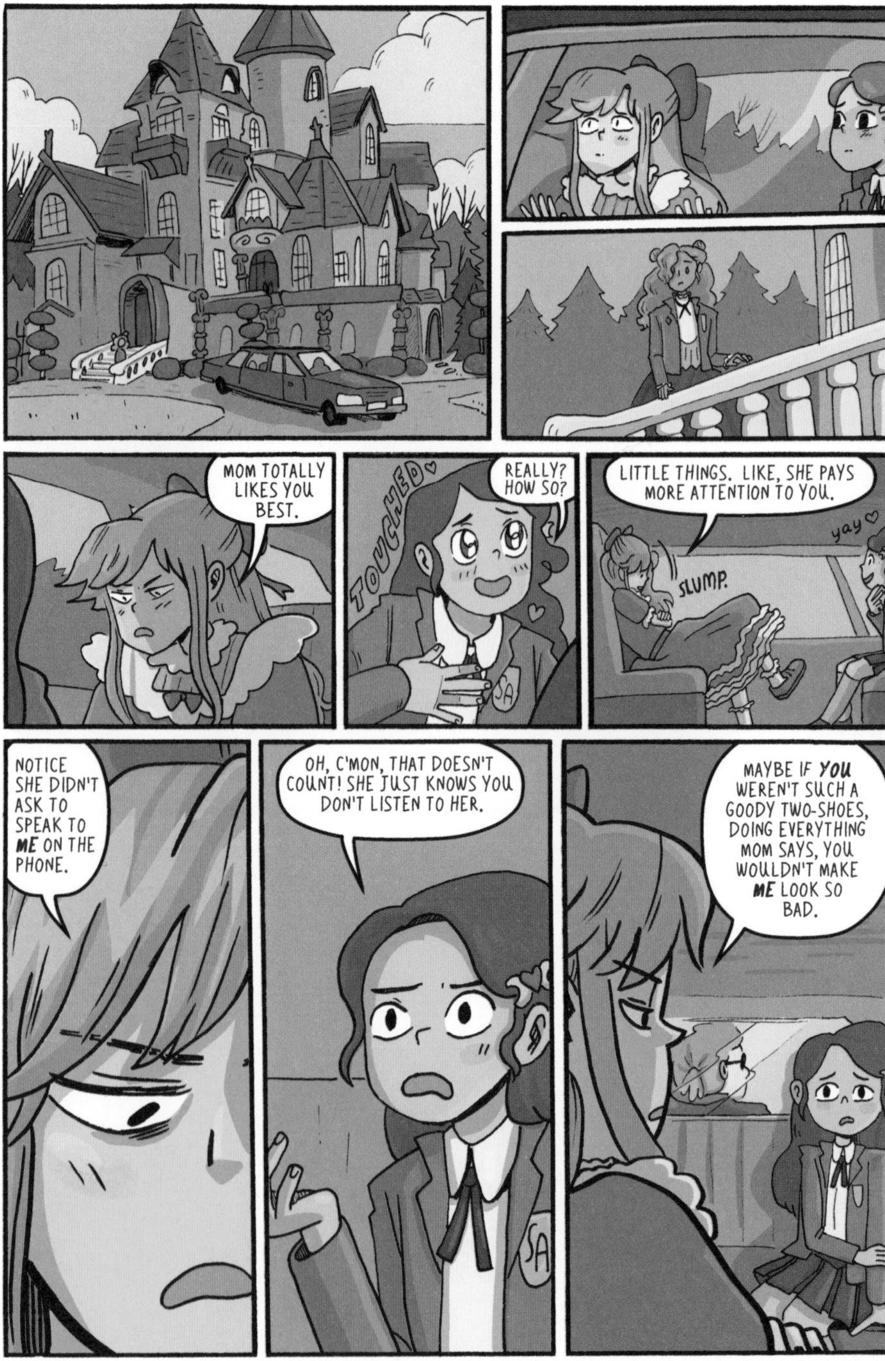
MOM TOTALLY LIKES YOU BEST.
TOUCHED
REALLY? HOW SO?
LITTLE THINGS. LIKE, SHE PAYS MORE ATTENTION TO YOU.
yay
SLUMP.
NOTICE SHE DIDN'T ASK TO SPEAK TO ME ON THE PHONE.
OH, C'MON, THAT DOESN'T COUNT! SHE JUST KNOWS YOU DON'T LISTEN TO HER.
MAYBE IF YOU WEREN'T SUCH A GOODY TWO-SHOES, DOING EVERYTHING MOM SAYS, YOU WOULDN'T MAKE ME LOOK SO BAD.

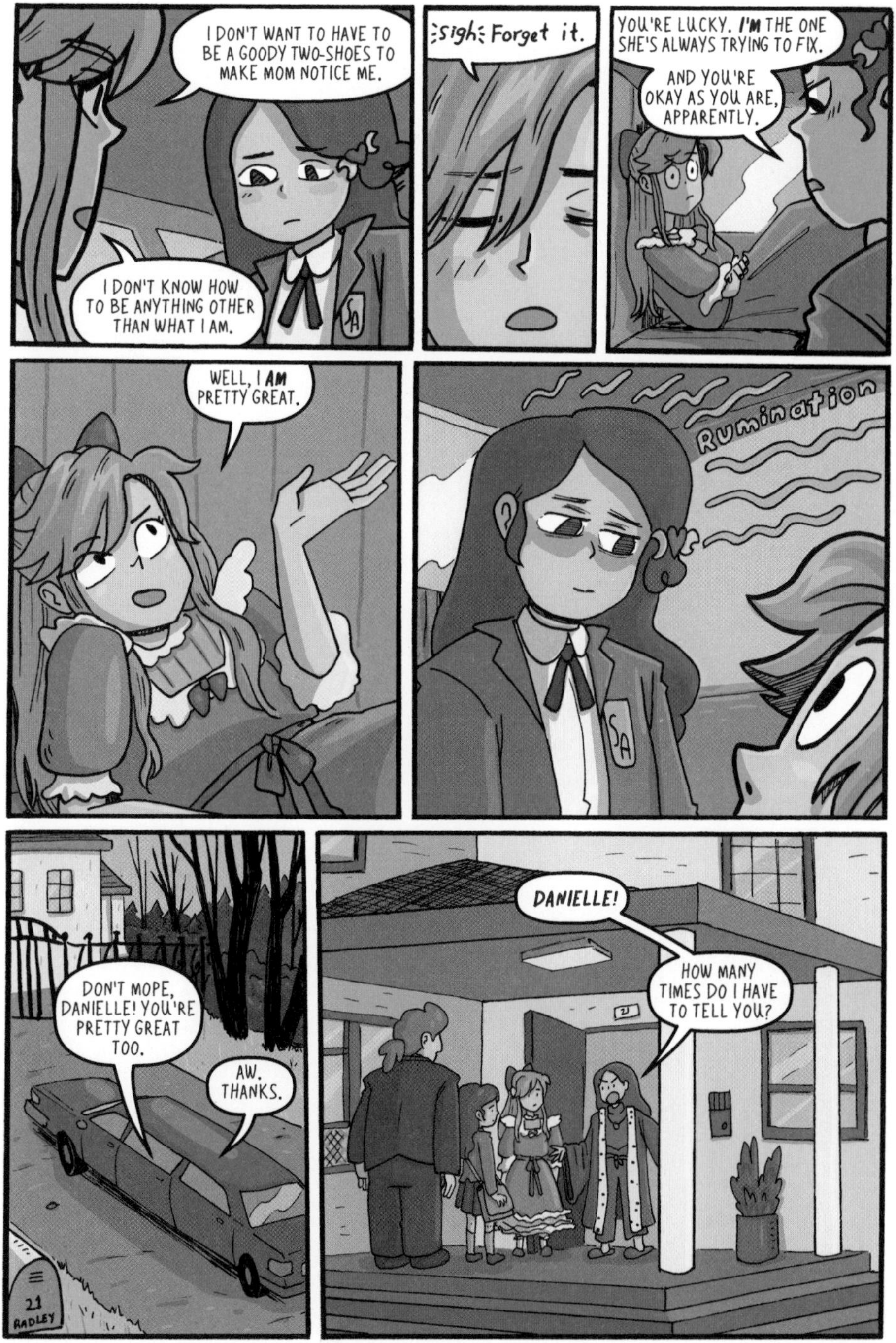
I DON'T WANT TO HAVE TO BE A GOODY TWO-SHOES TO MAKE MOM NOTICE ME.
I DON'T KNOW HOW TO BE ANYTHING OTHER THAN WHAT I AM.
sigh Forget it.
YOU'RE LUCKY. **I'M** THE ONE SHE'S ALWAYS TRYING TO FIX.
AND YOU'RE OKAY AS YOU ARE, APPARENTLY.
WELL, I **AM** PRETTY GREAT.
Rumination
DON'T MOPE, DANIELLE! YOU'RE PRETTY GREAT TOO.
AW. THANKS.
21 RADLEY
DANIELLE!
HOW MANY TIMES DO I HAVE TO TELL YOU?

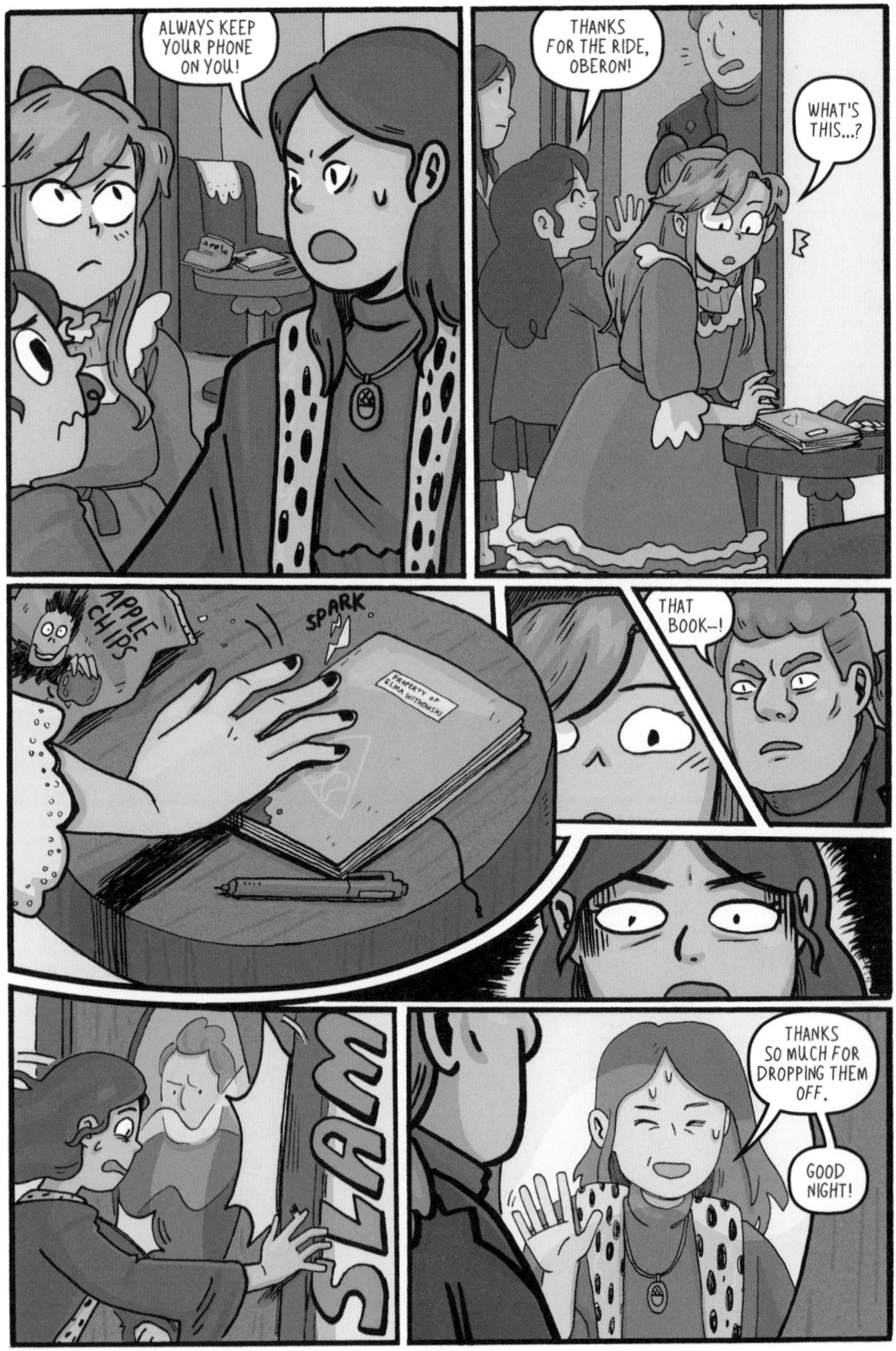
ALWAYS KEEP YOUR PHONE ON YOU!
THANKS FOR THE RIDE, OBERON!
WHAT'S THIS...?
APPLE CHIPS
SPARK
PROPERTY OF ELMA WITKOWSKI
THAT BOOK--!
SLAM
THANKS SO MUCH FOR DROPPING THEM OFF.
GOOD NIGHT!

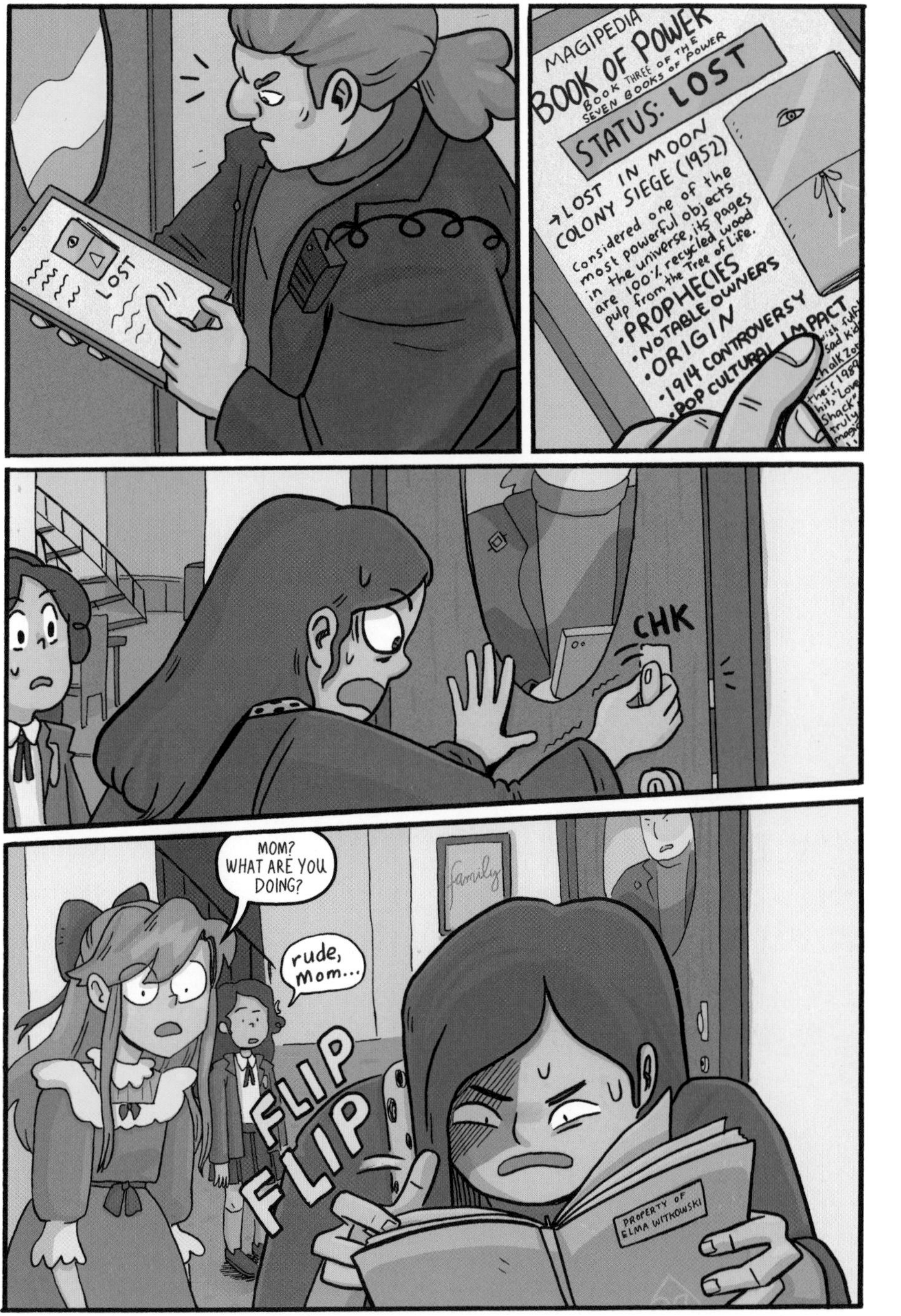
LOST
MAGIPEDIA
BOOK OF POWER
BOOK THREE OF THE SEVEN BOOKS OF POWER
STATUS: LOST
→LOST IN MOON COLONY SIEGE (1952)
Considered one of the most powerful objects in the universe, its pages are 100% recycled wood pulp from the Tree of Life.
•PROPHECIES
•NOTABLE OWNERS
•ORIGIN
•1914 CONTROVERSY
•POP CULTURAL IMPACT
CHK
MOM? WHAT ARE YOU DOING?
family
rude, Mom...
FLIP
FLIP
PROPERTY OF ELMA WITKOWSKI

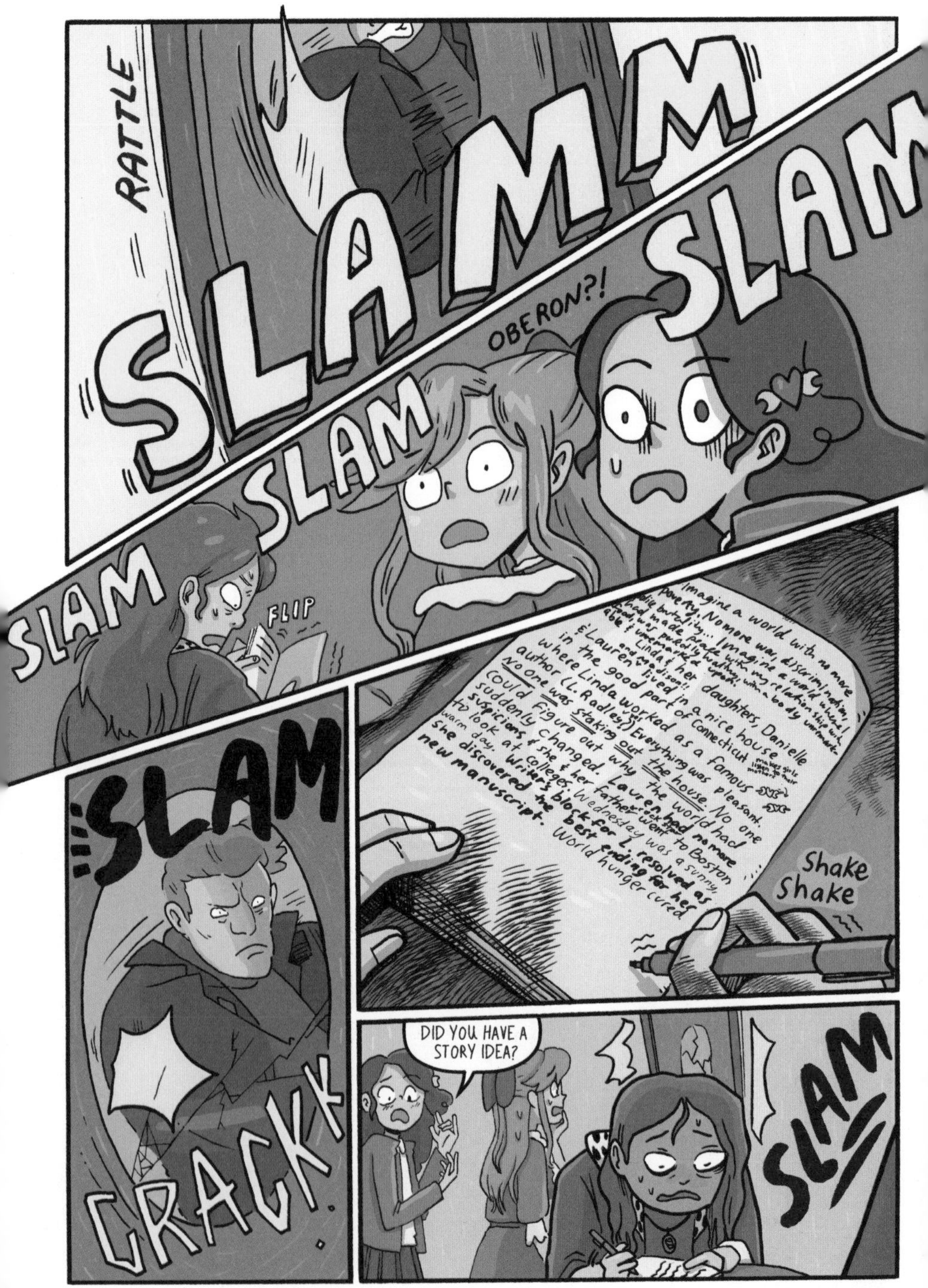
RATTLE
SLAMM
OBERON?!
SLAM
SLAM
SLAM
FLIP
SLAM
Imagine a world with no more
poverty. No more war, discrimination
Linda & her daughters, Danielle
& Lauren lived in a nice house
in the good part of Connecticut
where Linda workad as a famous
author (L. Radley!!) Everything was pleasant.
No one was staking out the house. No one
could figure out why the world had no more
suddenly changed. Lauren had
suspicions & she & her father went to Boston
to look at colleges. Wednesday was a sunny,
warm day. Writer's block for L. resolved as
she discovered the best ending for her
new manuscript. World hunger cured.
Shake
Shake
CRACKK.
DID YOU HAVE A STORY IDEA?
SLAM

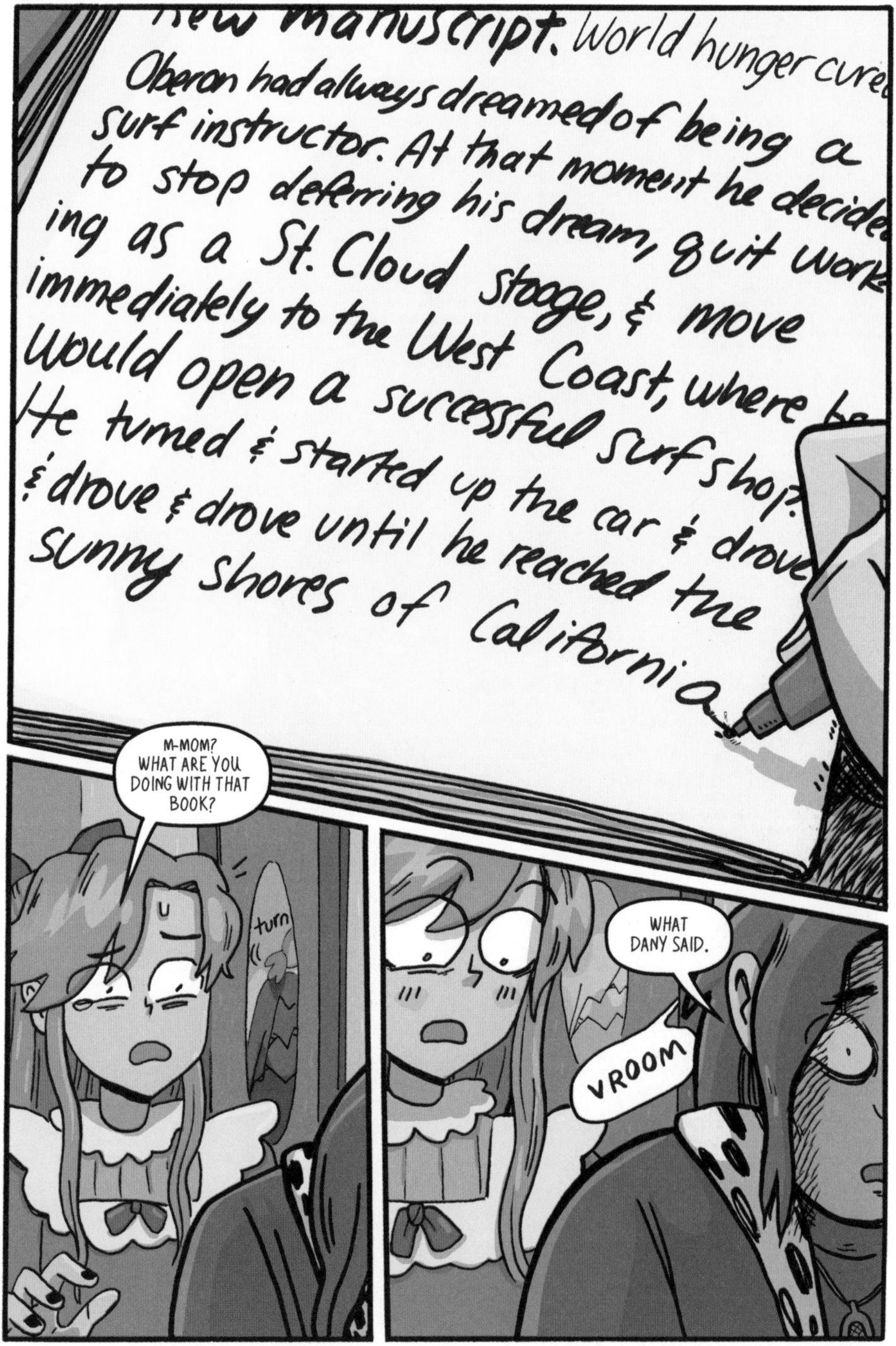
new manuscript. World hunger cure
Oberon had always dreamed of being a
surf instructor. At that moment he decide
to stop deferring his dream, quit work
ing as a St. Cloud stooge, & move
immediately to the West Coast, where
would open a successful surf shop.
He turned & started up the car & drove
& drove & drove until he reached the
sunny shores of California
M-MOM? WHAT ARE YOU DOING WITH THAT BOOK?
turn
WHAT DANY SAID.
VROOM

I HAD A STORY IDEA.

The next day, a beautiful fall day, Linda & the girls went to Melton to visit Tracy & get the magical sketch-books Tracy had taken from Aunt Elma's house.

HEY, LINDA?

I *REALLY* DON'T THINK YOU LEFT YOUR YEARBOOKS HERE, LIN.

I KNOW I DID.

I WOULD WEAR THAT.

hee hee

IN: POSTAGE
OUT: CATERWAUL
MAXI-MAXI DRESS
HAUTE CLOWNWEAR
GLOWING ORBS

BEST DR

WORST DRESSED

58

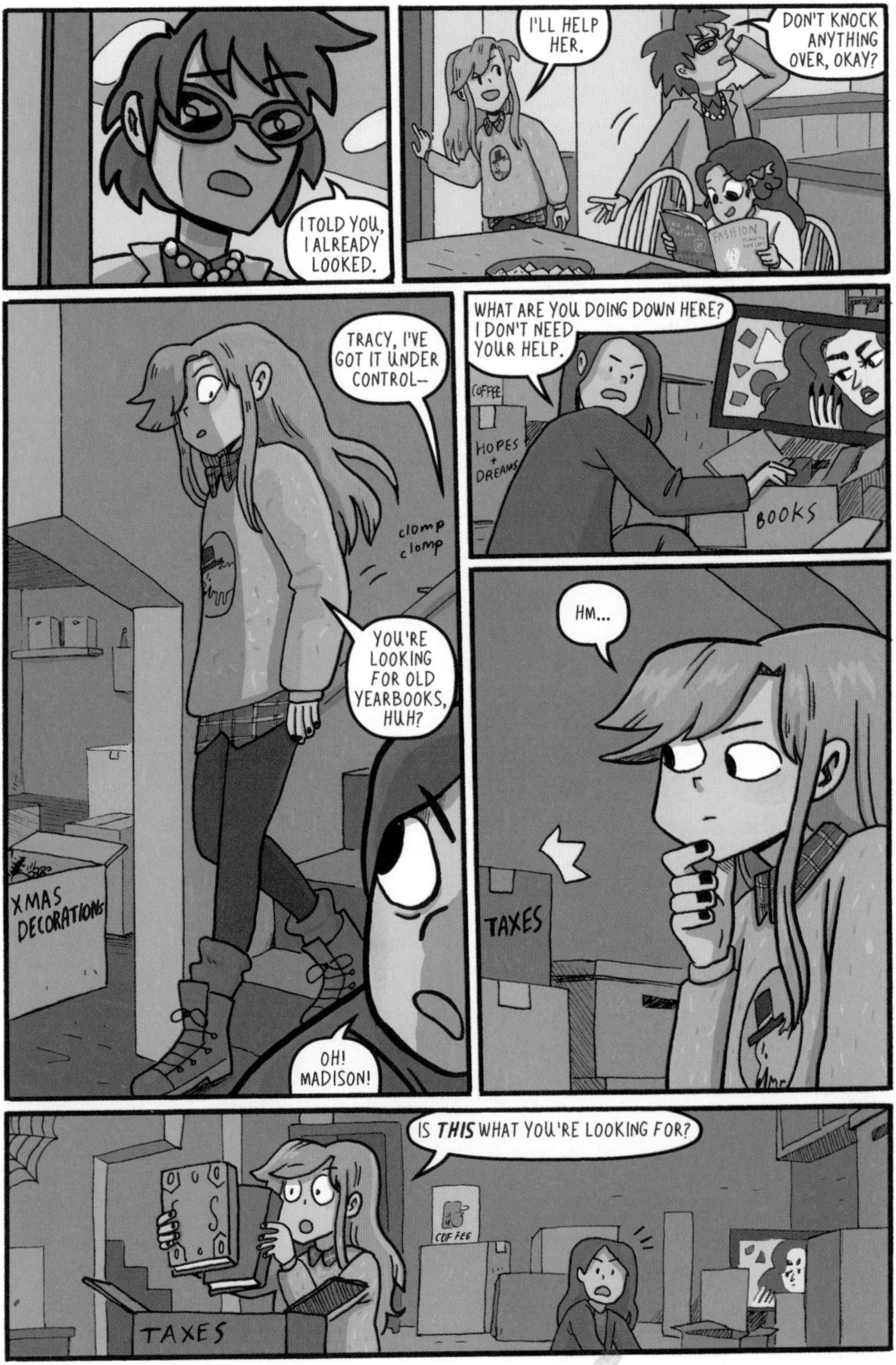
I TOLD YOU, I ALREADY LOOKED.
I'LL HELP HER.
DON'T KNOCK ANYTHING OVER, OKAY?
FASHION
TRACY, I'VE GOT IT UNDER CONTROL--
clomp clomp
XMAS DECORATIONS
YOU'RE LOOKING FOR OLD YEARBOOKS, HUH?
OH! MADISON!
WHAT ARE YOU DOING DOWN HERE? I DON'T NEED YOUR HELP.
COFFEE
HOPES + DREAMS
BOOKS
HM...
TAXES
IS THIS WHAT YOU'RE LOOKING FOR?
COFFEE
TAXES

MADISON! HOW DID YOU...

...FIND THESE?

SUMMER CLOTHES

TAXES

I'M PRETTY GOOD AT FINDING THINGS. THEY WERE AUNT ELMA'S, RIGHT?

Property of Elma Jablonski

THEY WERE.

SEE? I CAN BE A GOOD DAUGHTER SOMETIMES TOO.

YOU *KNOW* I LOVE YOU GIRLS EQUALLY.

I NEED TO BORROW THESE BOOKS. BUT I DON'T THINK TRACY'D UNDERSTAND.

SO LET'S KEEP THIS A SECRET, OKAY?

HON?

!!

villy espresso

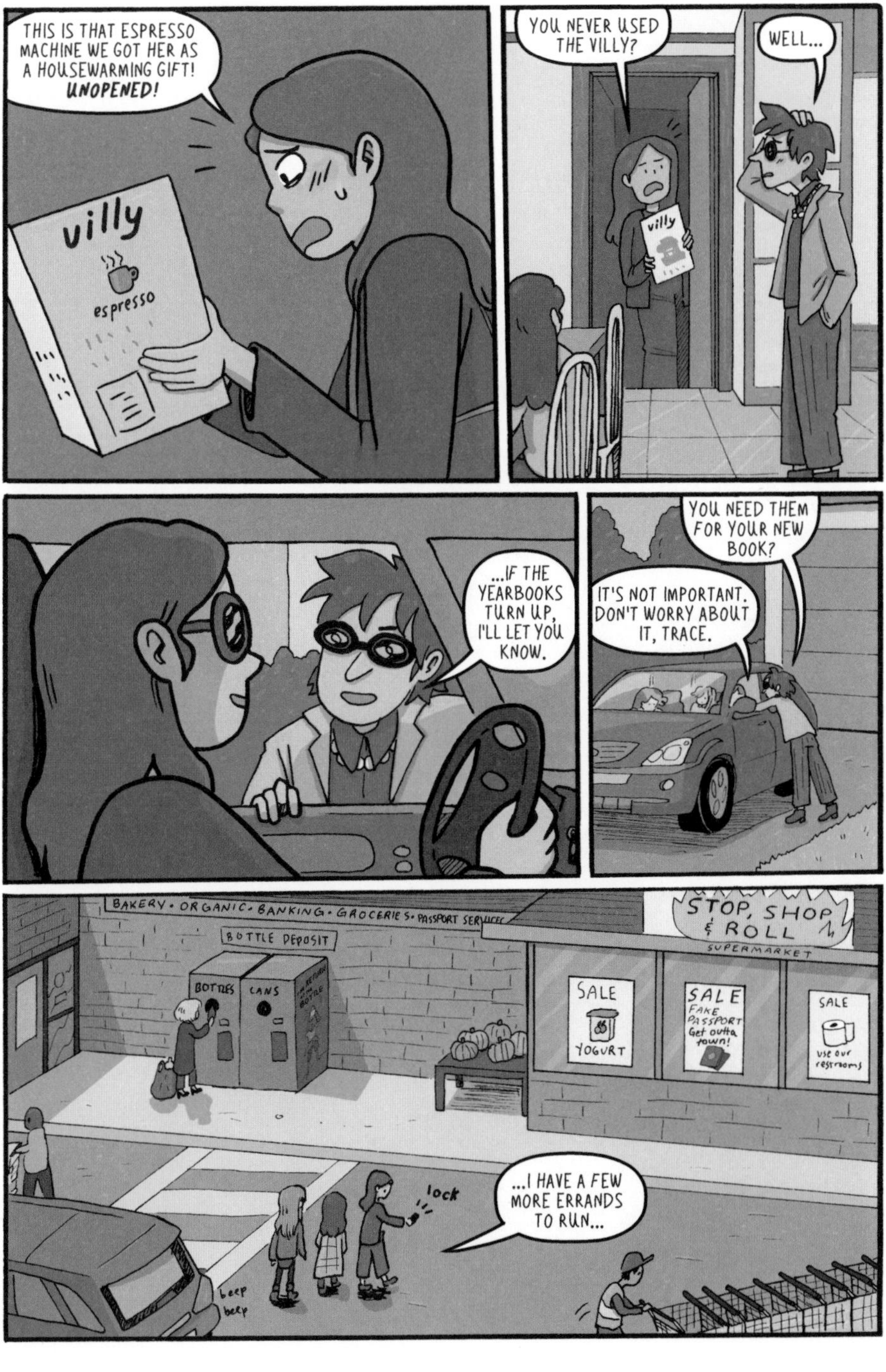
THIS IS THAT ESPRESSO MACHINE WE GOT HER AS A HOUSEWARMING GIFT! **UNOPENED!**
villy
espresso
YOU NEVER USED THE VILLY?
WELL...
villy
...IF THE YEARBOOKS TURN UP, I'LL LET YOU KNOW.
YOU NEED THEM FOR YOUR NEW BOOK?
IT'S NOT IMPORTANT. DON'T WORRY ABOUT IT, TRACE.
BAKERY • ORGANIC • BANKING • GROCERIES • PASSPORT
BOTTLE DEPOSIT
BOTTLES
CANS
STOP, SHOP & ROLL
SUPERMARKET
SALE
YOGURT
SALE
FAKE PASSPORT
Get outta town!
SALE
use our restrooms
lock
...I HAVE A FEW MORE ERRANDS TO RUN...
beep beep

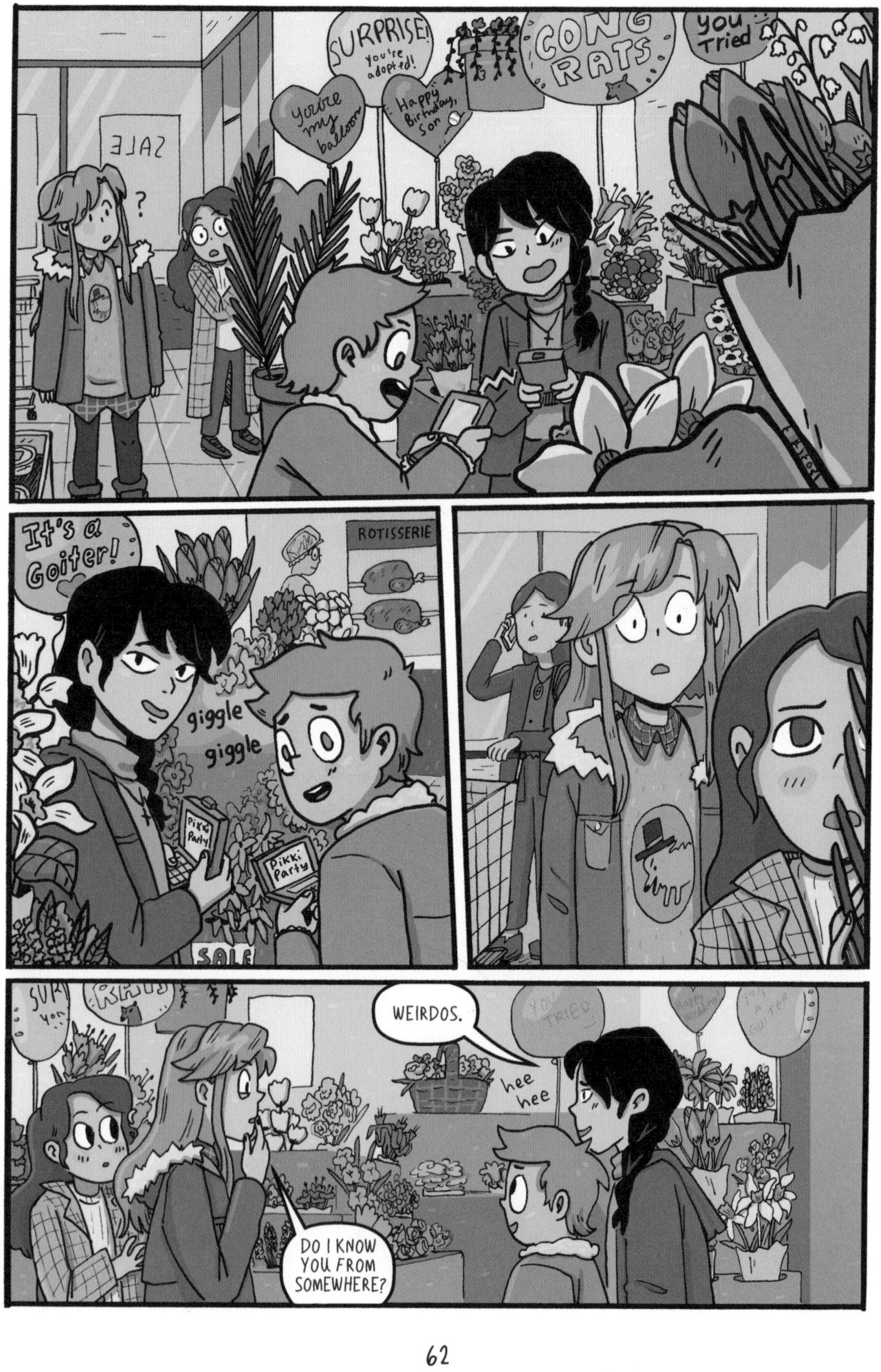
SURPRISE! you're adopted!
You're my balloon
Happy Birthday, Son
CONG RATS
you Tried
?
It's a Goiter!
ROTISSERIE
giggle
giggle
Pikki Party
Pikki Party
SALE
WEIRDOS.
hee hee
DO I KNOW YOU FROM SOMEWHERE?

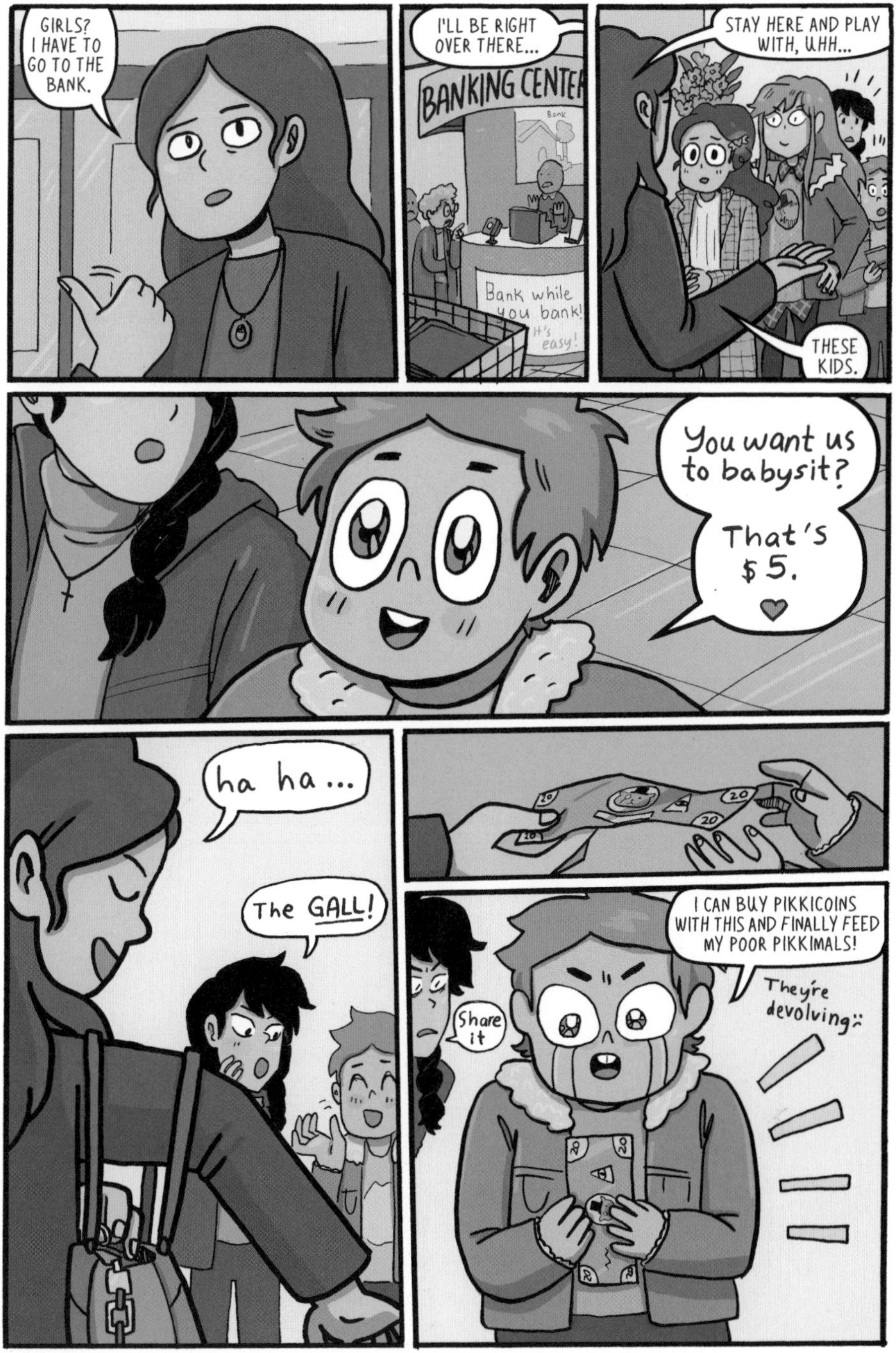
GIRLS? I HAVE TO GO TO THE BANK.
I'LL BE RIGHT OVER THERE...
BANKING CENTER
Bank
Bank while you bank!
It's easy!
STAY HERE AND PLAY WITH, UHH...
THESE KIDS.
You want us to babysit?
That's $5.
ha ha...
The GALL!
I CAN BUY PIKKICOINS WITH THIS AND FINALLY FEED MY POOR PIKKIMALS!
They're devolving
Share it

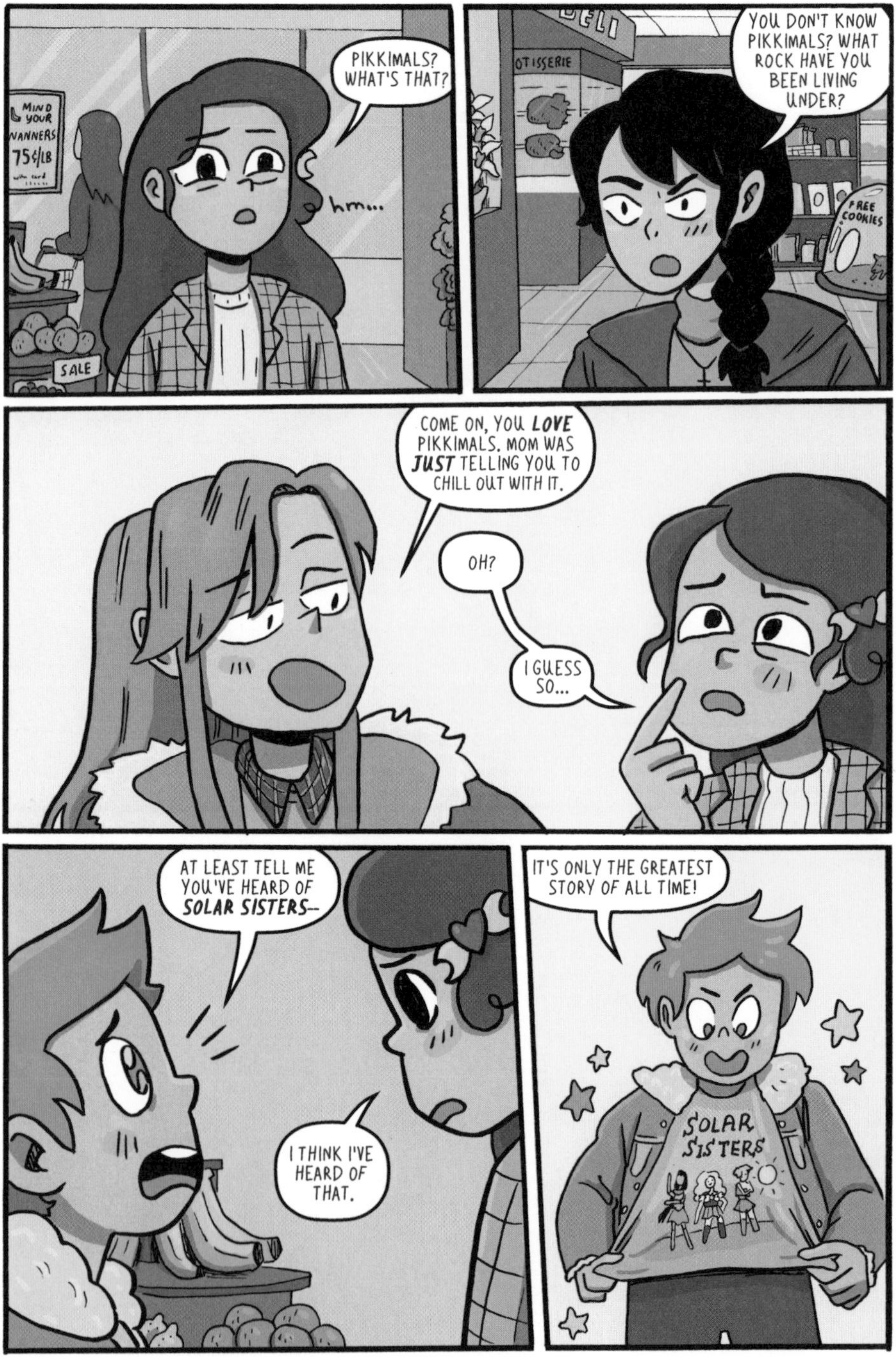

MIND YOUR NANNERS 75¢/LB
SALE
PIKKIMALS? WHAT'S THAT?
hm...
DELI
OTISSERIE
FREE COOKIES
YOU DON'T KNOW PIKKIMALS? WHAT ROCK HAVE YOU BEEN LIVING UNDER?
COME ON, YOU **LOVE** PIKKIMALS. MOM WAS **JUST** TELLING YOU TO CHILL OUT WITH IT.
OH?
I GUESS SO...
AT LEAST TELL ME YOU'VE HEARD OF **SOLAR SISTERS**--
I THINK I'VE HEARD OF THAT.
IT'S ONLY THE GREATEST STORY OF ALL TIME!
SOLAR SISTERS

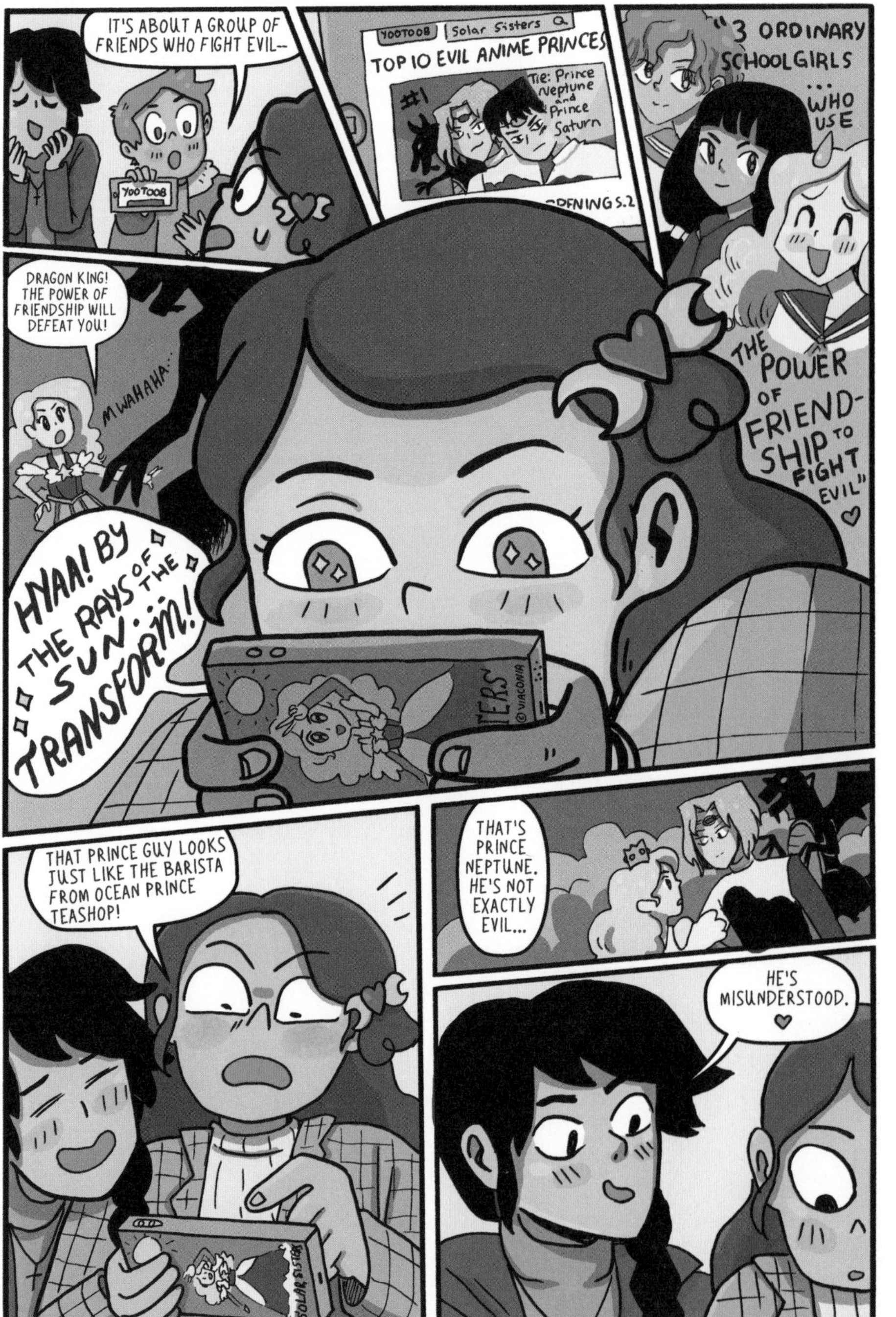
IT'S ABOUT A GROUP OF FRIENDS WHO FIGHT EVIL--
YOOTOOB
YOOTOOB
Solar Sisters
TOP 10 EVIL ANIME PRINCES
#1
Tie: Prince Neptune and Prince Saturn
OPENINGS S.2
"3 ORDINARY SCHOOLGIRLS ... WHO USE
THE POWER OF FRIENDSHIP TO FIGHT EVIL"
DRAGON KING! THE POWER OF FRIENDSHIP WILL DEFEAT YOU!
MWAHAHA...
HYAA! BY THE RAYS OF THE SUN... TRANSFORM!
©VIACONIA
THAT PRINCE GUY LOOKS JUST LIKE THE BARISTA FROM OCEAN PRINCE TEASHOP!
SOLAR SISTERS
THAT'S PRINCE NEPTUNE. HE'S NOT EXACTLY EVIL...
HE'S MISUNDERSTOOD.

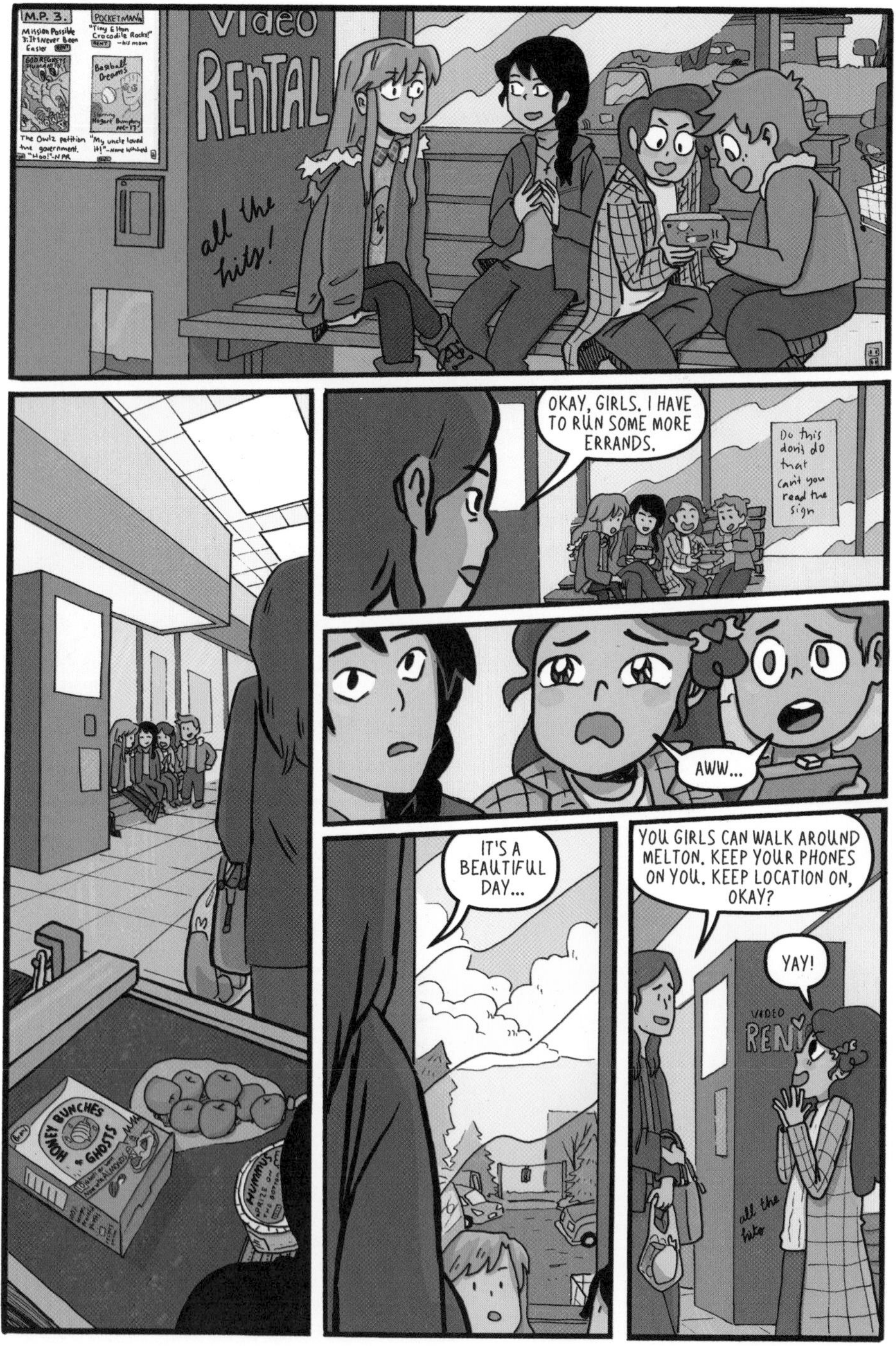
Video RENTAL
all the hits!
OKAY, GIRLS. I HAVE TO RUN SOME MORE ERRANDS.
Do this don't do that can't you read the sign
AWW...
HONEY BUNCHES OF GHOSTS
HUMMUS
IT'S A BEAUTIFUL DAY...
YOU GIRLS CAN WALK AROUND MELTON. KEEP YOUR PHONES ON YOU. KEEP LOCATION ON, OKAY?
YAY!
all the hits

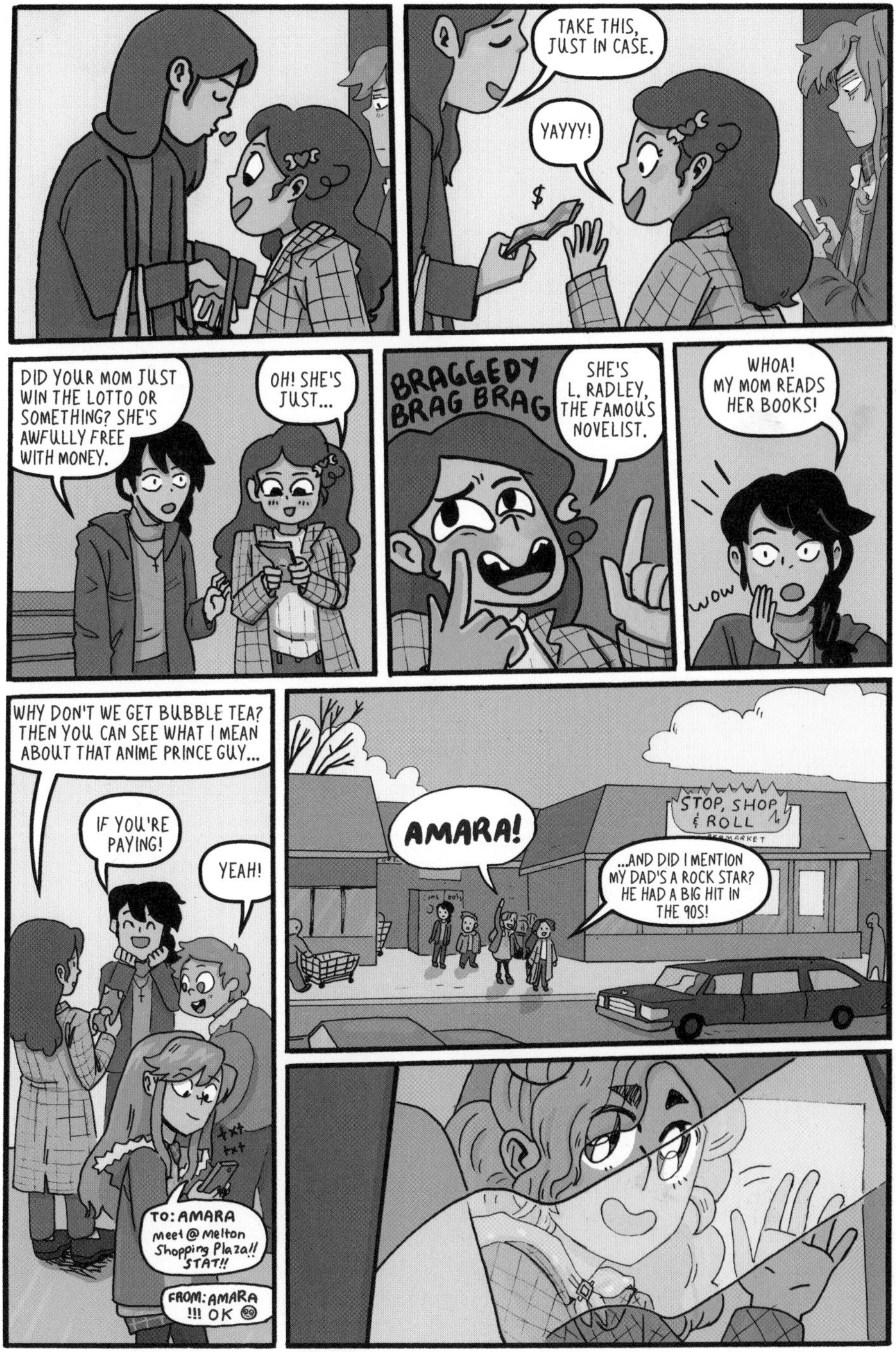
TAKE THIS, JUST IN CASE.
YAYYY!
$
DID YOUR MOM JUST WIN THE LOTTO OR SOMETHING? SHE'S AWFULLY FREE WITH MONEY.
OH! SHE'S JUST...
BRAGGEDY BRAG BRAG
SHE'S L. RADLEY, THE FAMOUS NOVELIST.
WHOA! MY MOM READS HER BOOKS!
WOW
WHY DON'T WE GET BUBBLE TEA? THEN YOU CAN SEE WHAT I MEAN ABOUT THAT ANIME PRINCE GUY...
IF YOU'RE PAYING!
YEAH!
txt
txt
TO: AMARA
Meet @ Melton Shopping Plaza!! STAT!!
FROM: AMARA
!!! OK
AMARA!
STOP, SHOP & ROLL
...AND DID I MENTION MY DAD'S A ROCK STAR? HE HAD A BIG HIT IN THE 90S!

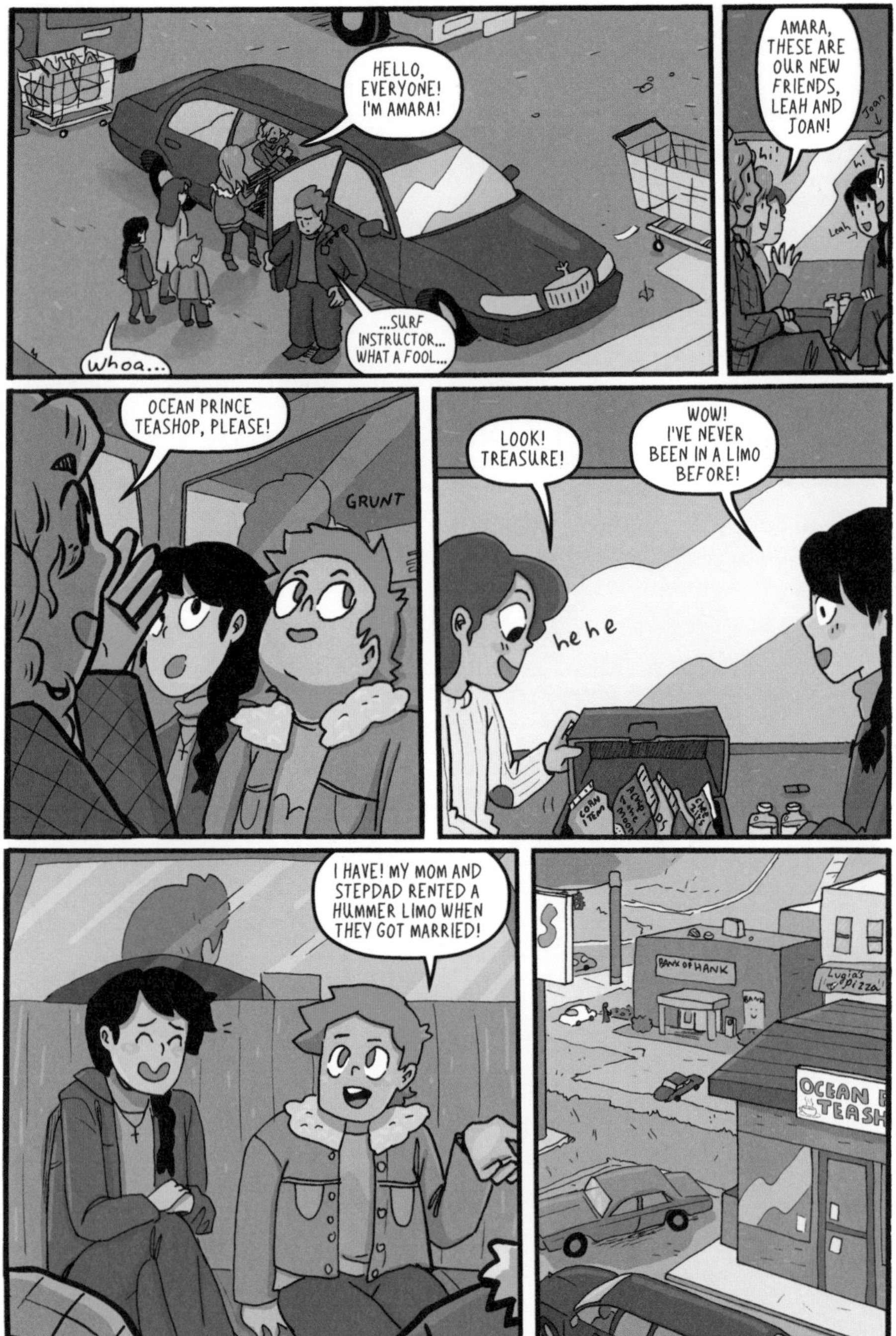

HELLO, EVERYONE! I'M AMARA!
...SURF INSTRUCTOR... WHAT A FOOL...
whoa...
AMARA, THESE ARE OUR NEW FRIENDS, LEAH AND JOAN!
hi!
hi
Joan
Leah
OCEAN PRINCE TEASHOP, PLEASE!
GRUNT
LOOK! TREASURE!
WOW! I'VE NEVER BEEN IN A LIMO BEFORE!
hehe
I HAVE! MY MOM AND STEPDAD RENTED A HUMMER LIMO WHEN THEY GOT MARRIED!
BANK OF HANK
Lugia's Pizza

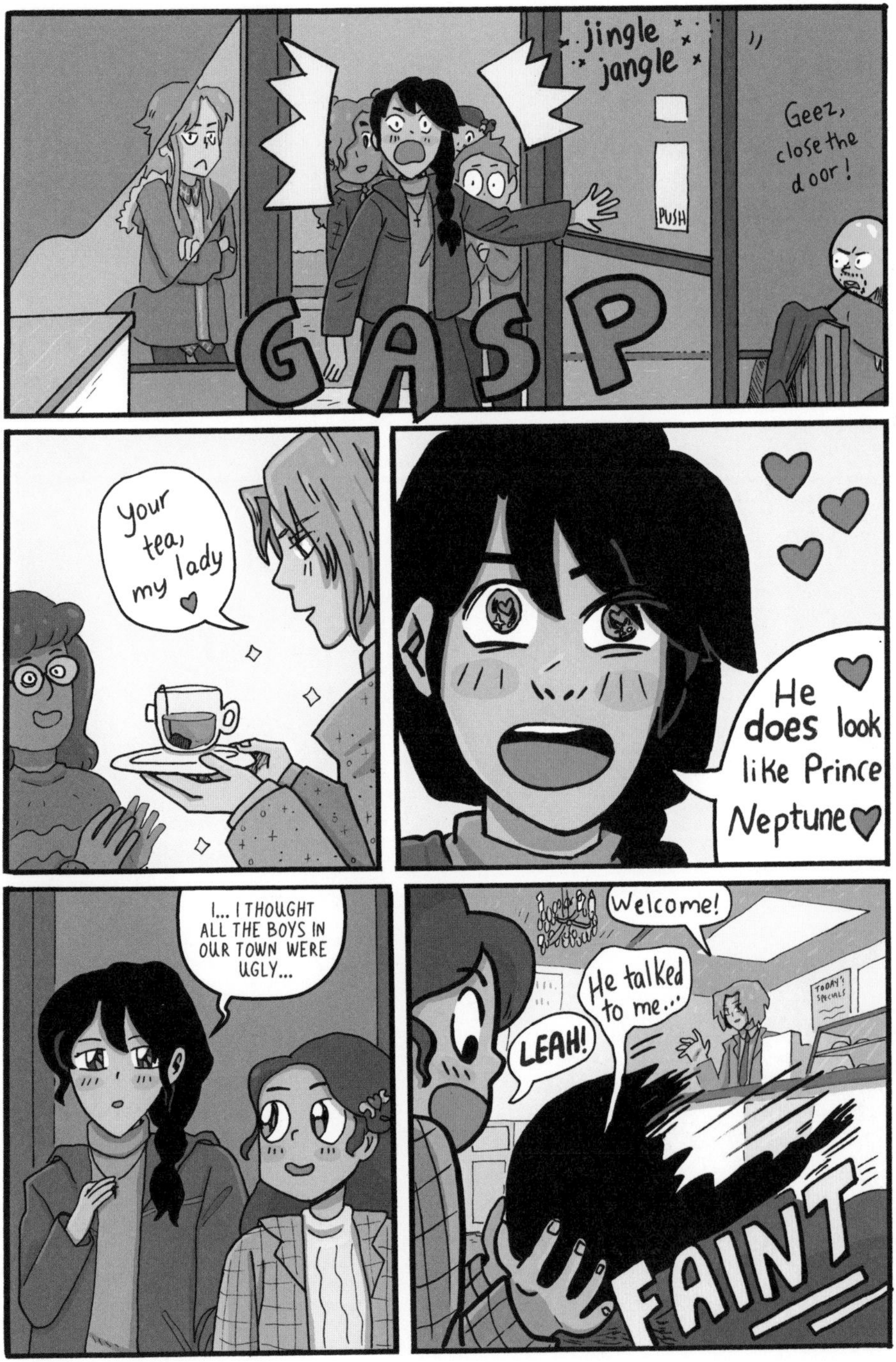
jingle
jangle
PUSH
Geez, close the door!
GASP
Your tea, my lady
He does look like Prince Neptune
I... I THOUGHT ALL THE BOYS IN OUR TOWN WERE UGLY...
Welcome!
He talked to me...
LEAH!
FAINT

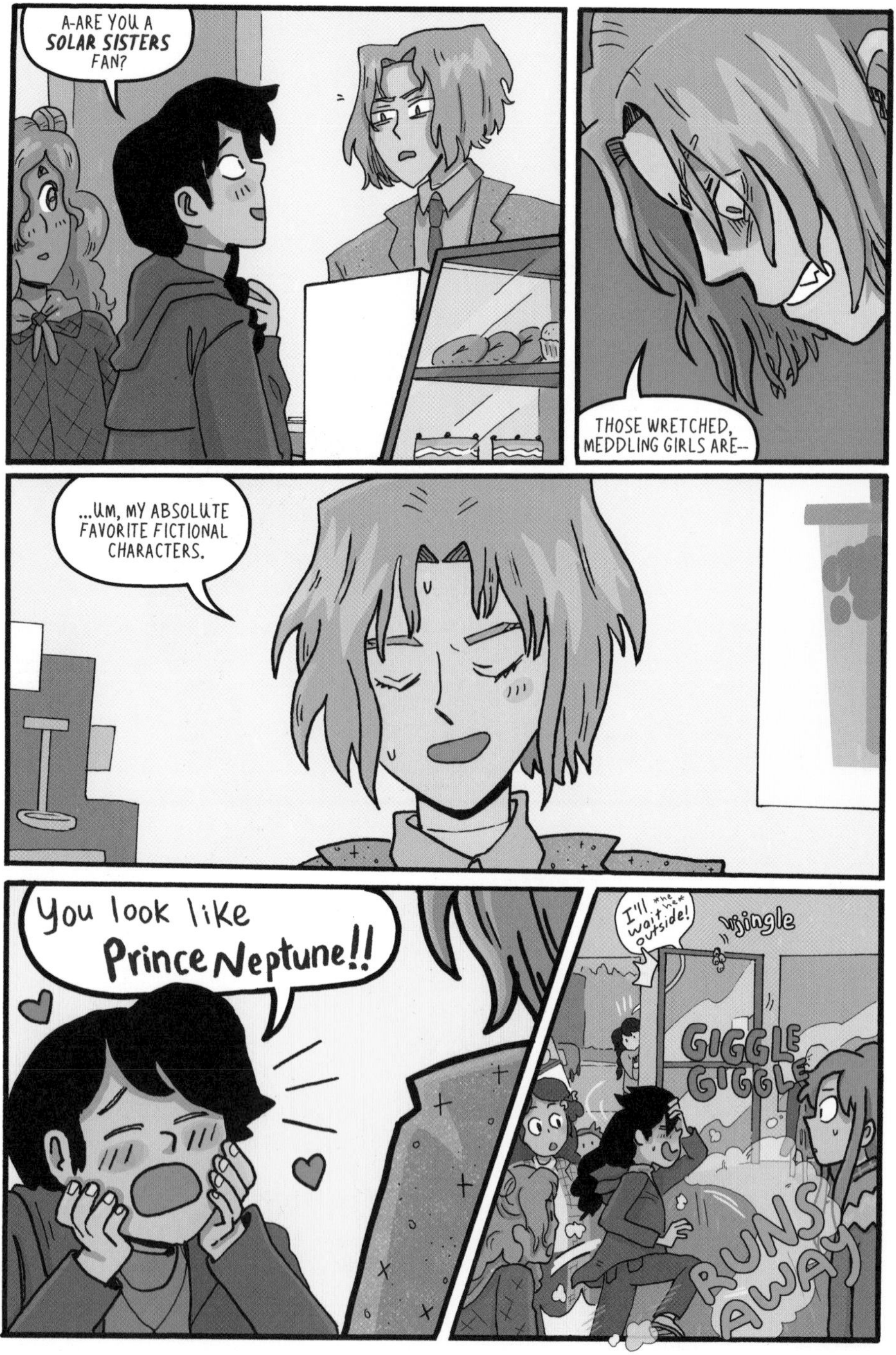
A-ARE YOU A SOLAR SISTERS FAN?
THOSE WRETCHED, MEDDLING GIRLS ARE--
...UM, MY ABSOLUTE FAVORITE FICTIONAL CHARACTERS.
You look like Prince Neptune!!
I'll *he he* wait outside!
jingle
GIGGLE GIGGLE
RUNS AWAY

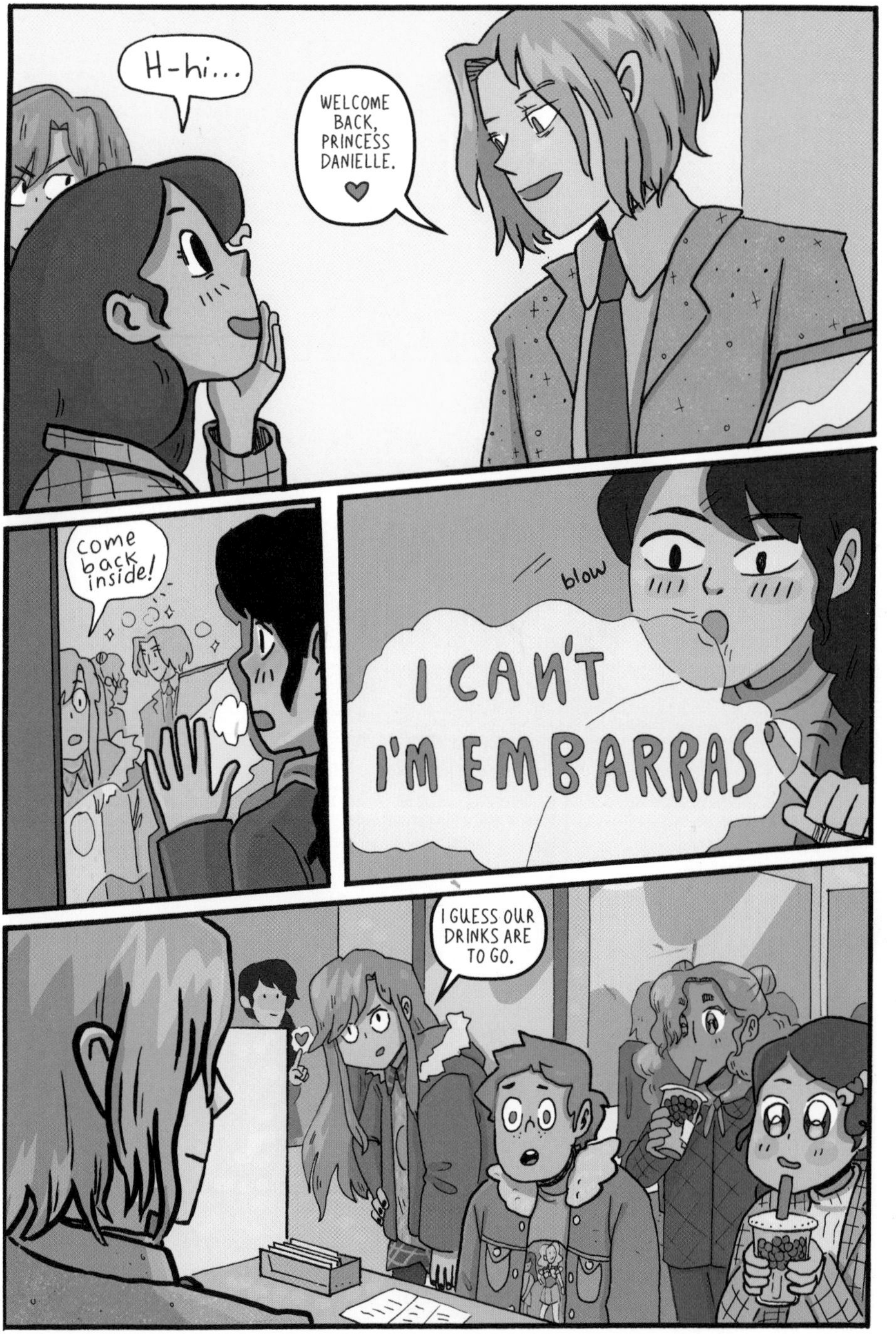
H-hi...
WELCOME BACK, PRINCESS DANIELLE.
come back inside!
blow
I CAN'T I'M EMBARRAS
I GUESS OUR DRINKS ARE TO GO.

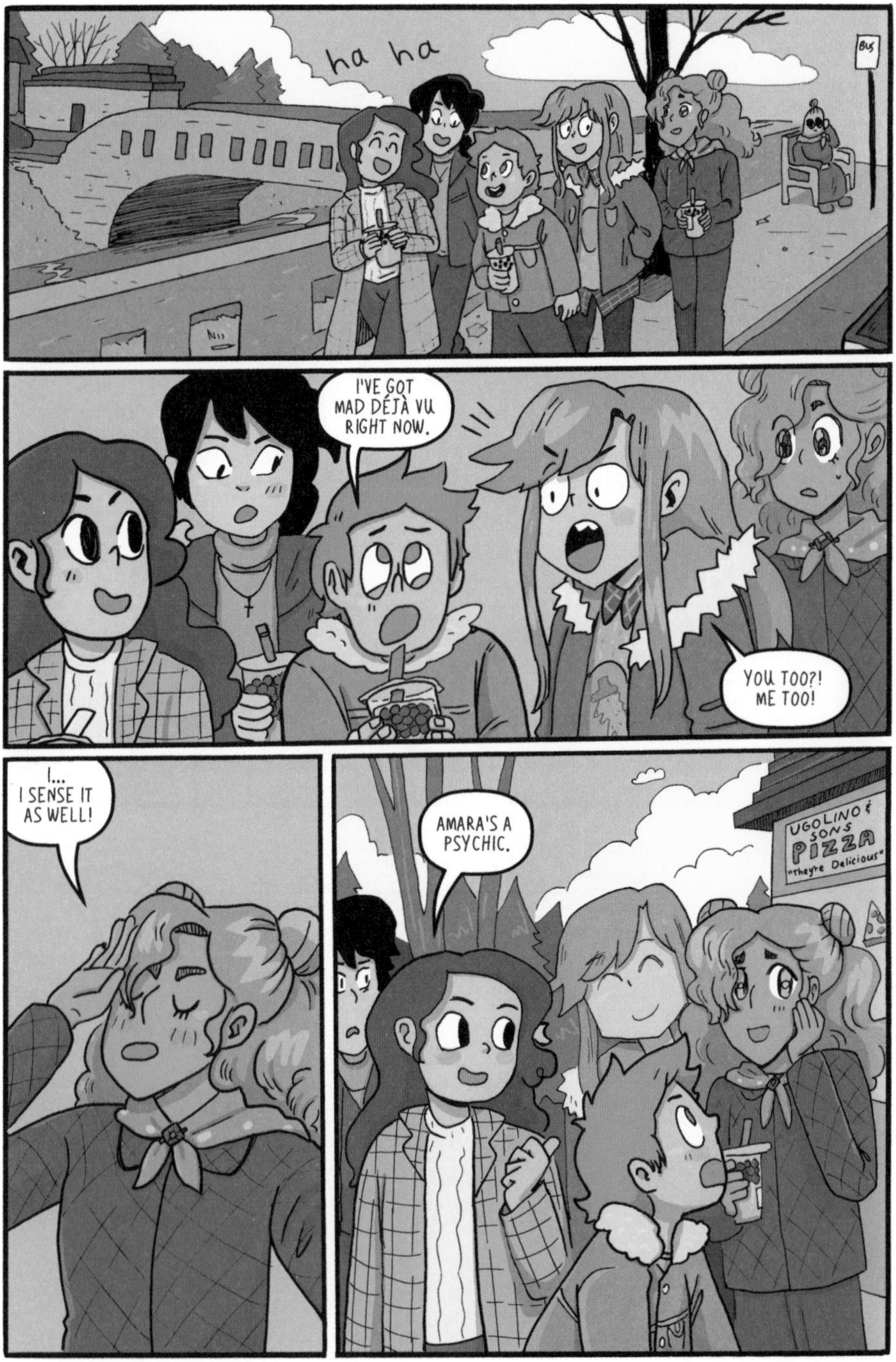
ha ha
BUS
I'VE GOT MAD DÉJÀ VU RIGHT NOW.
YOU TOO?! ME TOO!
I... I SENSE IT AS WELL!
AMARA'S A PSYCHIC.
UGOLINO & SONS PIZZA "They're Delicious"

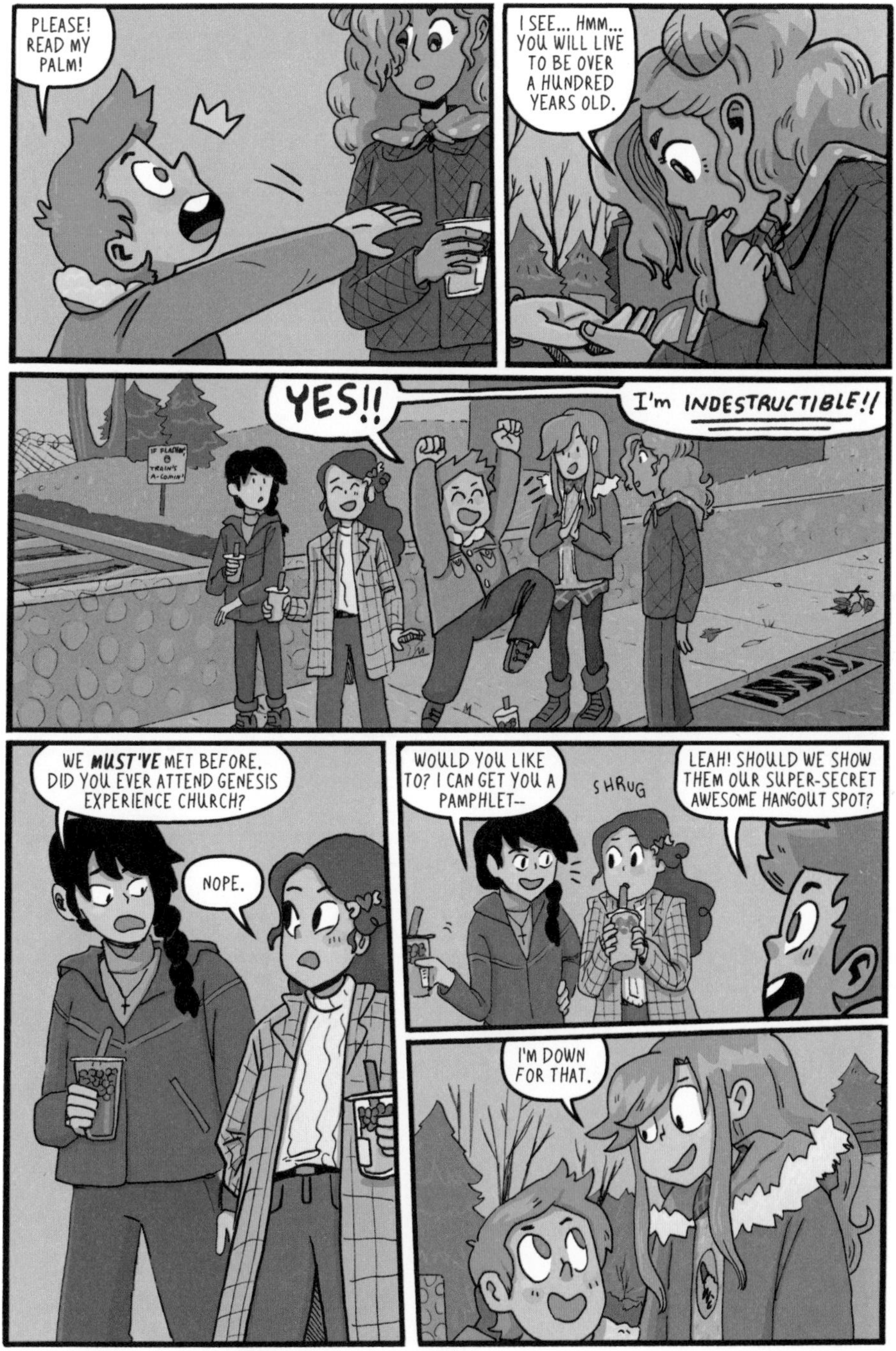
PLEASE! READ MY PALM!
I SEE... HMM... YOU WILL LIVE TO BE OVER A HUNDRED YEARS OLD.
YES!!
I'm INDESTRUCTIBLE!!
WE MUST'VE MET BEFORE. DID YOU EVER ATTEND GENESIS EXPERIENCE CHURCH?
NOPE.
WOULD YOU LIKE TO? I CAN GET YOU A PAMPHLET--
SHRUG
LEAH! SHOULD WE SHOW THEM OUR SUPER-SECRET AWESOME HANGOUT SPOT?
I'M DOWN FOR THAT.

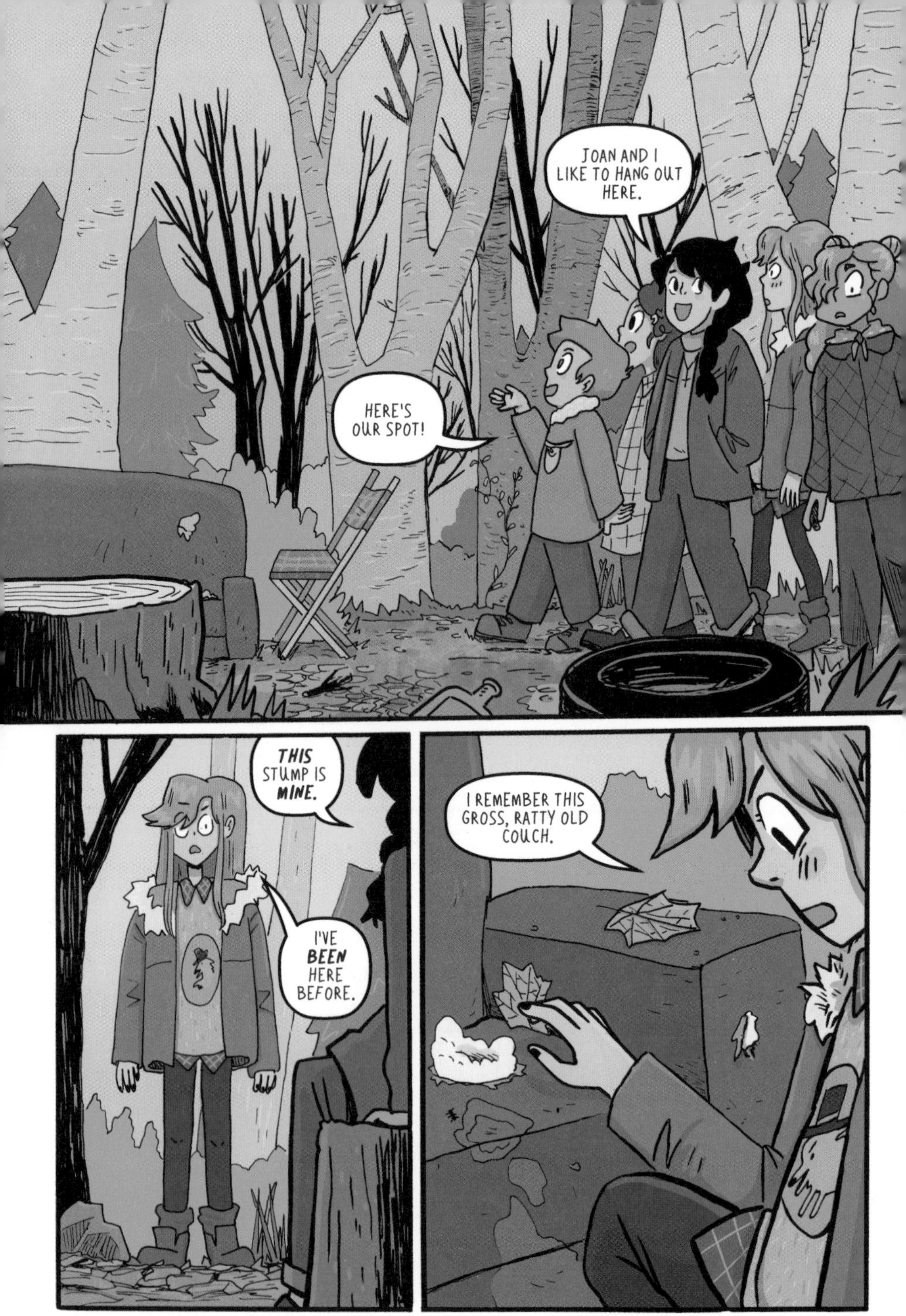
HERE'S OUR SPOT!
JOAN AND I LIKE TO HANG OUT HERE.
THIS STUMP IS **MINE.**
I'VE **BEEN** HERE BEFORE.
I REMEMBER THIS GROSS, RATTY OLD COUCH.

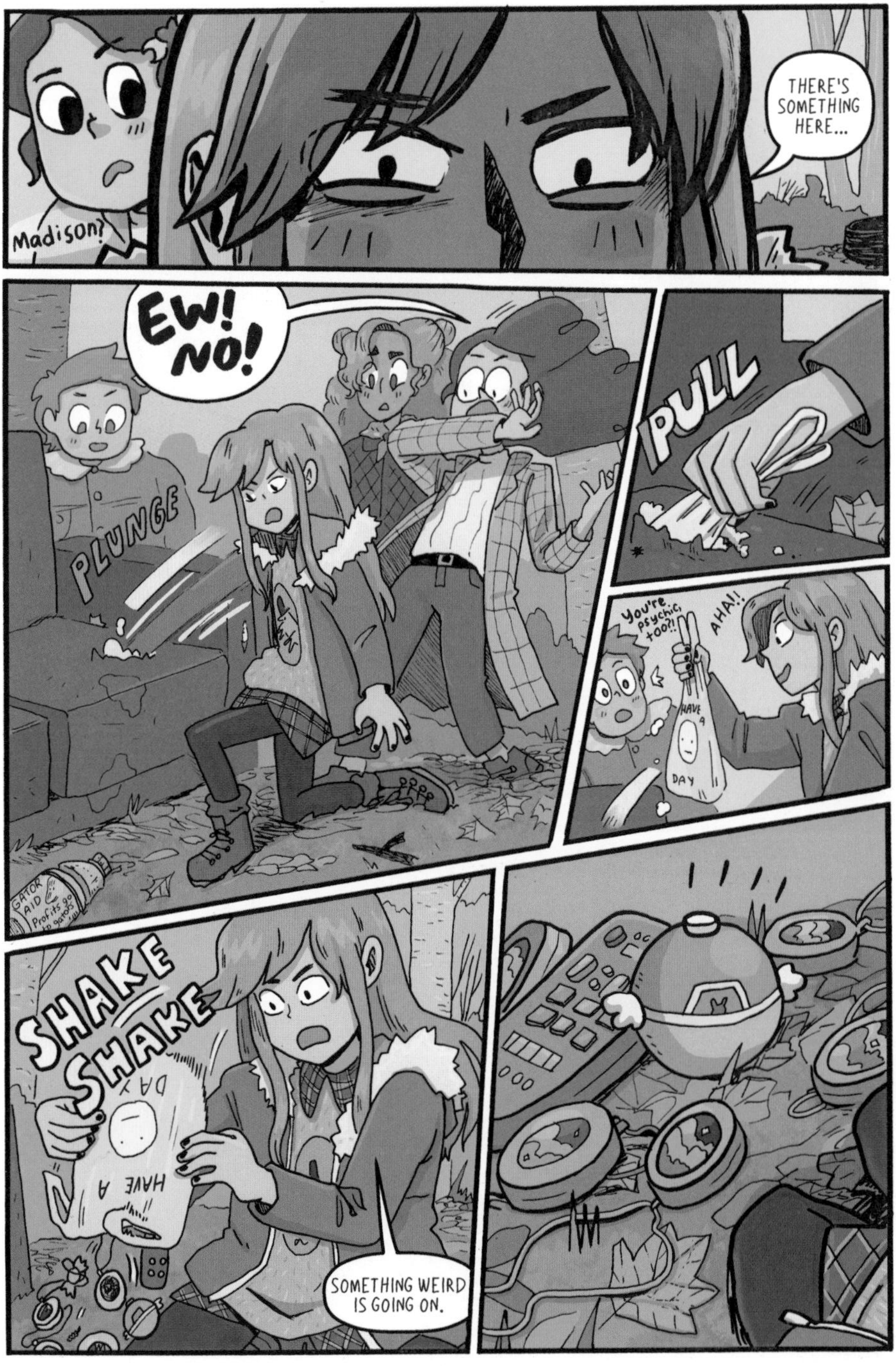
Madison?
THERE'S SOMETHING HERE...
EW! NO!
PLUNGE
GATOR AID
Profits go to gators
PULL
You're psychic, too?!
AHA!!
HAVE A DAY
SHAKE SHAKE
DAY
HAVE A
SOMETHING WEIRD IS GOING ON.

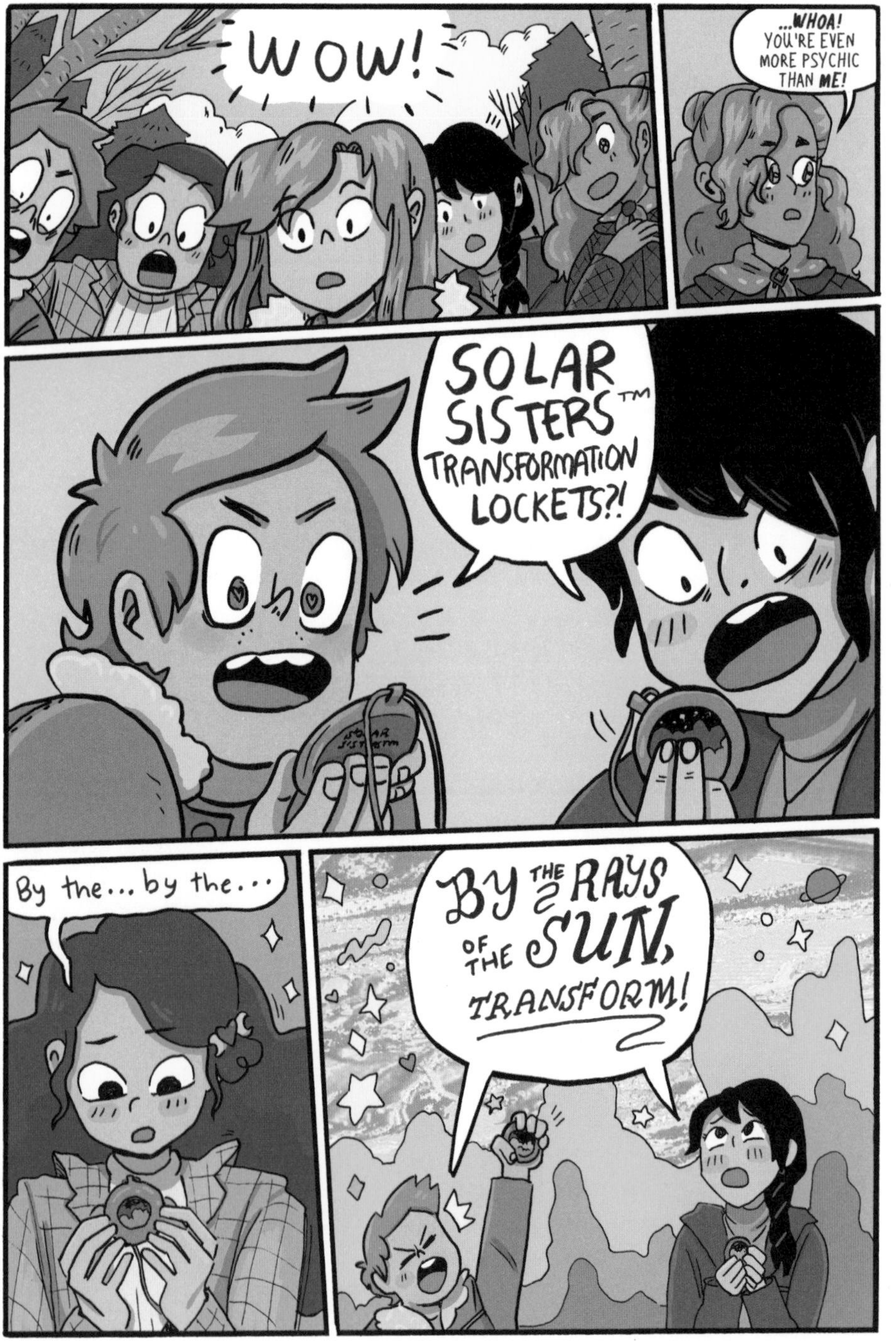
WOW!
...WHOA! YOU'RE EVEN MORE PSYCHIC THAN ME!
SOLAR SISTERS™ TRANSFORMATION LOCKETS?!
SOLAR SISTERS
By the... by the...
BY THE RAYS OF THE SUN, TRANSFORM!

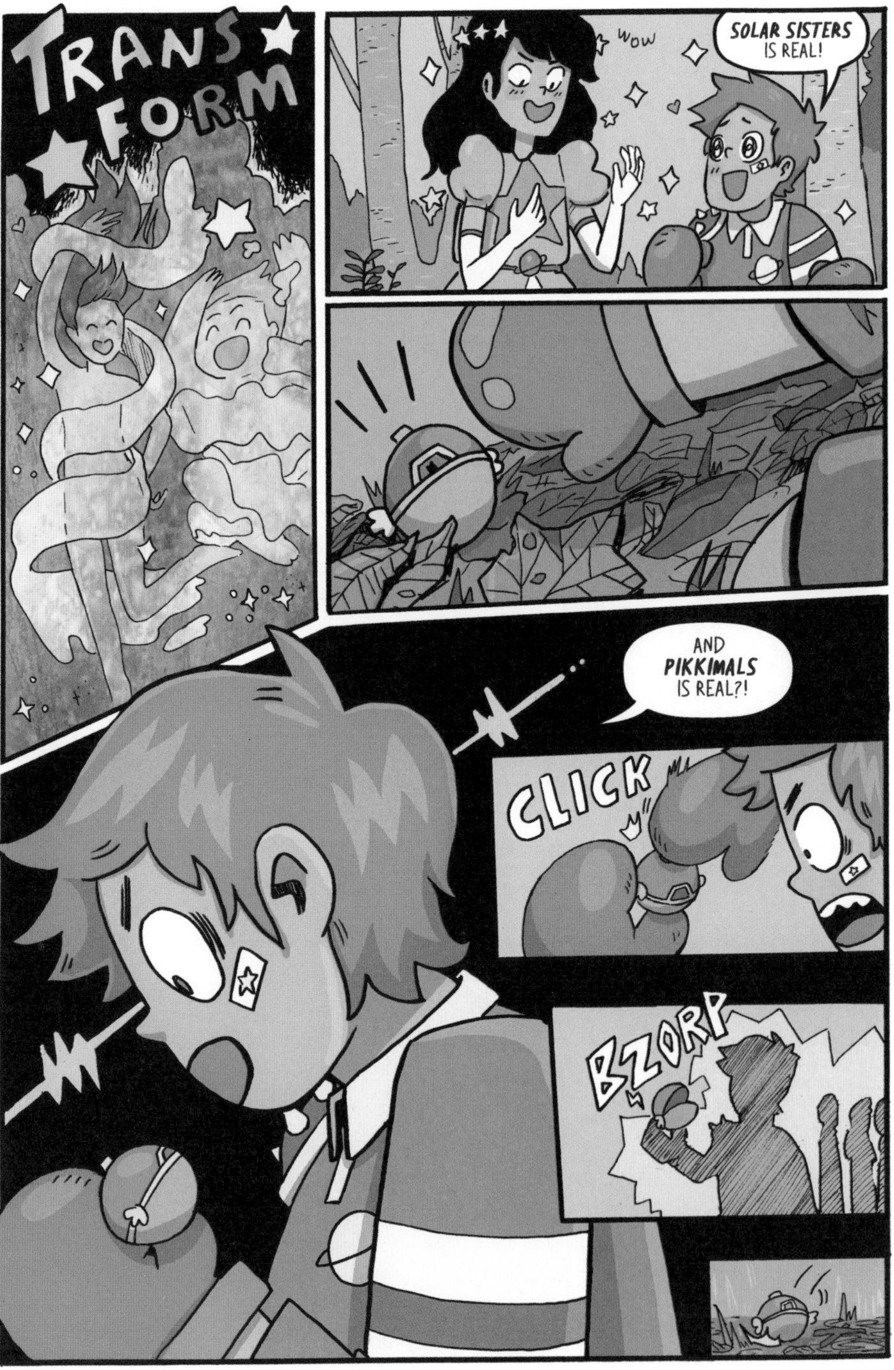
TRANS FORM
WOW
SOLAR SISTERS IS REAL!
AND PIKKIMALS IS REAL?!
CLICK
BZORP

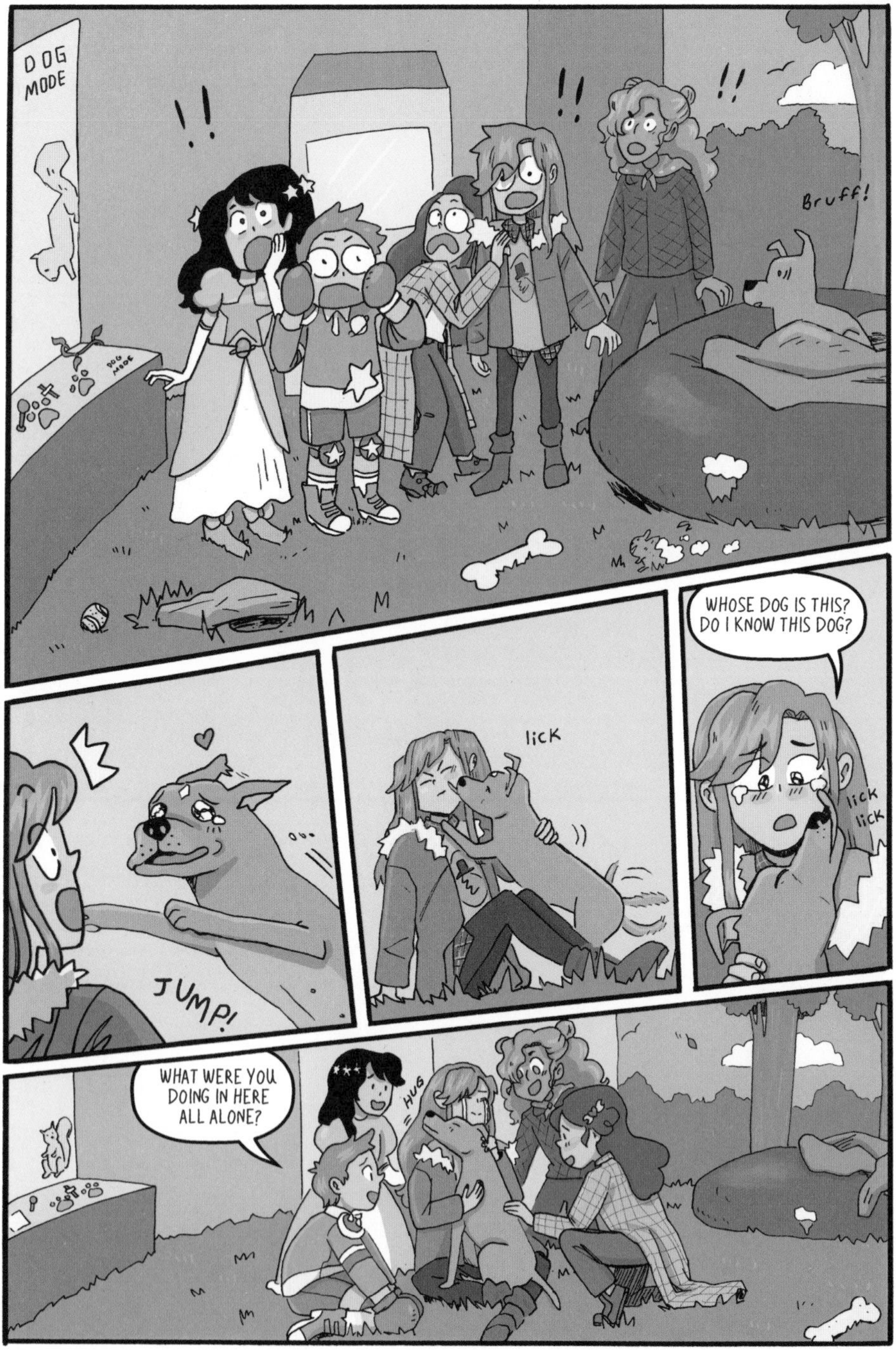
DOG MODE
DOG MODE
!!
!!
!!
Bruff!
WHOSE DOG IS THIS? DO I KNOW THIS DOG?
JUMP!
lick
lick lick
WHAT WERE YOU DOING IN HERE ALL ALONE?
HUG

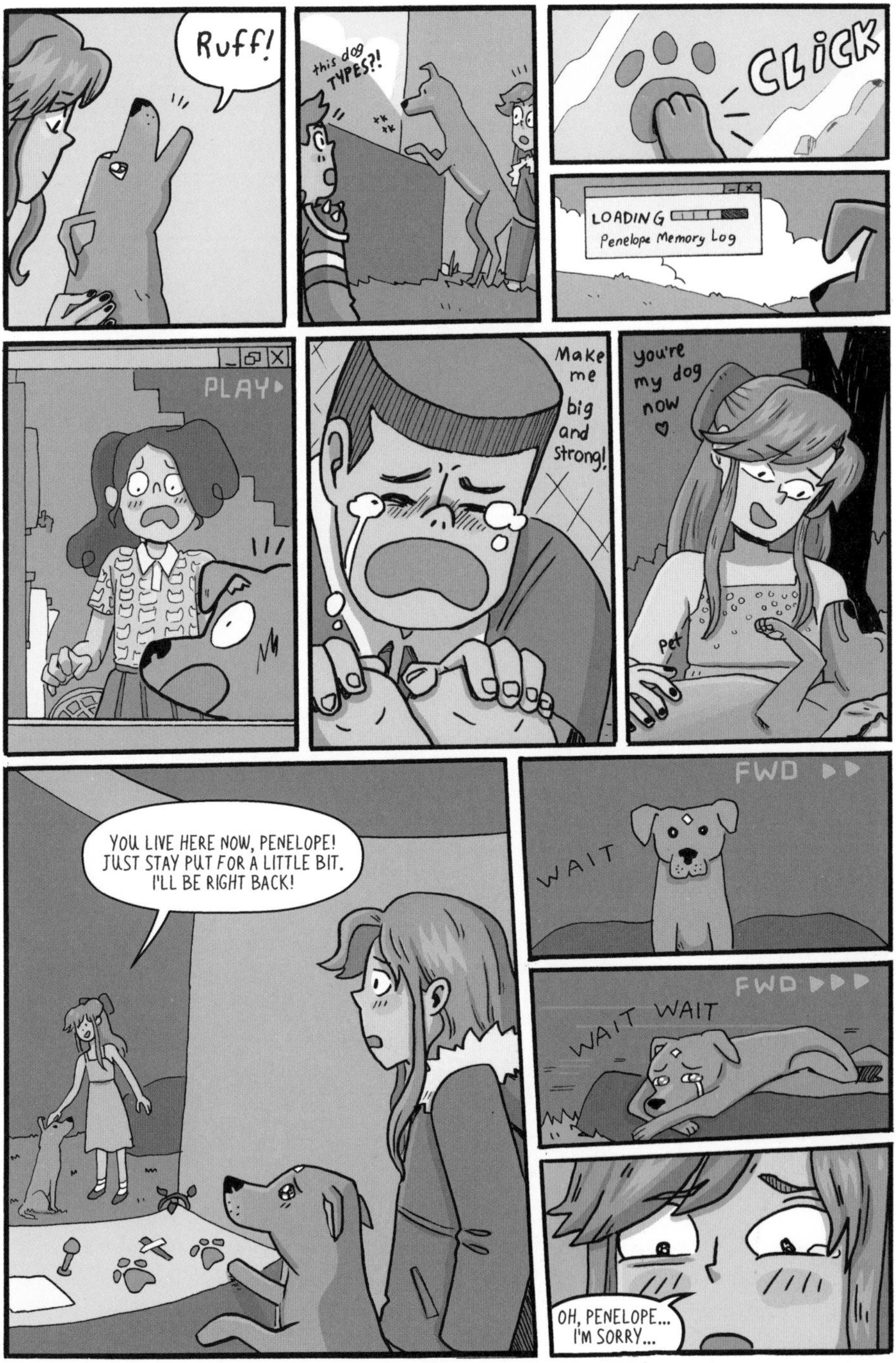

Ruff!
this dog TYPES?!
CLICK
LOADING
Penelope Memory Log
PLAY
Make me big and strong!
you're my dog now ♥
pet
YOU LIVE HERE NOW, PENELOPE! JUST STAY PUT FOR A LITTLE BIT. I'LL BE RIGHT BACK!
FWD
WAIT
FWD
WAIT WAIT
OH, PENELOPE... I'M SORRY...

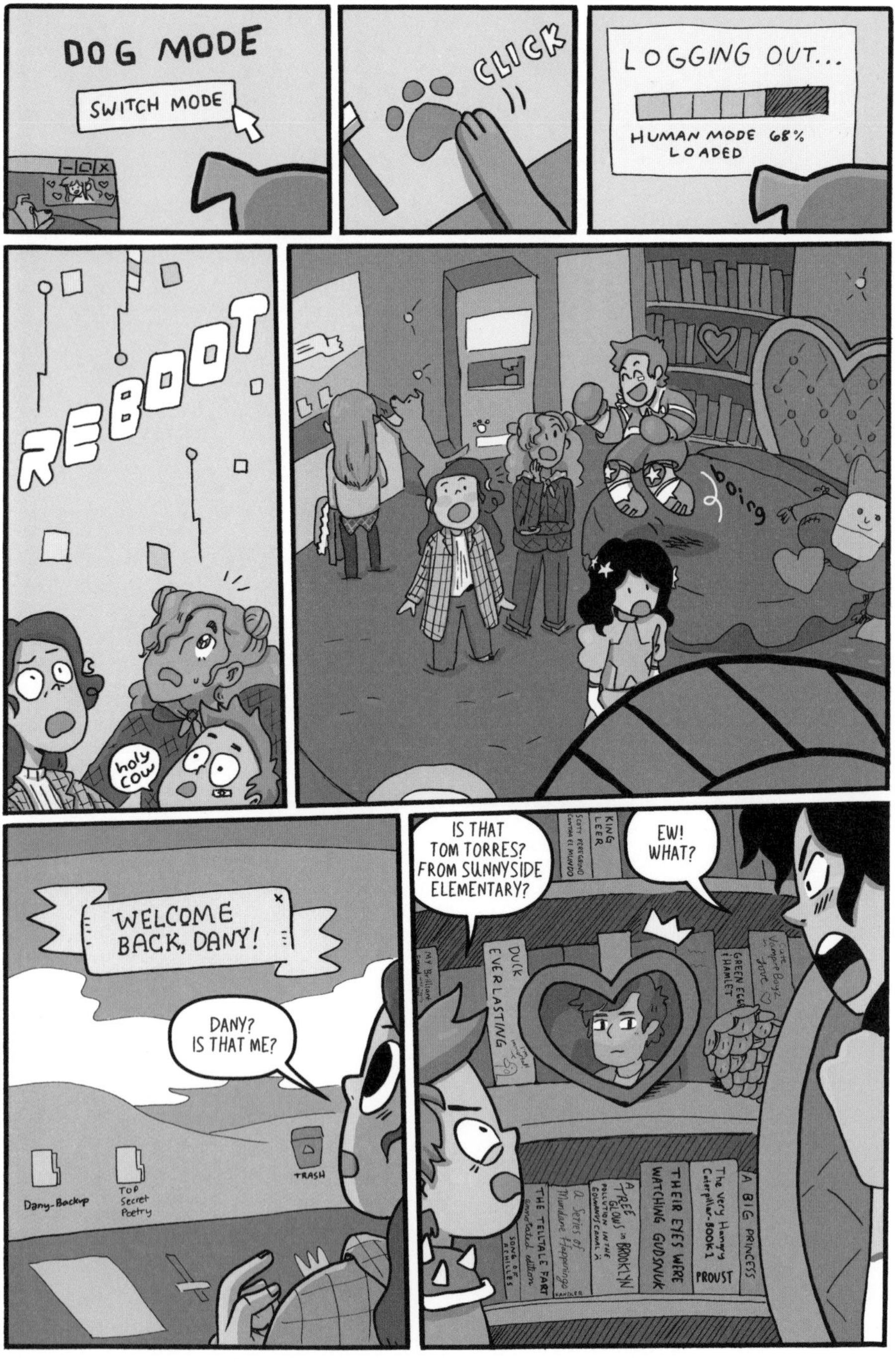
DOG MODE
SWITCH MODE
CLICK
LOGGING OUT...
HUMAN MODE 68% LOADED
REBOOT
holy cow
boing
WELCOME BACK, DANY!
DANY? IS THAT ME?
Dany-Backup
Top Secret Poetry
TRASH
IS THAT TOM TORRES? FROM SUNNYSIDE ELEMENTARY?
EW! WHAT?
KING LEER
DUCK EVERLASTING
GREEN EGGS & HAMLET
THE TELLTALE FART
A TREE GLOWS IN BROOKLYN
THEIR EYES WERE WATCHING GUDSNUK
The Very Hungry Caterpillar - BOOK 1
PROUST
A BIG PRINCESS

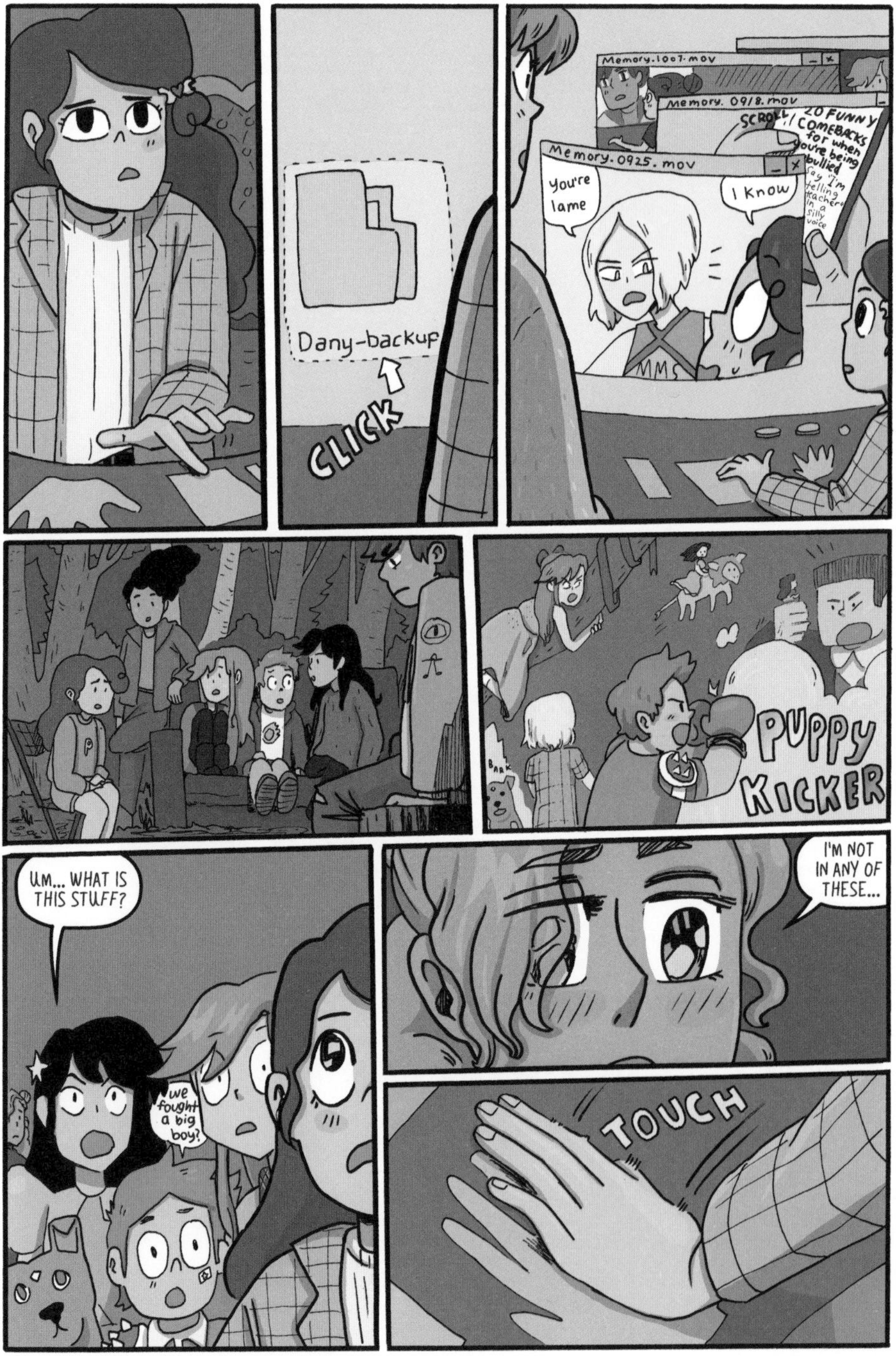
Dany-backup
CLICK
Memory.1007.mov
Memory.0918.mov
SCROLL
20 FUNNY COMEBACKS for when you're being bullied
Say "I'm telling teacher" in a silly voice
Memory.0925.mov
You're lame
I know
MMS
BARK
PUPPY KICKER
UM... WHAT IS THIS STUFF?
we fought a big boy?
I'M NOT IN ANY OF THESE...
TOUCH

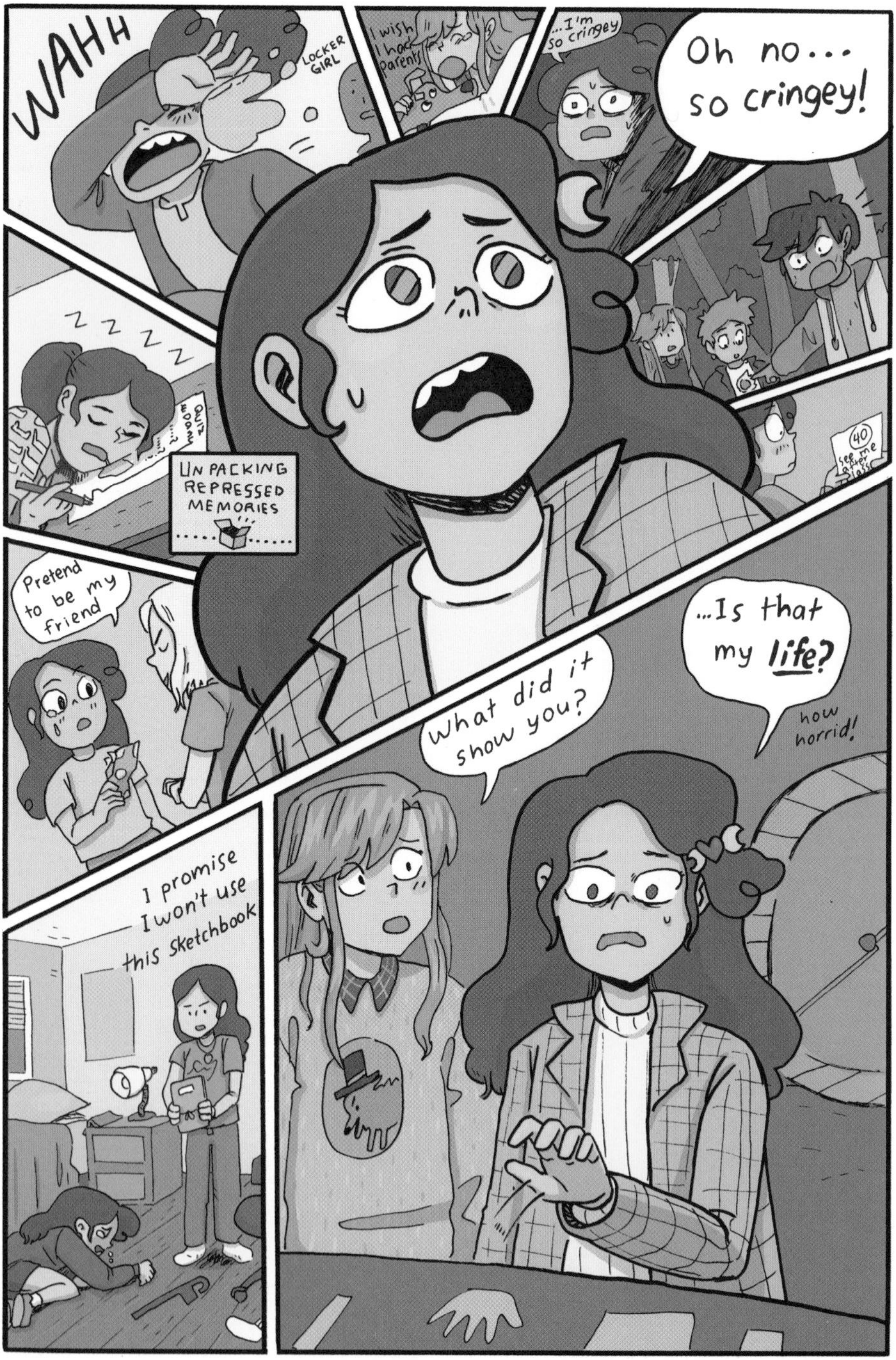

WAHH
LOCKER GIRL
I wish I had parents!
...I'm so cringey
Oh no... so cringey!
ZZZZ
QUIZ
UNPACKING REPRESSED MEMORIES
40 see me after class
Pretend to be my friend
...Is that my life?
how horrid!
What did it show you?
I promise I won't use this sketchbook

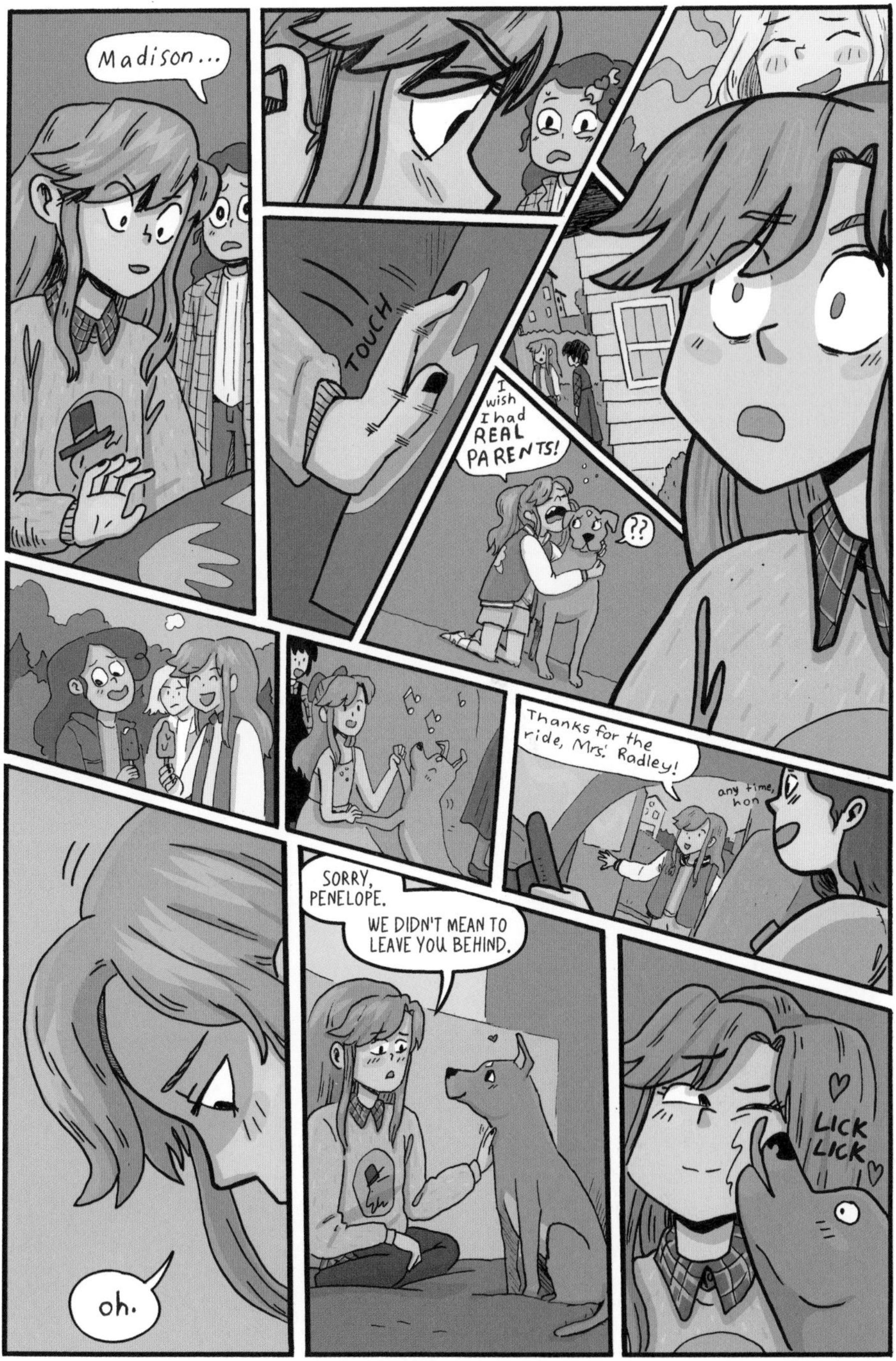
Madison...
TOUCH
I wish I had REAL PARENTS!
??
Thanks for the ride, Mrs. Radley!
any time, hon
SORRY, PENELOPE.
WE DIDN'T MEAN TO LEAVE YOU BEHIND.
LICK LICK
oh.

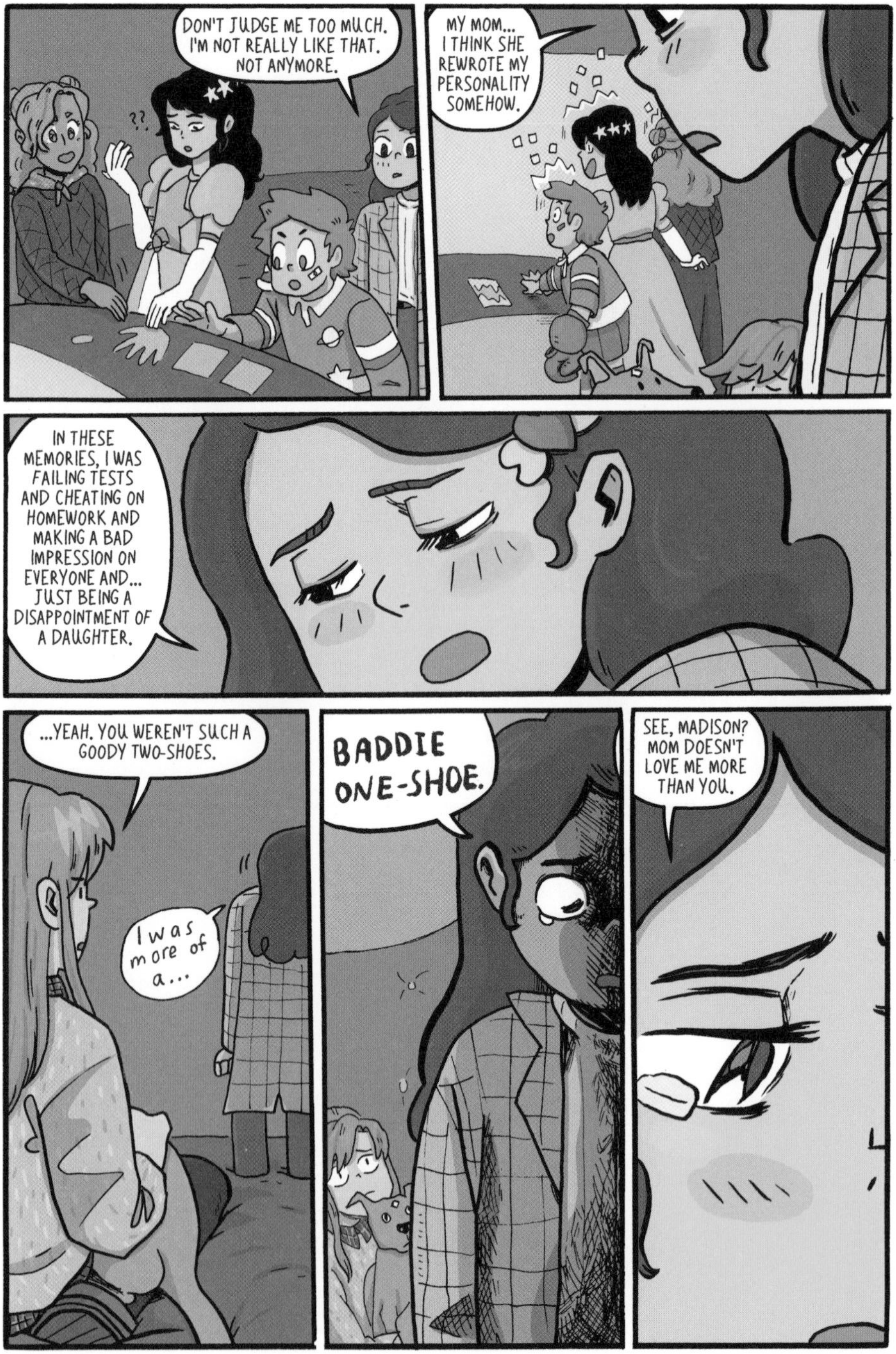
DON'T JUDGE ME TOO MUCH. I'M NOT REALLY LIKE THAT. NOT ANYMORE.
??
MY MOM... I THINK SHE REWROTE MY PERSONALITY SOMEHOW.
IN THESE MEMORIES, I WAS FAILING TESTS AND CHEATING ON HOMEWORK AND MAKING A BAD IMPRESSION ON EVERYONE AND... JUST BEING A DISAPPOINTMENT OF A DAUGHTER.
...YEAH. YOU WEREN'T SUCH A GOODY TWO-SHOES.
I was more of a...
BADDIE ONE-SHOE.
SEE, MADISON? MOM DOESN'T LOVE ME MORE THAN YOU.

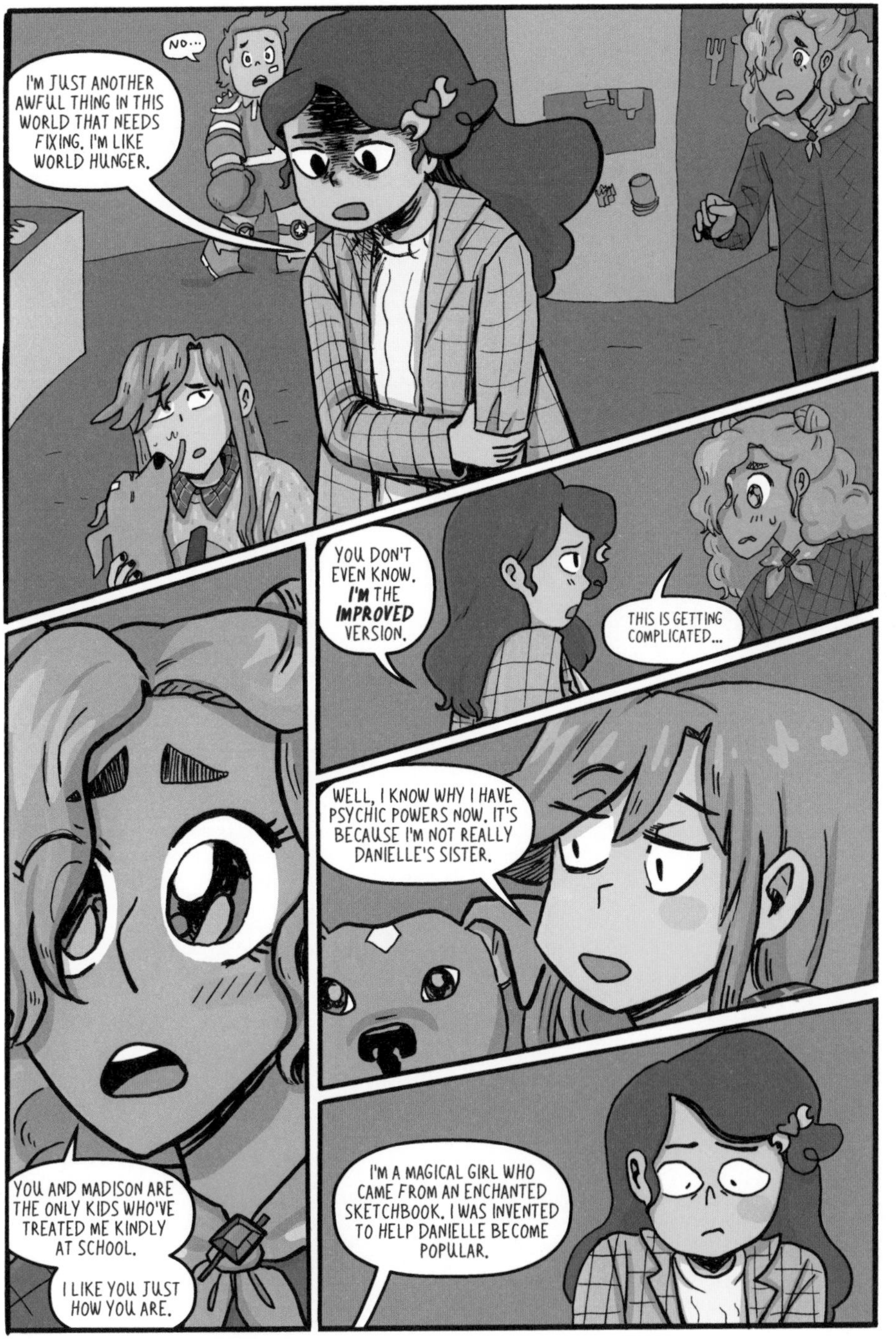

NO...
I'M JUST ANOTHER AWFUL THING IN THIS WORLD THAT NEEDS FIXING. I'M LIKE WORLD HUNGER.
YOU DON'T EVEN KNOW. I'M THE IMPROVED VERSION.
THIS IS GETTING COMPLICATED...
WELL, I KNOW WHY I HAVE PSYCHIC POWERS NOW. IT'S BECAUSE I'M NOT REALLY DANIELLE'S SISTER.
YOU AND MADISON ARE THE ONLY KIDS WHO'VE TREATED ME KINDLY AT SCHOOL.
I LIKE YOU JUST HOW YOU ARE.
I'M A MAGICAL GIRL WHO CAME FROM AN ENCHANTED SKETCHBOOK. I WAS INVENTED TO HELP DANIELLE BECOME POPULAR.

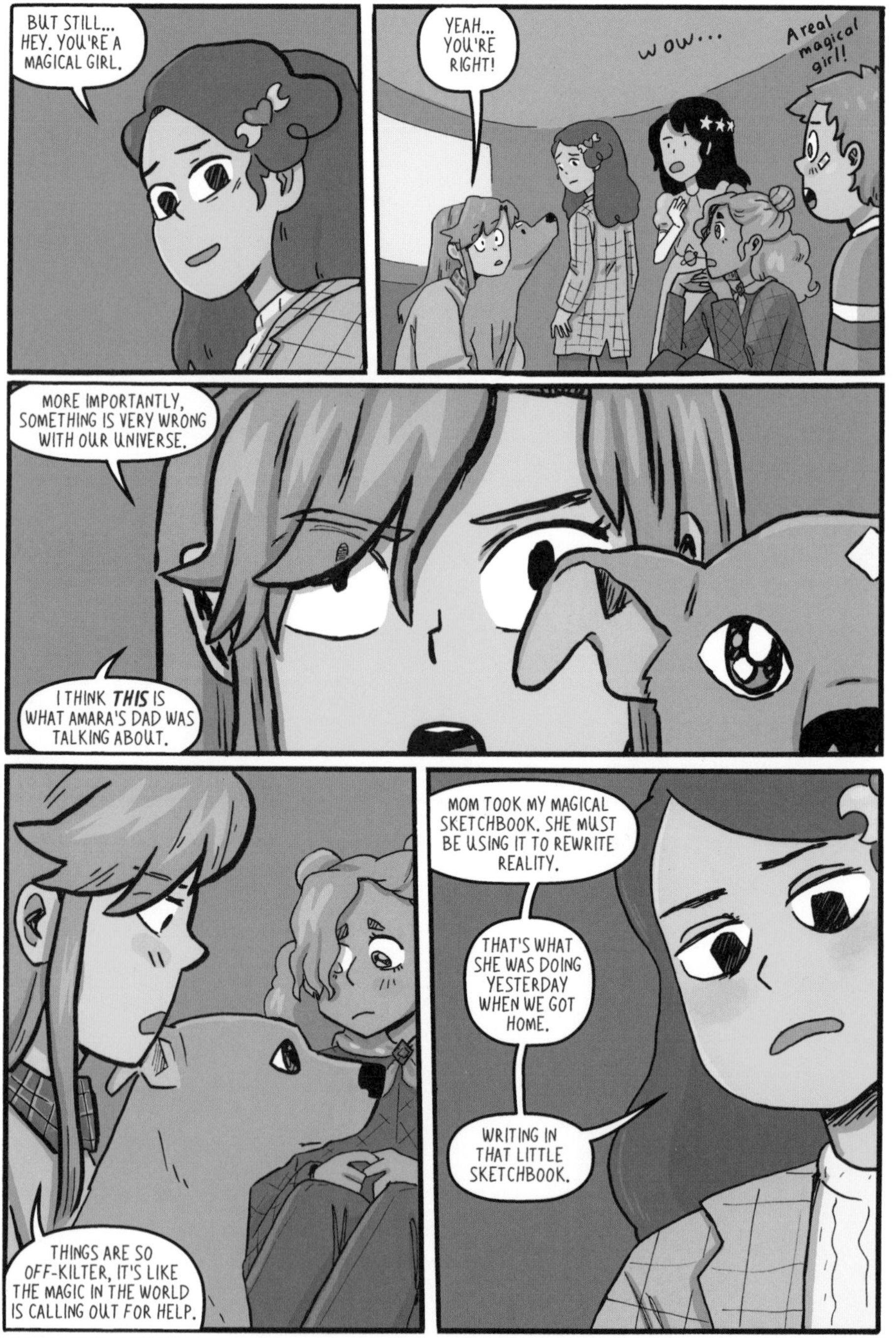
BUT STILL... HEY. YOU'RE A MAGICAL GIRL.
YEAH... YOU'RE RIGHT!
WOW...
A real magical girl!
MORE IMPORTANTLY, SOMETHING IS VERY WRONG WITH OUR UNIVERSE.
I THINK THIS IS WHAT AMARA'S DAD WAS TALKING ABOUT.
THINGS ARE SO OFF-KILTER, IT'S LIKE THE MAGIC IN THE WORLD IS CALLING OUT FOR HELP.
MOM TOOK MY MAGICAL SKETCHBOOK. SHE MUST BE USING IT TO REWRITE REALITY.
THAT'S WHAT SHE WAS DOING YESTERDAY WHEN WE GOT HOME.
WRITING IN THAT LITTLE SKETCHBOOK.

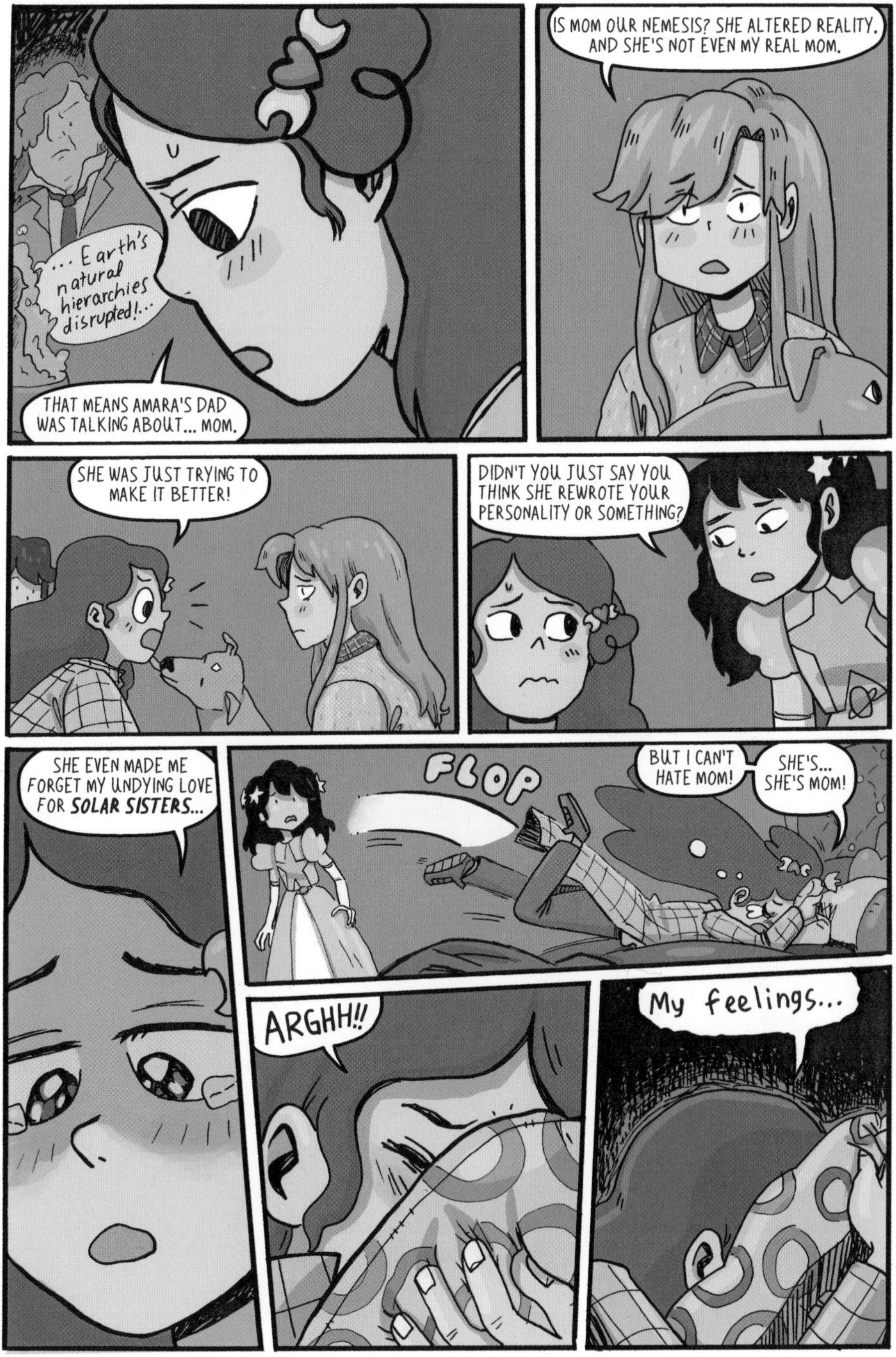
...Earth's natural hierarchies disrupted!...
THAT MEANS AMARA'S DAD WAS TALKING ABOUT... MOM.
IS MOM OUR NEMESIS? SHE ALTERED REALITY. AND SHE'S NOT EVEN MY REAL MOM.
SHE WAS JUST TRYING TO MAKE IT BETTER!
DIDN'T YOU JUST SAY YOU THINK SHE REWROTE YOUR PERSONALITY OR SOMETHING?
SHE EVEN MADE ME FORGET MY UNDYING LOVE FOR SOLAR SISTERS...
FLOP
BUT I CAN'T HATE MOM!
SHE'S... SHE'S MOM!
ARGHH!!
My feelings...

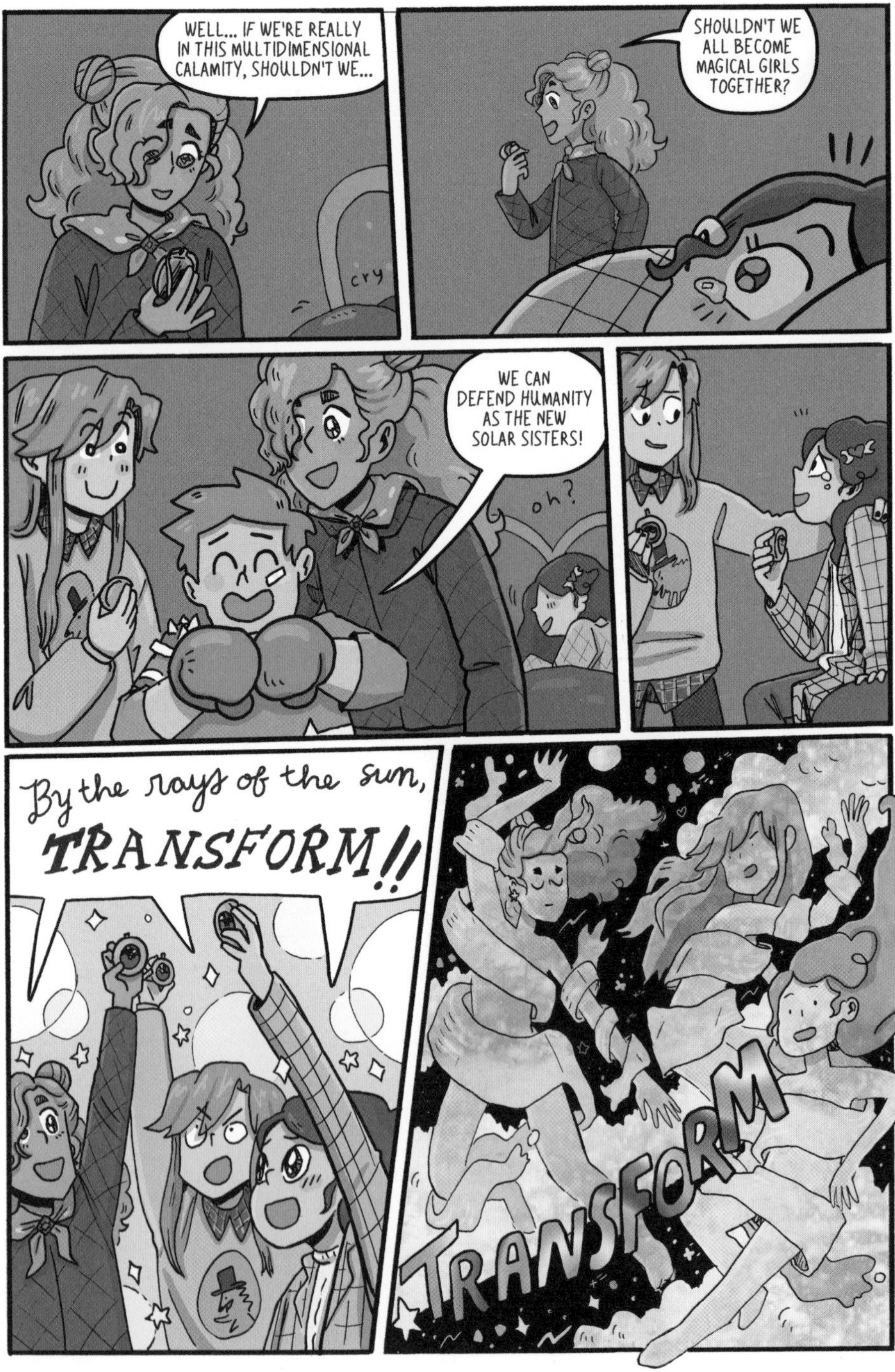
WELL... IF WE'RE REALLY IN THIS MULTIDIMENSIONAL CALAMITY, SHOULDN'T WE...
cry
SHOULDN'T WE ALL BECOME MAGICAL GIRLS TOGETHER?
WE CAN DEFEND HUMANITY AS THE NEW SOLAR SISTERS!
oh?
By the rays of the sun, TRANSFORM!!
TRANSFORM

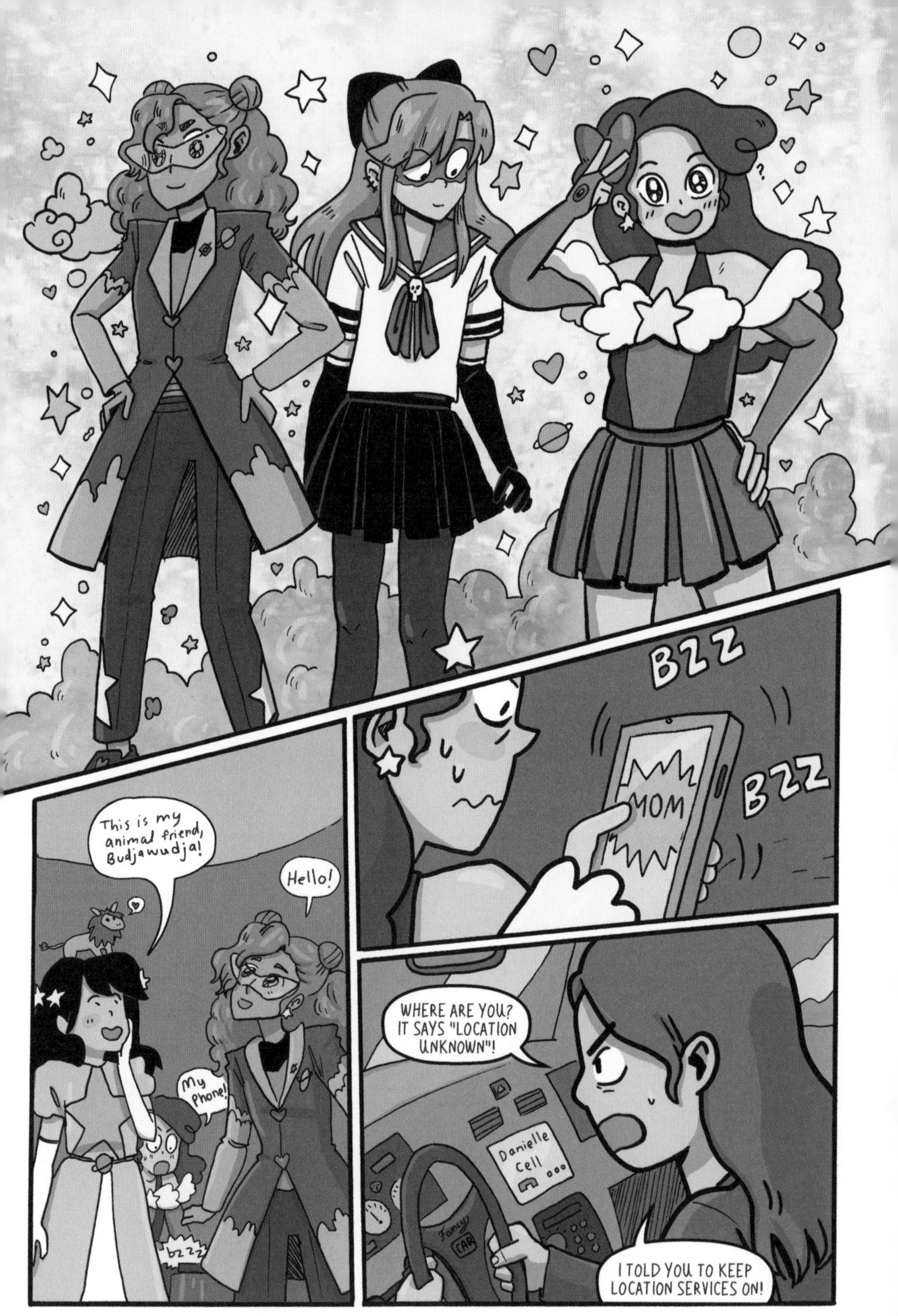
BZZ
BZZ
MOM
This is my animal friend, Budjawudja!
Hello!
My phone!
bzzz
WHERE ARE YOU? IT SAYS "LOCATION UNKNOWN"!
Danielle Cell
Fancy CAR
I TOLD YOU TO KEEP LOCATION SERVICES ON!

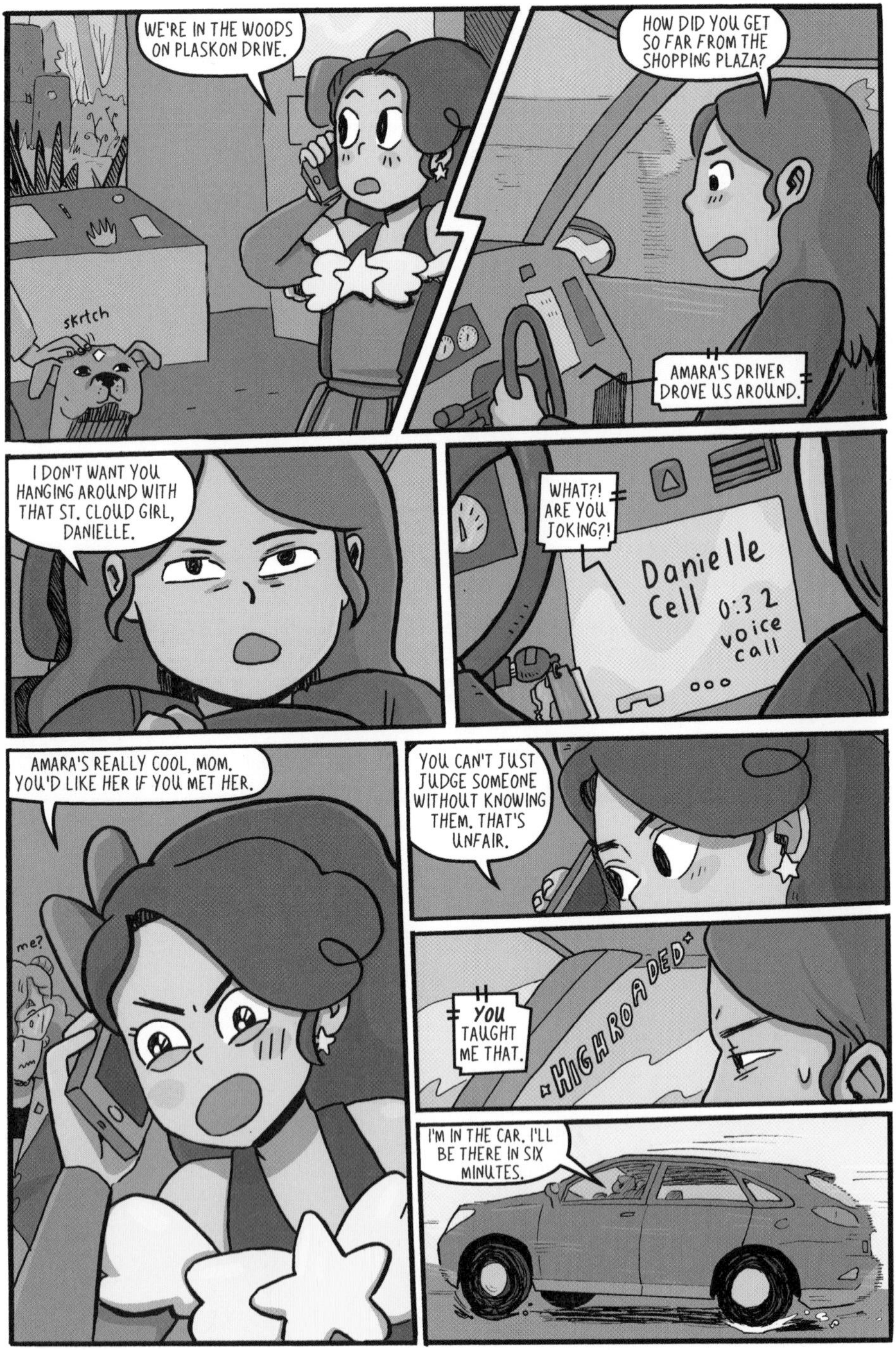
WE'RE IN THE WOODS ON PLASKON DRIVE.
skrtch
HOW DID YOU GET SO FAR FROM THE SHOPPING PLAZA?
AMARA'S DRIVER DROVE US AROUND.
I DON'T WANT YOU HANGING AROUND WITH THAT ST. CLOUD GIRL, DANIELLE.
WHAT?! ARE YOU JOKING?!
Danielle Cell 0:32 voice call
AMARA'S REALLY COOL, MOM. YOU'D LIKE HER IF YOU MET HER.
me?
YOU CAN'T JUST JUDGE SOMEONE WITHOUT KNOWING THEM. THAT'S UNFAIR.
YOU TAUGHT ME THAT.
HIGHROADED
I'M IN THE CAR. I'LL BE THERE IN SIX MINUTES.

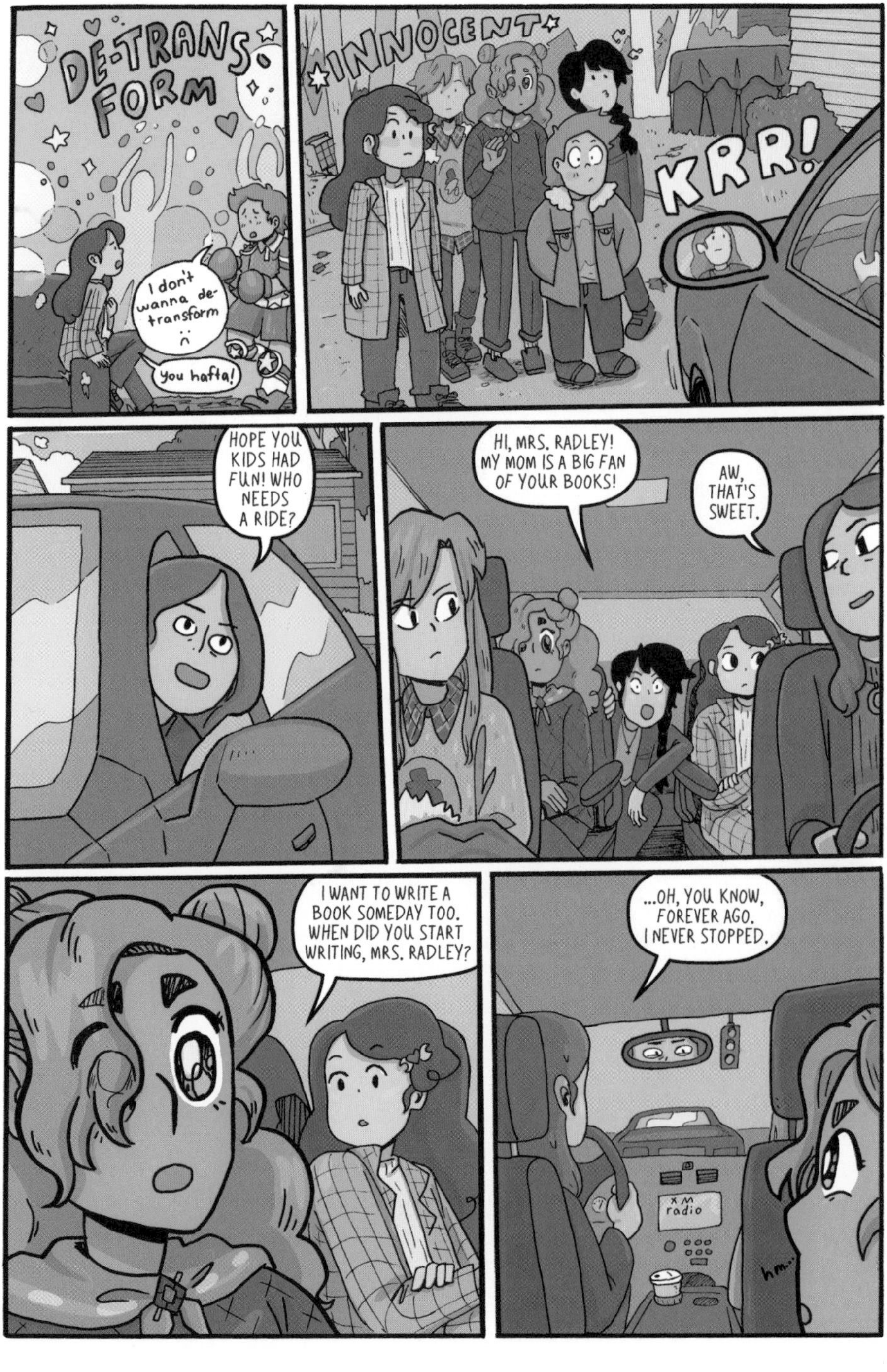
DE-TRANS-FORM
I don't wanna de-transform :(
You hafta!
INNOCENT
KRR!
HOPE YOU KIDS HAD FUN! WHO NEEDS A RIDE?
HI, MRS. RADLEY! MY MOM IS A BIG FAN OF YOUR BOOKS!
AW, THAT'S SWEET.
I WANT TO WRITE A BOOK SOMEDAY TOO. WHEN DID YOU START WRITING, MRS. RADLEY?
...OH, YOU KNOW, FOREVER AGO. I NEVER STOPPED.
XM radio
hm...

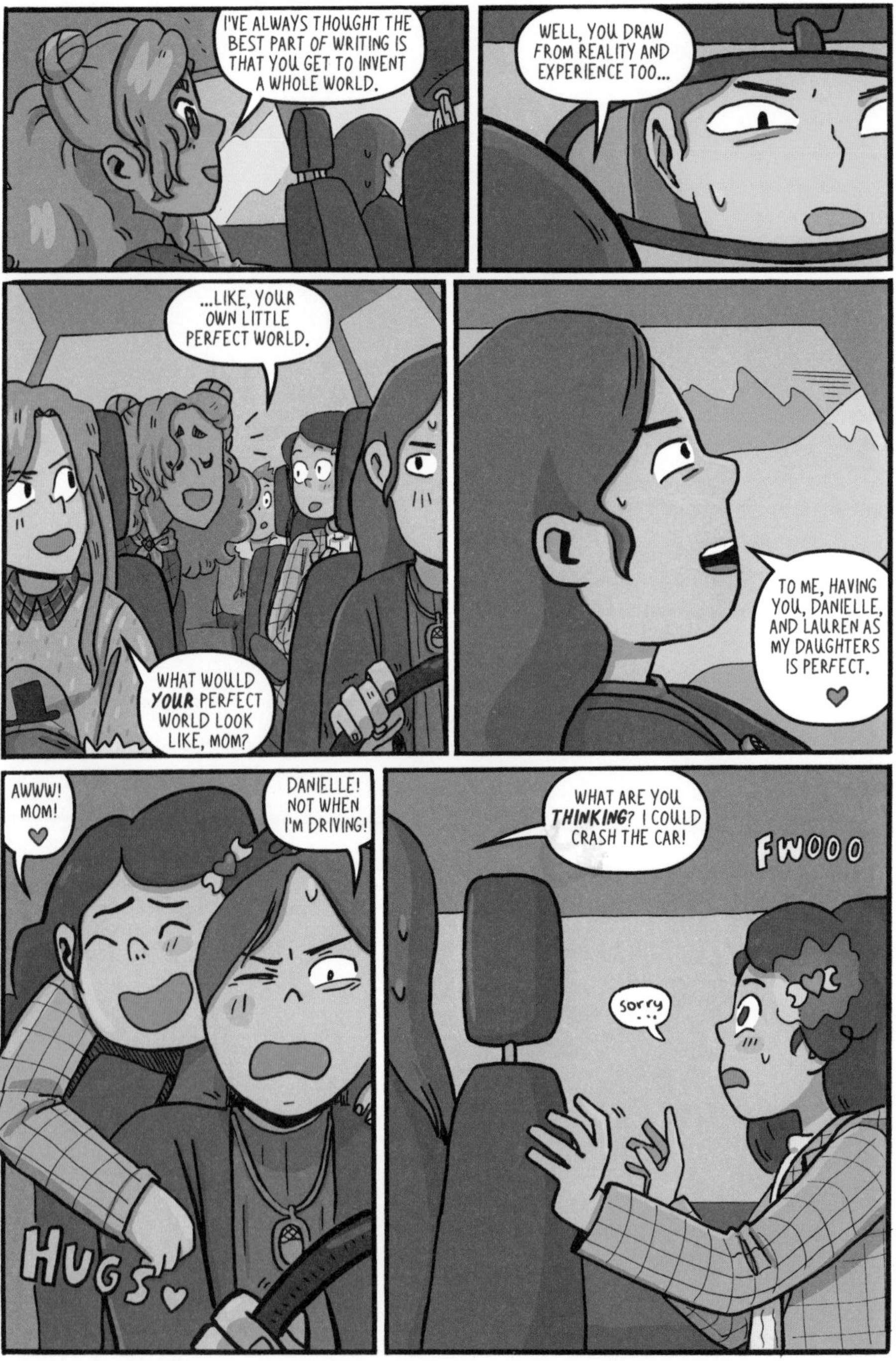
I'VE ALWAYS THOUGHT THE BEST PART OF WRITING IS THAT YOU GET TO INVENT A WHOLE WORLD.
WELL, YOU DRAW FROM REALITY AND EXPERIENCE TOO...
...LIKE, YOUR OWN LITTLE PERFECT WORLD.
WHAT WOULD **YOUR** PERFECT WORLD LOOK LIKE, MOM?
TO ME, HAVING YOU, DANIELLE, AND LAUREN AS MY DAUGHTERS IS PERFECT.
AWWW! MOM!
DANIELLE! NOT WHEN I'M DRIVING!
HUGS
WHAT ARE YOU ***THINKING***? I COULD CRASH THE CAR!
FWOOO
sorry...

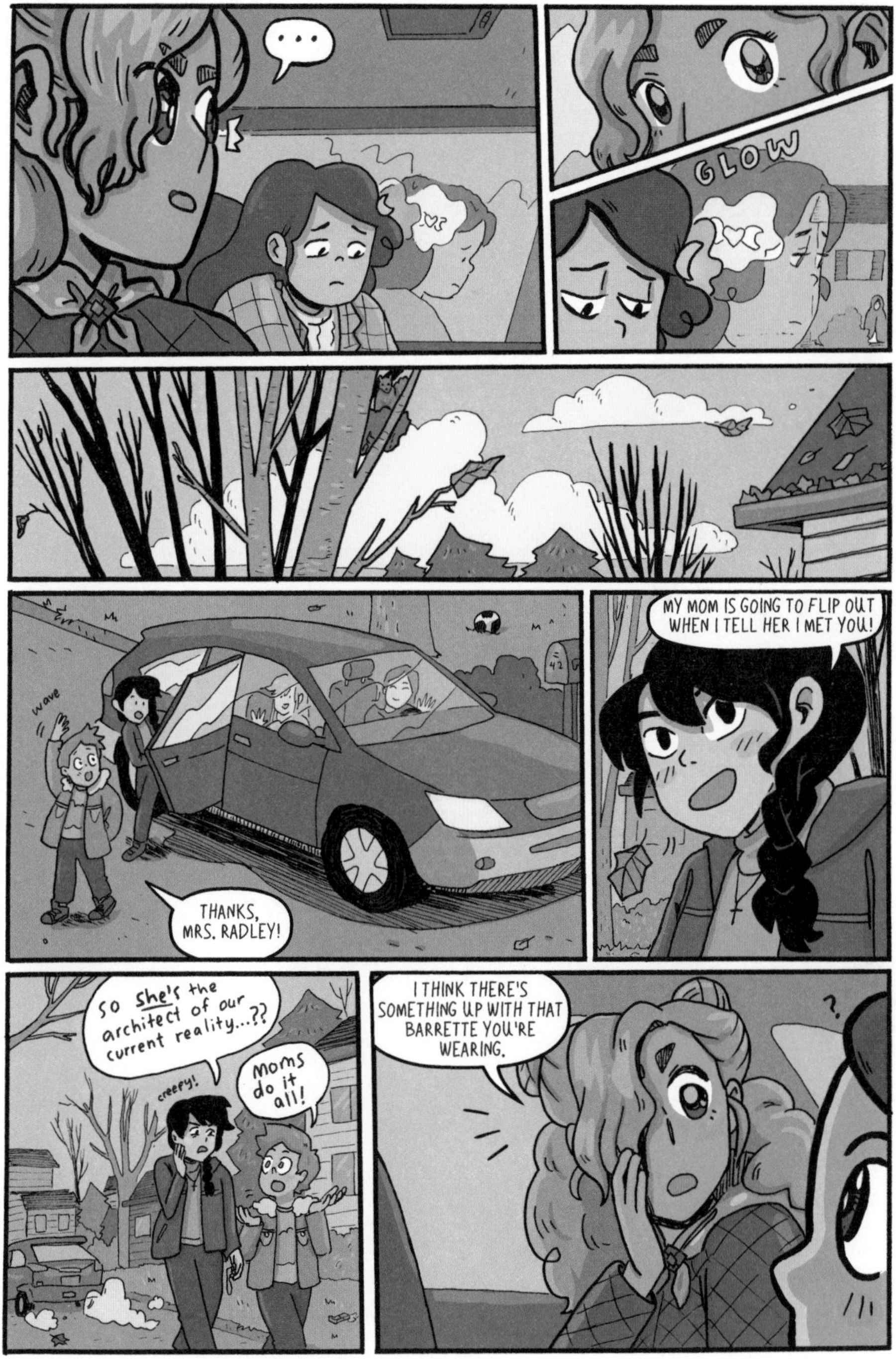
...
GLOW
wave
THANKS, MRS. RADLEY!
MY MOM IS GOING TO FLIP OUT WHEN I TELL HER I MET YOU!
So She's the architect of our current reality...??
creepy!
Moms do it all!
I THINK THERE'S SOMETHING UP WITH THAT BARRETTE YOU'RE WEARING.
?

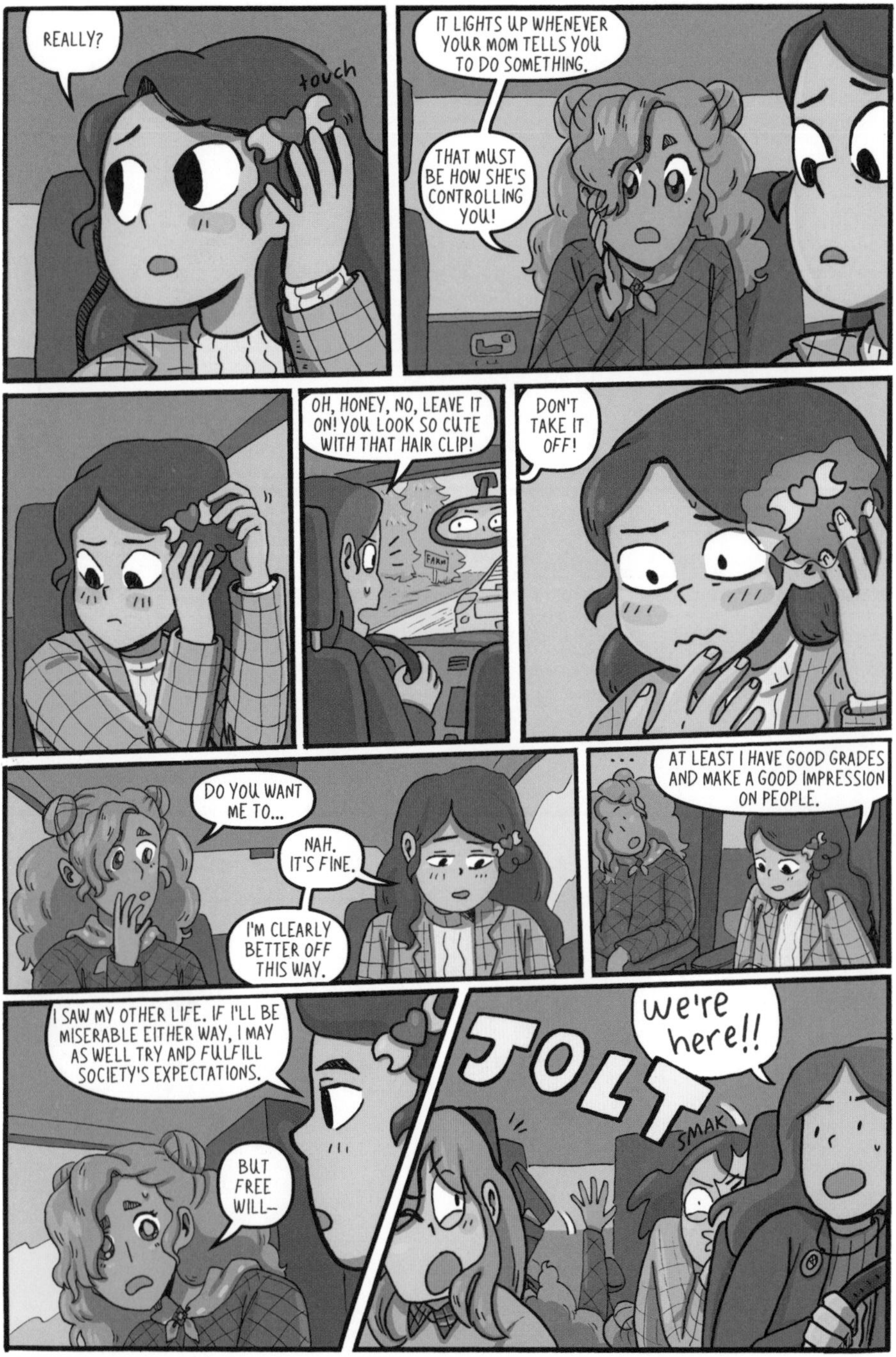

REALLY?
touch
IT LIGHTS UP WHENEVER YOUR MOM TELLS YOU TO DO SOMETHING.
THAT MUST BE HOW SHE'S CONTROLLING YOU!
OH, HONEY, NO, LEAVE IT ON! YOU LOOK SO CUTE WITH THAT HAIR CLIP!
FARM
DON'T TAKE IT OFF!
DO YOU WANT ME TO...
NAH. IT'S FINE.
I'M CLEARLY BETTER OFF THIS WAY.
...
AT LEAST I HAVE GOOD GRADES AND MAKE A GOOD IMPRESSION ON PEOPLE.
I SAW MY OTHER LIFE. IF I'LL BE MISERABLE EITHER WAY, I MAY AS WELL TRY AND FULFILL SOCIETY'S EXPECTATIONS.
BUT FREE WILL–
JOLT
we're here!!
SMAK

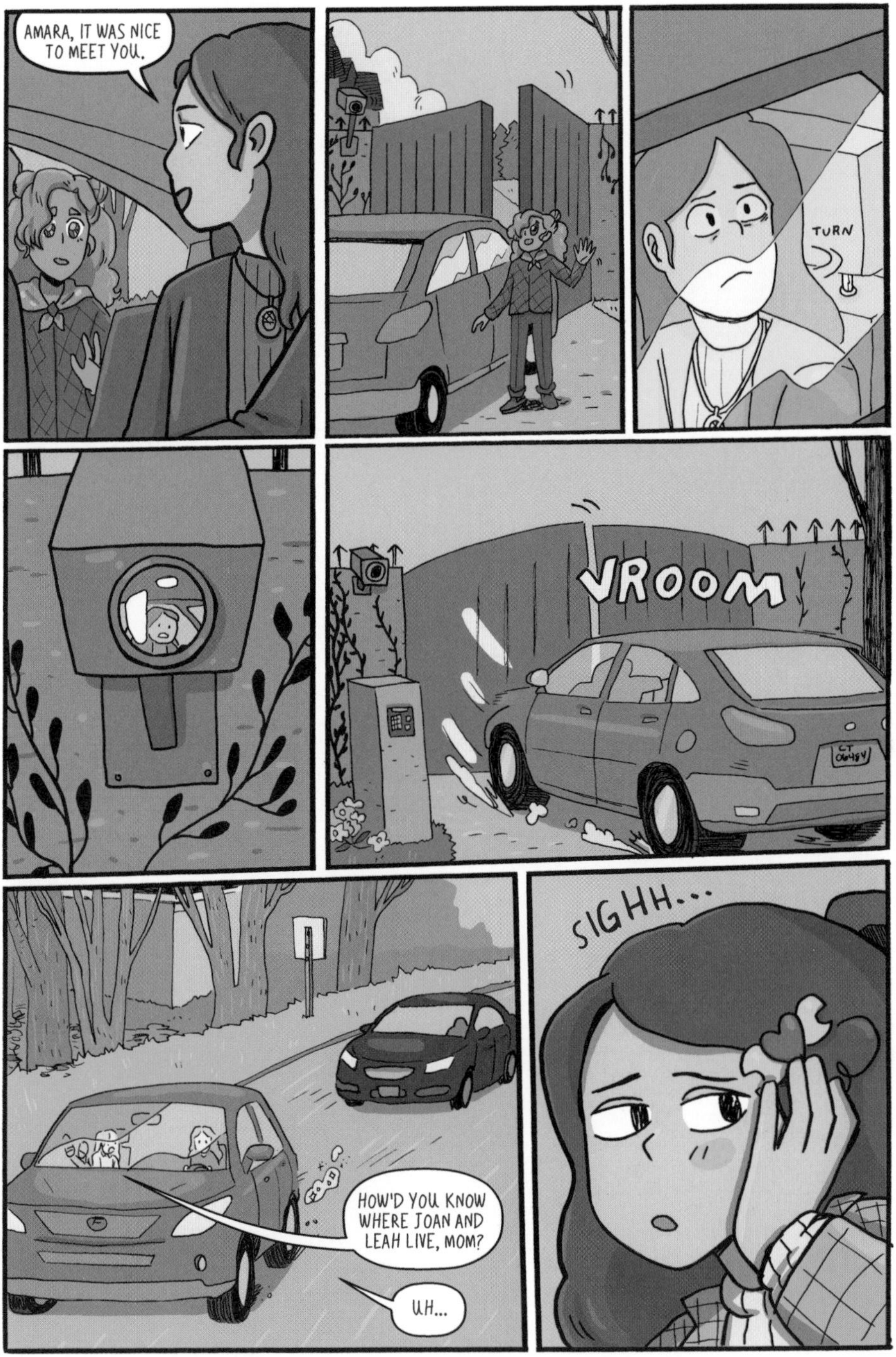
AMARA, IT WAS NICE TO MEET YOU.
TURN
VROOM
CT 06484
SIGHH...
HOW'D YOU KNOW WHERE JOAN AND LEAH LIVE, MOM?
UH...

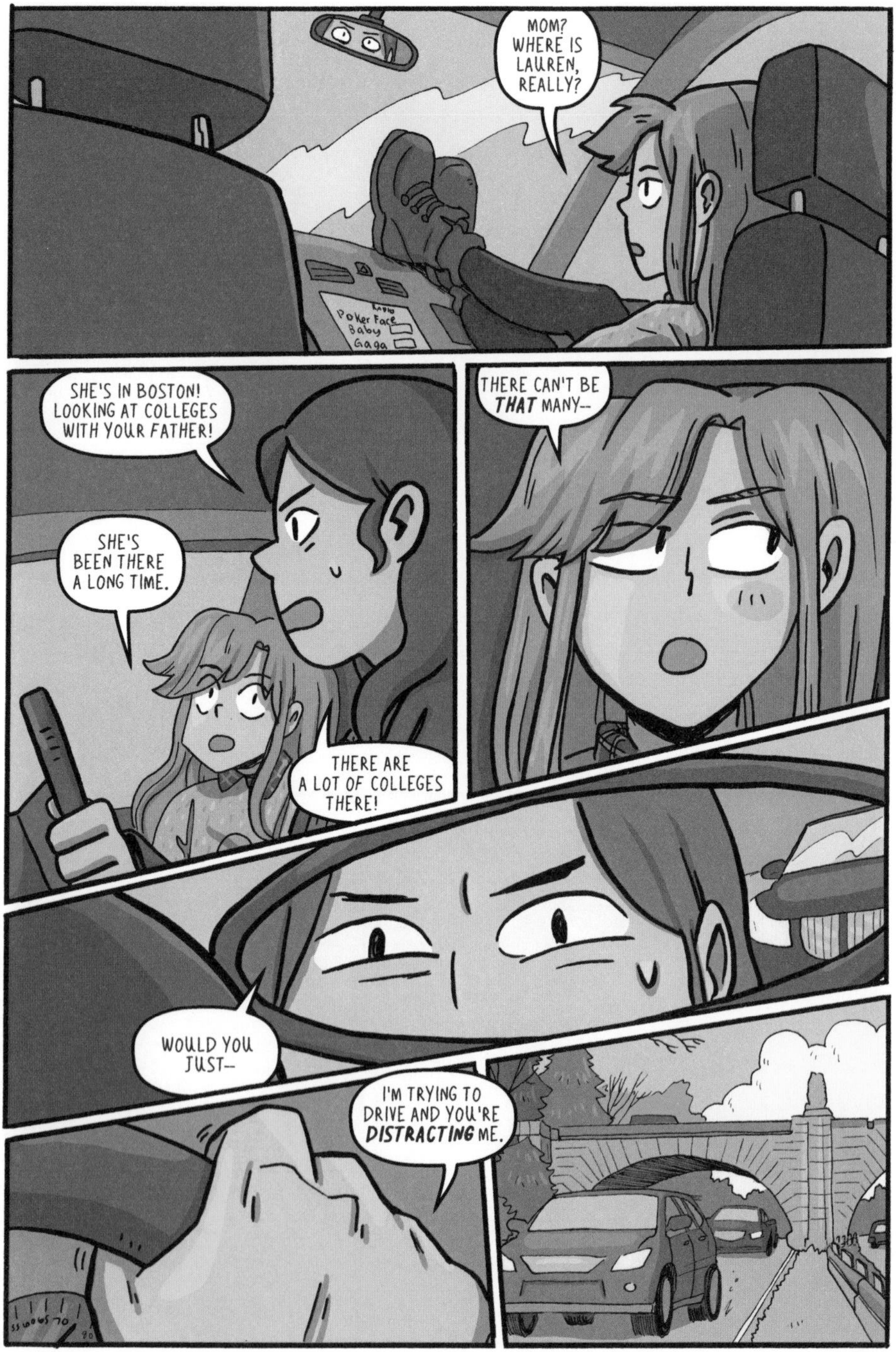
MOM? WHERE IS LAUREN, REALLY?
Radio
Poker Face
Baby
Gaga
SHE'S IN BOSTON! LOOKING AT COLLEGES WITH YOUR FATHER!
SHE'S BEEN THERE A LONG TIME.
THERE ARE A LOT OF COLLEGES THERE!
THERE CAN'T BE **THAT** MANY--
WOULD YOU JUST--
I'M TRYING TO DRIVE AND YOU'RE **DISTRACTING** ME.

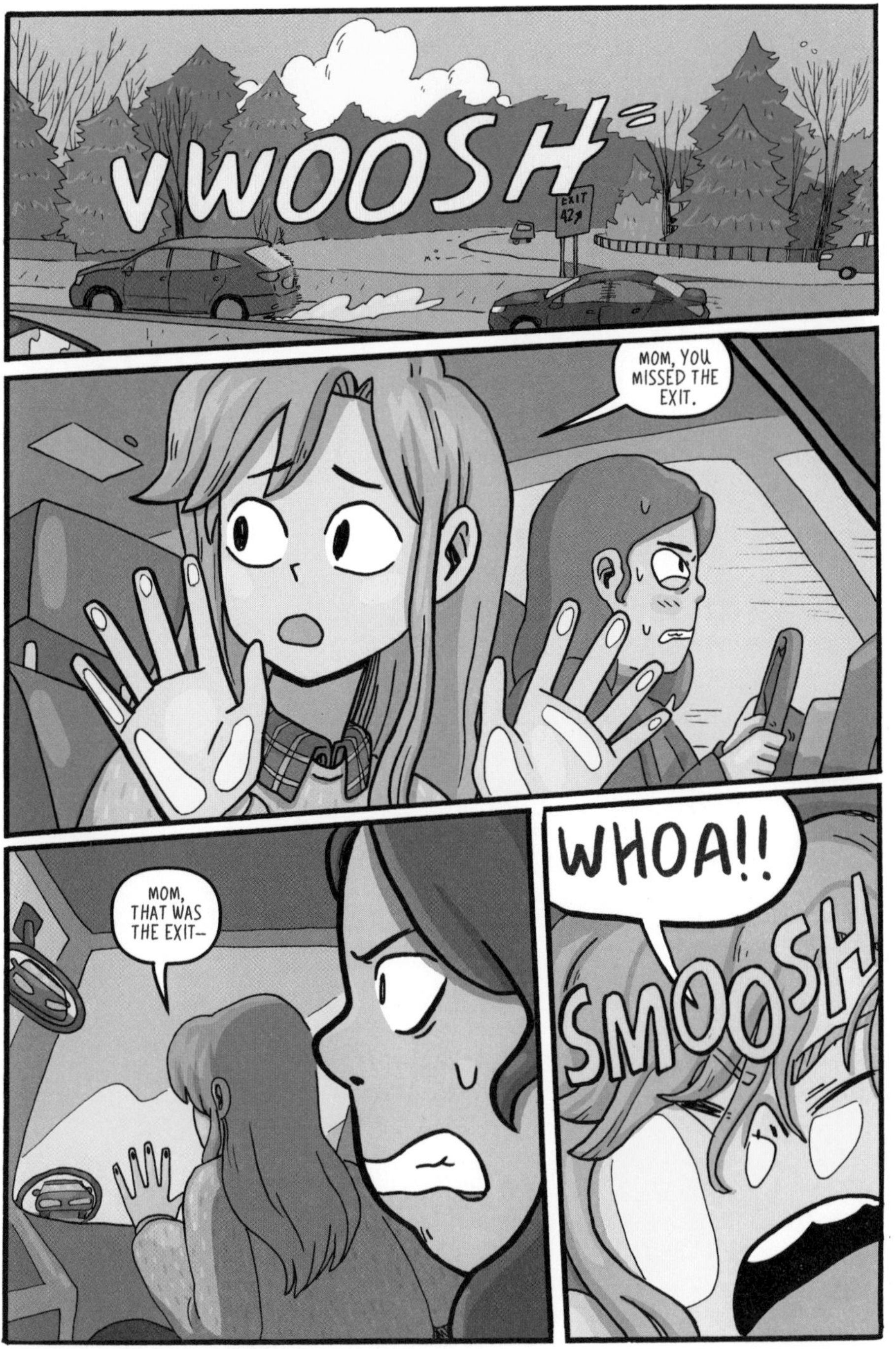
VWOOSH
EXIT 42
MOM, YOU MISSED THE EXIT.
MOM, THAT WAS THE EXIT--
WHOA!!
SMOOSH

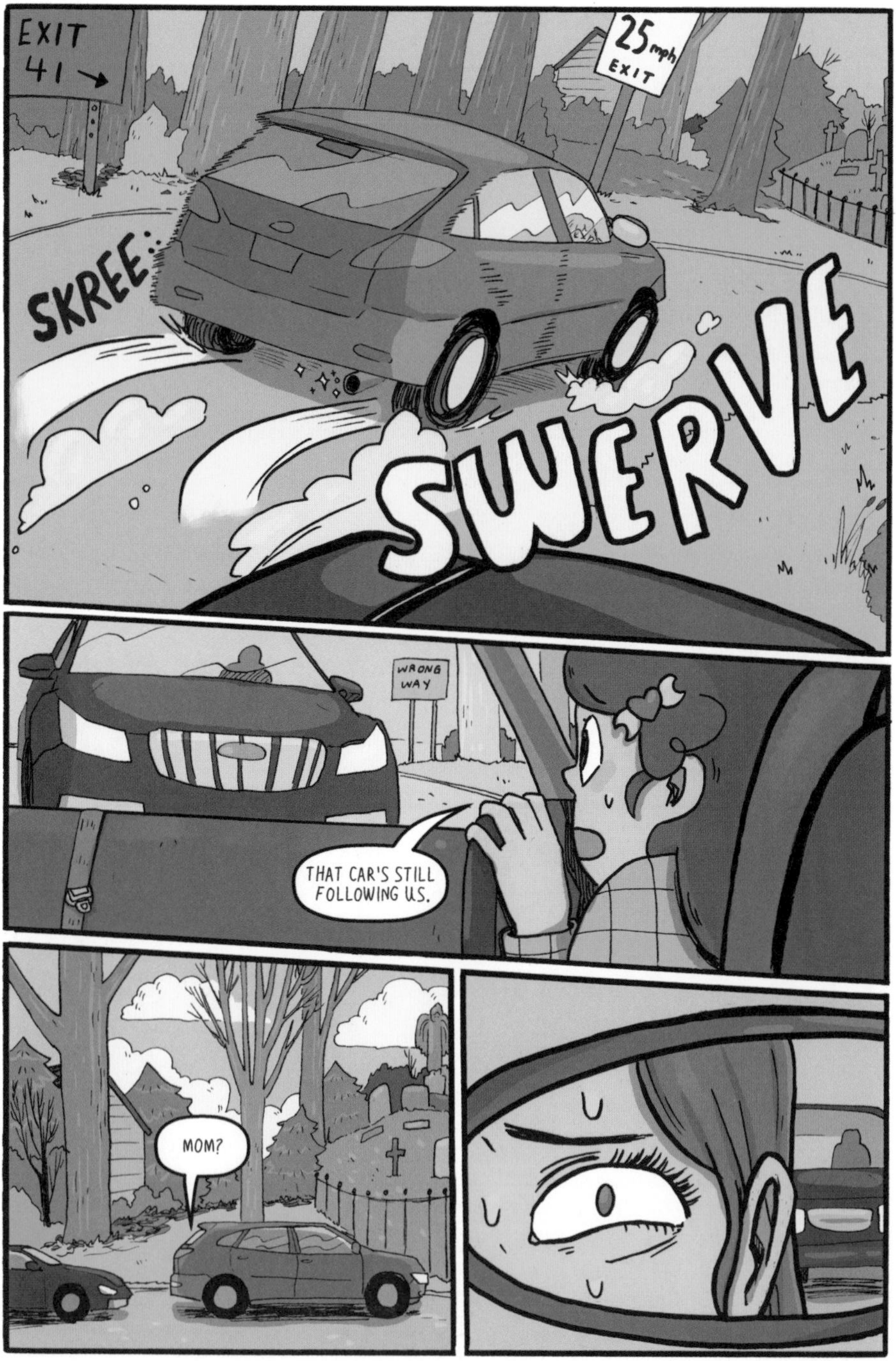
EXIT
41
25 mph
EXIT
SKREE
SWERVE
WRONG WAY
THAT CAR'S STILL FOLLOWING US.
MOM?

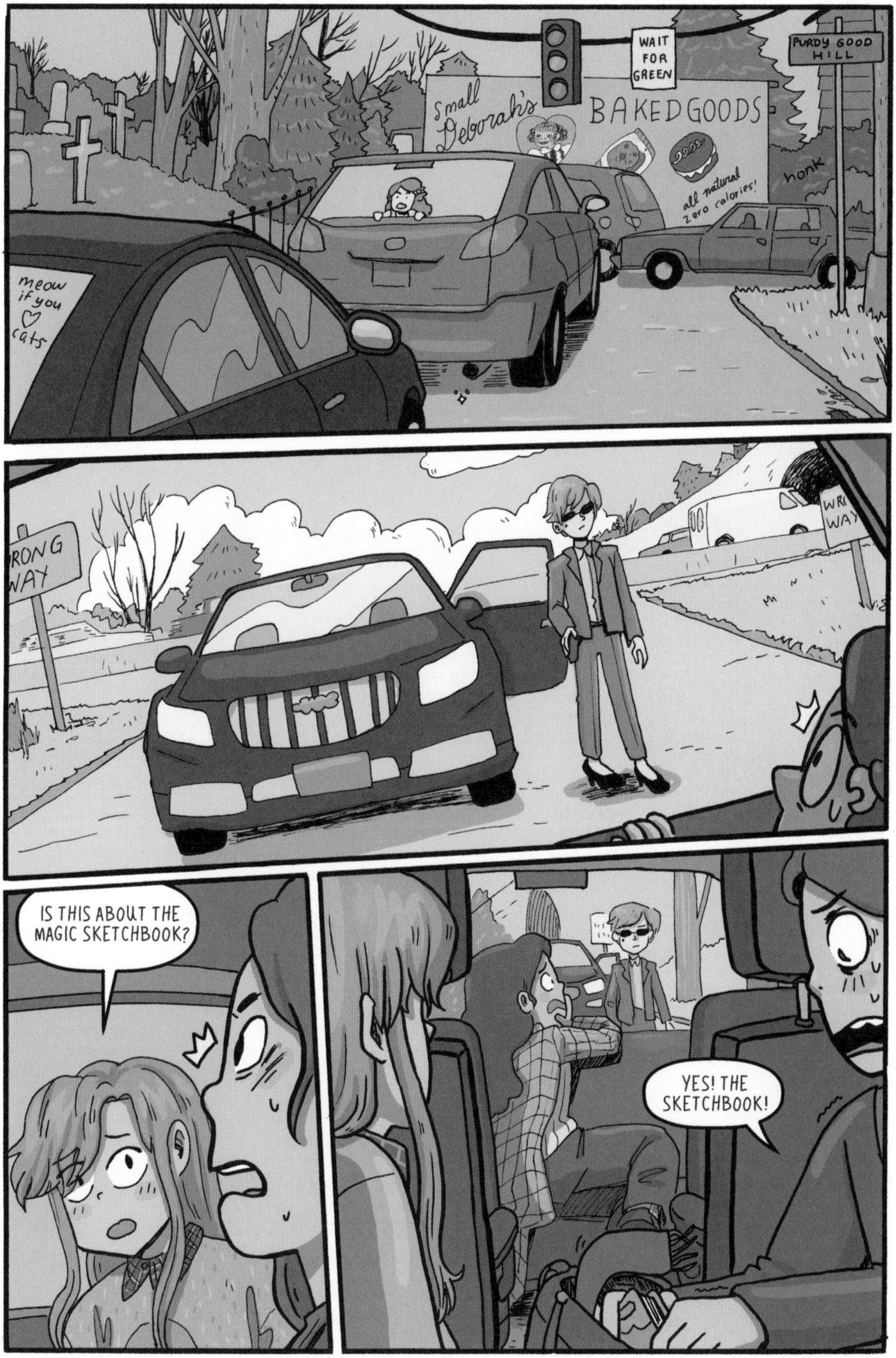
WAIT FOR GREEN
PURDY GOOD HILL
Small Deborah's
BAKED GOODS
all natural
zero calories!
honk
meow if you ♡ cats
WRONG WAY
IS THIS ABOUT THE MAGIC SKETCHBOOK?
YES! THE SKETCHBOOK!

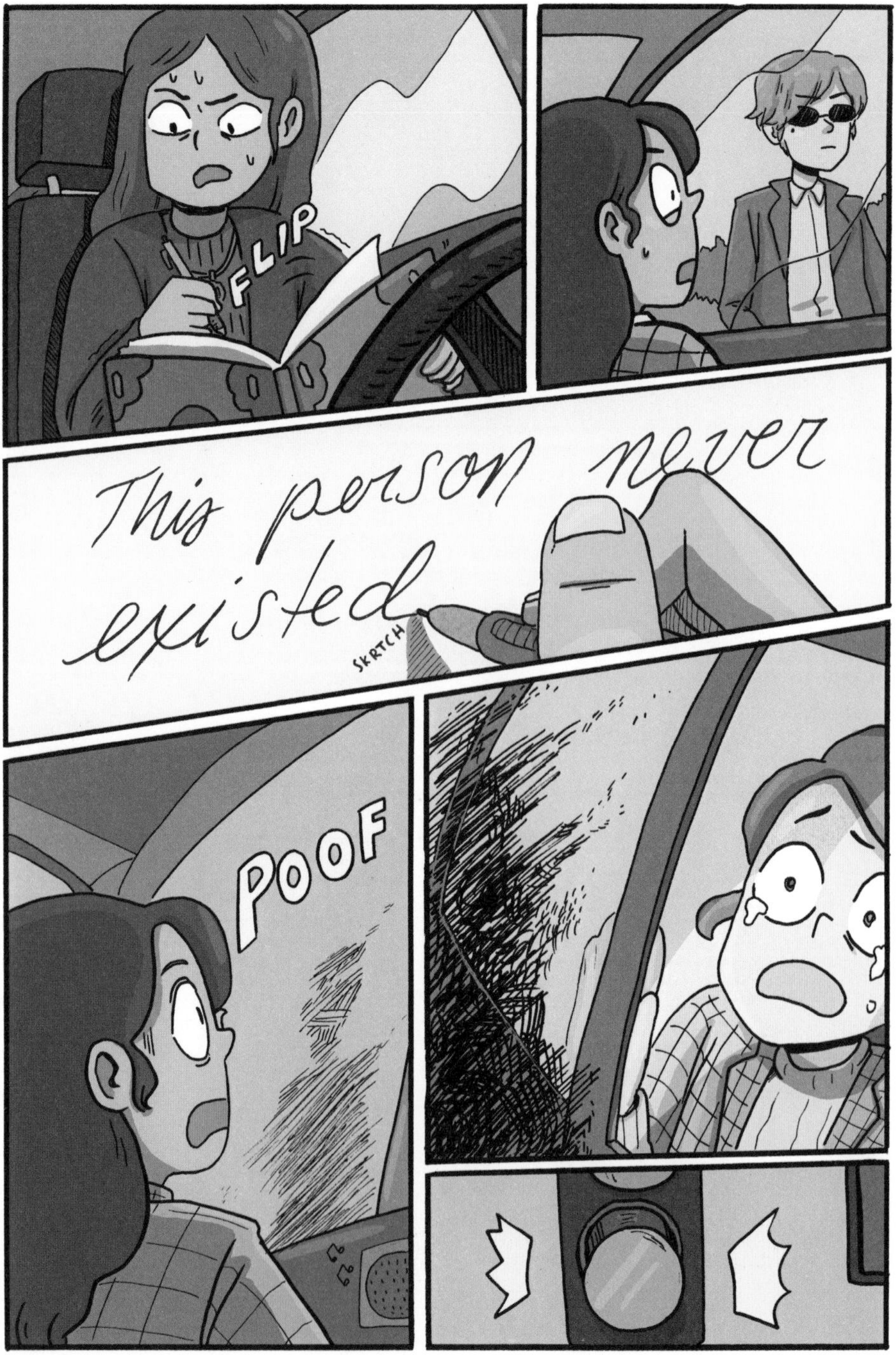
FLIP
This person never existed
SKRTCH
POOF

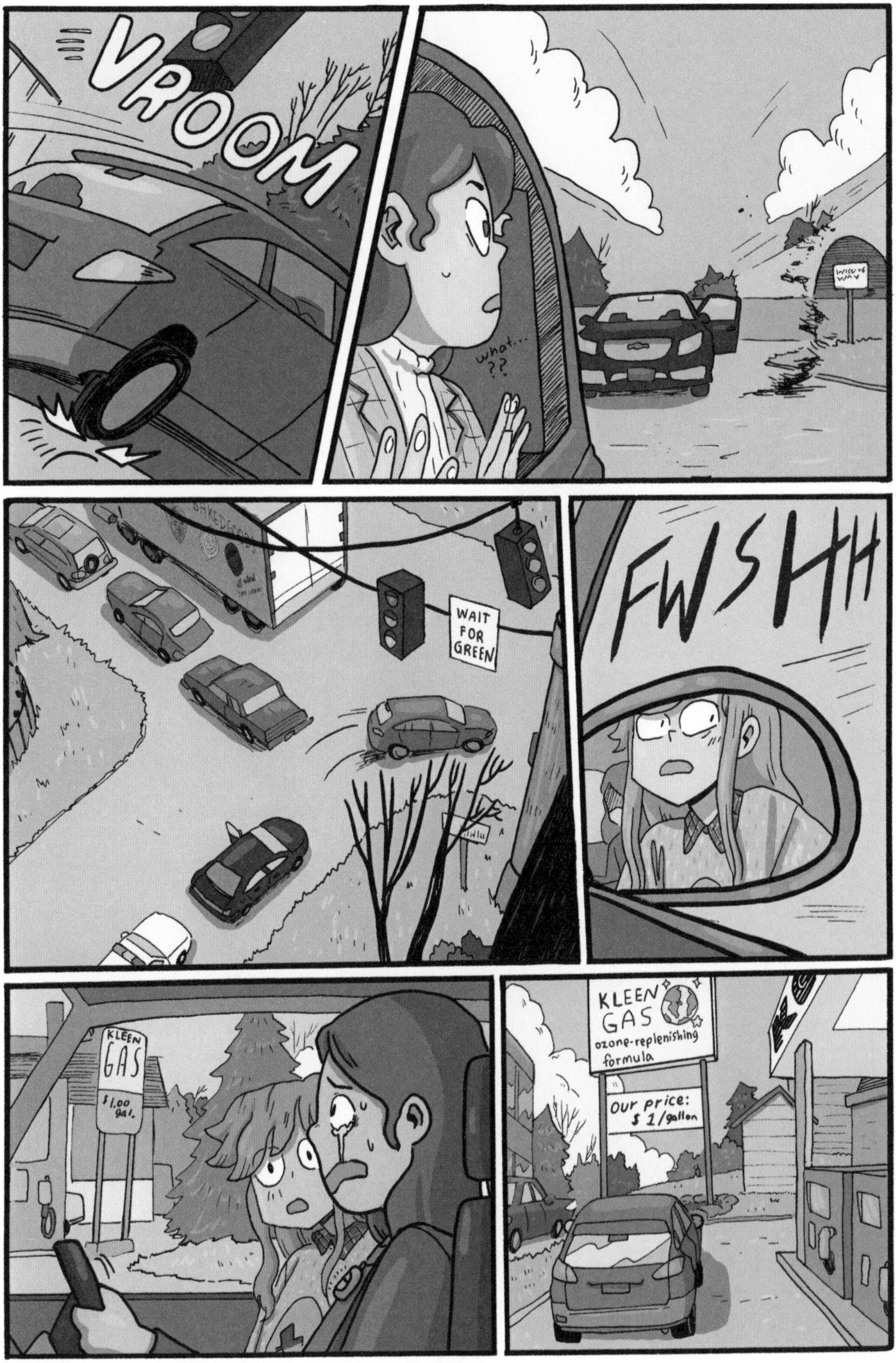
VROOM
what... ??
WAIT FOR GREEN
FWSHH
KLEEN GAS
$1.00 gal.
KLEEN GAS
ozone-replenishing formula
Our price:
$ 1/gallon

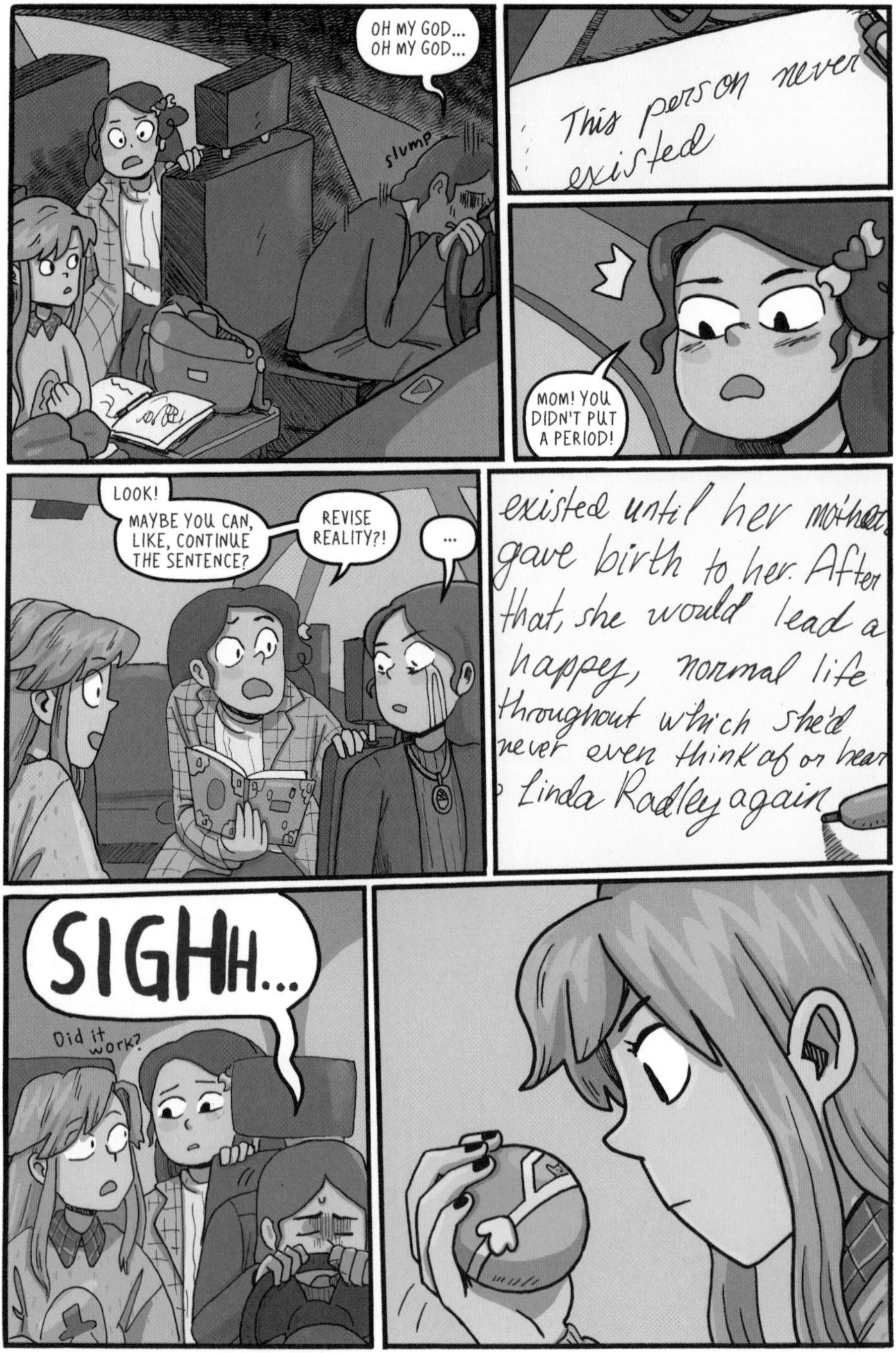
OH MY GOD...
OH MY GOD...
slump
This person never existed
MOM! YOU DIDN'T PUT A PERIOD!
LOOK!
MAYBE YOU CAN, LIKE, CONTINUE THE SENTENCE?
REVISE REALITY?!
...
existed until her mother gave birth to her. After that, she would lead a happy, normal life throughout which she'd never even think of or hear
Linda Radley again
SIGHH...
Did it work?

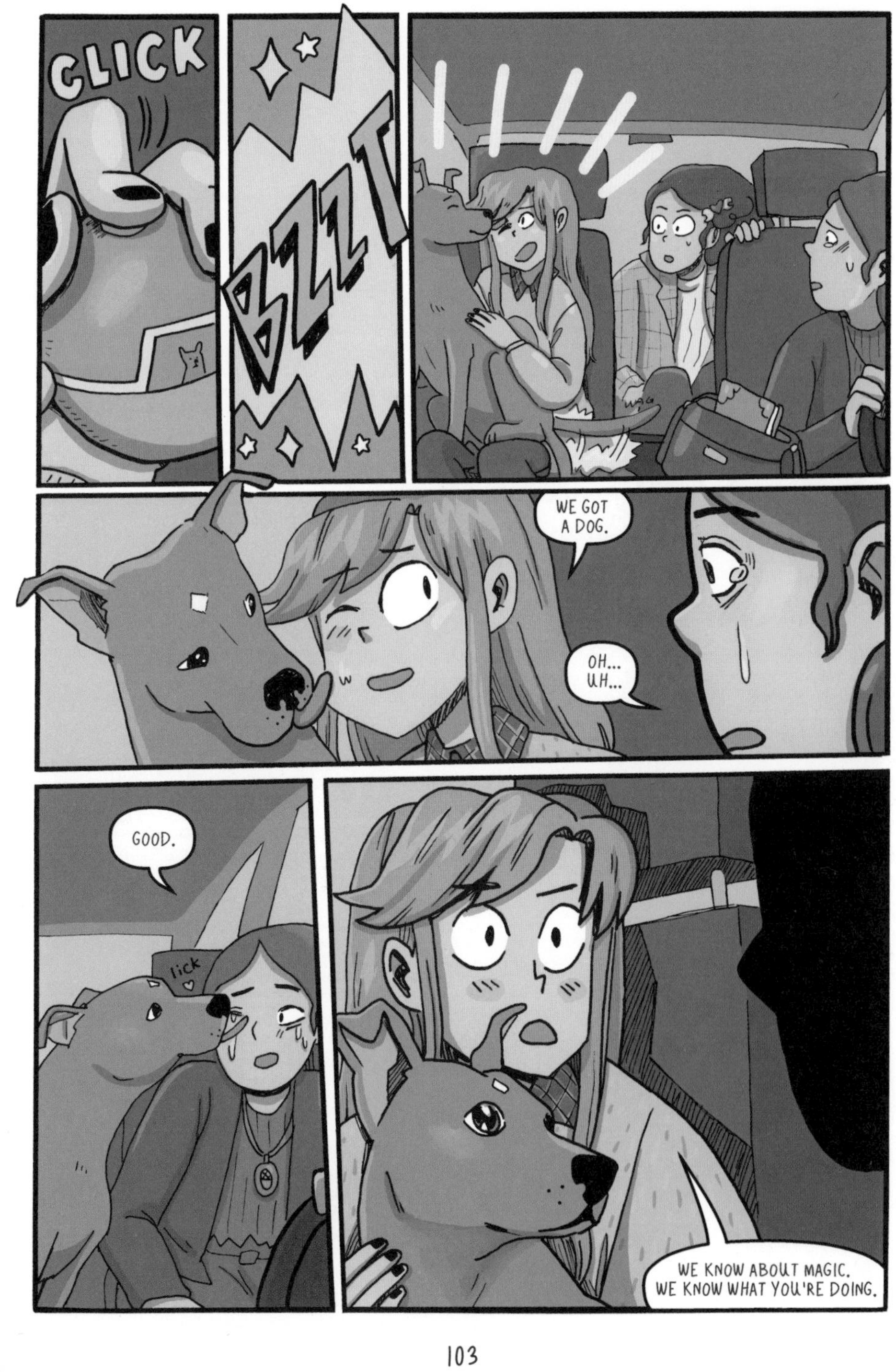
CLICK
BZZT
WAG
WE GOT A DOG.
OH... UH...
GOOD.
lick
WE KNOW ABOUT MAGIC. WE KNOW WHAT YOU'RE DOING.

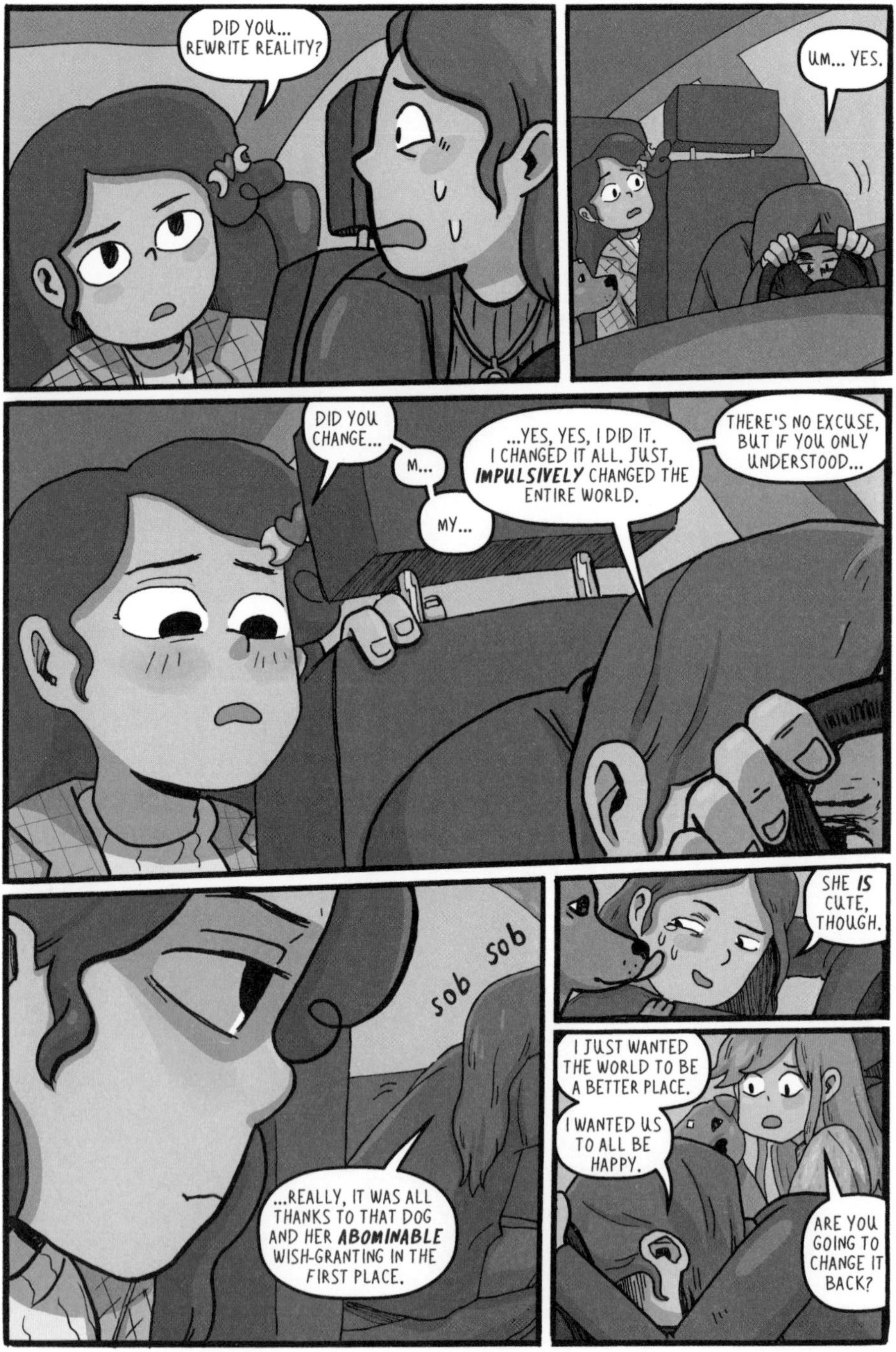
DID YOU... REWRITE REALITY?
UM... YES.
DID YOU CHANGE...
M...
MY...
...YES, YES, I DID IT. I CHANGED IT ALL. JUST, **IMPULSIVELY** CHANGED THE ENTIRE WORLD.
THERE'S NO EXCUSE, BUT IF YOU ONLY UNDERSTOOD...
sob sob
...REALLY, IT WAS ALL THANKS TO THAT DOG AND HER **ABOMINABLE** WISH-GRANTING IN THE FIRST PLACE.
SHE **IS** CUTE, THOUGH.
I JUST WANTED THE WORLD TO BE A BETTER PLACE.
I WANTED US TO ALL BE HAPPY.
ARE YOU GOING TO CHANGE IT BACK?

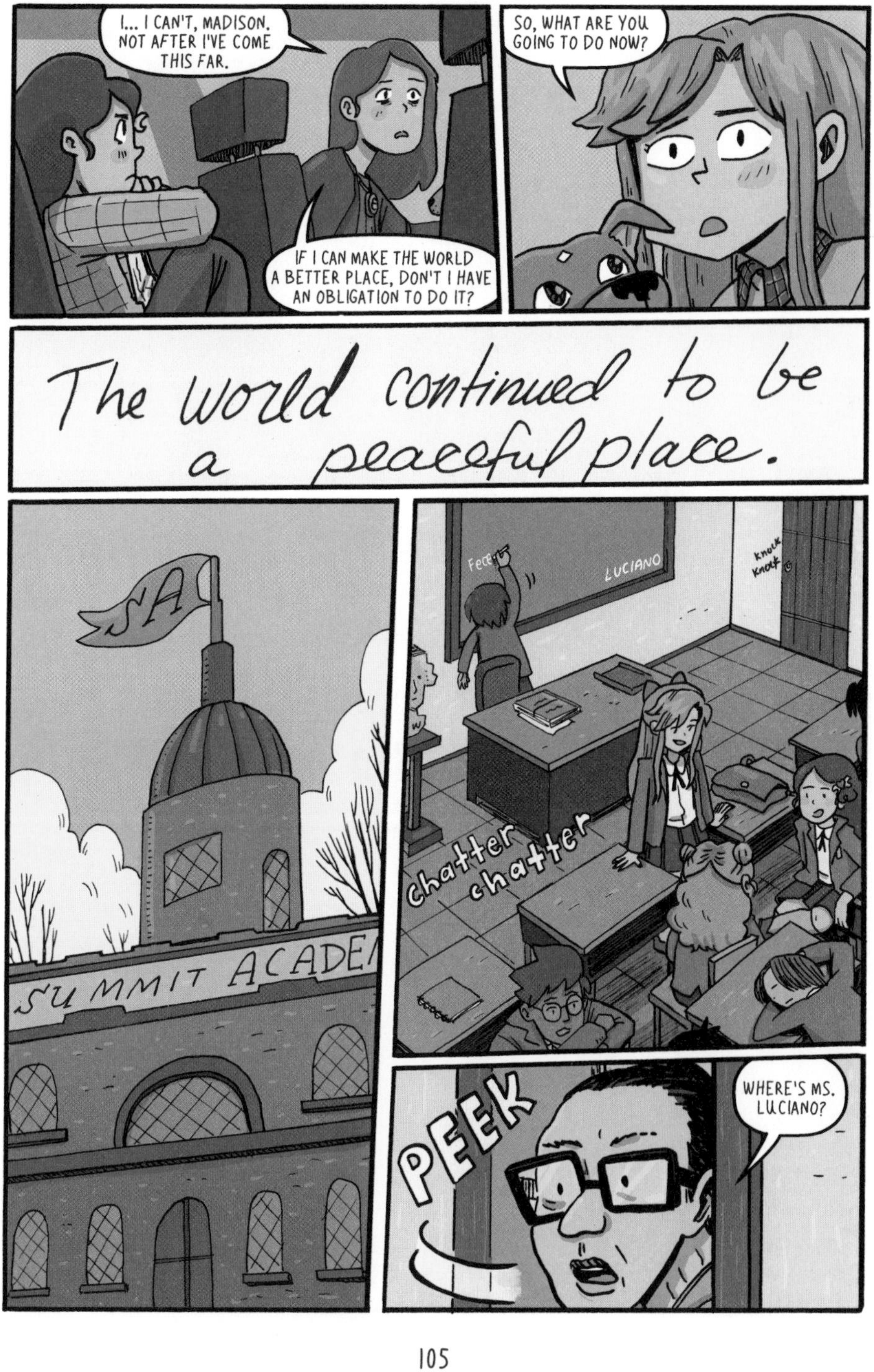
I... I CAN'T, MADISON. NOT AFTER I'VE COME THIS FAR.
IF I CAN MAKE THE WORLD A BETTER PLACE, DON'T I HAVE AN OBLIGATION TO DO IT?
SO, WHAT ARE YOU GOING TO DO NOW?
The world continued to be a peaceful place.
SA
SUMMIT ACADE
LUCIANO
knock knock
chatter chatter
PEEK
WHERE'S MS. LUCIANO?

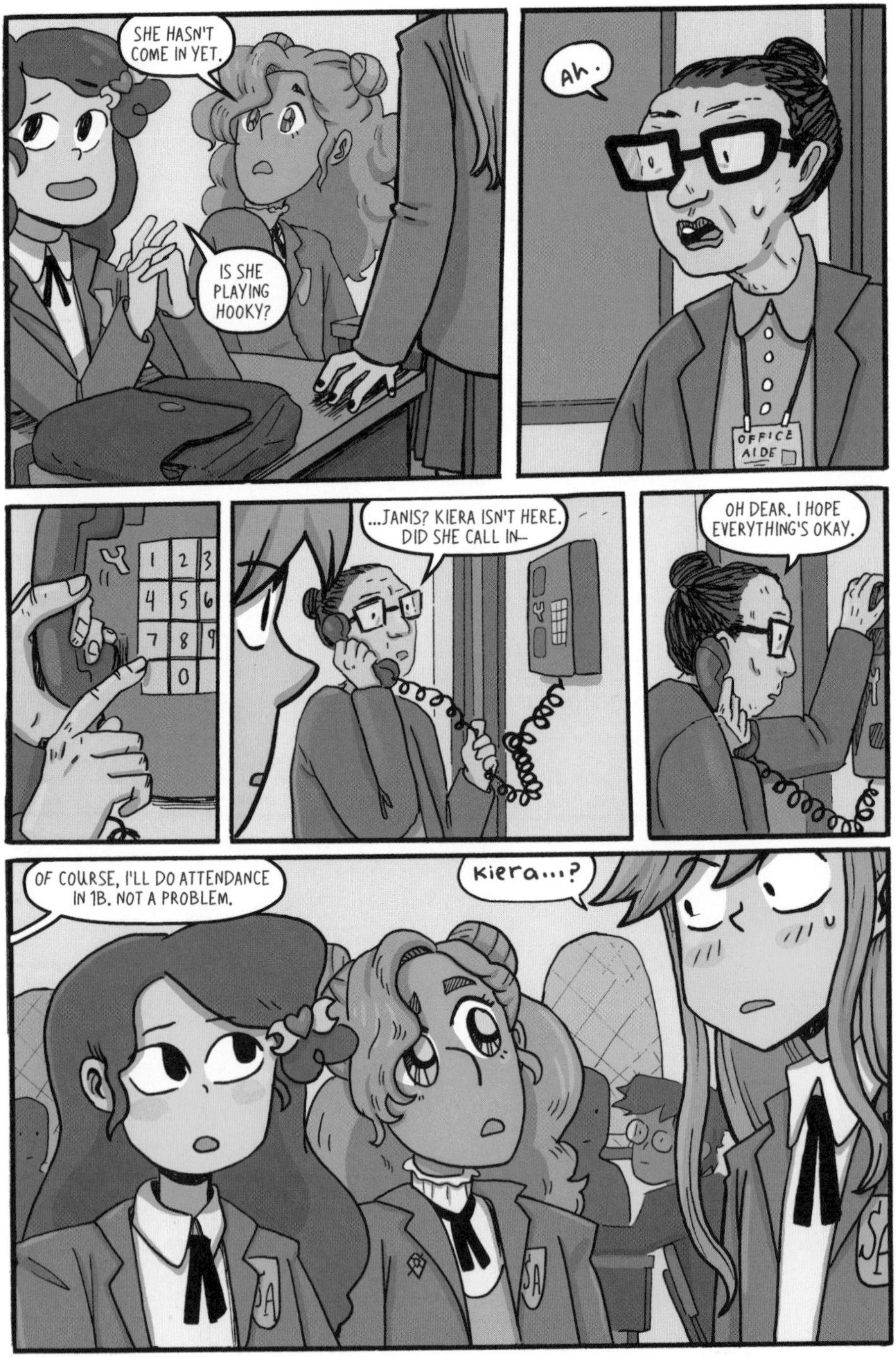
SHE HASN'T COME IN YET.
IS SHE PLAYING HOOKY?
Ah.
OFFICE AIDE
...JANIS? KIERA ISN'T HERE. DID SHE CALL IN—
OH DEAR. I HOPE EVERYTHING'S OKAY.
OF COURSE, I'LL DO ATTENDANCE IN 1B. NOT A PROBLEM.
Kiera...?

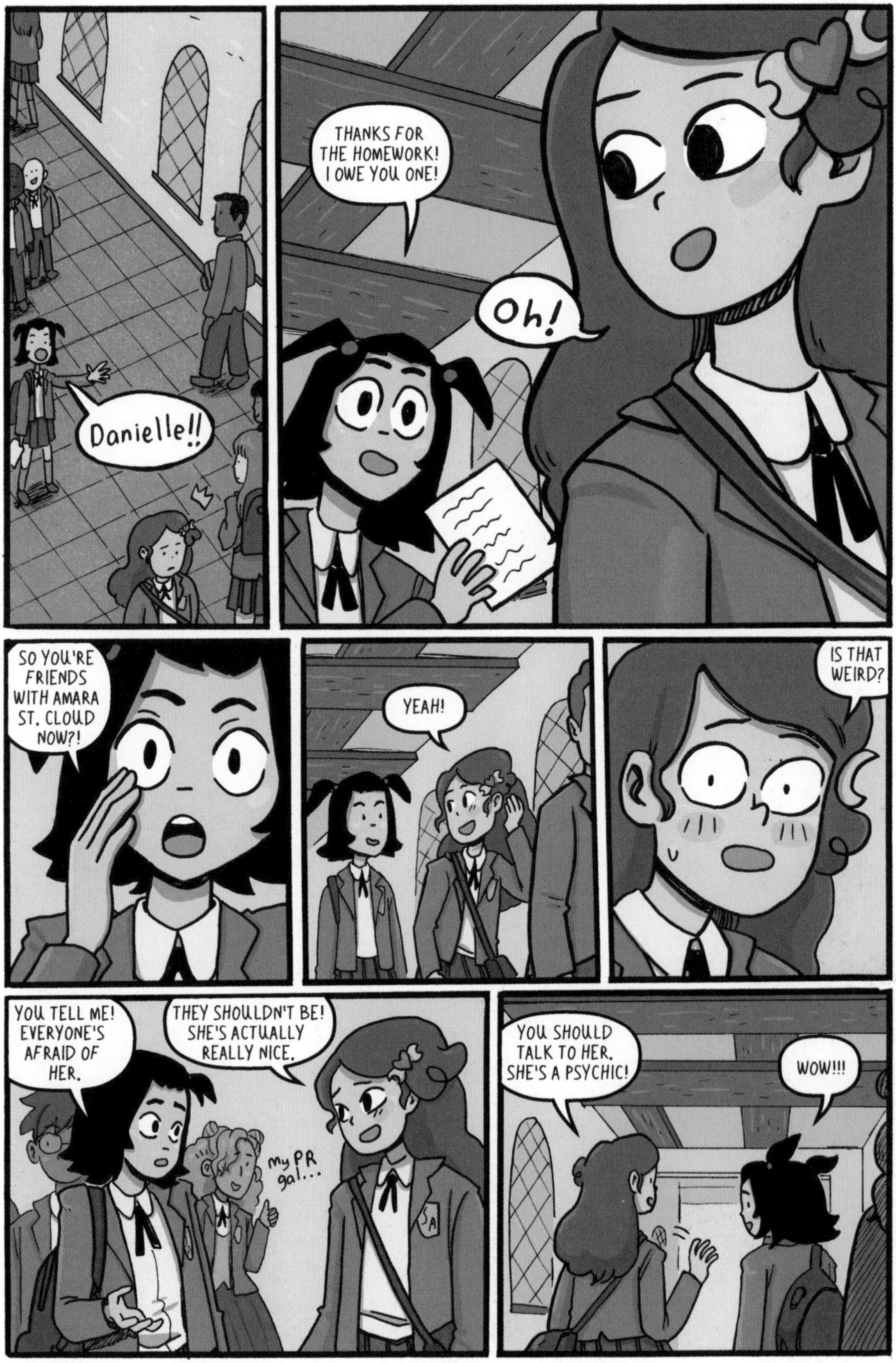
Danielle!!
THANKS FOR THE HOMEWORK! I OWE YOU ONE!
Oh!
SO YOU'RE FRIENDS WITH AMARA ST. CLOUD NOW?!
YEAH!
IS THAT WEIRD?
YOU TELL ME! EVERYONE'S AFRAID OF HER.
THEY SHOULDN'T BE! SHE'S ACTUALLY REALLY NICE.
my PR gal...
YOU SHOULD TALK TO HER. SHE'S A PSYCHIC!
WOW!!!

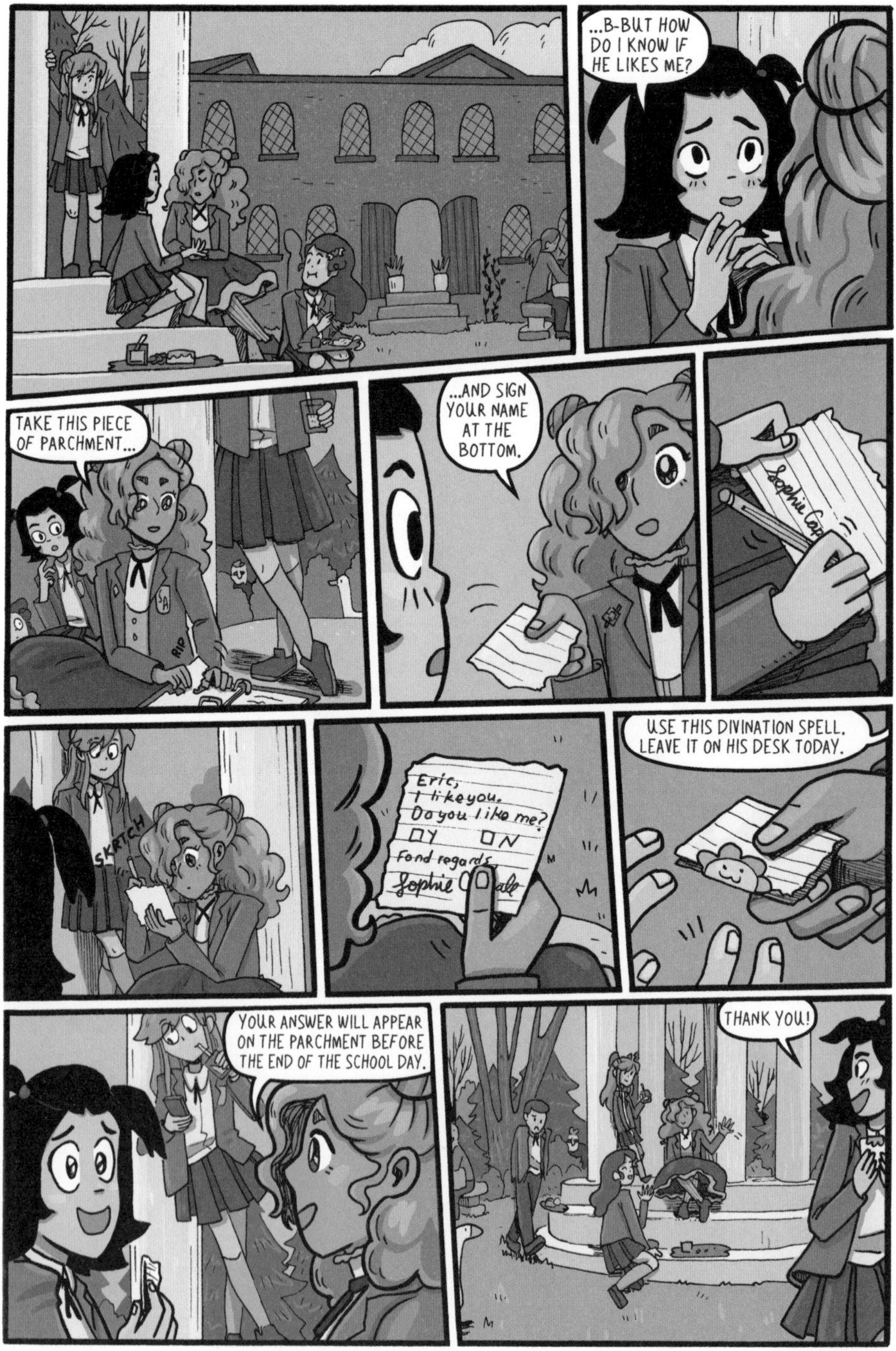
...B-BUT HOW DO I KNOW IF HE LIKES ME?
TAKE THIS PIECE OF PARCHMENT...
...AND SIGN YOUR NAME AT THE BOTTOM.
SKRTCH
Eric,
I like you.
Do you like me?
☐Y ☐N
Fond regards,
USE THIS DIVINATION SPELL. LEAVE IT ON HIS DESK TODAY.
YOUR ANSWER WILL APPEAR ON THE PARCHMENT BEFORE THE END OF THE SCHOOL DAY.
THANK YOU!

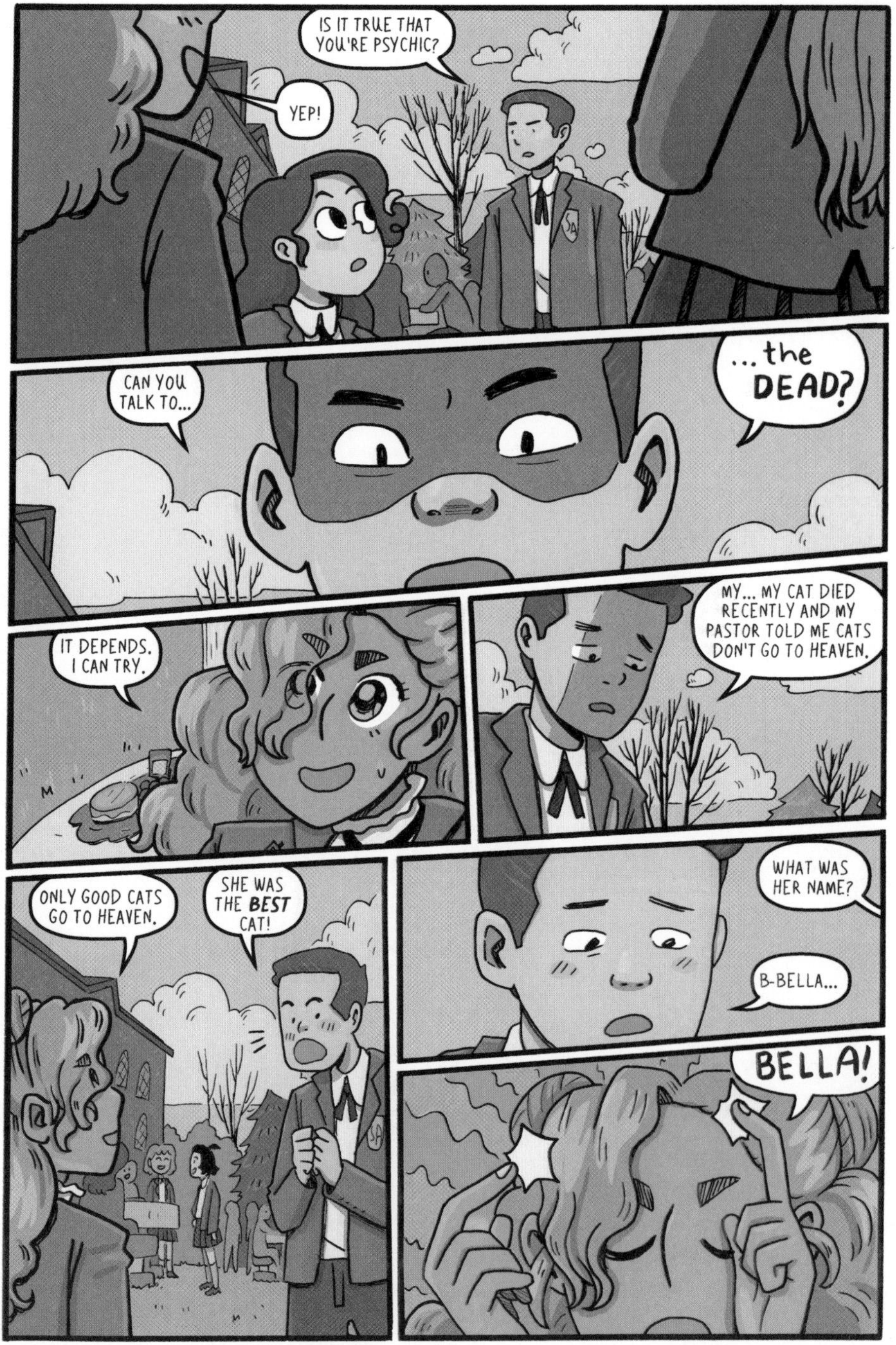
IS IT TRUE THAT YOU'RE PSYCHIC?
YEP!
CAN YOU TALK TO...
...the DEAD?
IT DEPENDS. I CAN TRY.
MY... MY CAT DIED RECENTLY AND MY PASTOR TOLD ME CATS DON'T GO TO HEAVEN.
ONLY GOOD CATS GO TO HEAVEN.
SHE WAS THE **BEST** CAT!
WHAT WAS HER NAME?
B-BELLA...
BELLA!

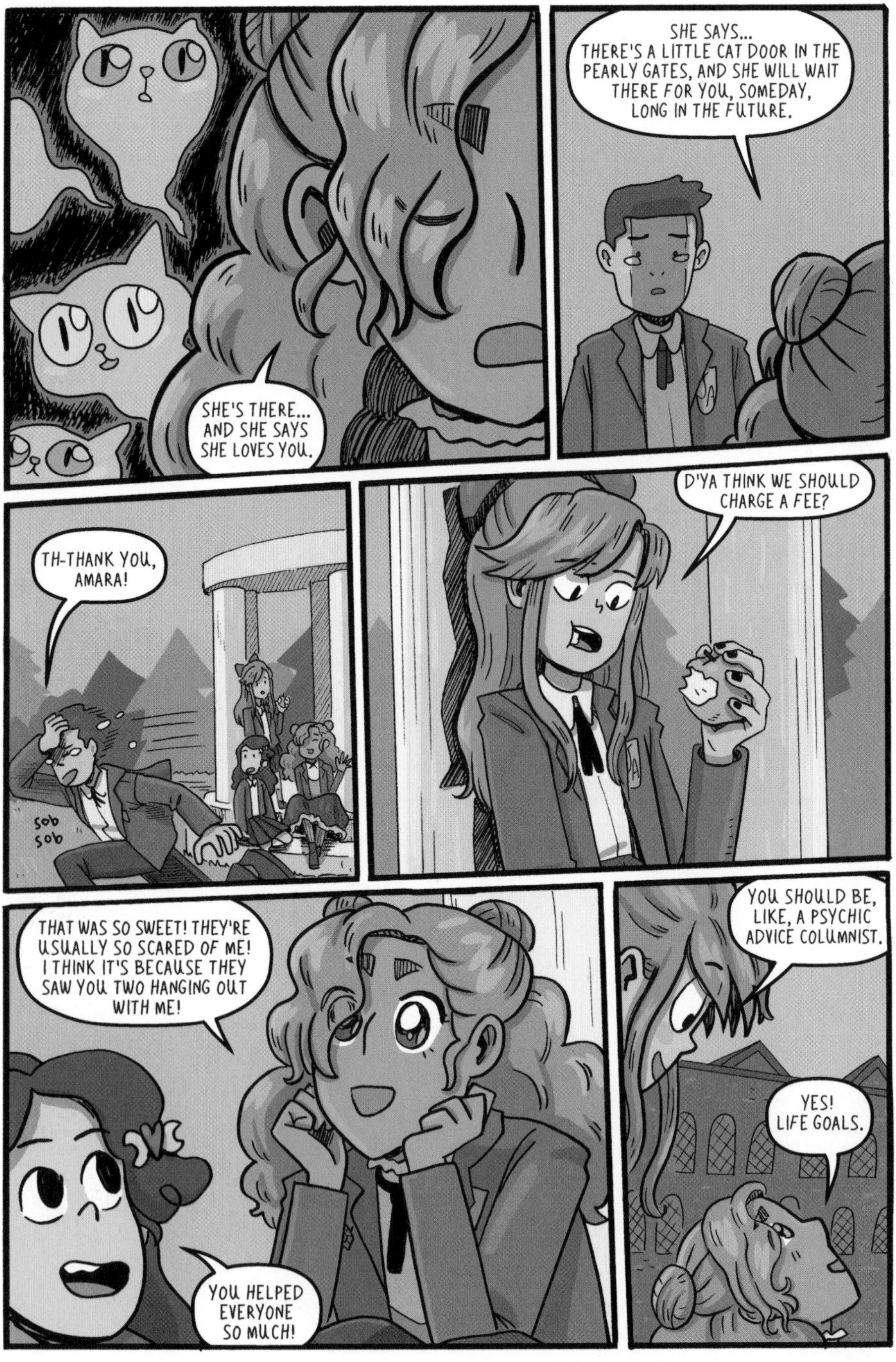
SHE'S THERE... AND SHE SAYS SHE LOVES YOU.
SHE SAYS... THERE'S A LITTLE CAT DOOR IN THE PEARLY GATES, AND SHE WILL WAIT THERE FOR YOU, SOMEDAY, LONG IN THE FUTURE.
TH-THANK YOU, AMARA!
sob sob
D'YA THINK WE SHOULD CHARGE A FEE?
THAT WAS SO SWEET! THEY'RE USUALLY SO SCARED OF ME! I THINK IT'S BECAUSE THEY SAW YOU TWO HANGING OUT WITH ME!
YOU HELPED EVERYONE SO MUCH!
YOU SHOULD BE, LIKE, A PSYCHIC ADVICE COLUMNIST.
YES! LIFE GOALS.

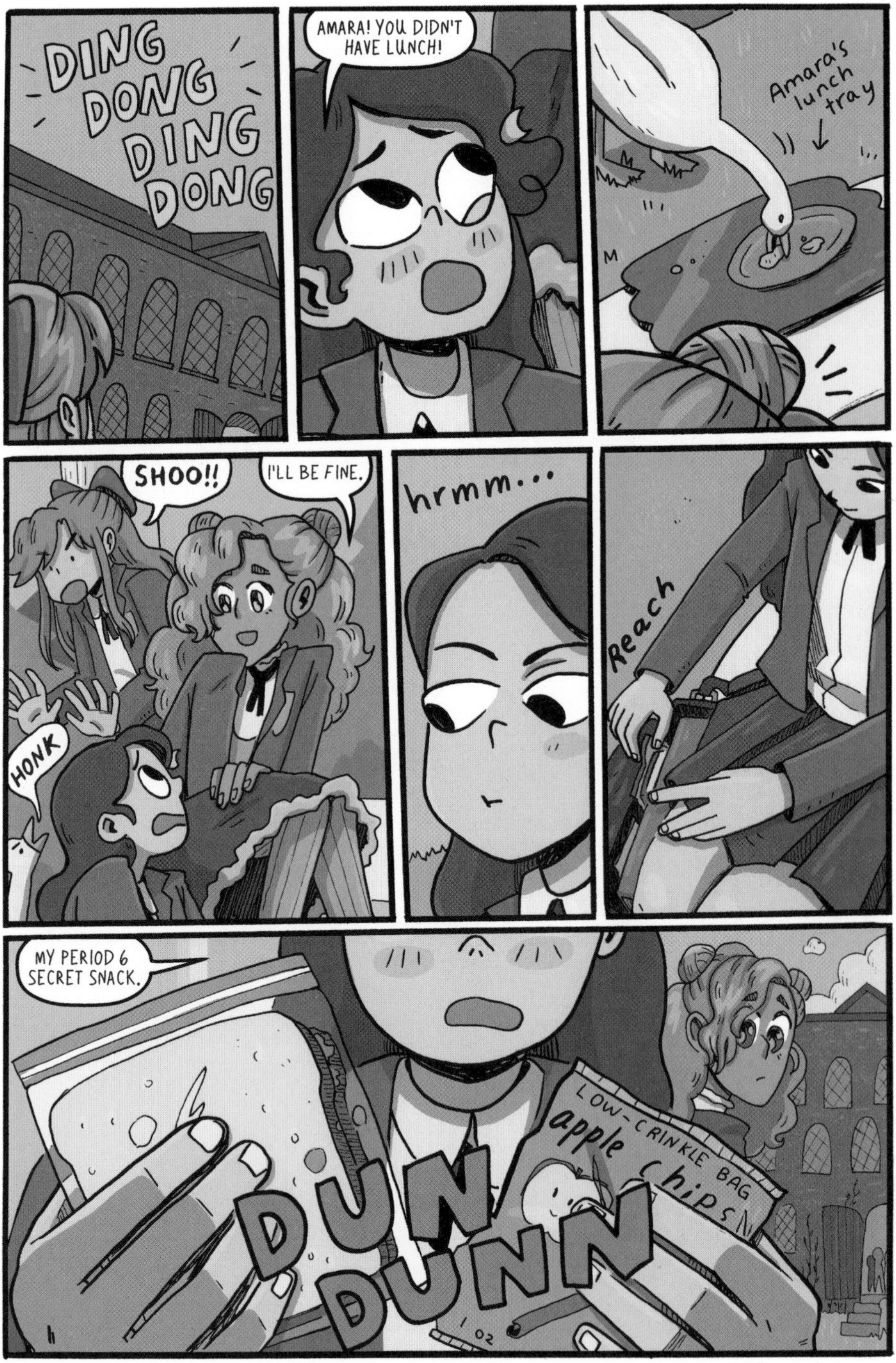
DING DONG DING DONG
AMARA! YOU DIDN'T HAVE LUNCH!
Amara's lunch tray
SHOO!!
I'LL BE FINE.
HONK
hrmm...
Reach
MY PERIOD 6 SECRET SNACK.
LOW-CRINKLE BAG apple chips
DUN DUNN

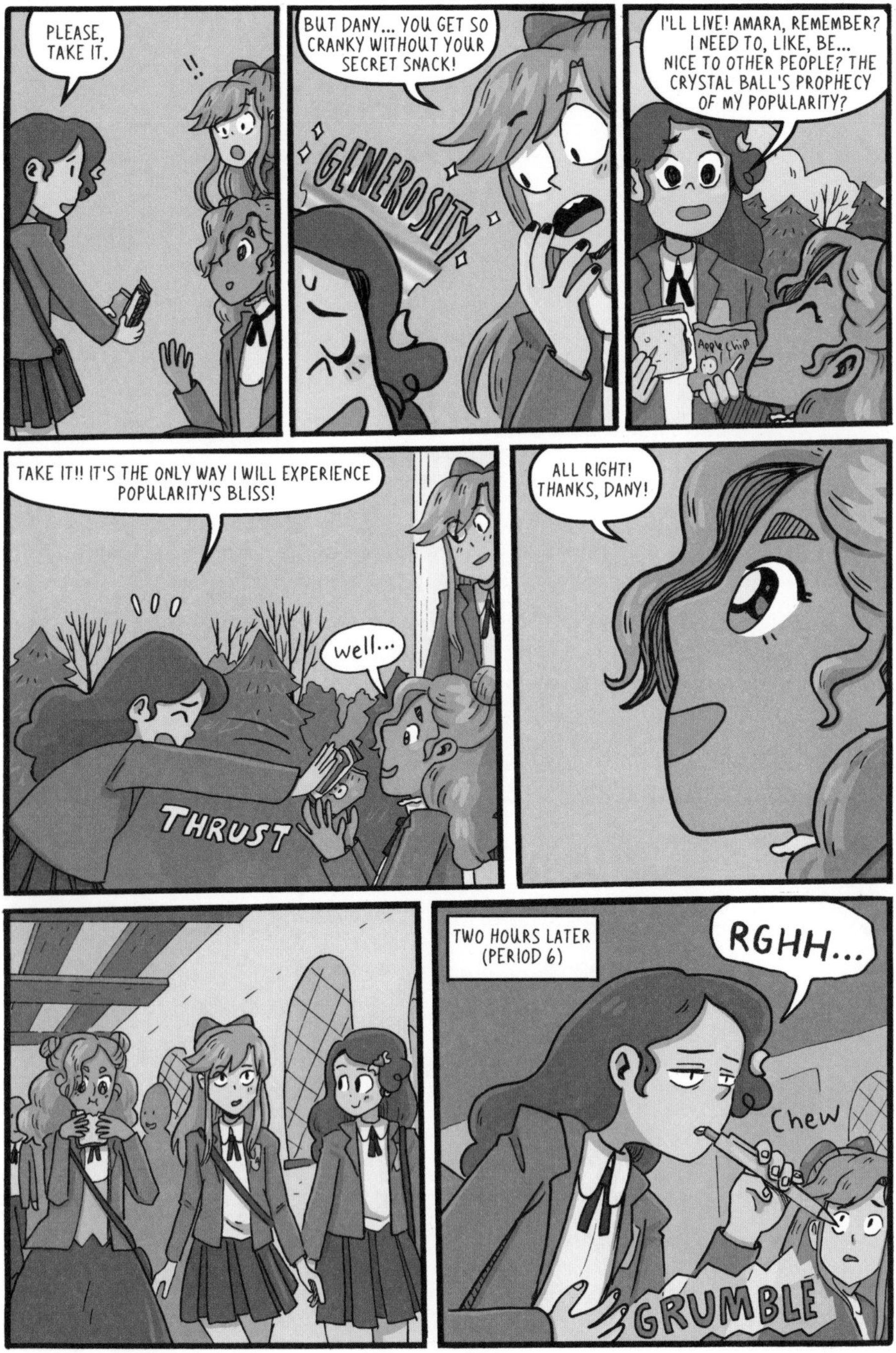
PLEASE, TAKE IT.
!!
BUT DANY... YOU GET SO CRANKY WITHOUT YOUR SECRET SNACK!
GENEROSITY
I'LL LIVE! AMARA, REMEMBER? I NEED TO, LIKE, BE... NICE TO OTHER PEOPLE? THE CRYSTAL BALL'S PROPHECY OF MY POPULARITY?
Apple Chips
TAKE IT!! IT'S THE ONLY WAY I WILL EXPERIENCE POPULARITY'S BLISS!
well...
THRUST
ALL RIGHT! THANKS, DANY!
TWO HOURS LATER (PERIOD 6)
RGHH...
Chew
GRUMBLE

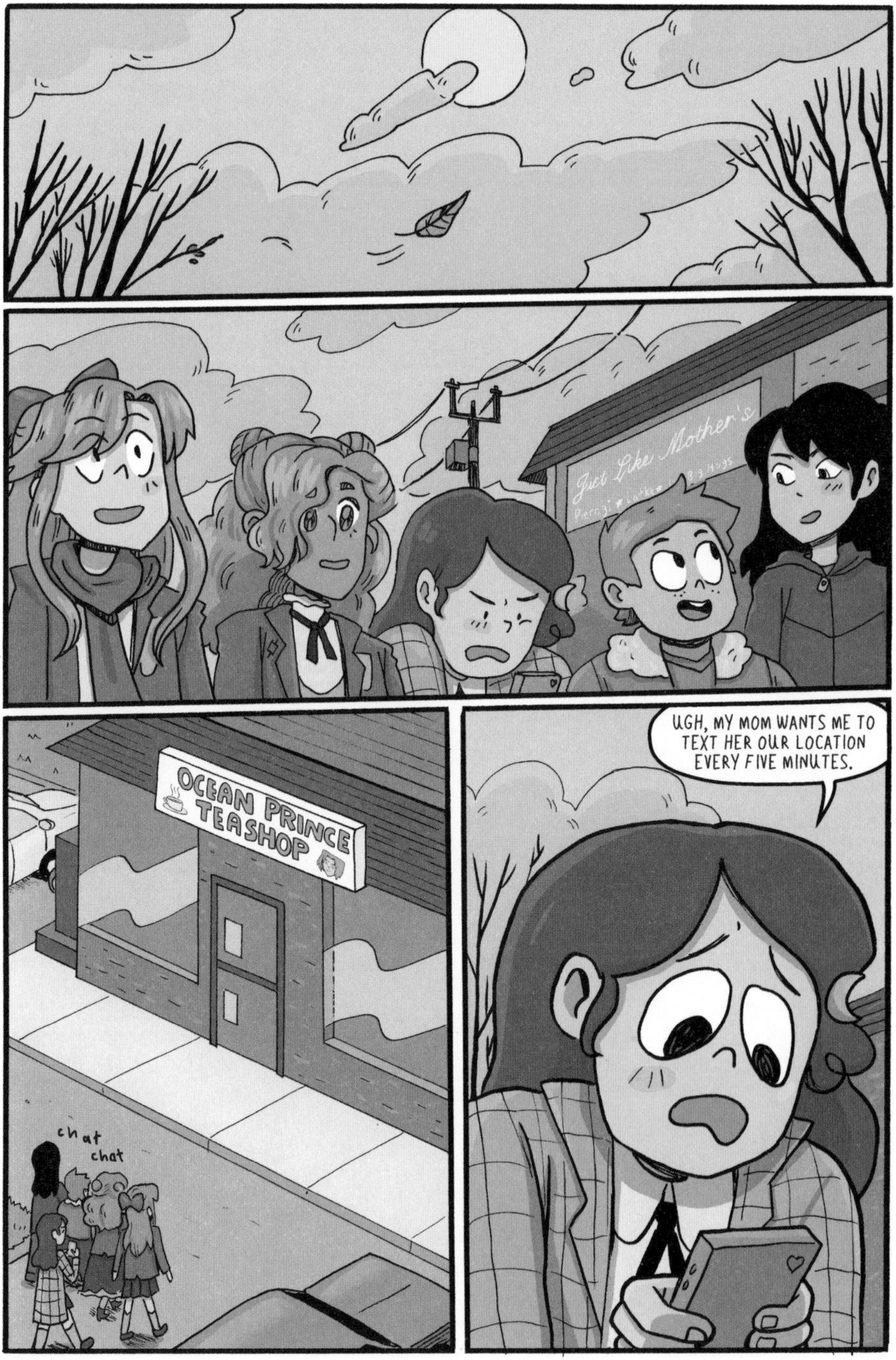
Just Like Mother's
OCEAN PRINCE TEASHOP
chat chat
UGH, MY MOM WANTS ME TO TEXT HER OUR LOCATION EVERY FIVE MINUTES.

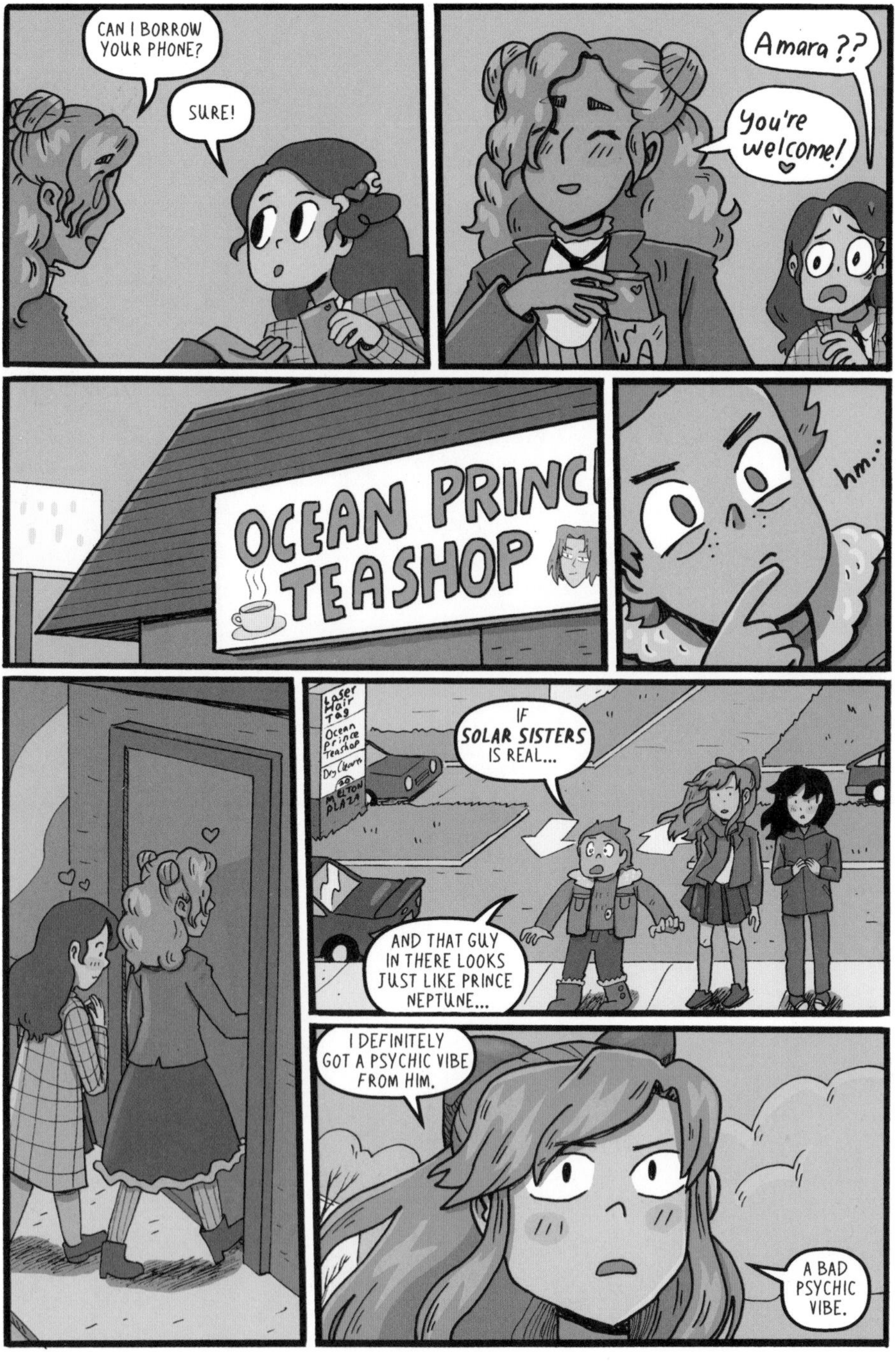
CAN I BORROW YOUR PHONE?
SURE!
Amara??
You're welcome!
OCEAN PRINC
TEASHOP
hm...
Laser Hair Tag
Ocean Prince Teashop
Dry Cleaners
MELTON PLAZA
IF SOLAR SISTERS IS REAL...
AND THAT GUY IN THERE LOOKS JUST LIKE PRINCE NEPTUNE...
I DEFINITELY GOT A PSYCHIC VIBE FROM HIM.
A BAD PSYCHIC VIBE.

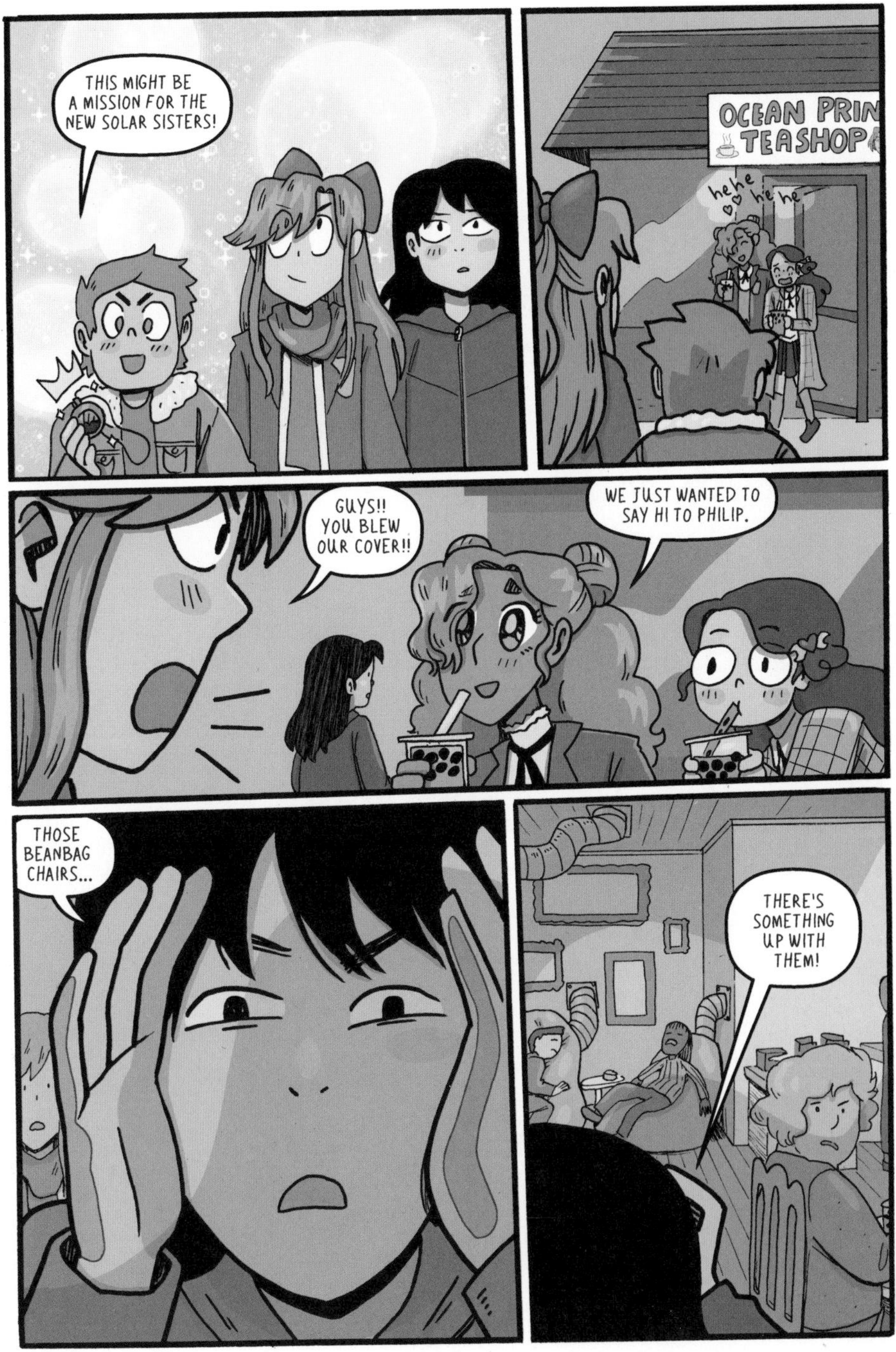
THIS MIGHT BE A MISSION FOR THE NEW SOLAR SISTERS!
OCEAN PRIN
TEASHOP
hehe
hehe
GUYS!! YOU BLEW OUR COVER!!
WE JUST WANTED TO SAY HI TO PHILIP.
THOSE BEANBAG CHAIRS...
THERE'S SOMETHING UP WITH THEM!

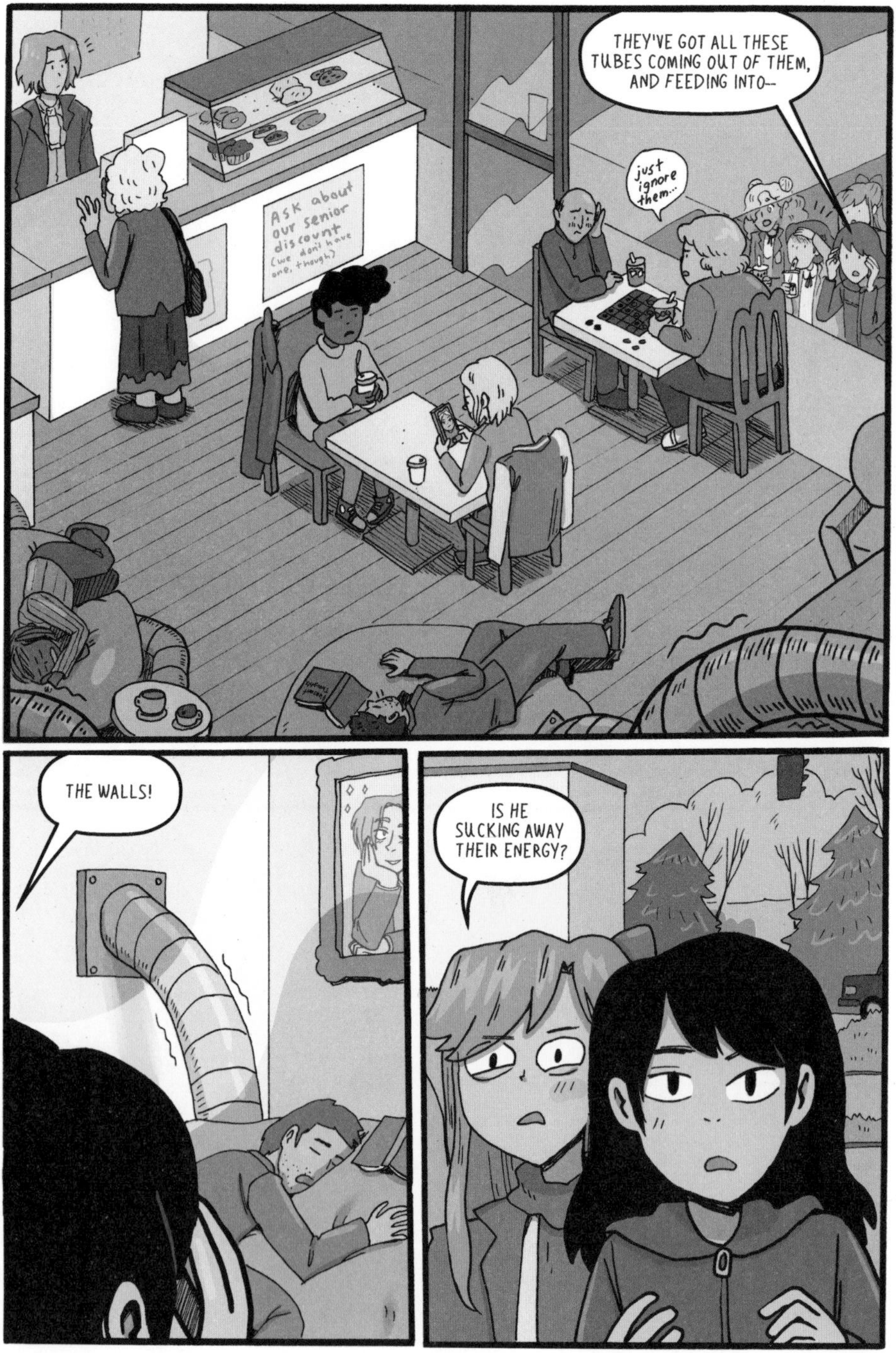
ASK about our senior discount (we don't have one, though)
THEY'VE GOT ALL THESE TUBES COMING OUT OF THEM, AND FEEDING INTO--
just ignore them...
THE WALLS!
IS HE SUCKING AWAY THEIR ENERGY?

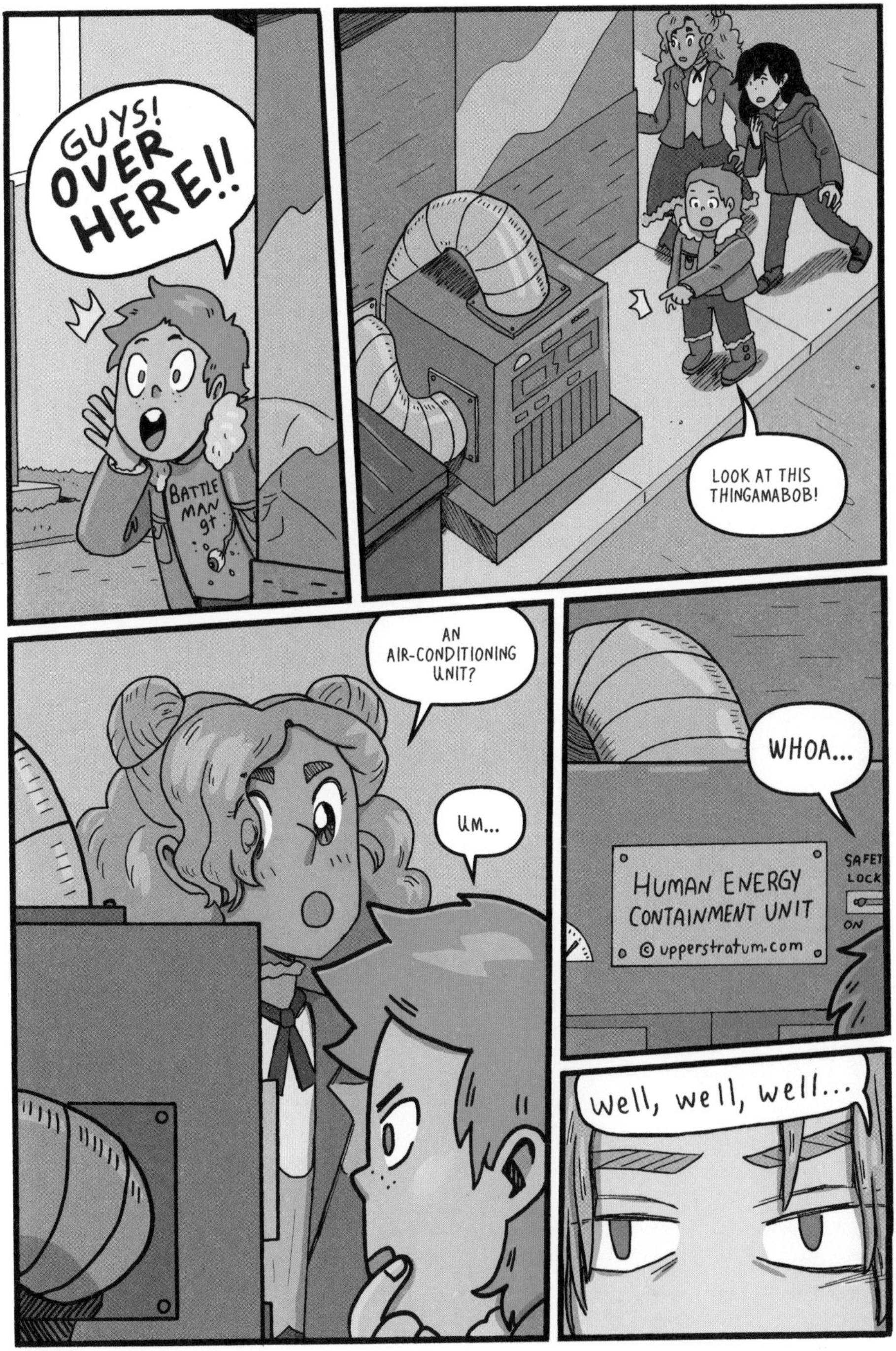
GUYS! OVER HERE!!
BATTLE MAN gt
LOOK AT THIS THINGAMABOB!
AN AIR-CONDITIONING UNIT?
UM...
WHOA...
HUMAN ENERGY CONTAINMENT UNIT
© upperstratum.com
SAFETY LOCK
ON
well, well, well...

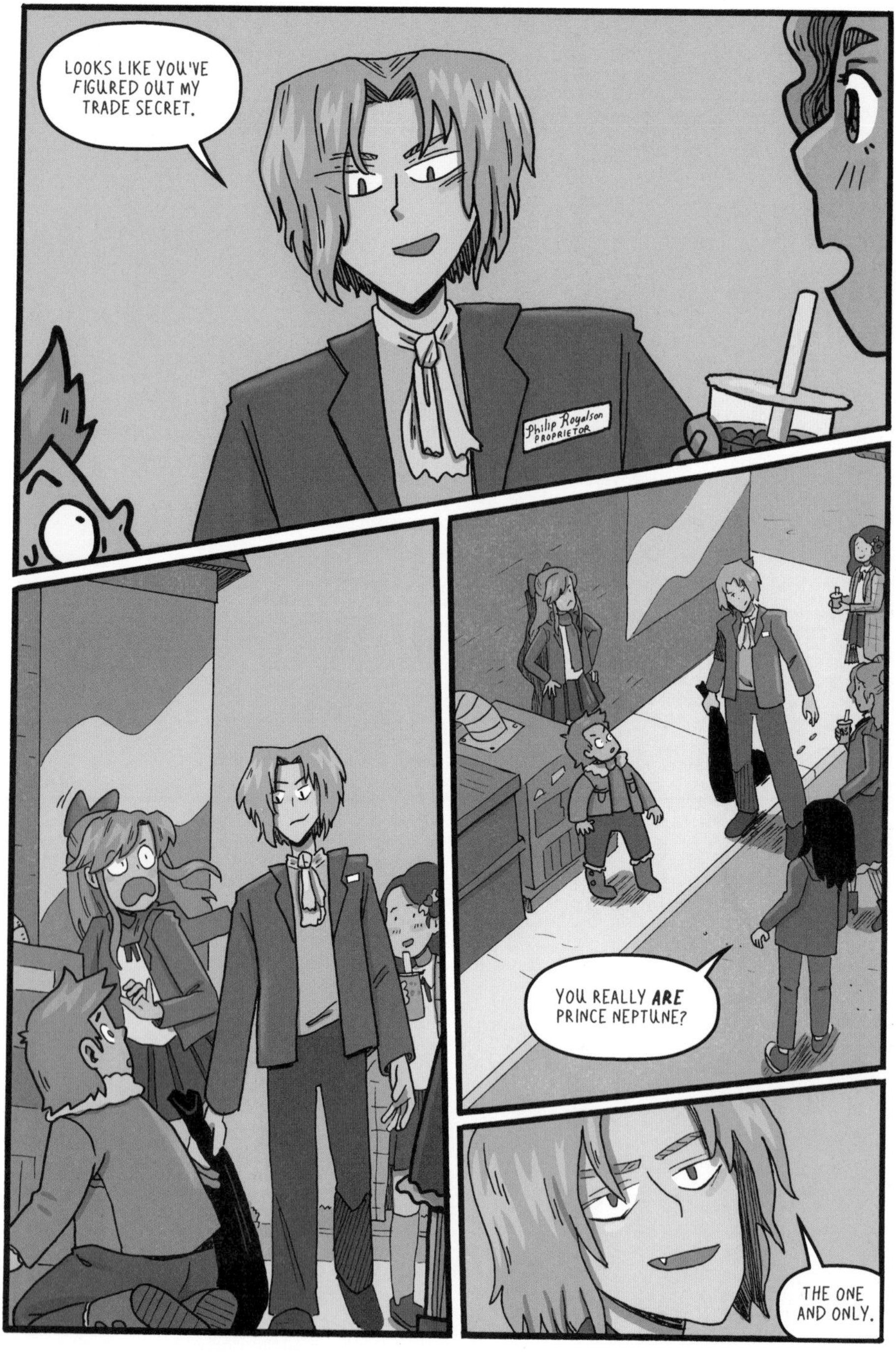
LOOKS LIKE YOU'VE FIGURED OUT MY TRADE SECRET.
Philip Royalson PROPRIETOR
YOU REALLY **ARE** PRINCE NEPTUNE?
THE ONE AND ONLY.

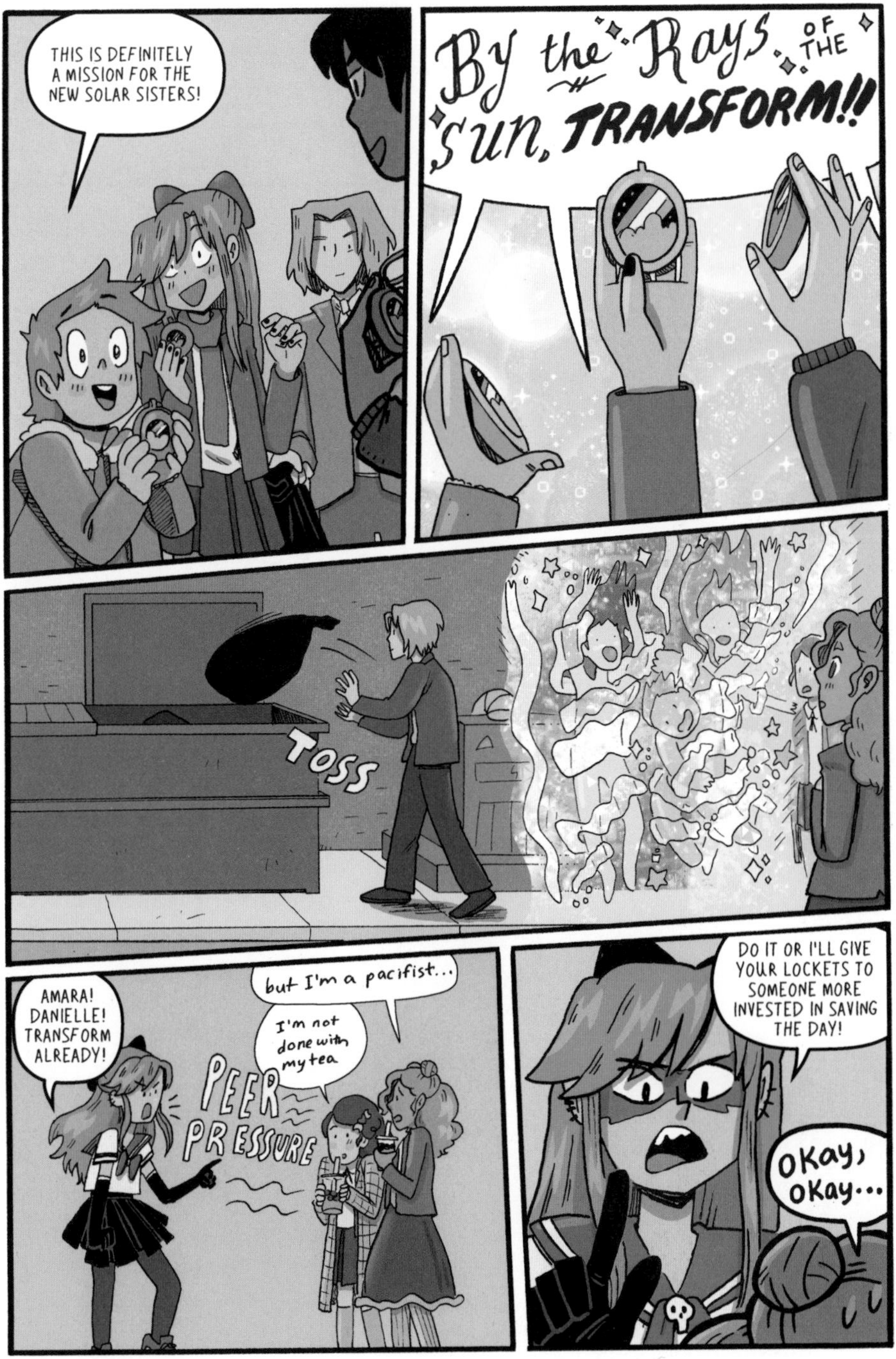
THIS IS DEFINITELY A MISSION FOR THE NEW SOLAR SISTERS!
By the Rays of the Sun, TRANSFORM!!
TOSS
AMARA! DANIELLE! TRANSFORM ALREADY!
but I'm a pacifist...
I'm not done with my tea
PEER PRESSURE
DO IT OR I'LL GIVE YOUR LOCKETS TO SOMEONE MORE INVESTED IN SAVING THE DAY!
OKay, OKay...

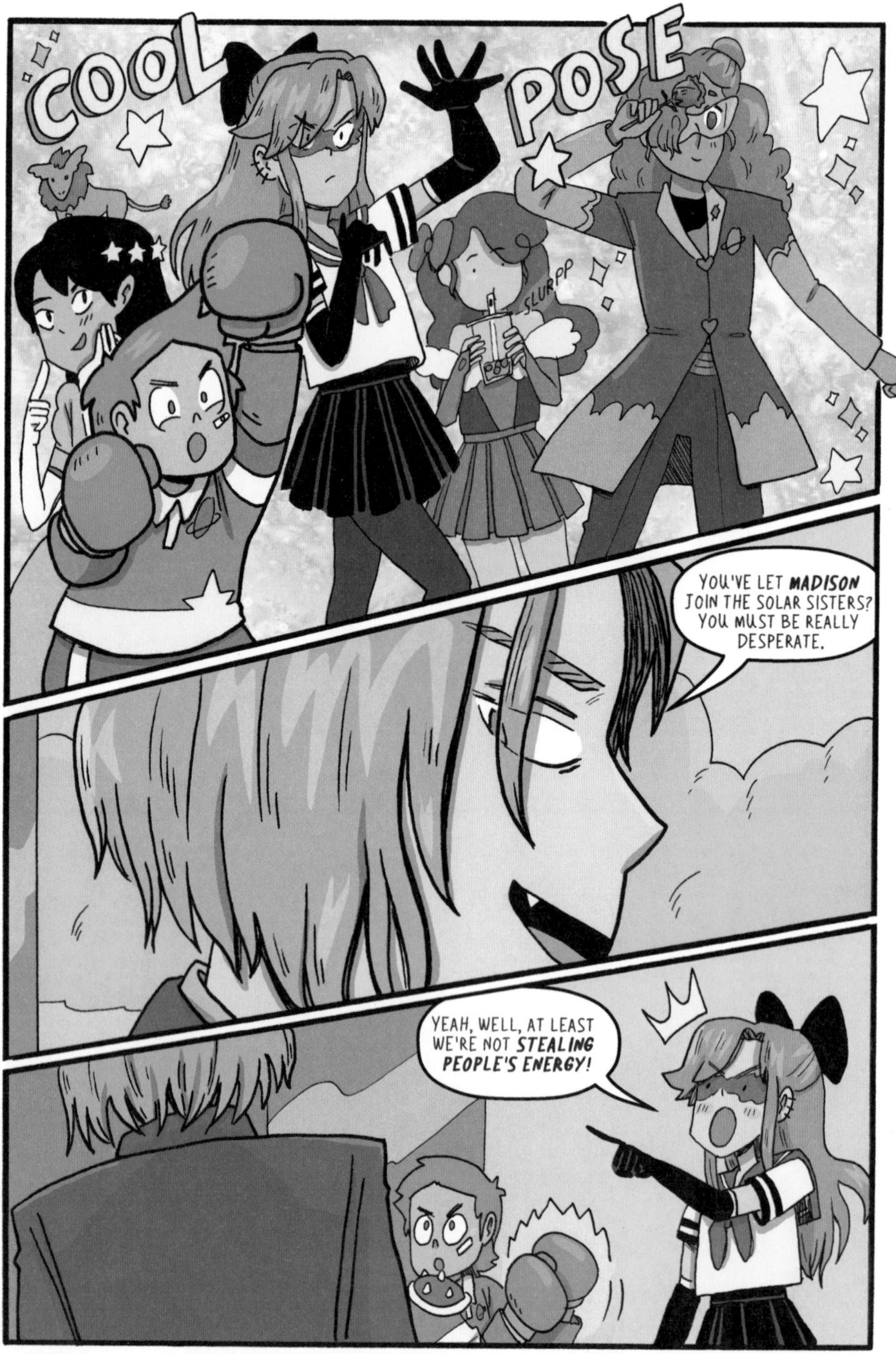
COOL POSE
SLURPP
YOU'VE LET MADISON JOIN THE SOLAR SISTERS? YOU MUST BE REALLY DESPERATE.
YEAH, WELL, AT LEAST WE'RE NOT STEALING PEOPLE'S ENERGY!

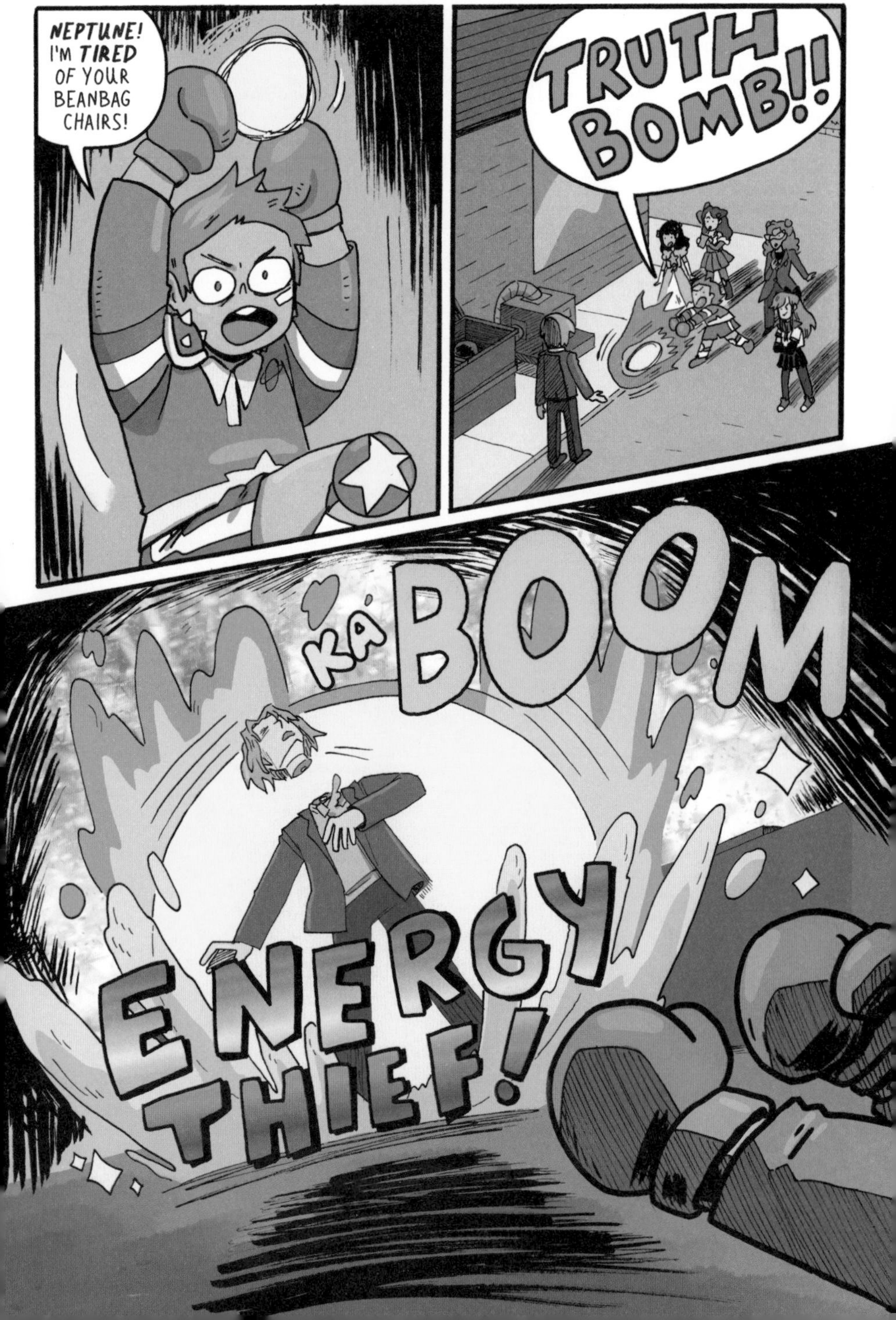
NEPTUNE! I'M TIRED OF YOUR BEANBAG CHAIRS!
TRUTH BOMB!!
KA BOOM
ENERGY THIEF!

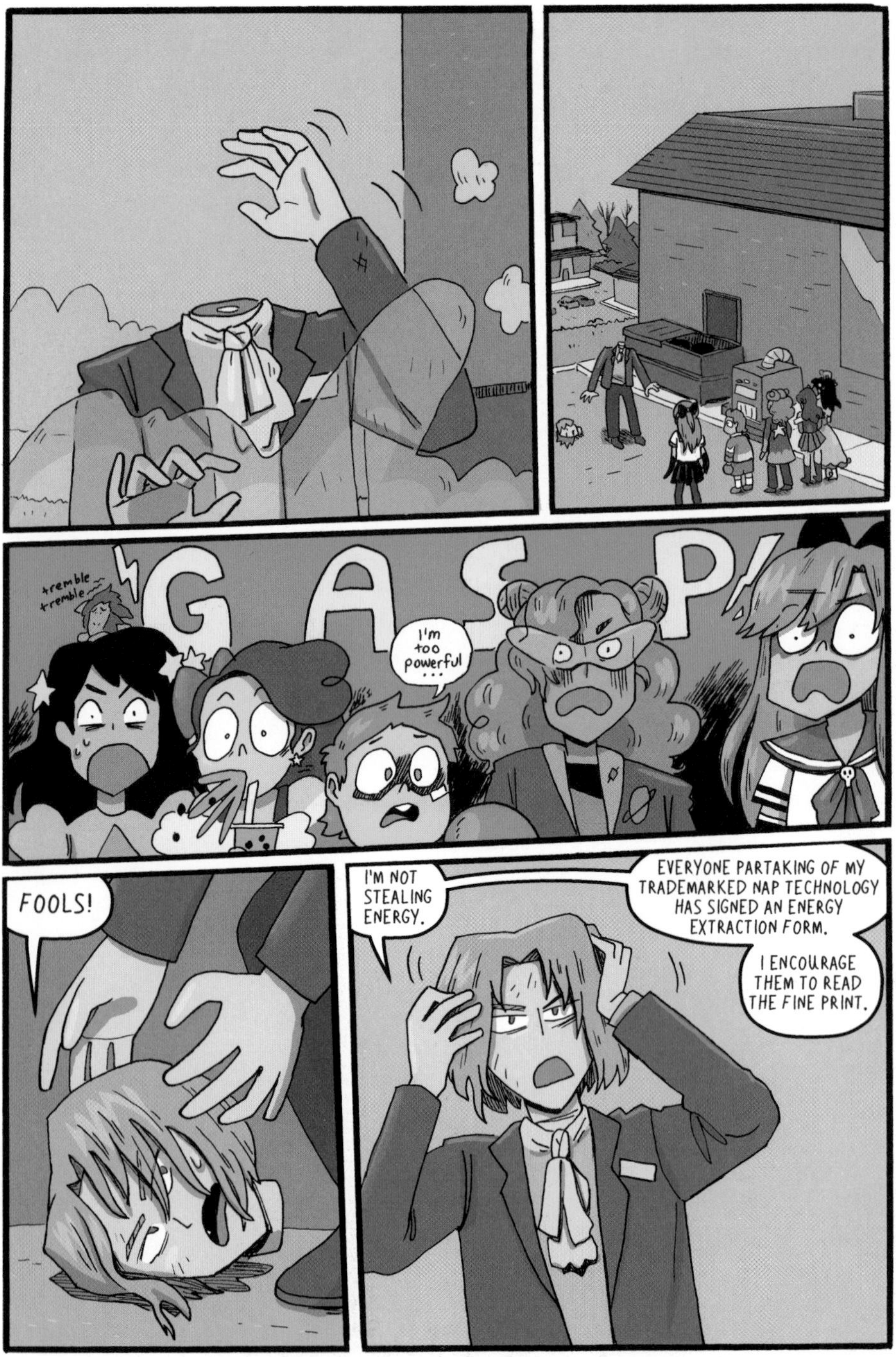
tremble tremble
GASP!
I'm too powerful...
FOOLS!
I'M NOT STEALING ENERGY.
EVERYONE PARTAKING OF MY TRADEMARKED NAP TECHNOLOGY HAS SIGNED AN ENERGY EXTRACTION FORM.
I ENCOURAGE THEM TO READ THE FINE PRINT.

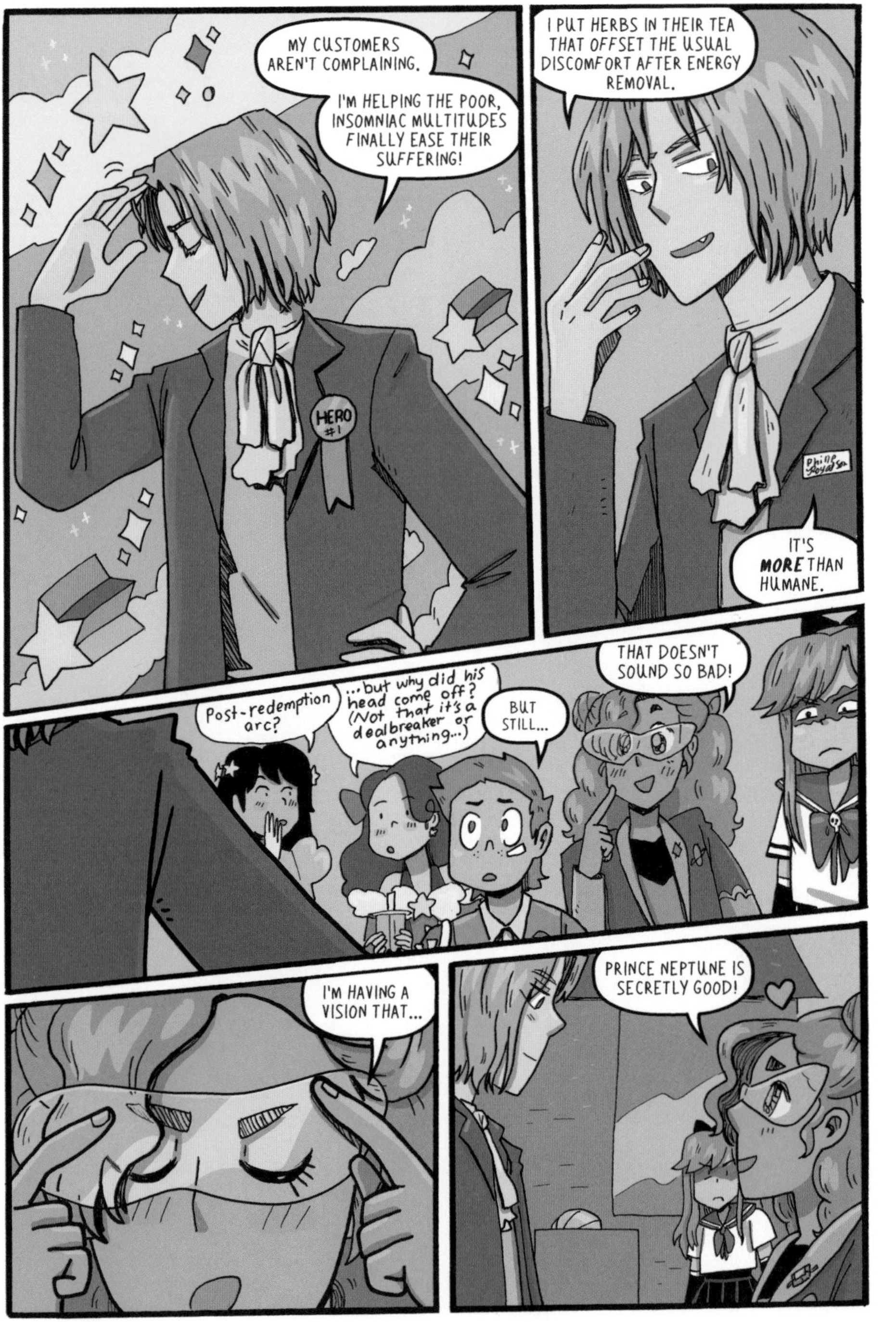
MY CUSTOMERS AREN'T COMPLAINING.
I'M HELPING THE POOR, INSOMNIAC MULTITUDES FINALLY EASE THEIR SUFFERING!
HERO #1
I PUT HERBS IN THEIR TEA THAT OFFSET THE USUAL DISCOMFORT AFTER ENERGY REMOVAL.
IT'S **MORE** THAN HUMANE.
Post-redemption arc?
...but why did his head come off? (Not that it's a dealbreaker or anything...)
BUT STILL...
THAT DOESN'T SOUND SO BAD!
I'M HAVING A VISION THAT...
PRINCE NEPTUNE IS SECRETLY GOOD!

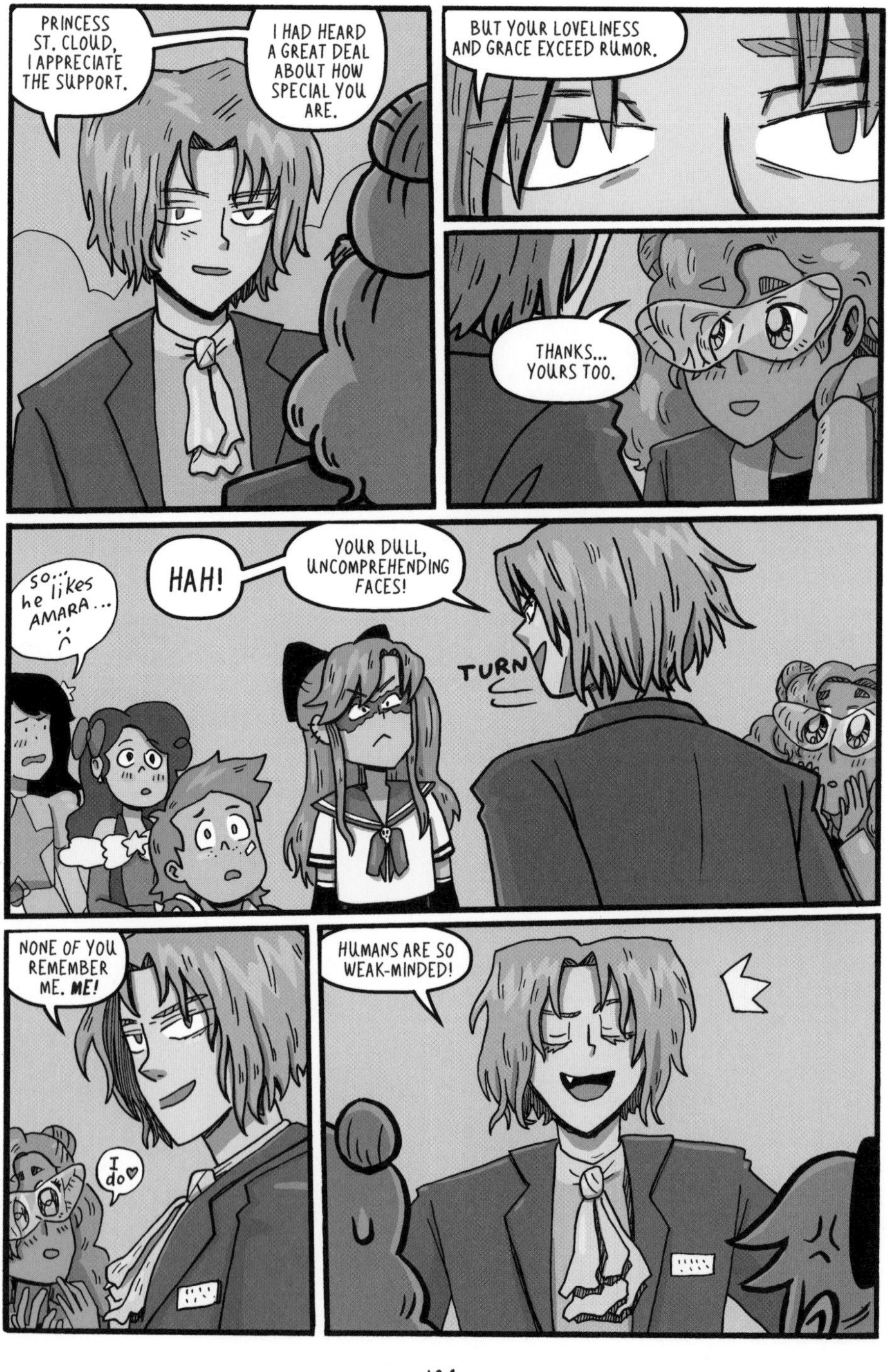
PRINCESS ST. CLOUD, I APPRECIATE THE SUPPORT.
I HAD HEARD A GREAT DEAL ABOUT HOW SPECIAL YOU ARE.
BUT YOUR LOVELINESS AND GRACE EXCEED RUMOR.
THANKS... YOURS TOO.
HAH!
YOUR DULL, UNCOMPREHENDING FACES!
so... he likes AMARA...
TURN
NONE OF YOU REMEMBER ME. **ME!**
I do♥
HUMANS ARE SO WEAK-MINDED!

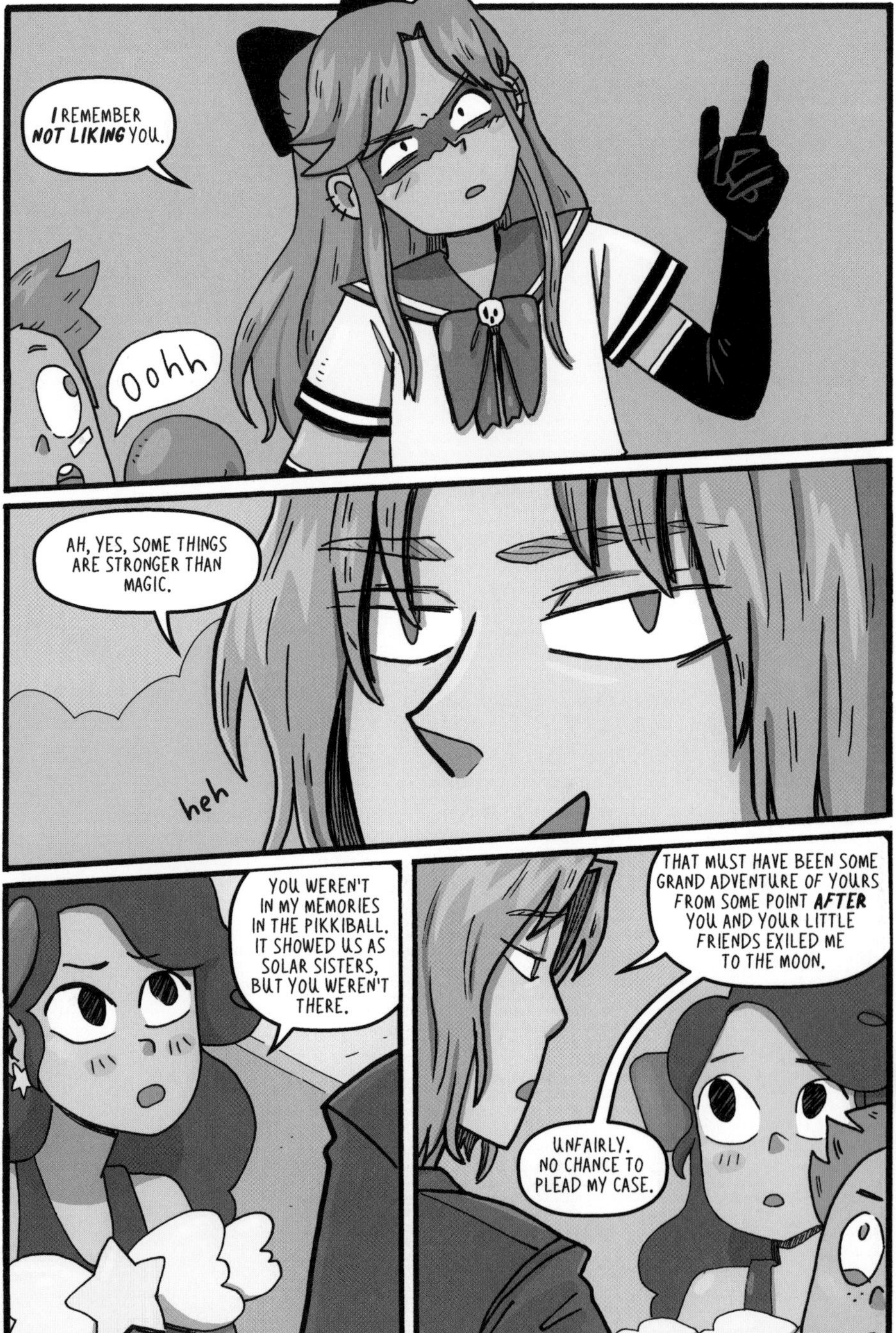
I REMEMBER **NOT LIKING** YOU.
oohh
AH, YES, SOME THINGS ARE STRONGER THAN MAGIC.
heh
YOU WEREN'T IN MY MEMORIES IN THE PIKKIBALL. IT SHOWED US AS SOLAR SISTERS, BUT YOU WEREN'T THERE.
THAT MUST HAVE BEEN SOME GRAND ADVENTURE OF YOURS FROM SOME POINT **AFTER** YOU AND YOUR LITTLE FRIENDS EXILED ME TO THE MOON.
UNFAIRLY. NO CHANCE TO PLEAD MY CASE.

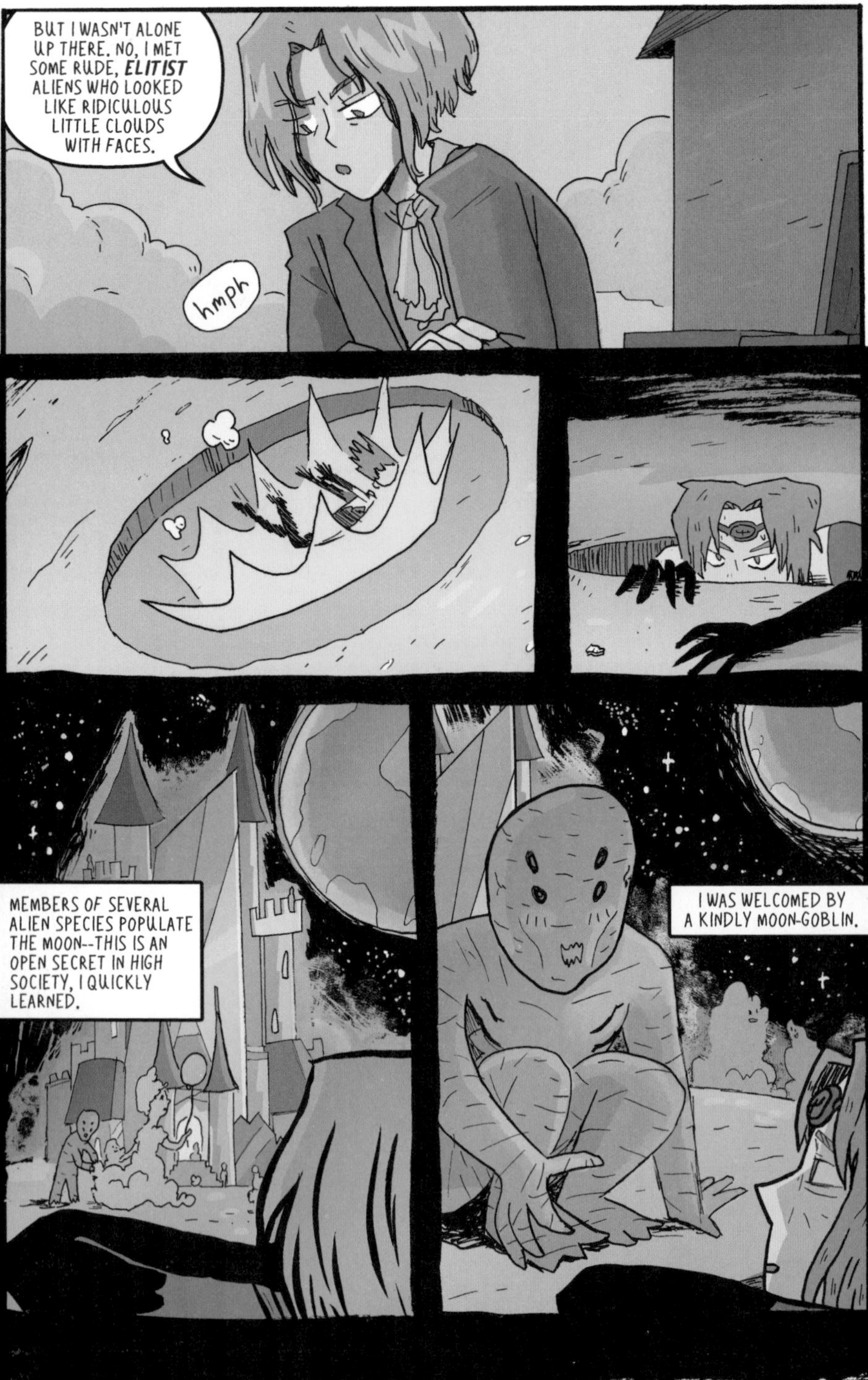
BUT I WASN'T ALONE UP THERE. NO, I MET SOME RUDE, ***ELITIST*** ALIENS WHO LOOKED LIKE RIDICULOUS LITTLE CLOUDS WITH FACES.
hmph
MEMBERS OF SEVERAL ALIEN SPECIES POPULATE THE MOON--THIS IS AN OPEN SECRET IN HIGH SOCIETY, I QUICKLY LEARNED.
I WAS WELCOMED BY A KINDLY MOON-GOBLIN.

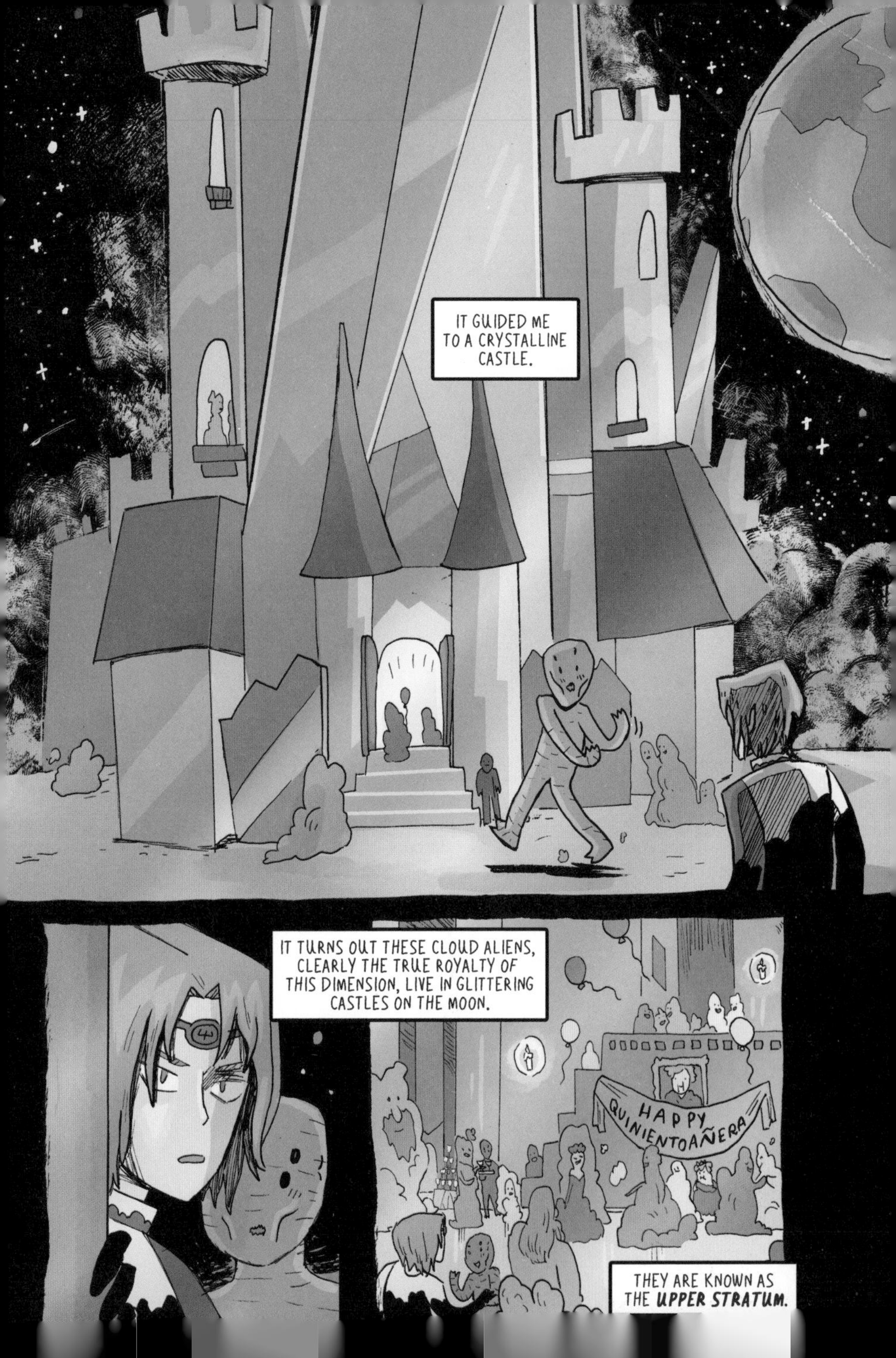
IT GUIDED ME TO A CRYSTALLINE CASTLE.
IT TURNS OUT THESE CLOUD ALIENS, CLEARLY THE TRUE ROYALTY OF THIS DIMENSION, LIVE IN GLITTERING CASTLES ON THE MOON.
HAPPY QUINIENTOAÑERA
THEY ARE KNOWN AS THE **UPPER STRATUM.**

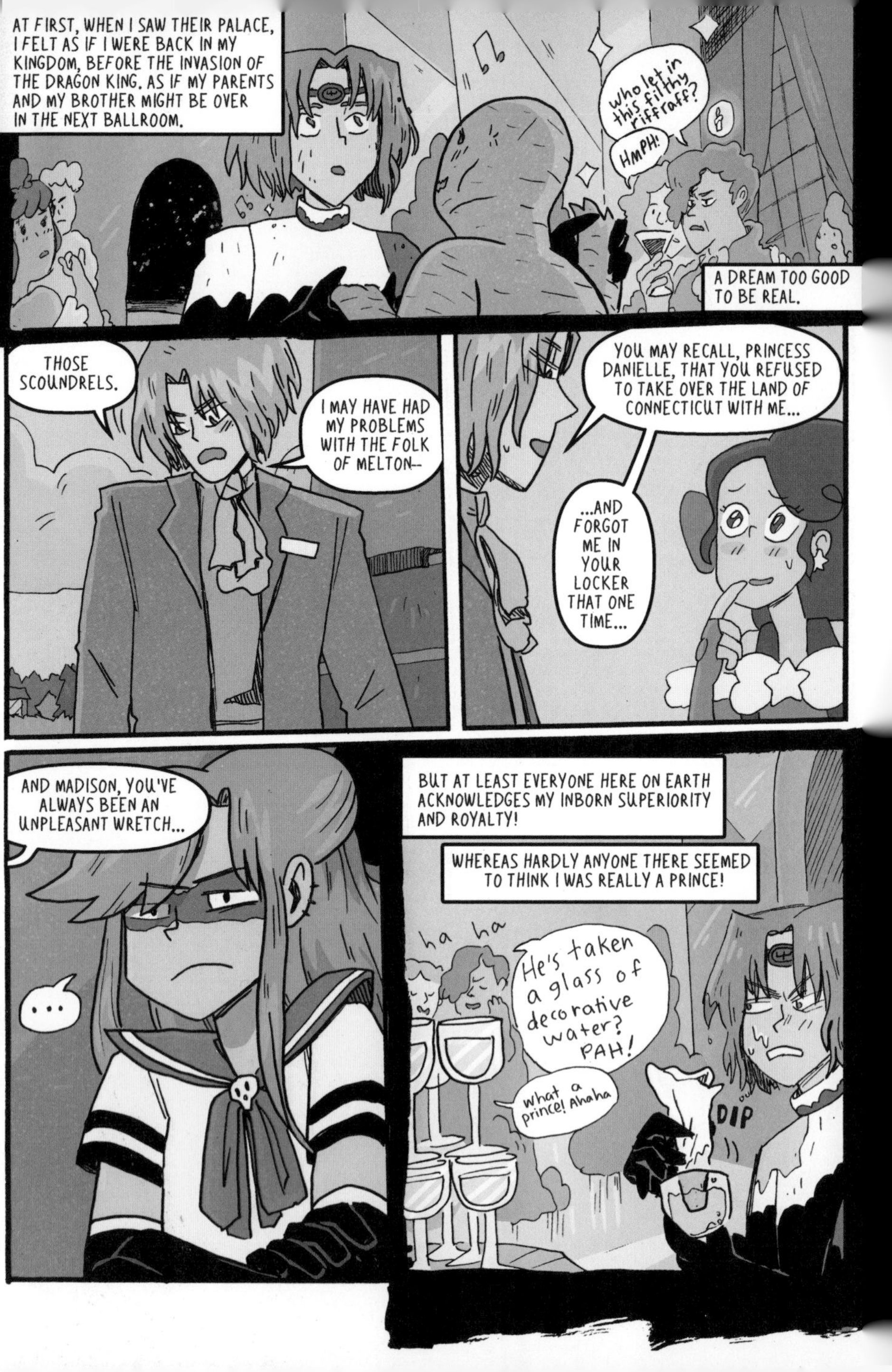
AT FIRST, WHEN I SAW THEIR PALACE, I FELT AS IF I WERE BACK IN MY KINGDOM, BEFORE THE INVASION OF THE DRAGON KING. AS IF MY PARENTS AND MY BROTHER MIGHT BE OVER IN THE NEXT BALLROOM.
who let in this filthy riffraff?
HMPH!
A DREAM TOO GOOD TO BE REAL.
THOSE SCOUNDRELS.
I MAY HAVE HAD MY PROBLEMS WITH THE FOLK OF MELTON--
YOU MAY RECALL, PRINCESS DANIELLE, THAT YOU REFUSED TO TAKE OVER THE LAND OF CONNECTICUT WITH ME...
...AND FORGOT ME IN YOUR LOCKER THAT ONE TIME...
AND MADISON, YOU'VE ALWAYS BEEN AN UNPLEASANT WRETCH...
...
BUT AT LEAST EVERYONE HERE ON EARTH ACKNOWLEDGES MY INBORN SUPERIORITY AND ROYALTY!
WHEREAS HARDLY ANYONE THERE SEEMED TO THINK I WAS REALLY A PRINCE!
ha ha
He's taken a glass of decorative water? PAH!
what a prince! Ahaha
DIP

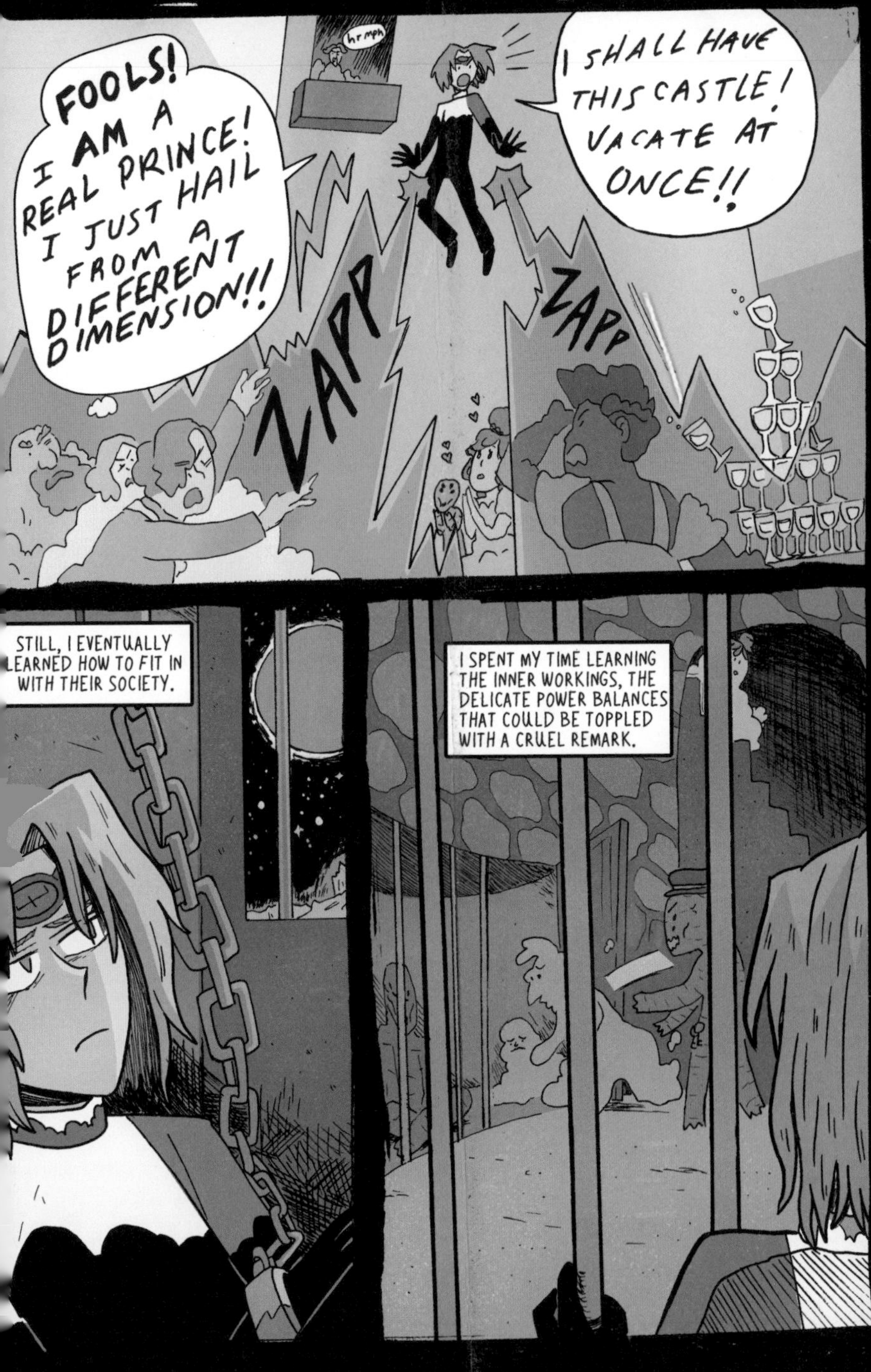
hrmph
FOOLS! I AM A REAL PRINCE! I JUST HAIL FROM A DIFFERENT DIMENSION!!
I SHALL HAVE THIS CASTLE! VACATE AT ONCE!!
ZAPP
ZAPP
STILL, I EVENTUALLY LEARNED HOW TO FIT IN WITH THEIR SOCIETY.
I SPENT MY TIME LEARNING THE INNER WORKINGS, THE DELICATE POWER BALANCES THAT COULD BE TOPPLED WITH A CRUEL REMARK.

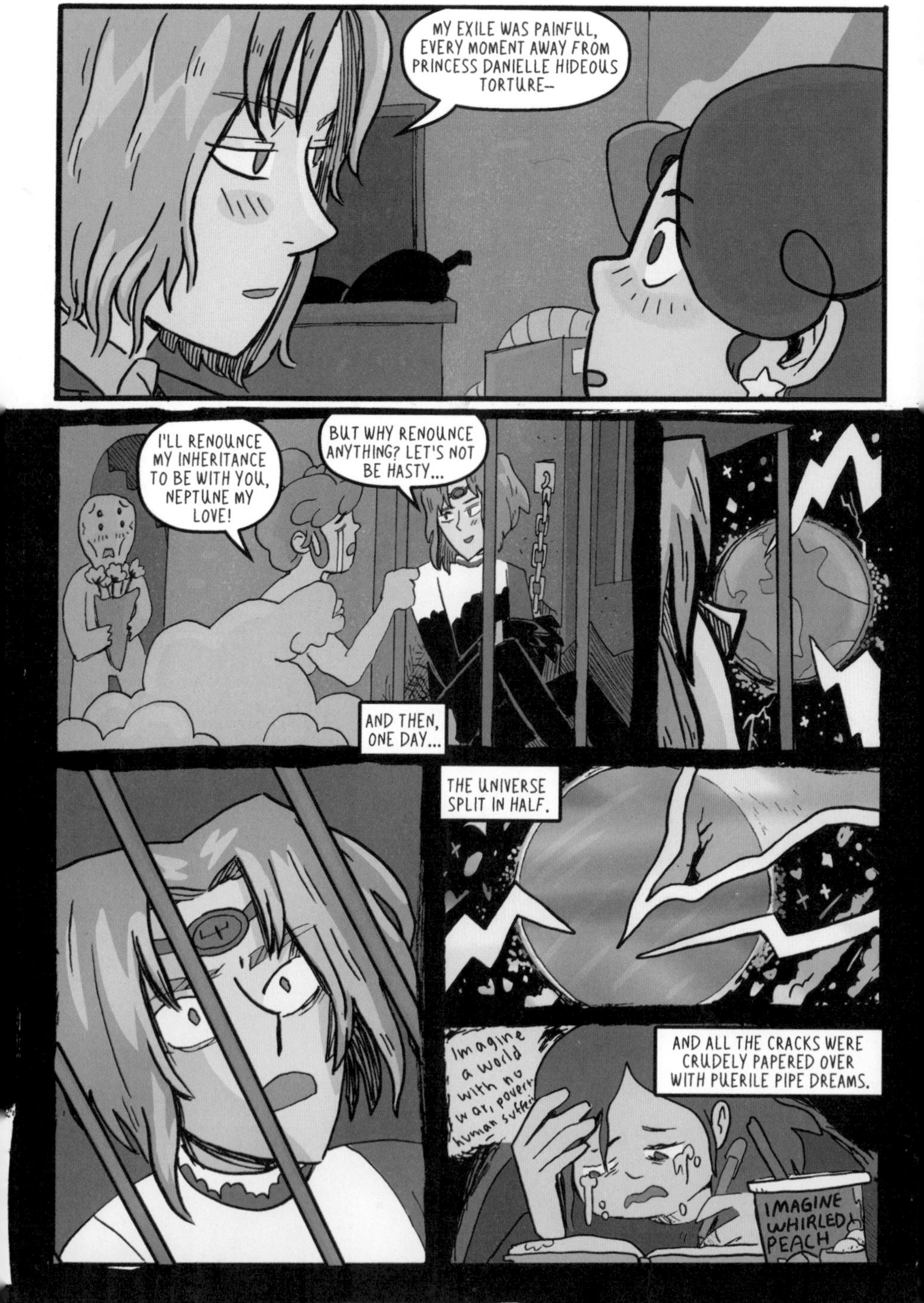
MY EXILE WAS PAINFUL, EVERY MOMENT AWAY FROM PRINCESS DANIELLE HIDEOUS TORTURE--
I'LL RENOUNCE MY INHERITANCE TO BE WITH YOU, NEPTUNE MY LOVE!
BUT WHY RENOUNCE ANYTHING? LET'S NOT BE HASTY...
AND THEN, ONE DAY...
THE UNIVERSE SPLIT IN HALF.
Imagine a world with no war, povert human suffer
AND ALL THE CRACKS WERE CRUDELY PAPERED OVER WITH PUERILE PIPE DREAMS.
IMAGINE WHIRLED PEACH

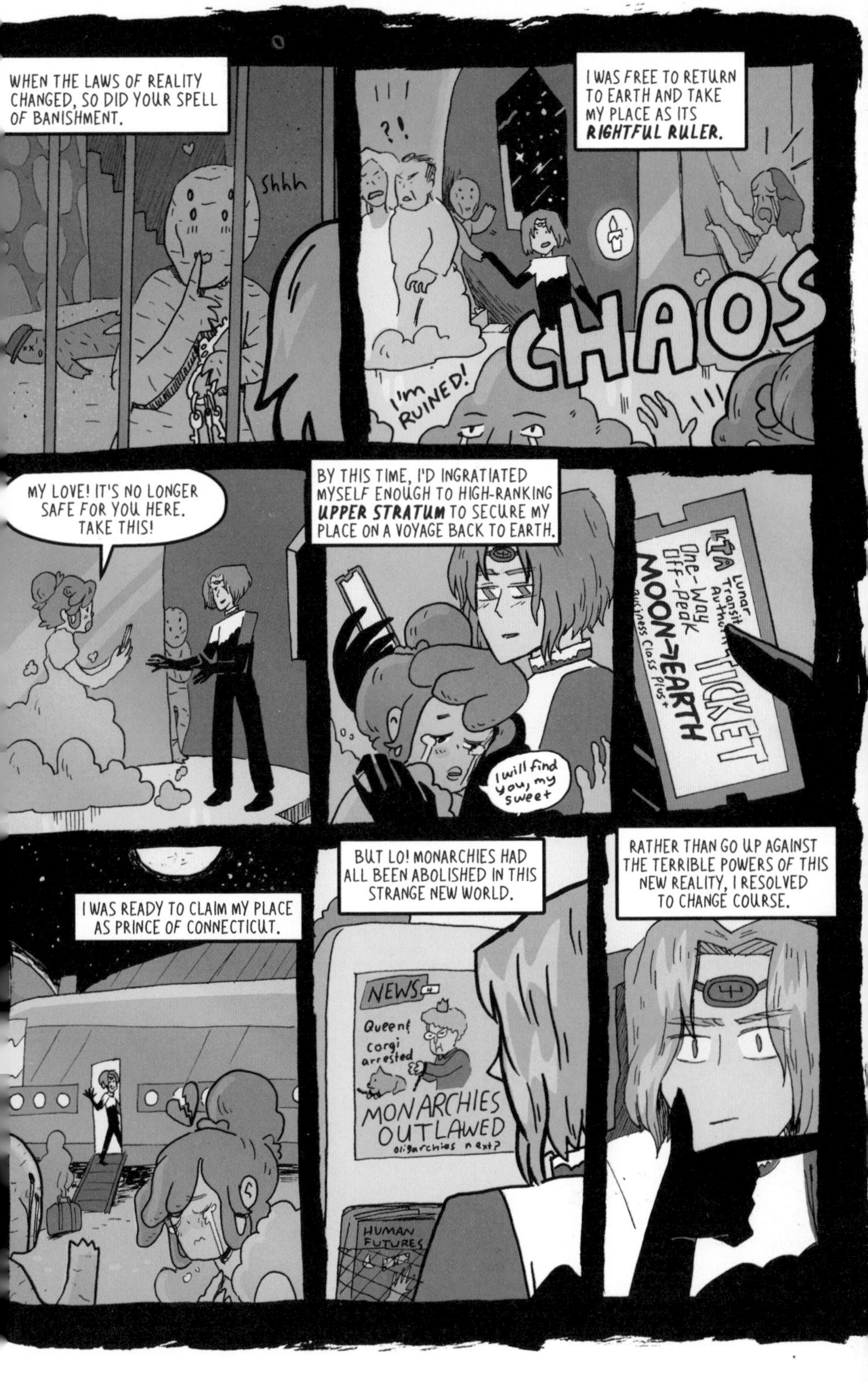
WHEN THE LAWS OF REALITY CHANGED, SO DID YOUR SPELL OF BANISHMENT.
Shhh
?!
I WAS FREE TO RETURN TO EARTH AND TAKE MY PLACE AS ITS **RIGHTFUL RULER.**
CHAOS
I'm RUINED!
MY LOVE! IT'S NO LONGER SAFE FOR YOU HERE. TAKE THIS!
BY THIS TIME, I'D INGRATIATED MYSELF ENOUGH TO HIGH-RANKING **UPPER STRATUM** TO SECURE MY PLACE ON A VOYAGE BACK TO EARTH.
I will find you, my sweet
LTA Lunar Transit Authority
TICKET
One-Way Off-Peak
MOON→EARTH
Business Class Plus+
I WAS READY TO CLAIM MY PLACE AS PRINCE OF CONNECTICUT.
BUT LO! MONARCHIES HAD ALL BEEN ABOLISHED IN THIS STRANGE NEW WORLD.
NEWS
Queen & corgi arrested
MONARCHIES OUTLAWED
oligarchies next?
HUMAN FUTURES
RATHER THAN GO UP AGAINST THE TERRIBLE POWERS OF THIS NEW REALITY, I RESOLVED TO CHANGE COURSE.

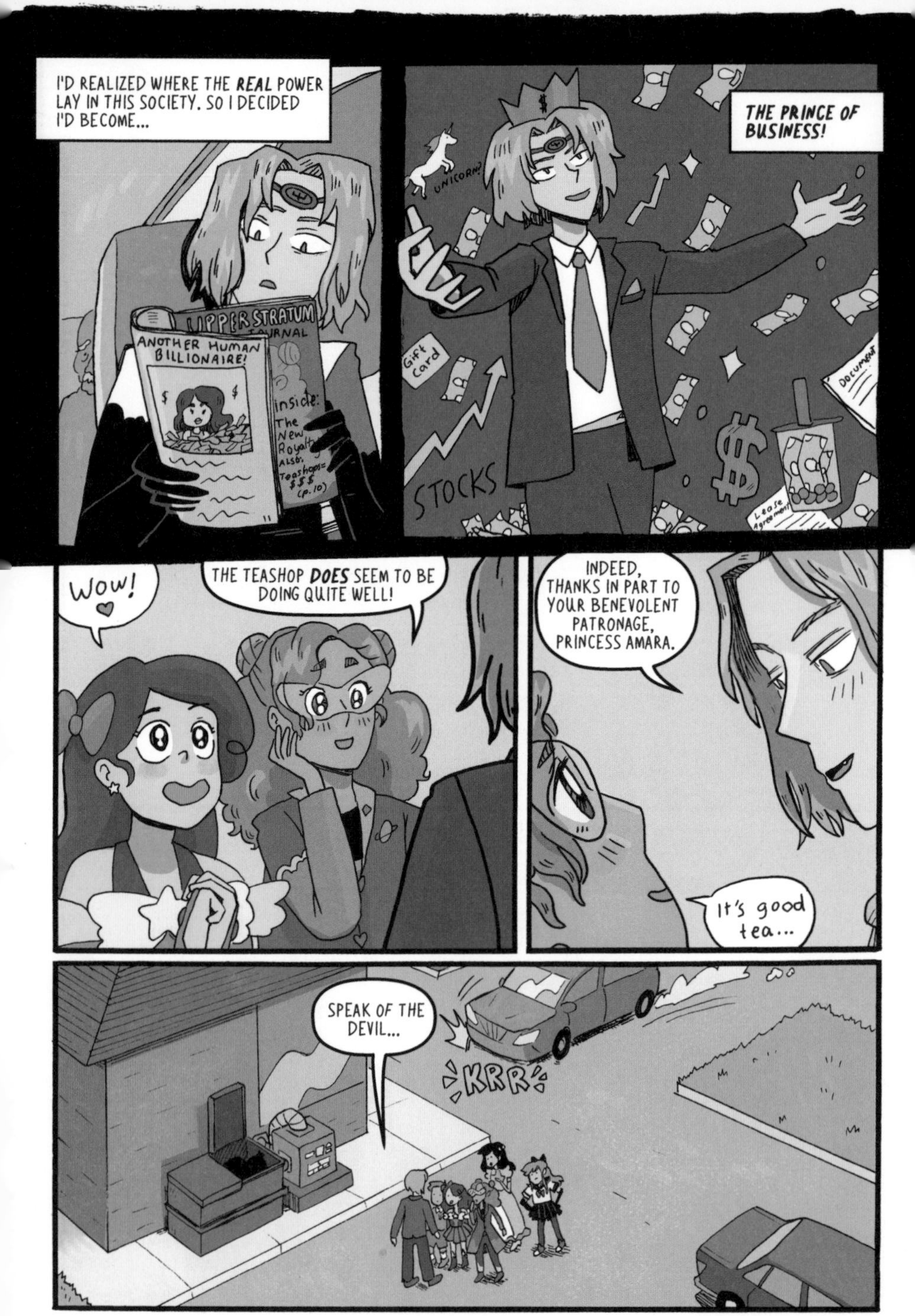
I'D REALIZED WHERE THE **REAL** POWER LAY IN THIS SOCIETY. SO I DECIDED I'D BECOME...
UPPER STRATUM JOURNAL
ANOTHER HUMAN BILLIONAIRE!
inside: The New Royalty
ALSO: Teashops = $$$ (p.10)
THE PRINCE OF BUSINESS!
UNICORN?
Gift Card
Document
STOCKS
Lease Agreement
Wow!
THE TEASHOP **DOES** SEEM TO BE DOING QUITE WELL!
INDEED, THANKS IN PART TO YOUR BENEVOLENT PATRONAGE, PRINCESS AMARA.
It's good tea...
SPEAK OF THE DEVIL...
KRR

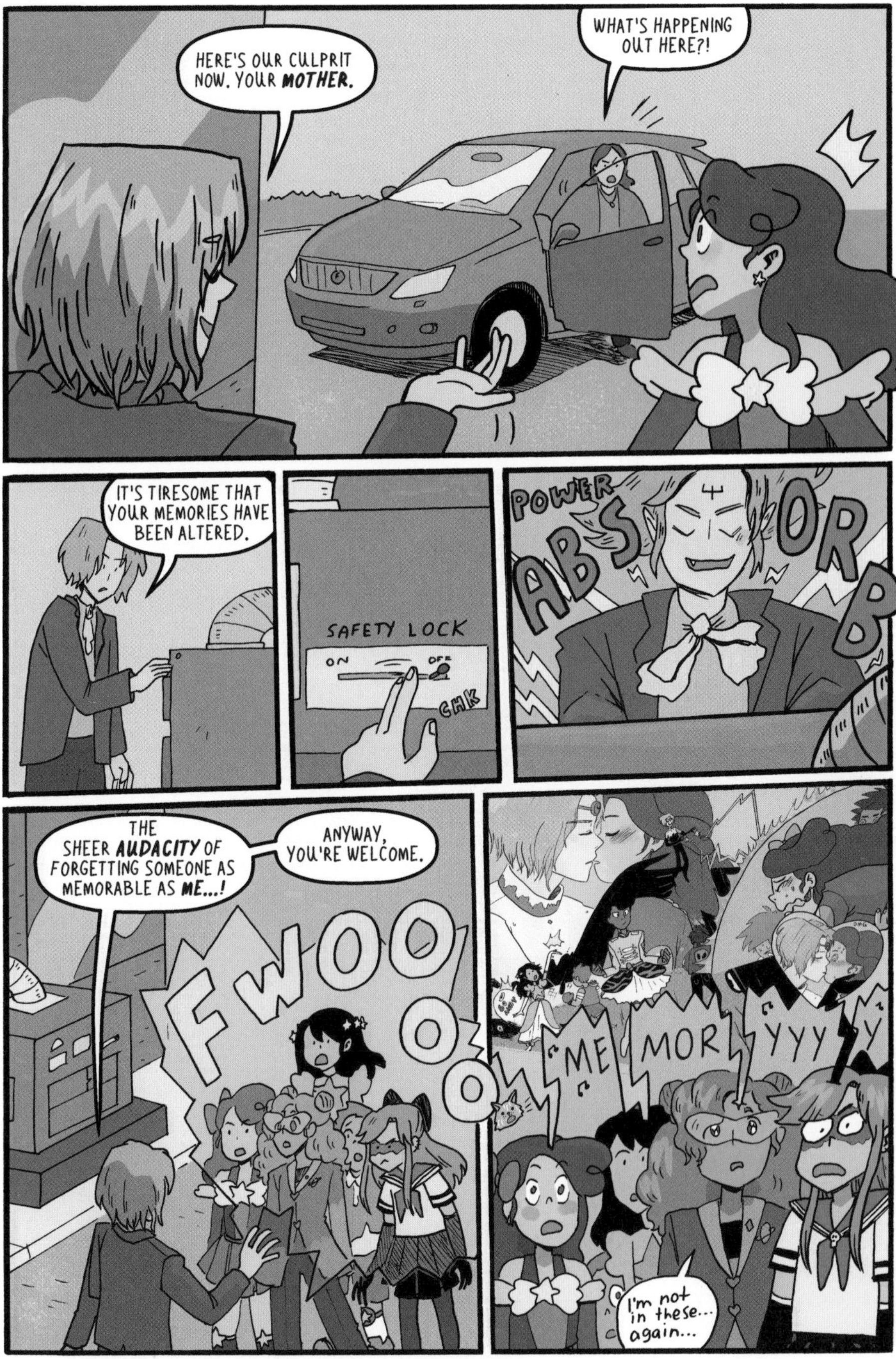

HERE'S OUR CULPRIT NOW. YOUR **MOTHER.**
WHAT'S HAPPENING OUT HERE?!
IT'S TIRESOME THAT YOUR MEMORIES HAVE BEEN ALTERED.
SAFETY LOCK
ON
OFF
CHK
POWER ABSORB
THE SHEER **AUDACITY** OF FORGETTING SOMEONE AS MEMORABLE AS **ME...!**
ANYWAY, YOU'RE WELCOME.
FWOOOO
MEMORYYYY
I'm not in these... again...

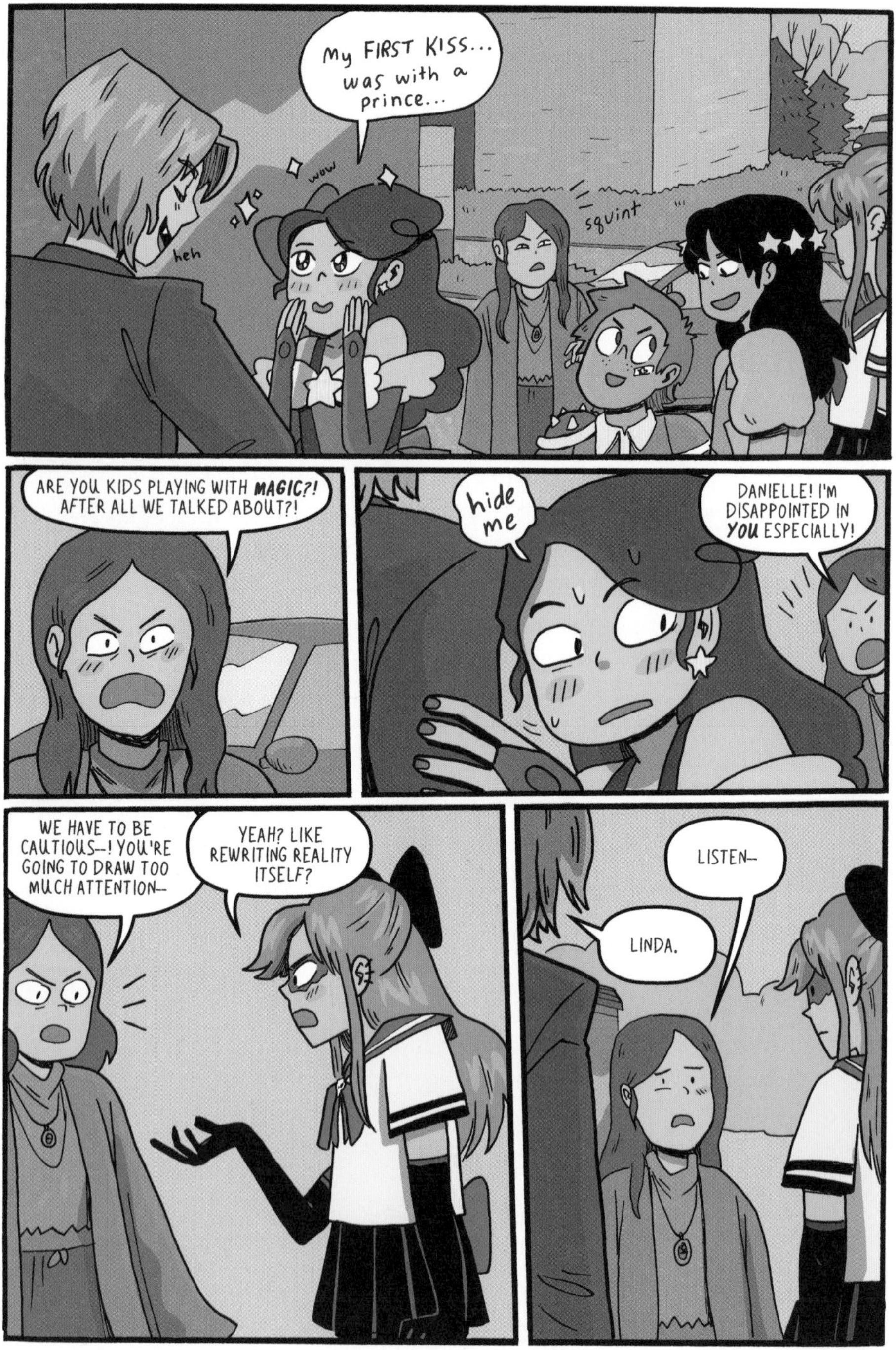
My FIRST KISS... was with a prince...
wow
heh
squint
ARE YOU KIDS PLAYING WITH MAGIC?! AFTER ALL WE TALKED ABOUT?!
hide me
DANIELLE! I'M DISAPPOINTED IN YOU ESPECIALLY!
WE HAVE TO BE CAUTIOUS--! YOU'RE GOING TO DRAW TOO MUCH ATTENTION--
YEAH? LIKE REWRITING REALITY ITSELF?
LISTEN--
LINDA.

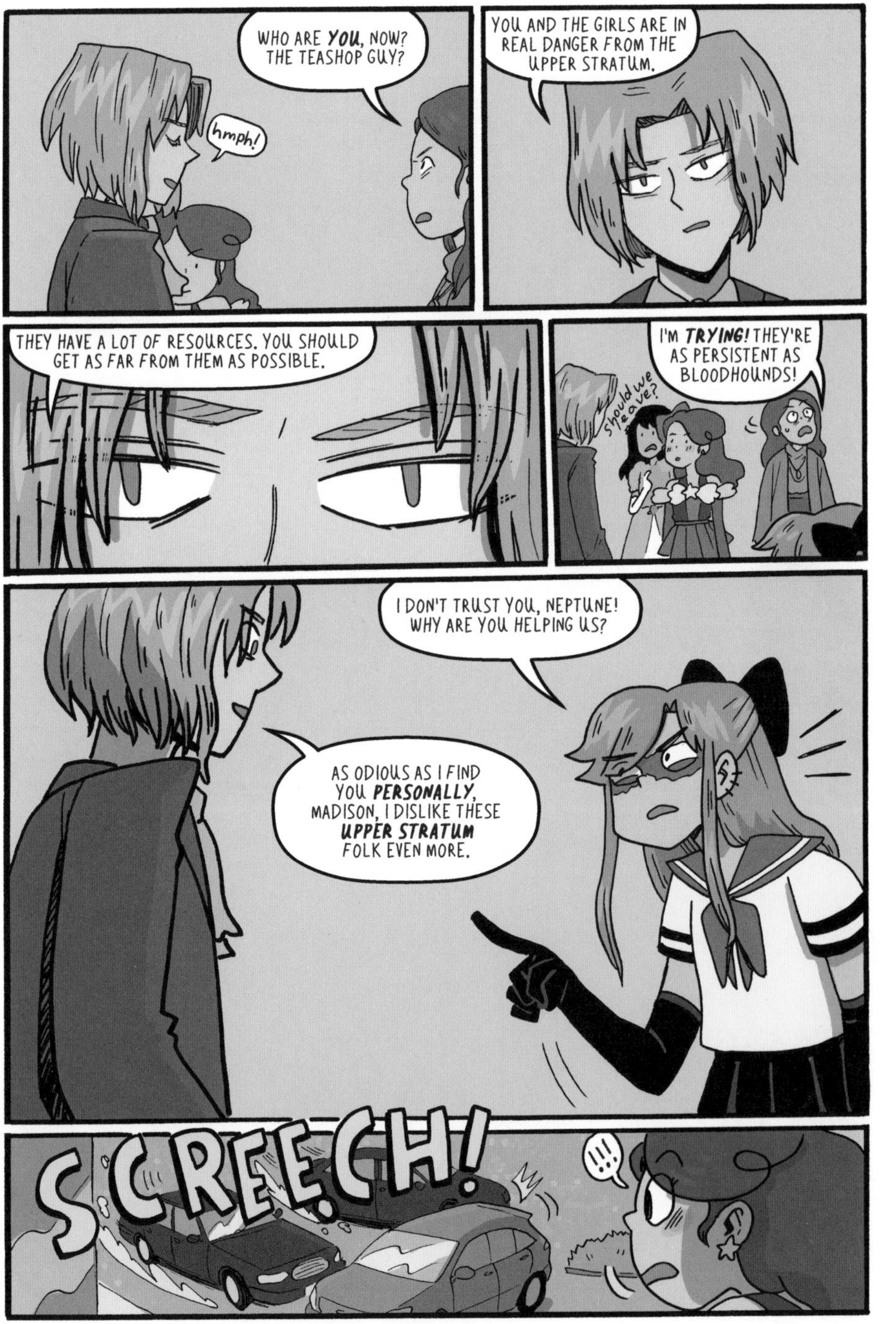
WHO ARE YOU, NOW? THE TEASHOP GUY?
hmph!
YOU AND THE GIRLS ARE IN REAL DANGER FROM THE UPPER STRATUM.
THEY HAVE A LOT OF RESOURCES. YOU SHOULD GET AS FAR FROM THEM AS POSSIBLE.
I'M TRYING! THEY'RE AS PERSISTENT AS BLOODHOUNDS!
Should we leave?
I DON'T TRUST YOU, NEPTUNE! WHY ARE YOU HELPING US?
AS ODIOUS AS I FIND YOU PERSONALLY, MADISON, I DISLIKE THESE UPPER STRATUM FOLK EVEN MORE.
SCREECH!
!!!

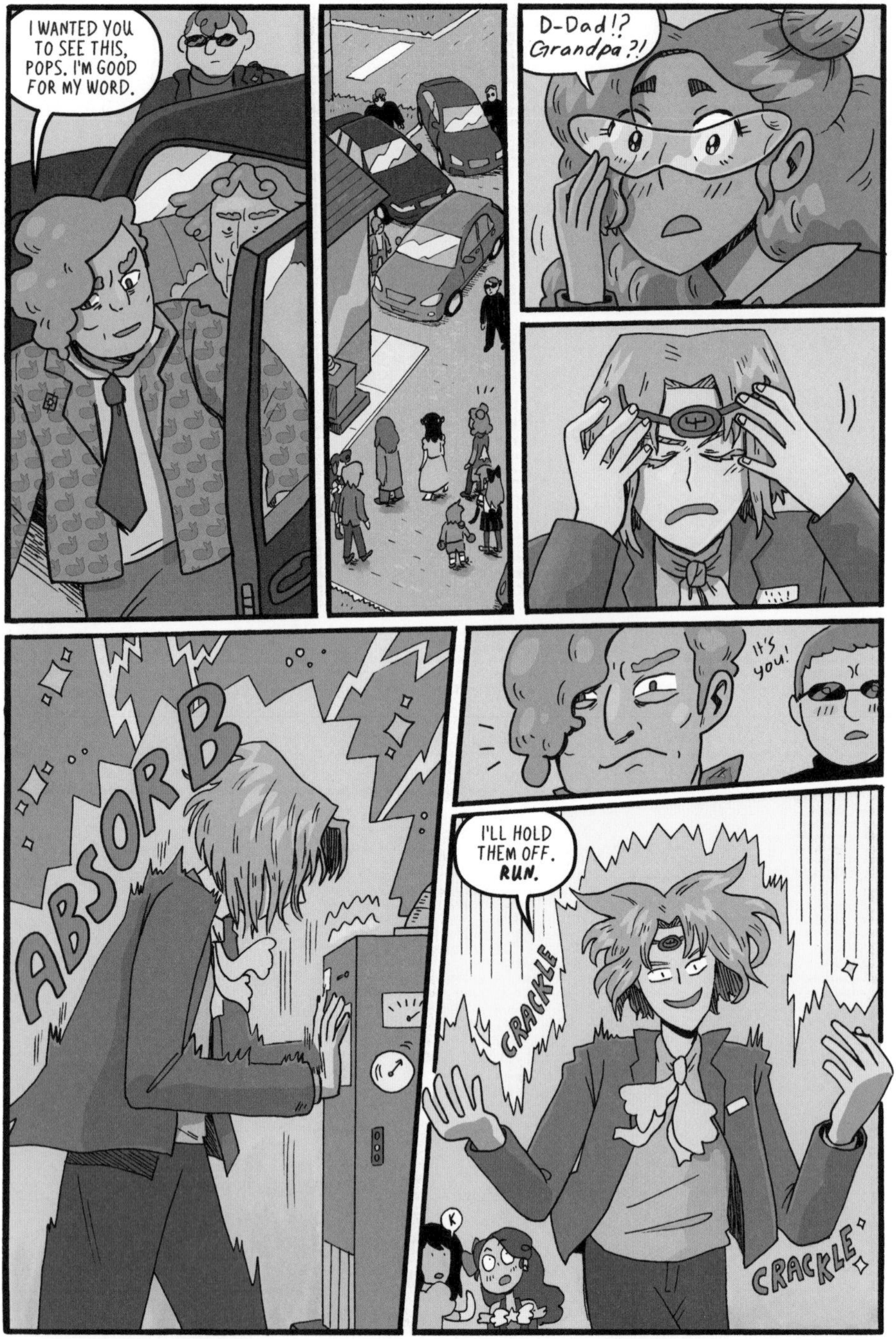
I WANTED YOU TO SEE THIS, POPS. I'M GOOD FOR MY WORD.
D-Dad!? Grandpa?!
ABSORB
It's you!
I'LL HOLD THEM OFF. **RUN.**
CRACKLE
CRACKLE
K

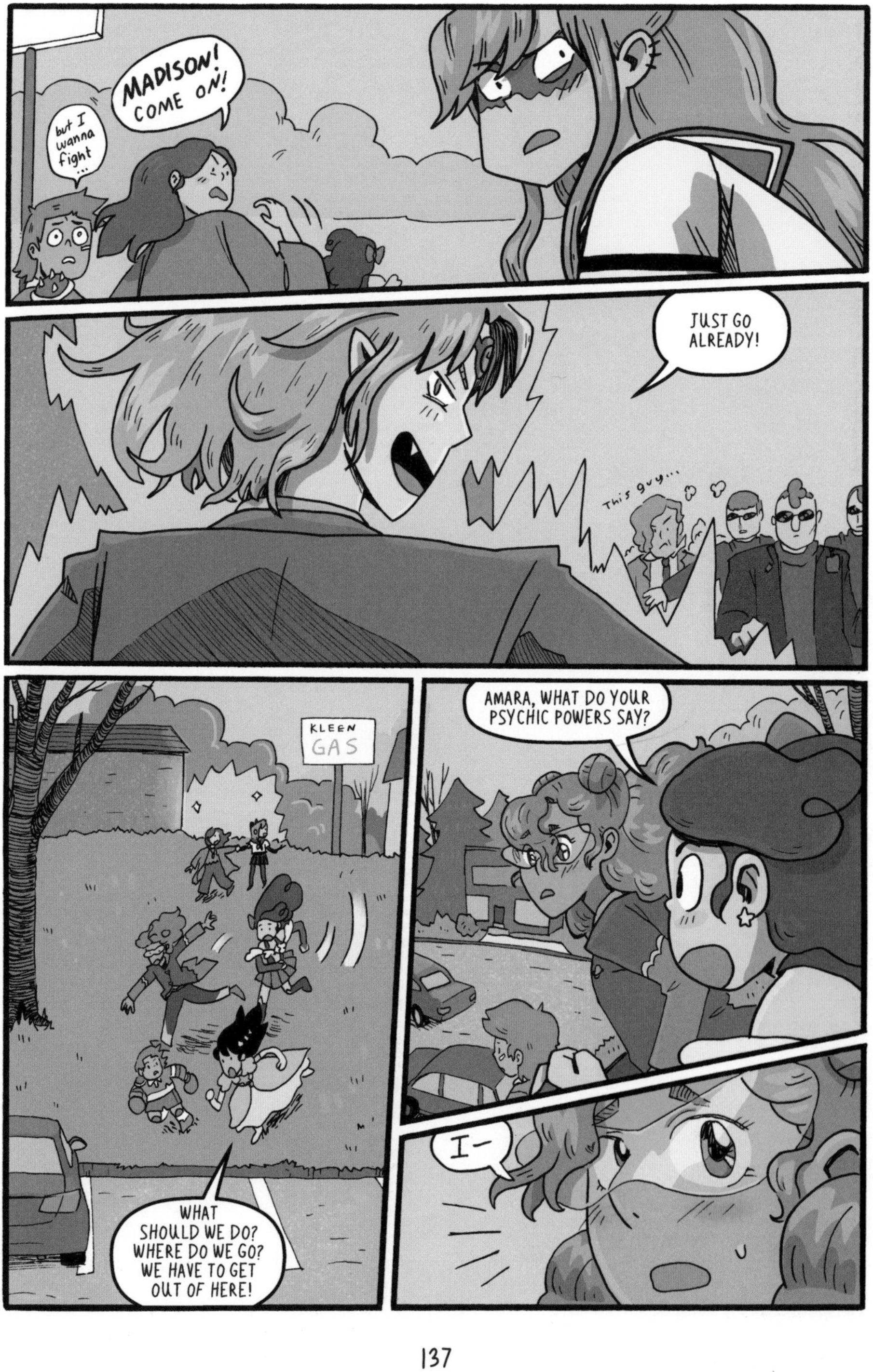
MADISON! COME ON!
but I wanna fight...
JUST GO ALREADY!
This guy...
KLEEN GAS
WHAT SHOULD WE DO? WHERE DO WE GO? WE HAVE TO GET OUT OF HERE!
AMARA, WHAT DO YOUR PSYCHIC POWERS SAY?
I—

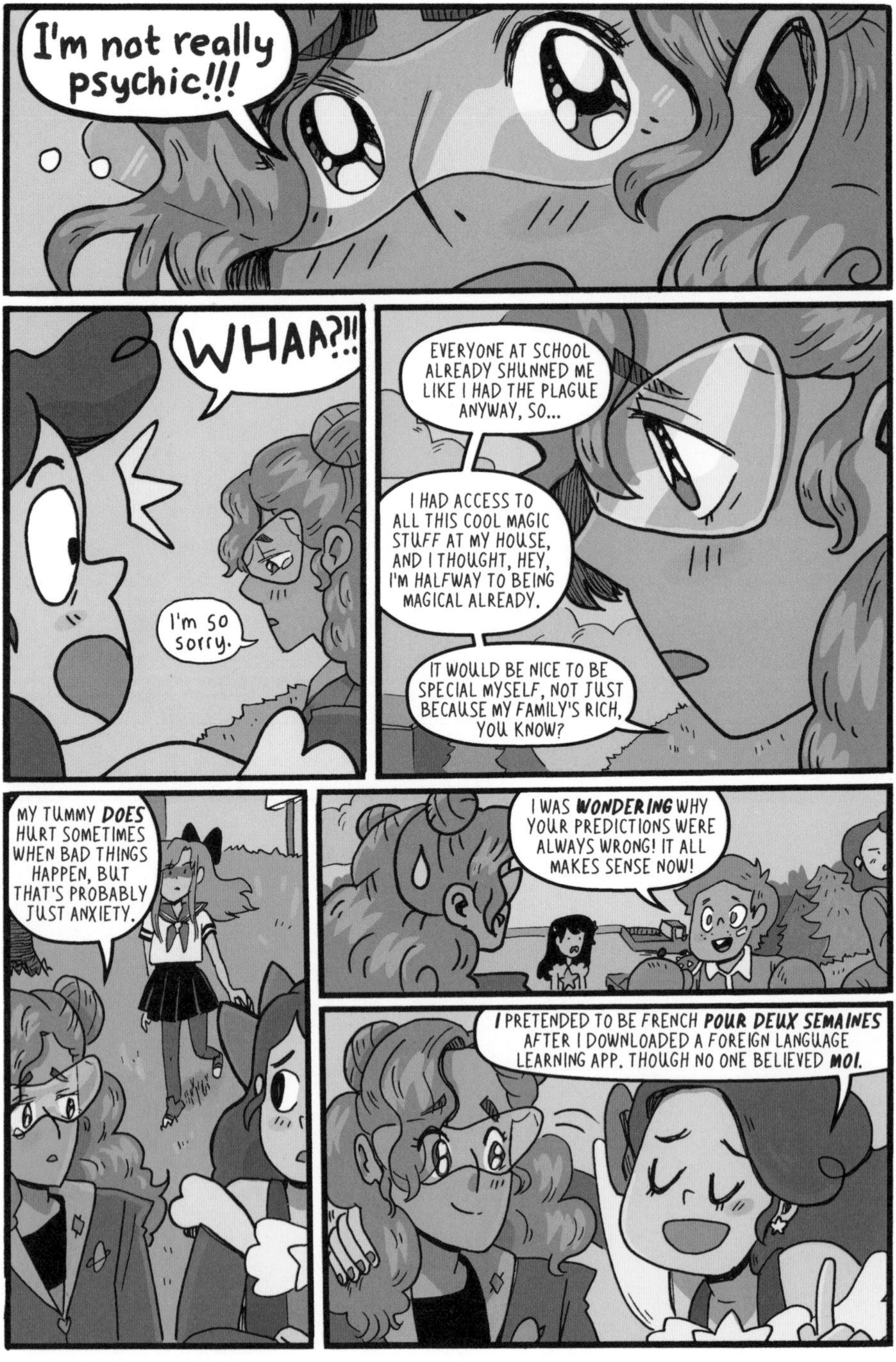
I'm not really psychic!!!
WHAA?!!
I'm so sorry.
EVERYONE AT SCHOOL ALREADY SHUNNED ME LIKE I HAD THE PLAGUE ANYWAY, SO...
I HAD ACCESS TO ALL THIS COOL MAGIC STUFF AT MY HOUSE, AND I THOUGHT, HEY, I'M HALFWAY TO BEING MAGICAL ALREADY.
IT WOULD BE NICE TO BE SPECIAL MYSELF, NOT JUST BECAUSE MY FAMILY'S RICH, YOU KNOW?
MY TUMMY **DOES** HURT SOMETIMES WHEN BAD THINGS HAPPEN, BUT THAT'S PROBABLY JUST ANXIETY.
I WAS **WONDERING** WHY YOUR PREDICTIONS WERE ALWAYS WRONG! IT ALL MAKES SENSE NOW!
I PRETENDED TO BE FRENCH **POUR DEUX SEMAINES** AFTER I DOWNLOADED A FOREIGN LANGUAGE LEARNING APP. THOUGH NO ONE BELIEVED **MOI**.

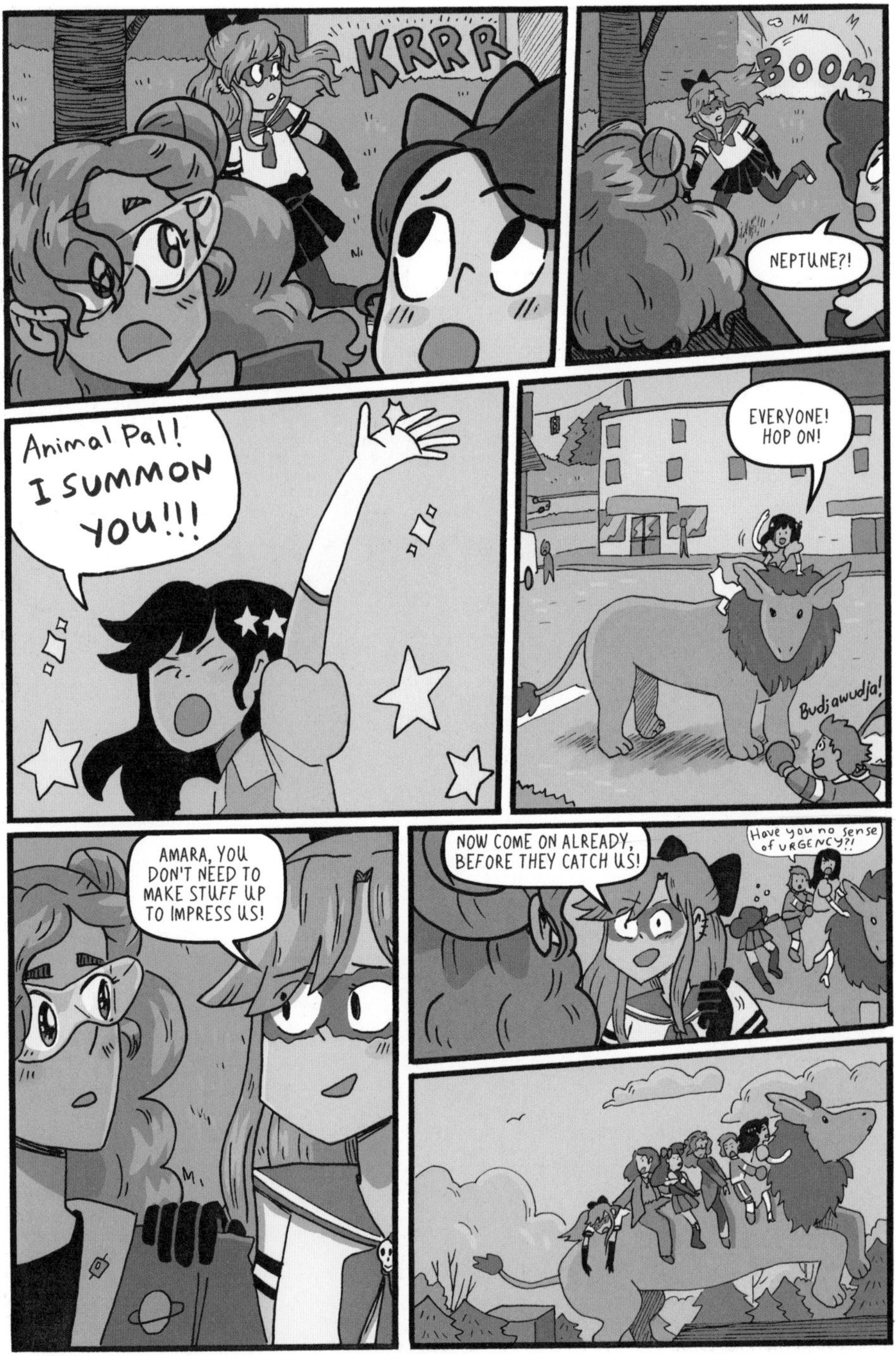
KRRR
BOOM
NEPTUNE?!
Animal Pal! I SUMMON YOU!!!
EVERYONE! HOP ON!
Budjawudja!
AMARA, YOU DON'T NEED TO MAKE STUFF UP TO IMPRESS US!
NOW COME ON ALREADY, BEFORE THEY CATCH US!
Have you no sense of URGENCY?!

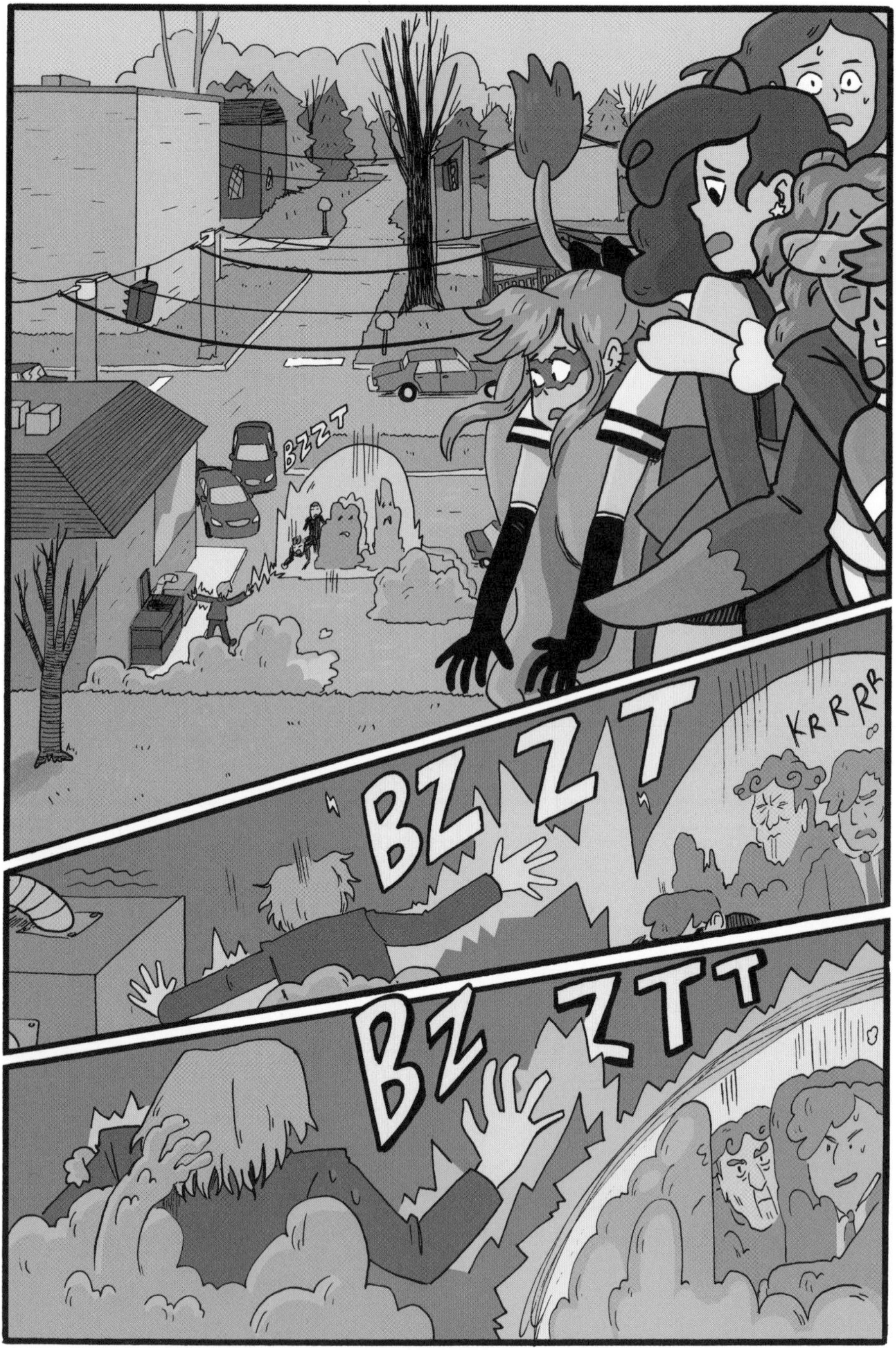
BZZT
BZ Z T
KRRRR
BZ ZTT

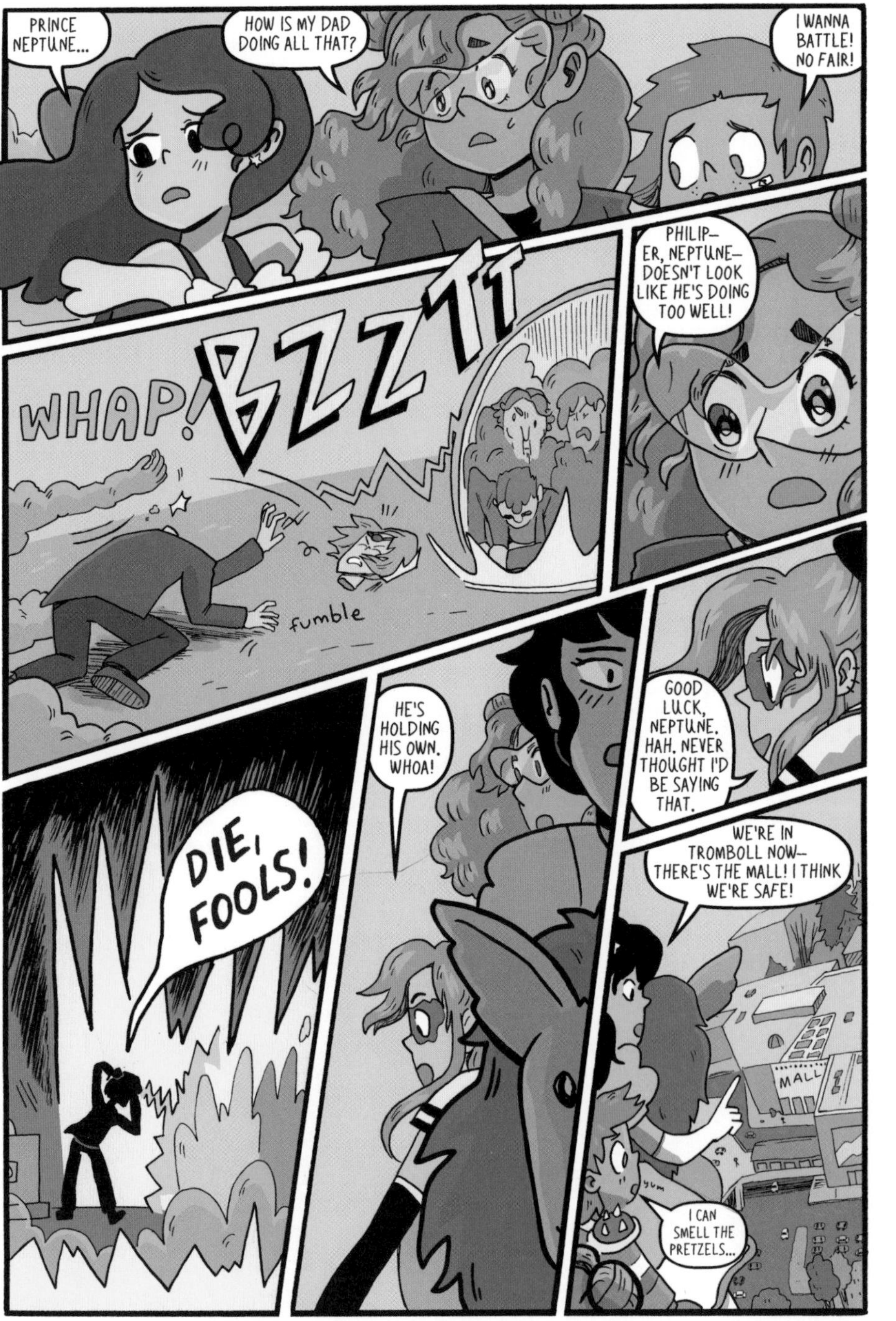
PRINCE NEPTUNE...
HOW IS MY DAD DOING ALL THAT?
I WANNA BATTLE! NO FAIR!
WHAP!
BZZTT
fumble
PHILIP— ER, NEPTUNE— DOESN'T LOOK LIKE HE'S DOING TOO WELL!
GOOD LUCK, NEPTUNE. HAH. NEVER THOUGHT I'D BE SAYING THAT.
DIE, FOOLS!
HE'S HOLDING HIS OWN. WHOA!
WE'RE IN TROMBOLL NOW— THERE'S THE MALL! I THINK WE'RE SAFE!
MALL
yum
I CAN SMELL THE PRETZELS...

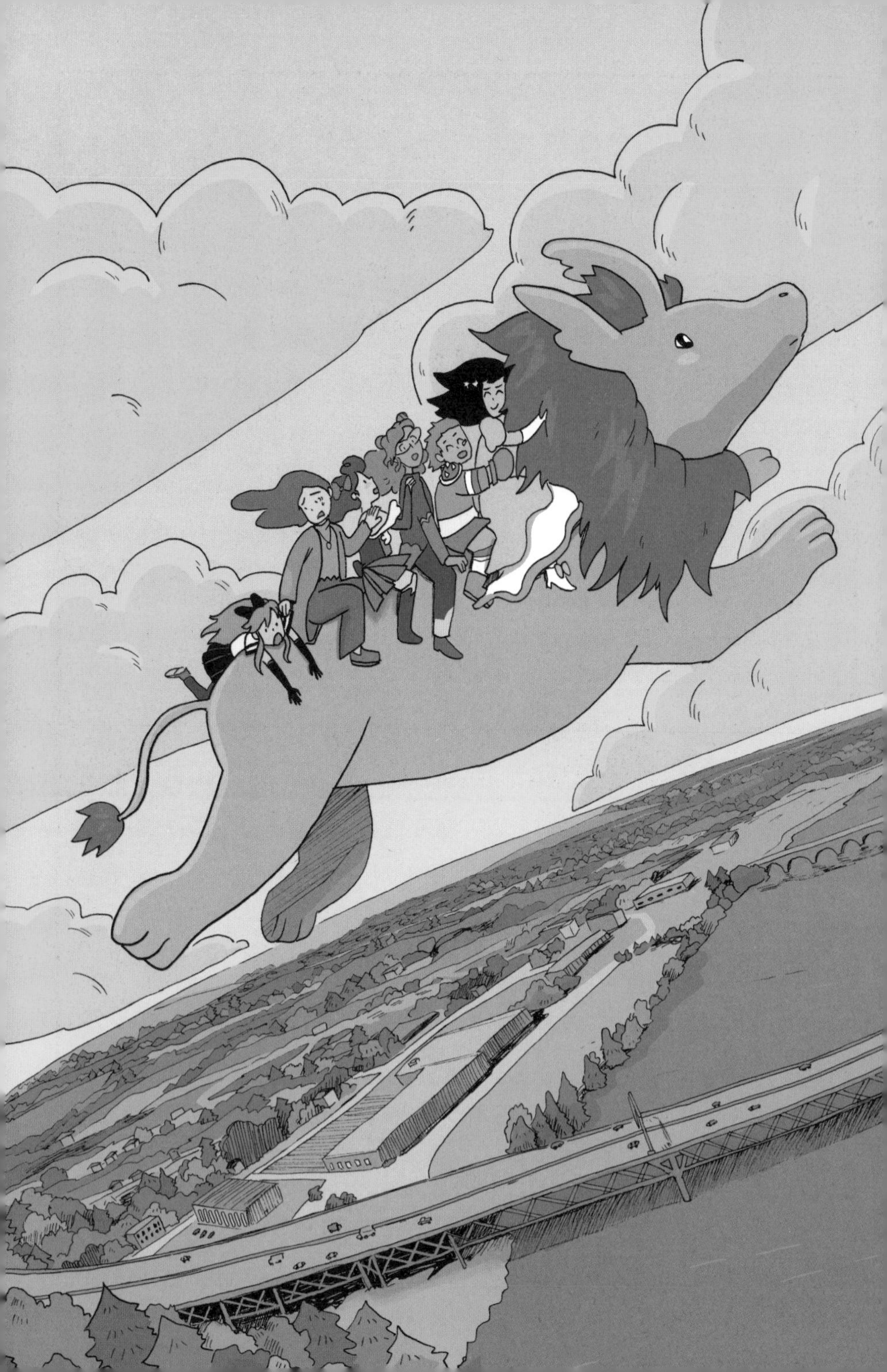

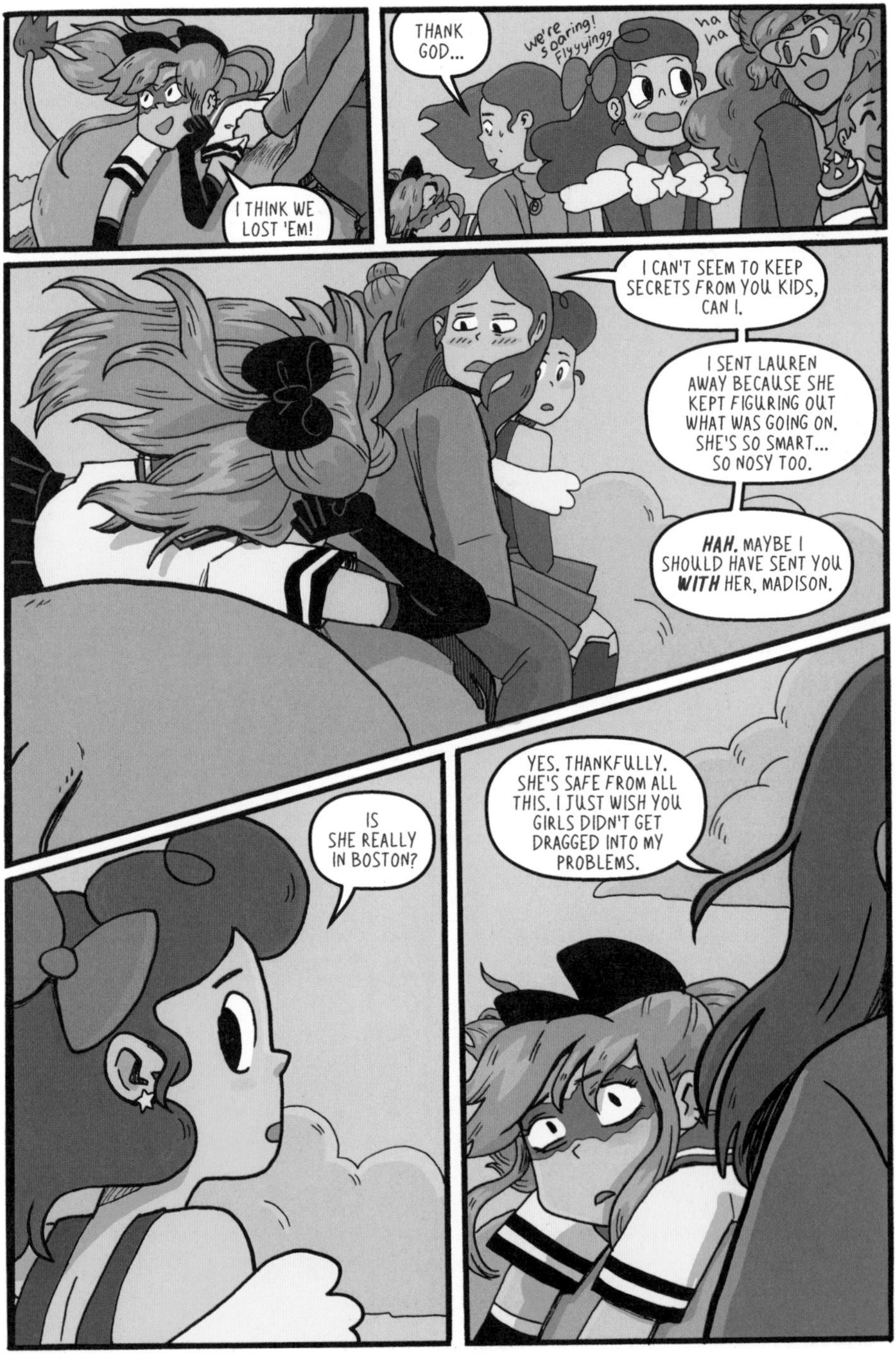
I THINK WE LOST 'EM!
THANK GOD...
we're soaring! Flyyyingg
ha ha
I CAN'T SEEM TO KEEP SECRETS FROM YOU KIDS, CAN I.
I SENT LAUREN AWAY BECAUSE SHE KEPT FIGURING OUT WHAT WAS GOING ON. SHE'S SO SMART... SO NOSY TOO.
HAH. MAYBE I SHOULD HAVE SENT YOU **WITH** HER, MADISON.
IS SHE REALLY IN BOSTON?
YES. THANKFULLY. SHE'S SAFE FROM ALL THIS. I JUST WISH YOU GIRLS DIDN'T GET DRAGGED INTO MY PROBLEMS.

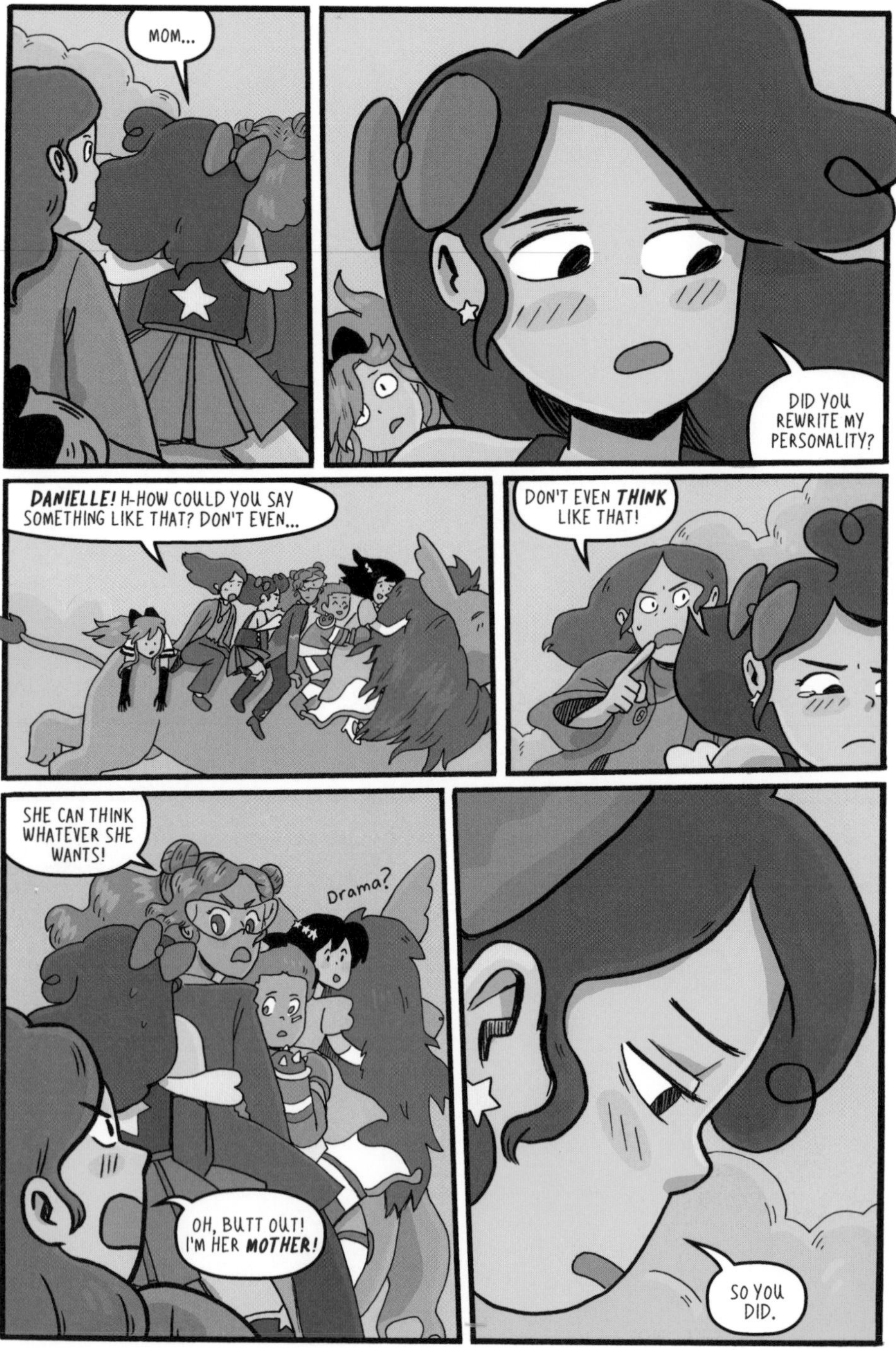
MOM...
DID YOU REWRITE MY PERSONALITY?
DANIELLE! H-HOW COULD YOU SAY SOMETHING LIKE THAT? DON'T EVEN...
DON'T EVEN **THINK** LIKE THAT!
SHE CAN THINK WHATEVER SHE WANTS!
Drama?
OH, BUTT OUT! I'M HER **MOTHER**!
SO YOU DID.

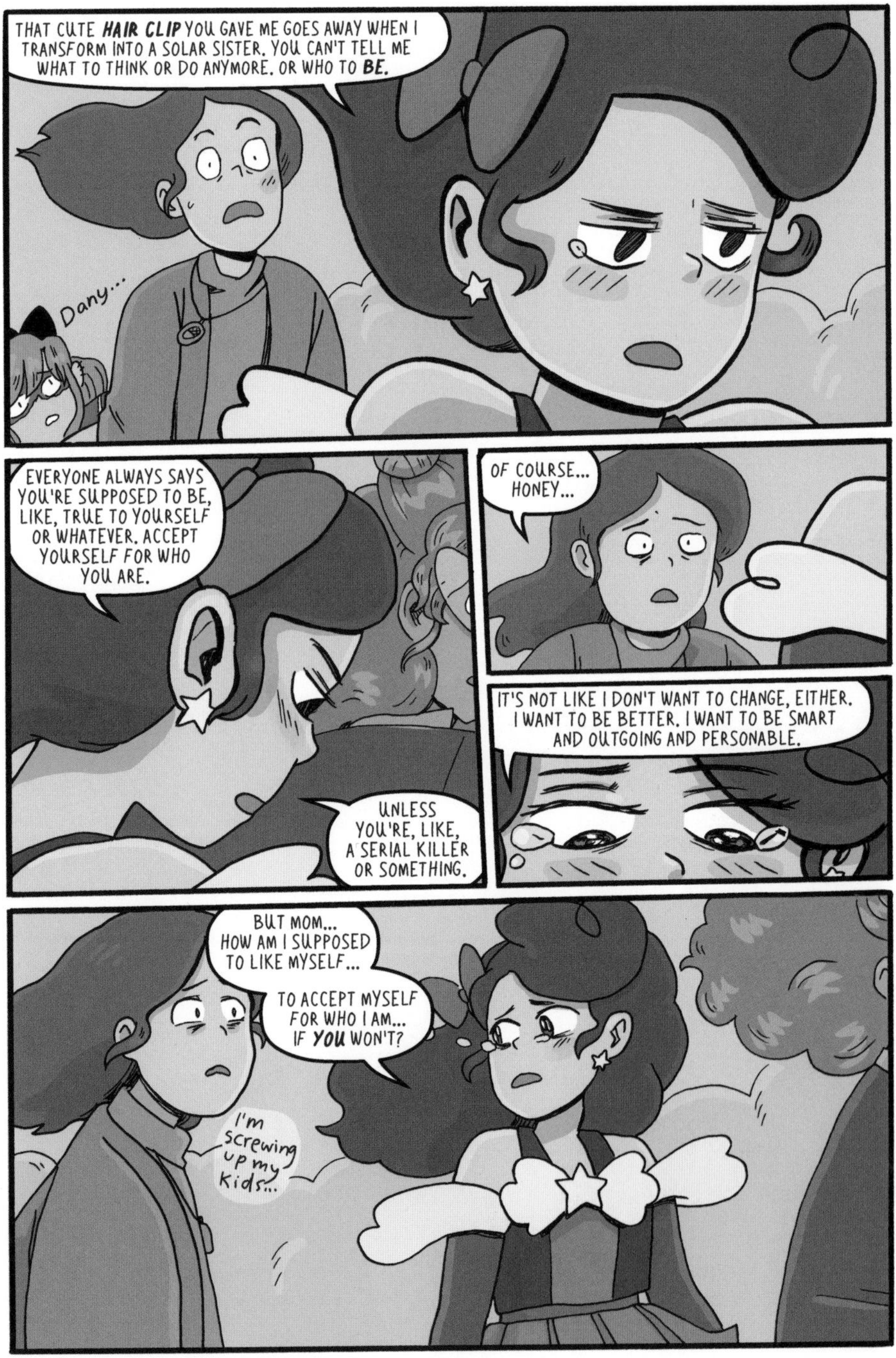
THAT CUTE HAIR CLIP YOU GAVE ME GOES AWAY WHEN I TRANSFORM INTO A SOLAR SISTER. YOU CAN'T TELL ME WHAT TO THINK OR DO ANYMORE. OR WHO TO BE.
Dany...
EVERYONE ALWAYS SAYS YOU'RE SUPPOSED TO BE, LIKE, TRUE TO YOURSELF OR WHATEVER. ACCEPT YOURSELF FOR WHO YOU ARE.
UNLESS YOU'RE, LIKE, A SERIAL KILLER OR SOMETHING.
OF COURSE... HONEY...
IT'S NOT LIKE I DON'T WANT TO CHANGE, EITHER. I WANT TO BE BETTER. I WANT TO BE SMART AND OUTGOING AND PERSONABLE.
BUT MOM... HOW AM I SUPPOSED TO LIKE MYSELF...
TO ACCEPT MYSELF FOR WHO I AM... IF YOU WON'T?
I'm screwing up my kids...

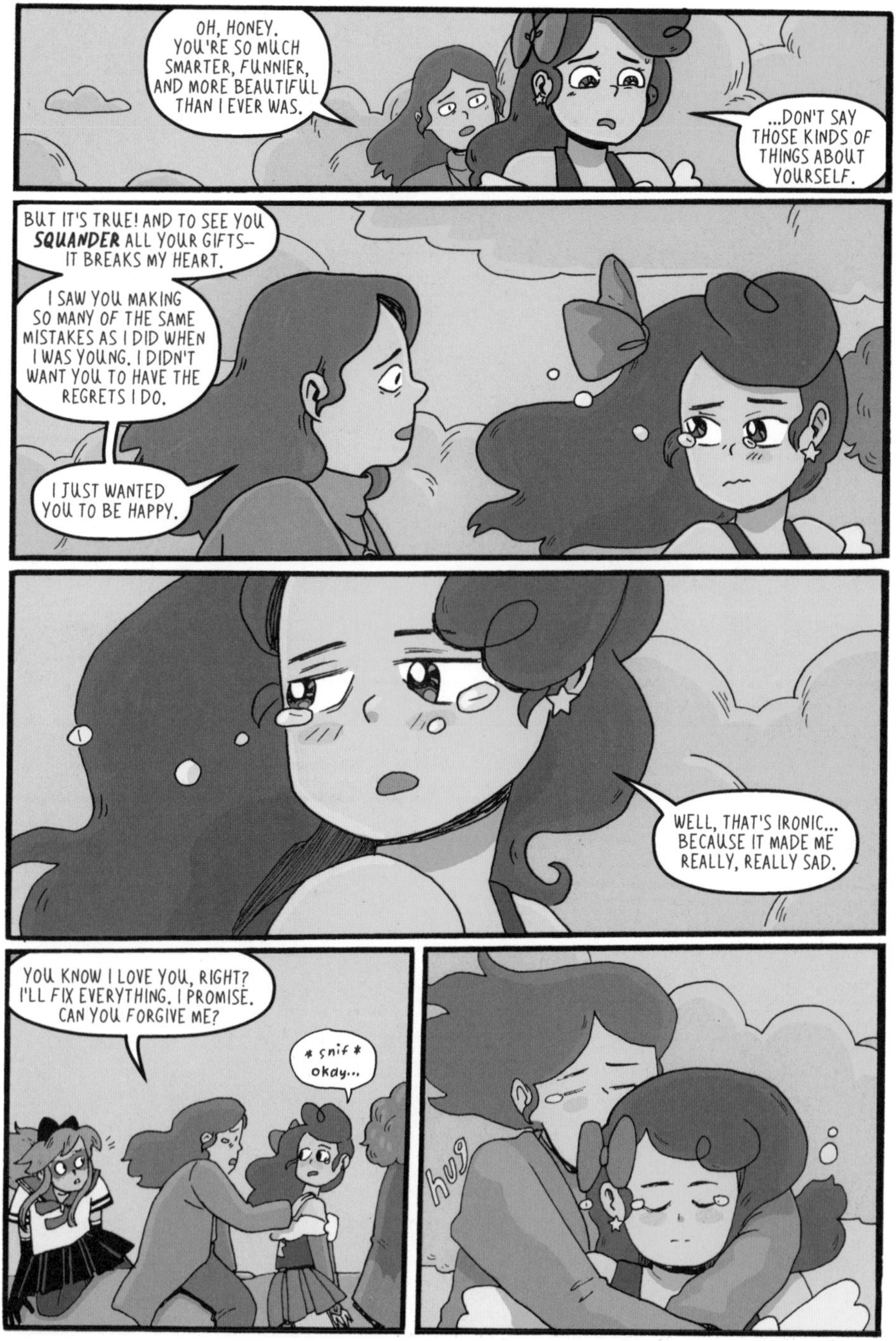
OH, HONEY. YOU'RE SO MUCH SMARTER, FUNNIER, AND MORE BEAUTIFUL THAN I EVER WAS.
...DON'T SAY THOSE KINDS OF THINGS ABOUT YOURSELF.
BUT IT'S TRUE! AND TO SEE YOU SQUANDER ALL YOUR GIFTS-- IT BREAKS MY HEART.
I SAW YOU MAKING SO MANY OF THE SAME MISTAKES AS I DID WHEN I WAS YOUNG. I DIDN'T WANT YOU TO HAVE THE REGRETS I DO.
I JUST WANTED YOU TO BE HAPPY.
WELL, THAT'S IRONIC... BECAUSE IT MADE ME REALLY, REALLY SAD.
YOU KNOW I LOVE YOU, RIGHT? I'LL FIX EVERYTHING. I PROMISE. CAN YOU FORGIVE ME?
* snif * okay...
hug

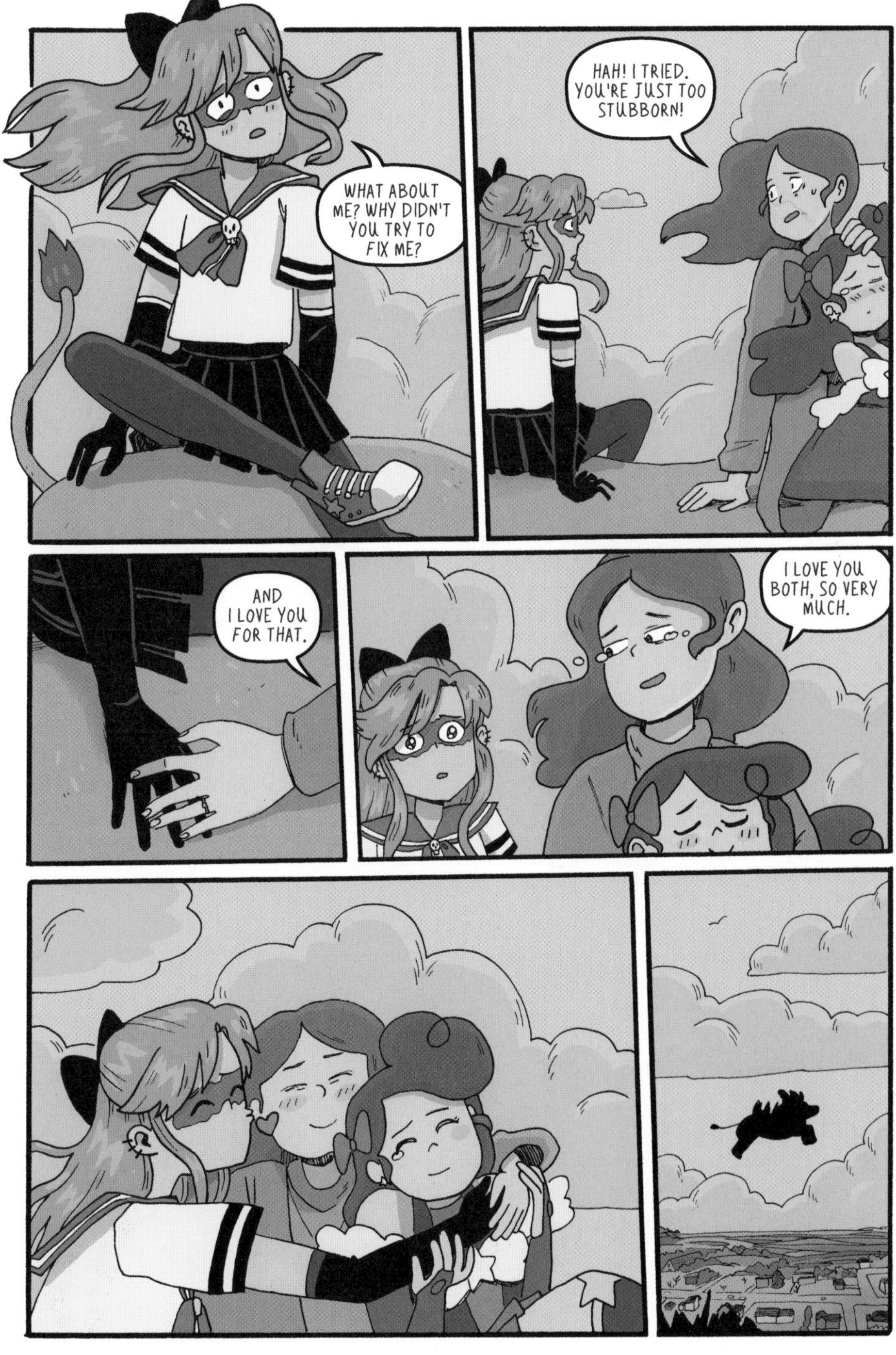
WHAT ABOUT ME? WHY DIDN'T YOU TRY TO FIX ME?
HAH! I TRIED. YOU'RE JUST TOO STUBBORN!
AND I LOVE YOU FOR THAT.
I LOVE YOU BOTH, SO VERY MUCH.

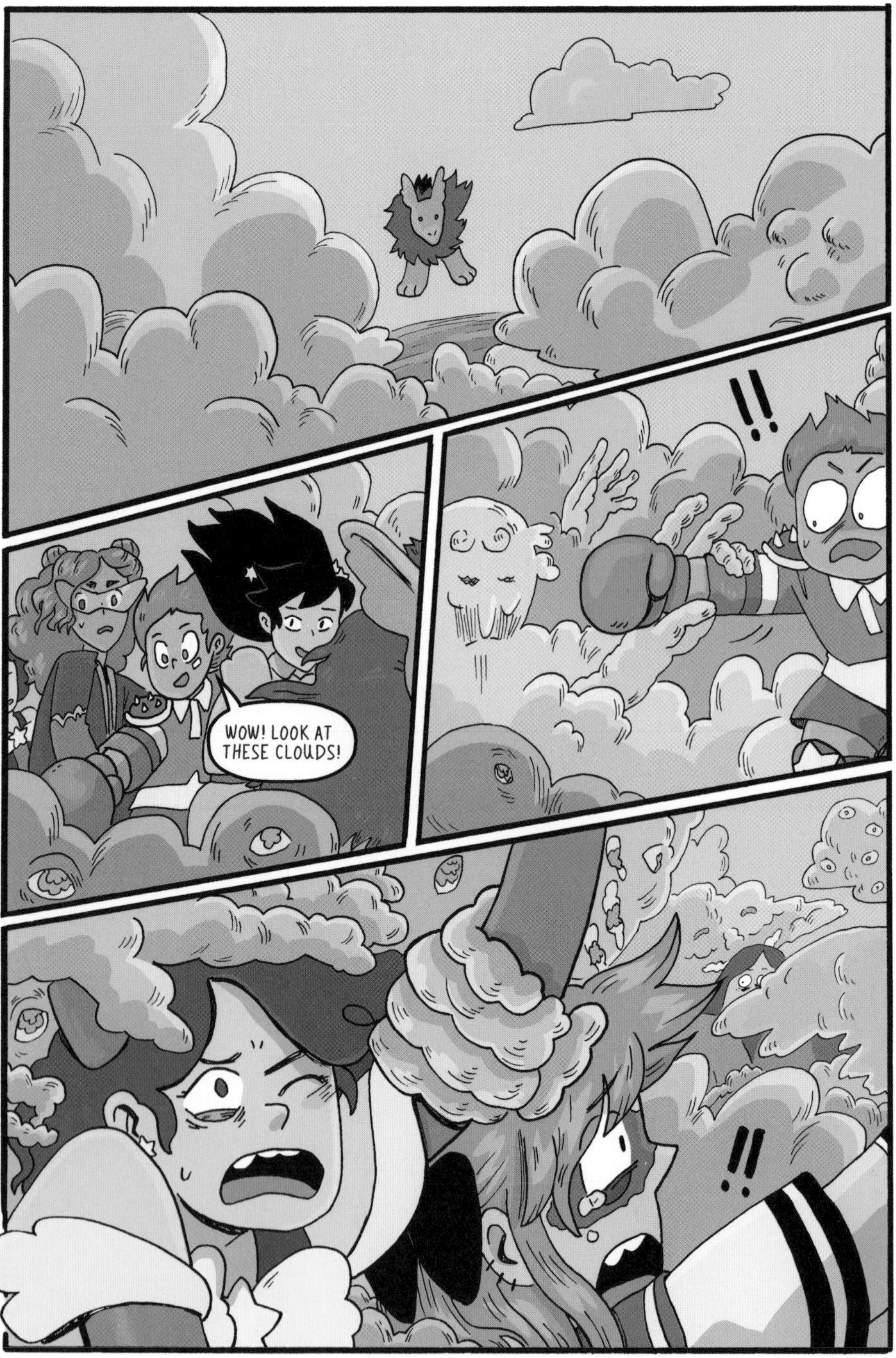
!!
WOW! LOOK AT THESE CLOUDS!
!!

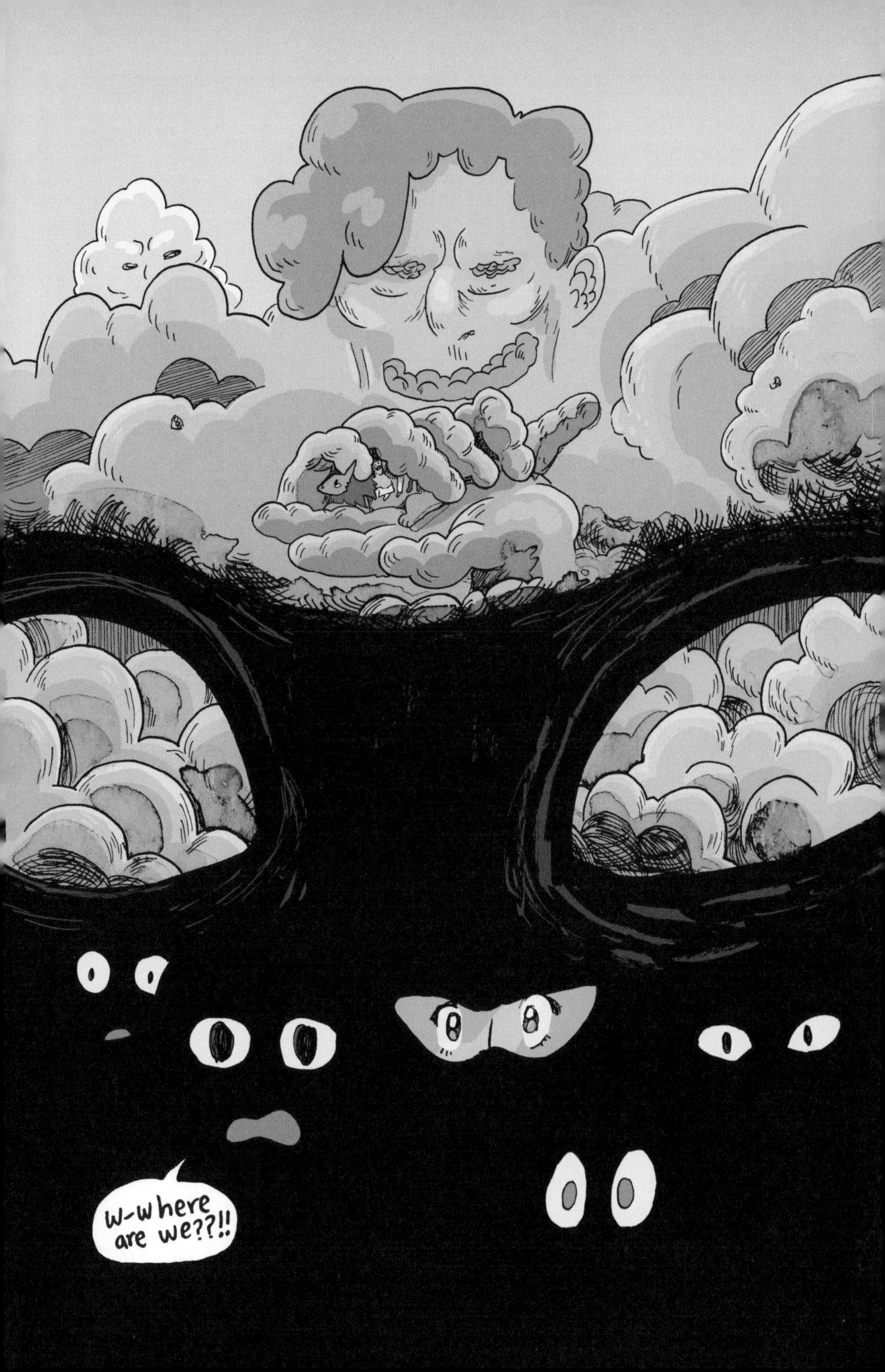
W-Where are we??!!

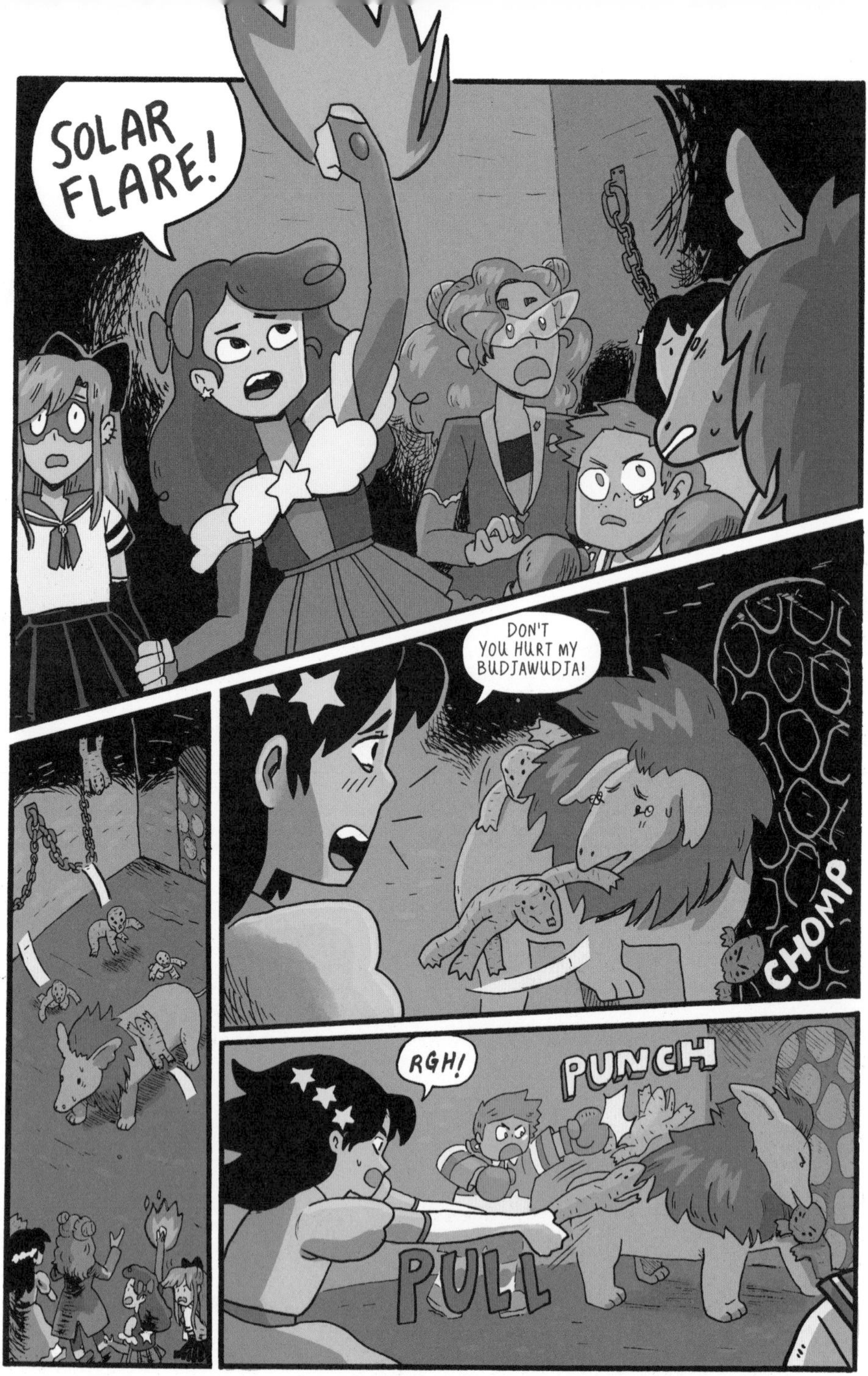
SOLAR FLARE!
DON'T YOU HURT MY BUDJAWUDJA!
CHOMP
RGH!
PUNCH
PULL

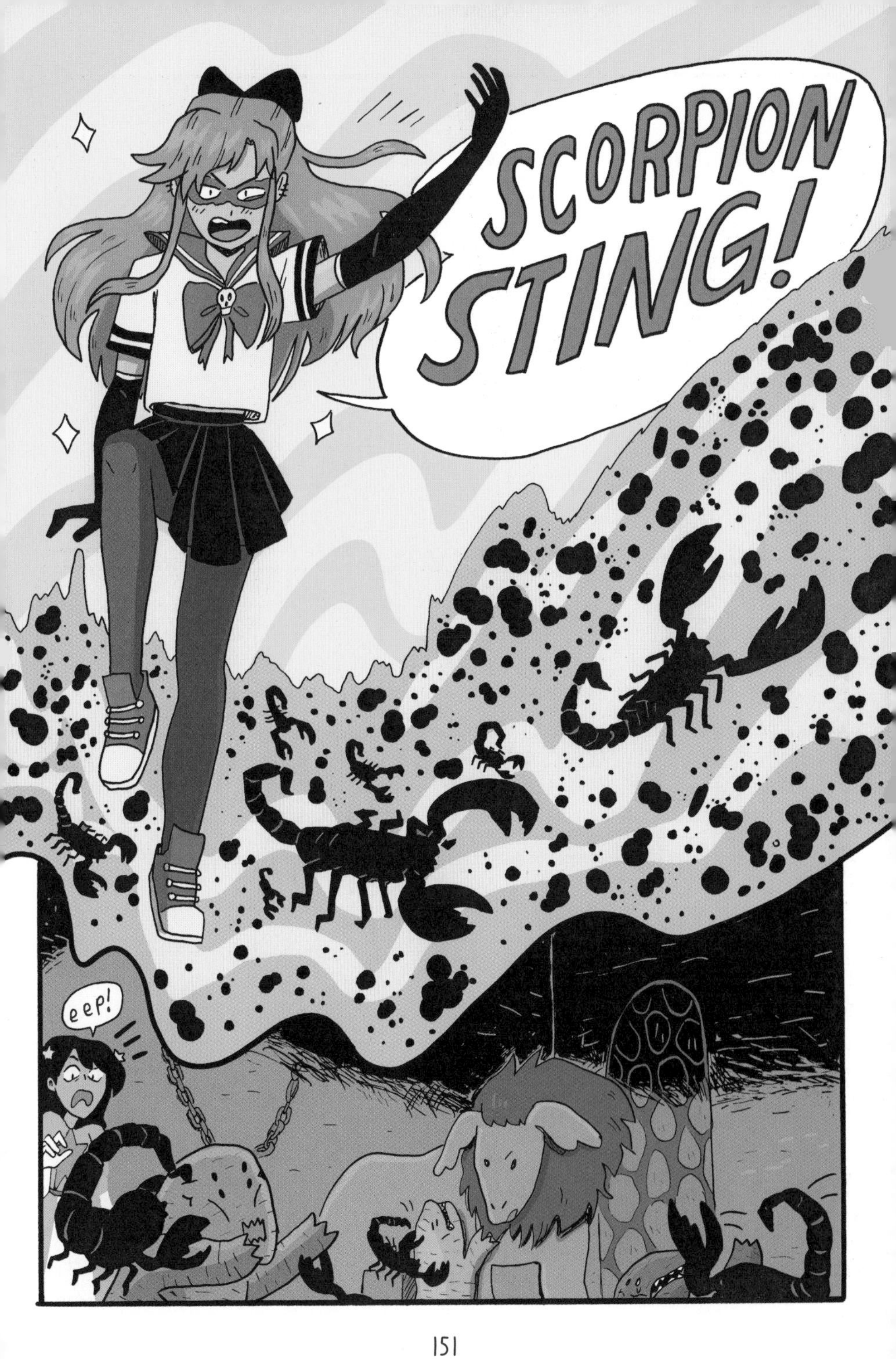
SCORPION STING!
eep!

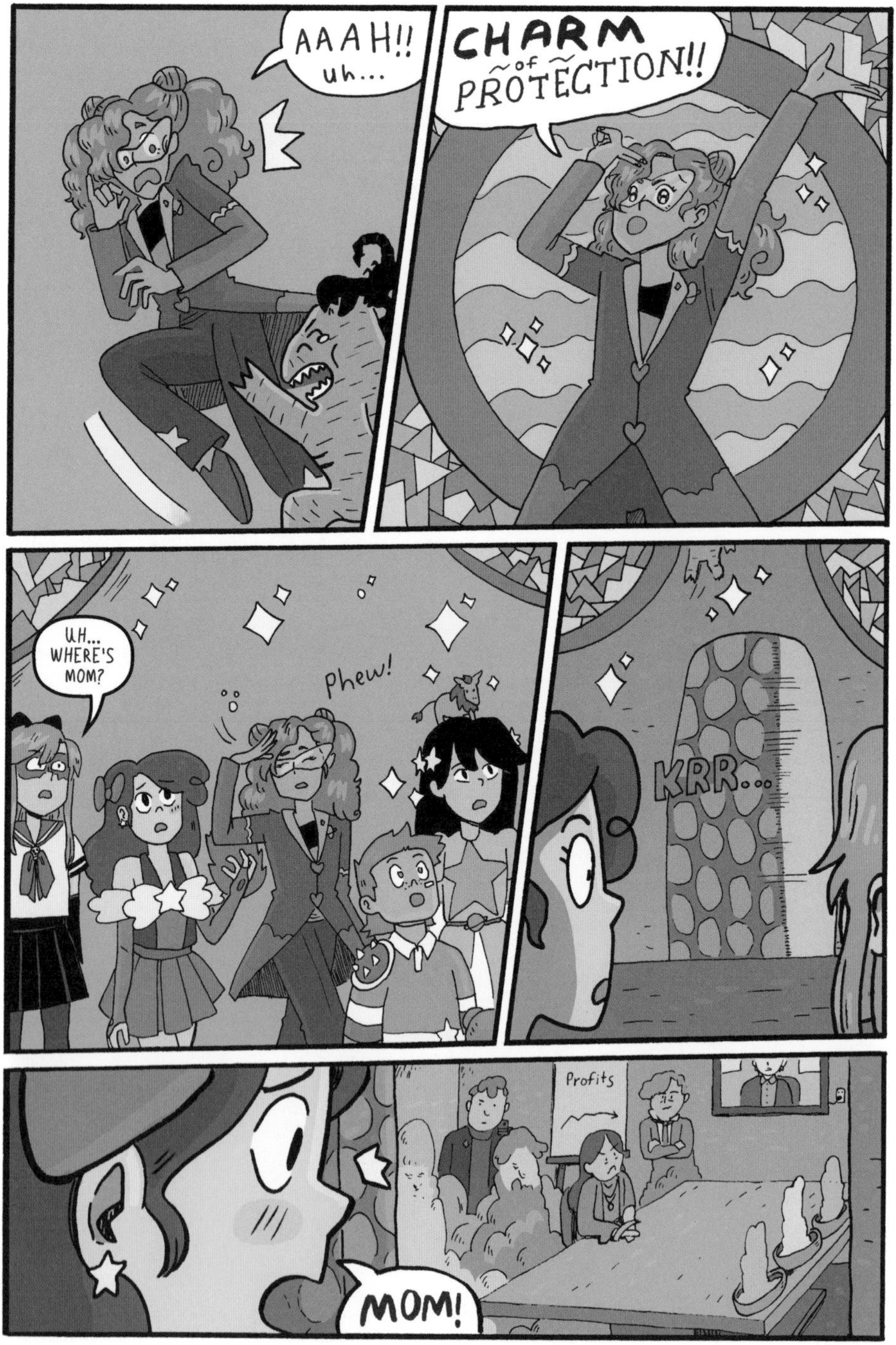
AAAH!!
uh...
CHARM of PROTECTION!!
UH... WHERE'S MOM?
Phew!
KRR...
Profits
MOM!

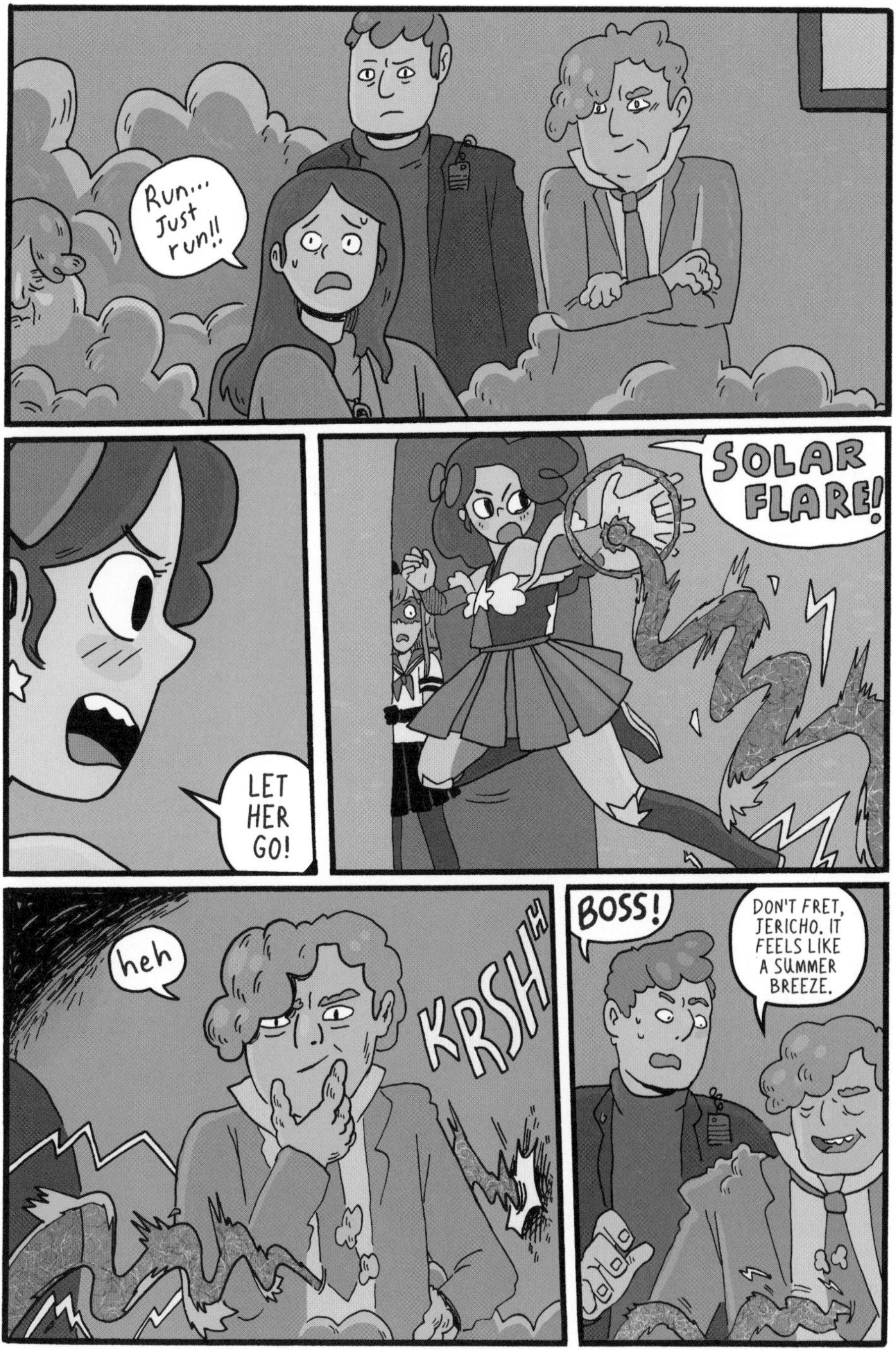
Run... Just run!!
LET HER GO!
SOLAR FLARE!
heh
KRSH^H
BOSS!
DON'T FRET, JERICHO. IT FEELS LIKE A SUMMER BREEZE.

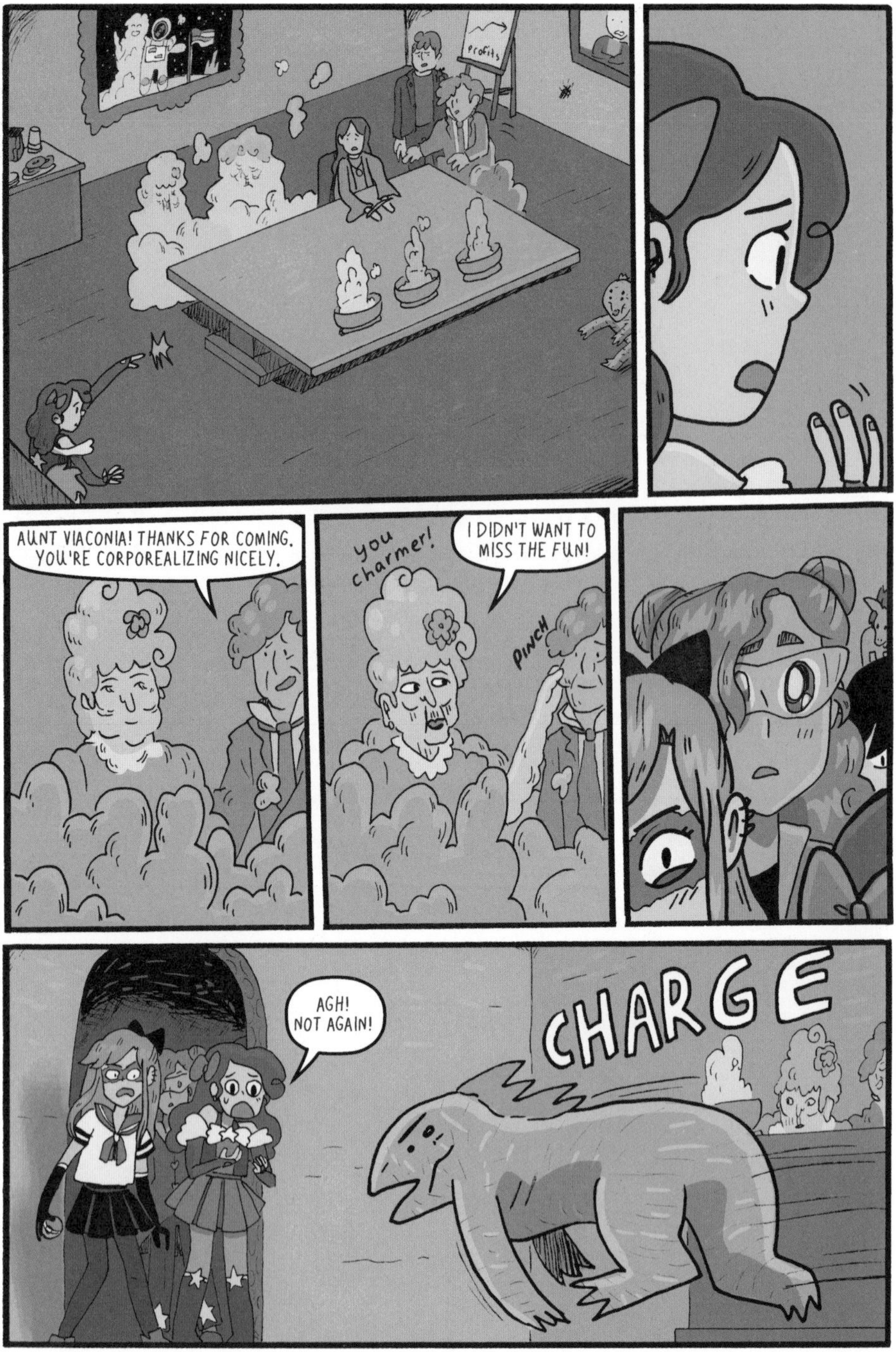
profits
AUNT VIACONIA! THANKS FOR COMING. YOU'RE CORPOREALIZING NICELY.
you charmer!
I DIDN'T WANT TO MISS THE FUN!
PINCH
AGH! NOT AGAIN!
CHARGE

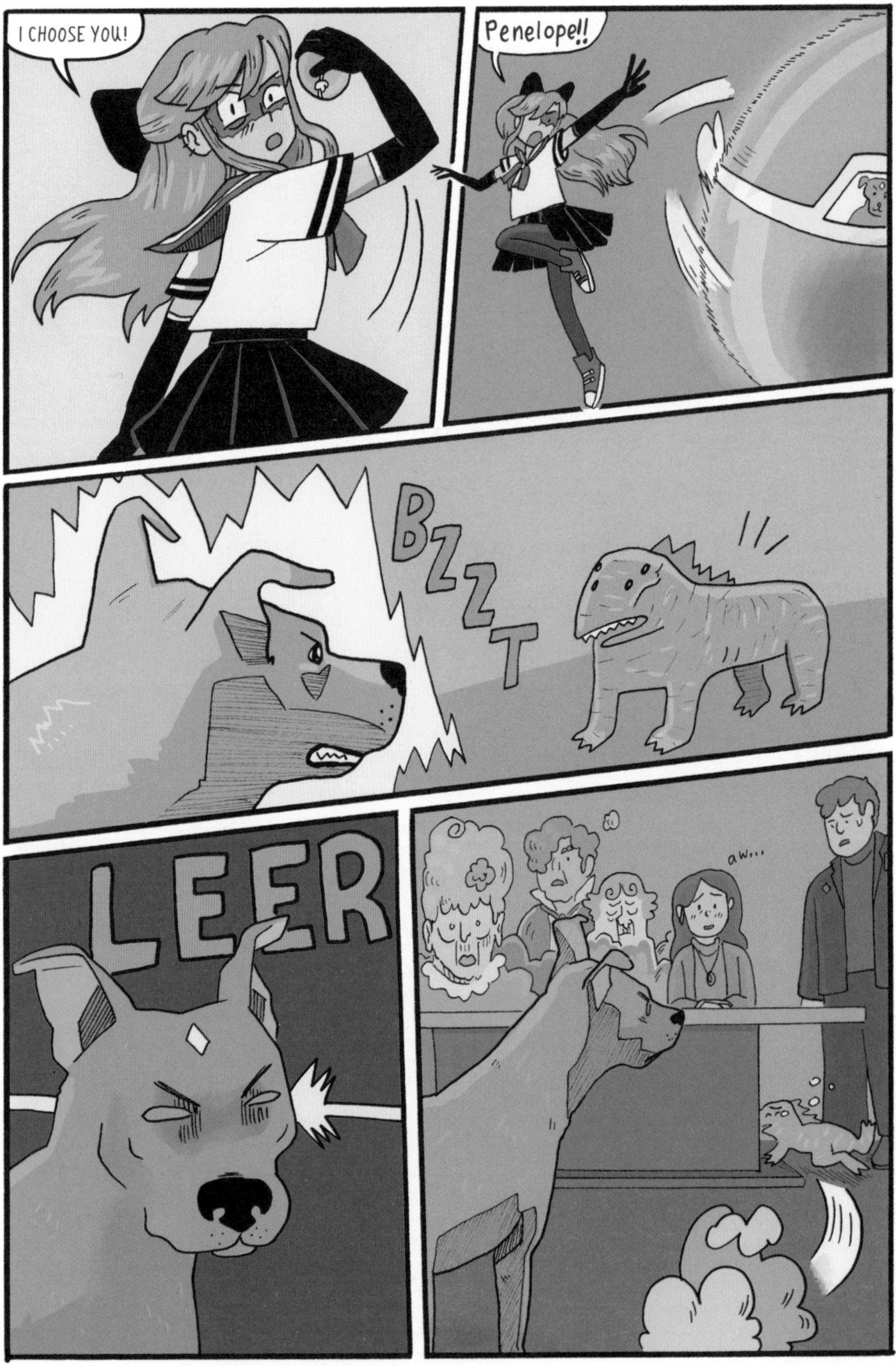

I CHOOSE YOU!
Penelope!!
BZZT
LEER
aw...

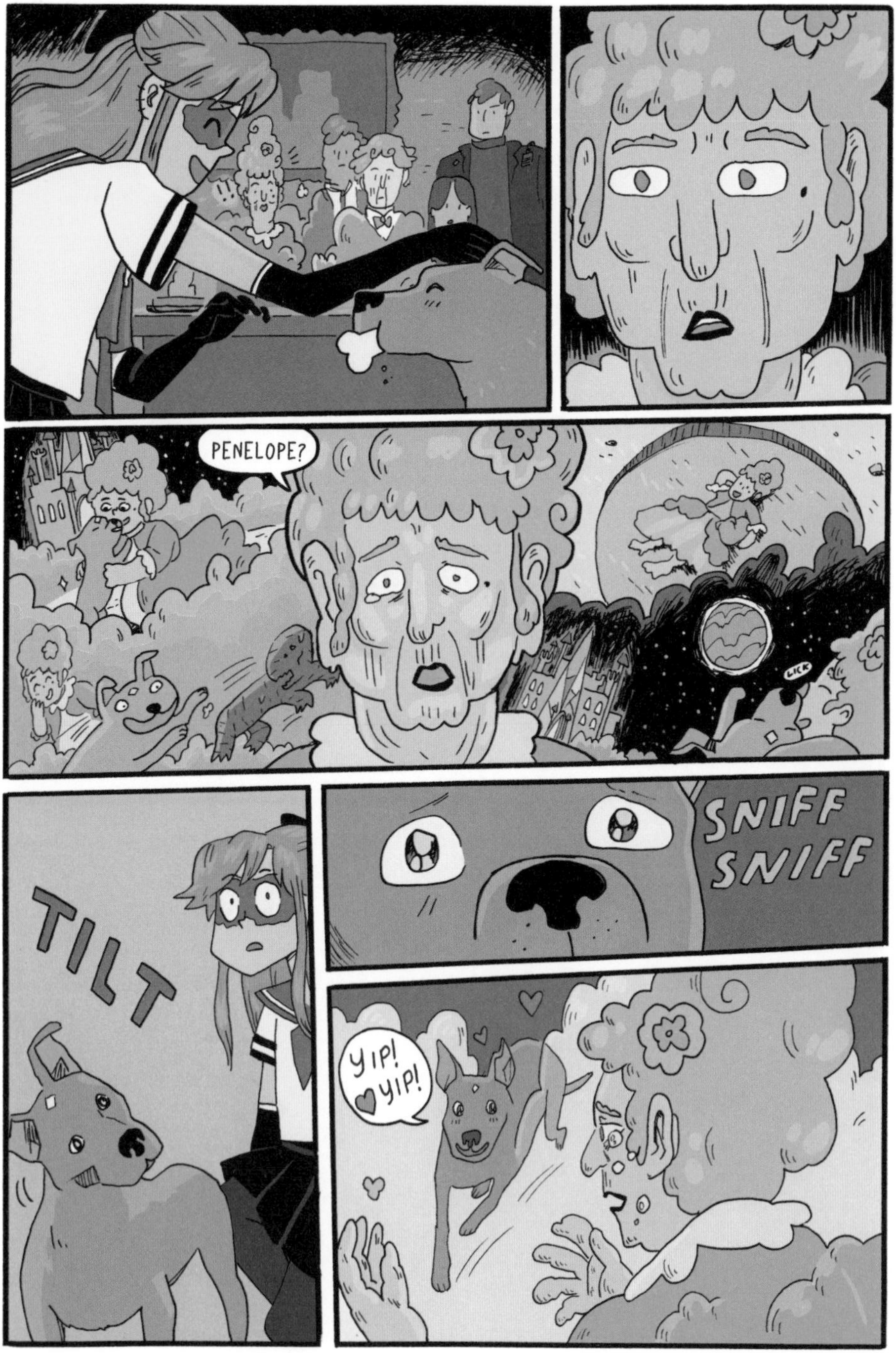
PENELOPE?
LICK
SNIFF SNIFF
TILT
YIP! YIP!

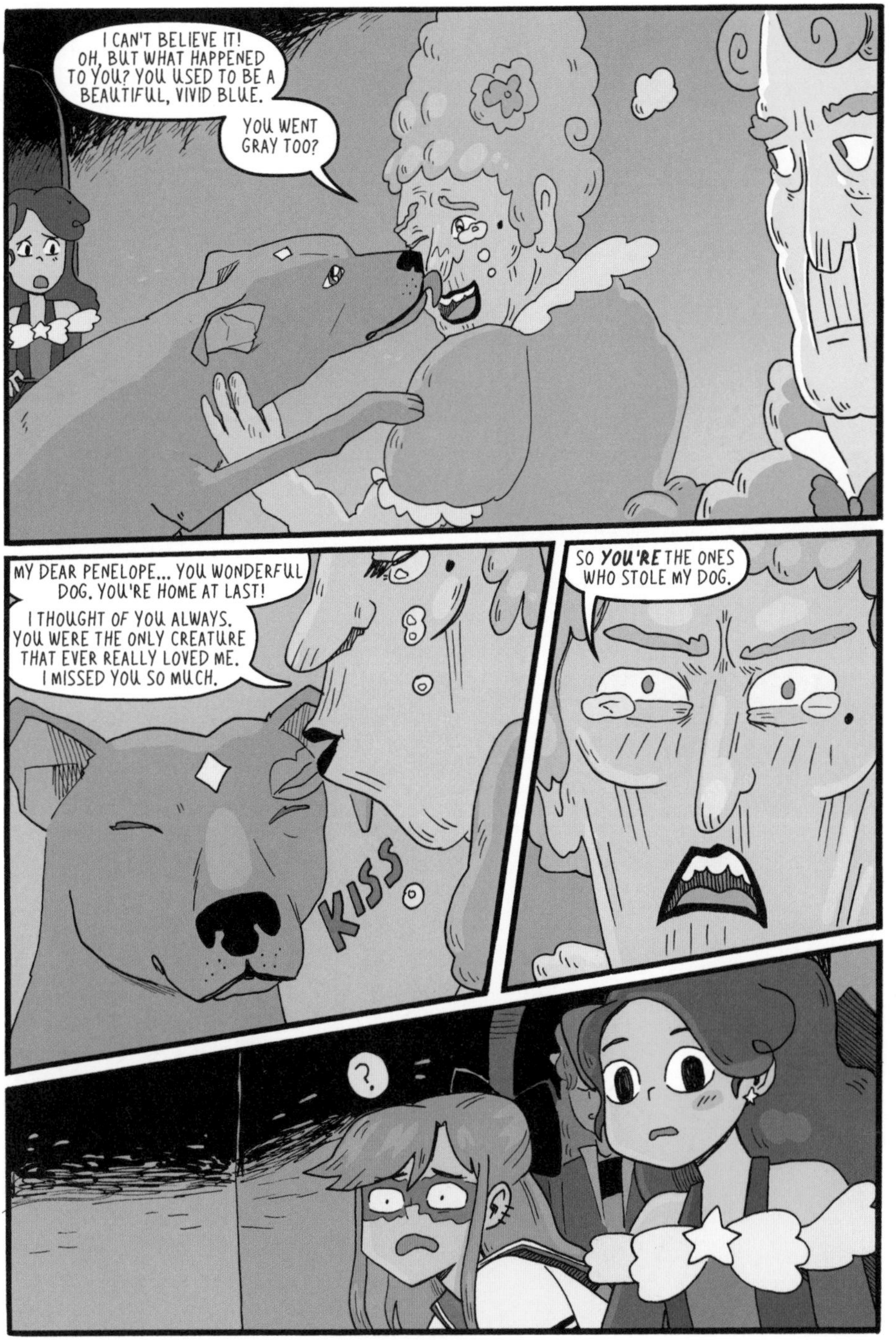
I CAN'T BELIEVE IT! OH, BUT WHAT HAPPENED TO YOU? YOU USED TO BE A BEAUTIFUL, VIVID BLUE.
YOU WENT GRAY TOO?
MY DEAR PENELOPE... YOU WONDERFUL DOG. YOU'RE HOME AT LAST!
I THOUGHT OF YOU ALWAYS. YOU WERE THE ONLY CREATURE THAT EVER REALLY LOVED ME. I MISSED YOU SO MUCH.
KISS
SO **YOU'RE** THE ONES WHO STOLE MY DOG.
?

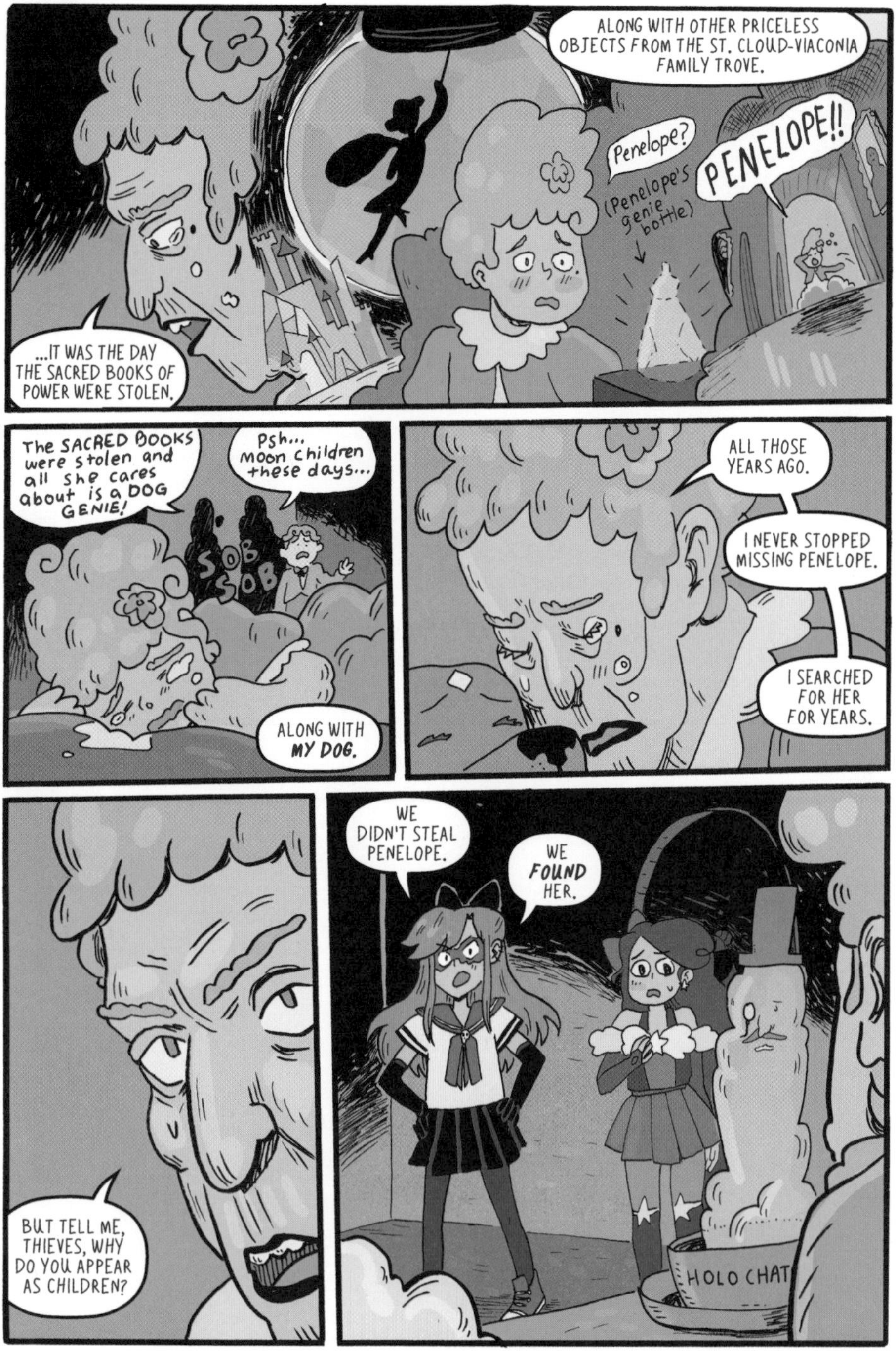
ALONG WITH OTHER PRICELESS OBJECTS FROM THE ST. CLOUD-VIACONIA FAMILY TROVE.
Penelope?
(Penelope's genie bottle)
PENELOPE!!
...IT WAS THE DAY THE SACRED BOOKS OF POWER WERE STOLEN.
The SACRED BOOKS were stolen and all she cares about is a DOG GENIE!
Psh... moon children these days...
SOB SOB
ALONG WITH **MY DOG.**
ALL THOSE YEARS AGO.
I NEVER STOPPED MISSING PENELOPE.
I SEARCHED FOR HER FOR YEARS.
BUT TELL ME, THIEVES, WHY DO YOU APPEAR AS CHILDREN?
WE DIDN'T STEAL PENELOPE.
WE **FOUND** HER.
HOLO CHAT

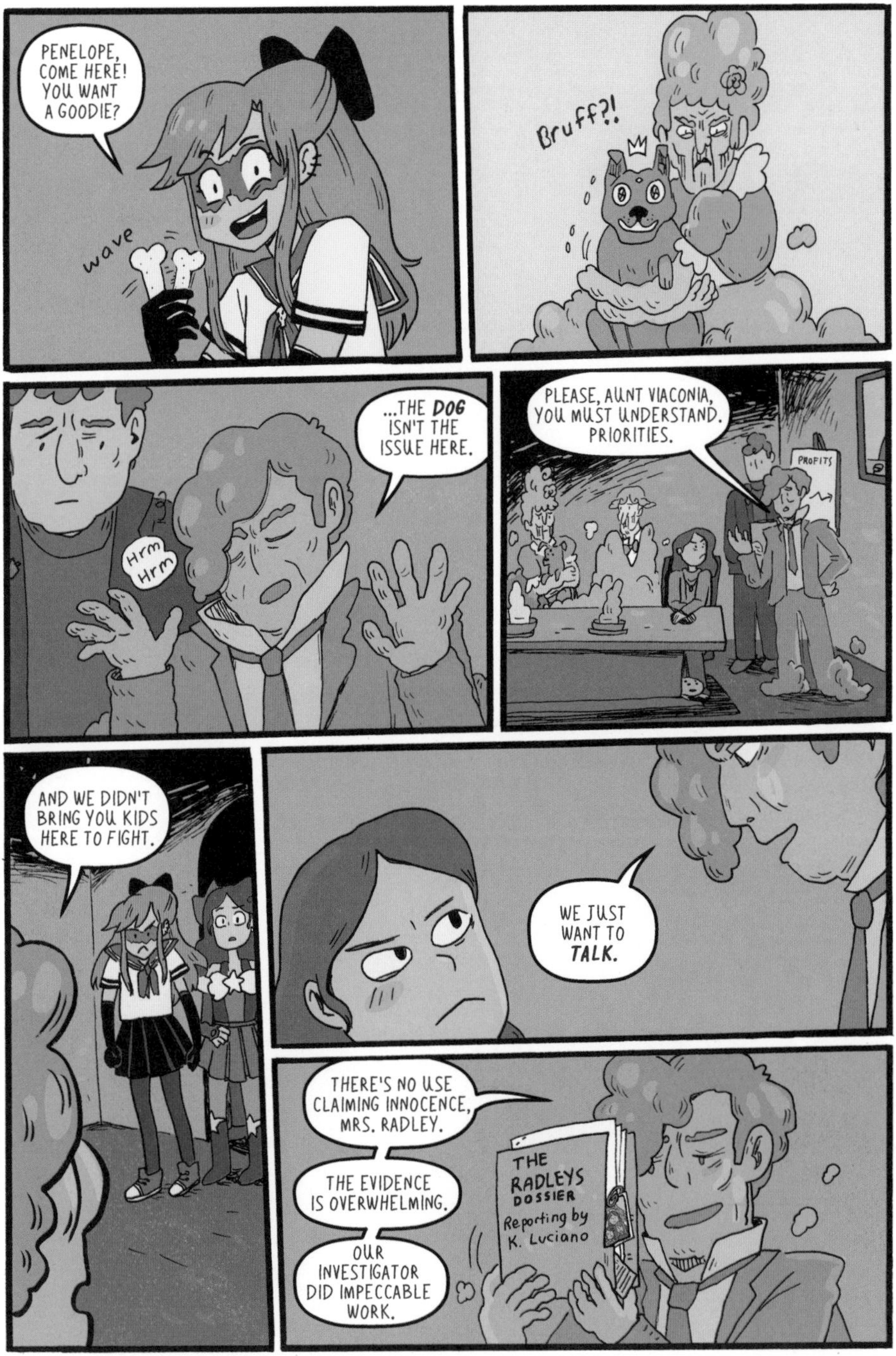
PENELOPE, COME HERE! YOU WANT A GOODIE?
wave
Bruff?!
...THE DOG ISN'T THE ISSUE HERE.
Hrm Hrm
PLEASE, AUNT VIACONIA, YOU MUST UNDERSTAND. PRIORITIES.
PROFITS
AND WE DIDN'T BRING YOU KIDS HERE TO FIGHT.
WE JUST WANT TO TALK.
THERE'S NO USE CLAIMING INNOCENCE, MRS. RADLEY.
THE EVIDENCE IS OVERWHELMING.
OUR INVESTIGATOR DID IMPECCABLE WORK.
THE RADLEYS DOSSIER
Reporting by K. Luciano

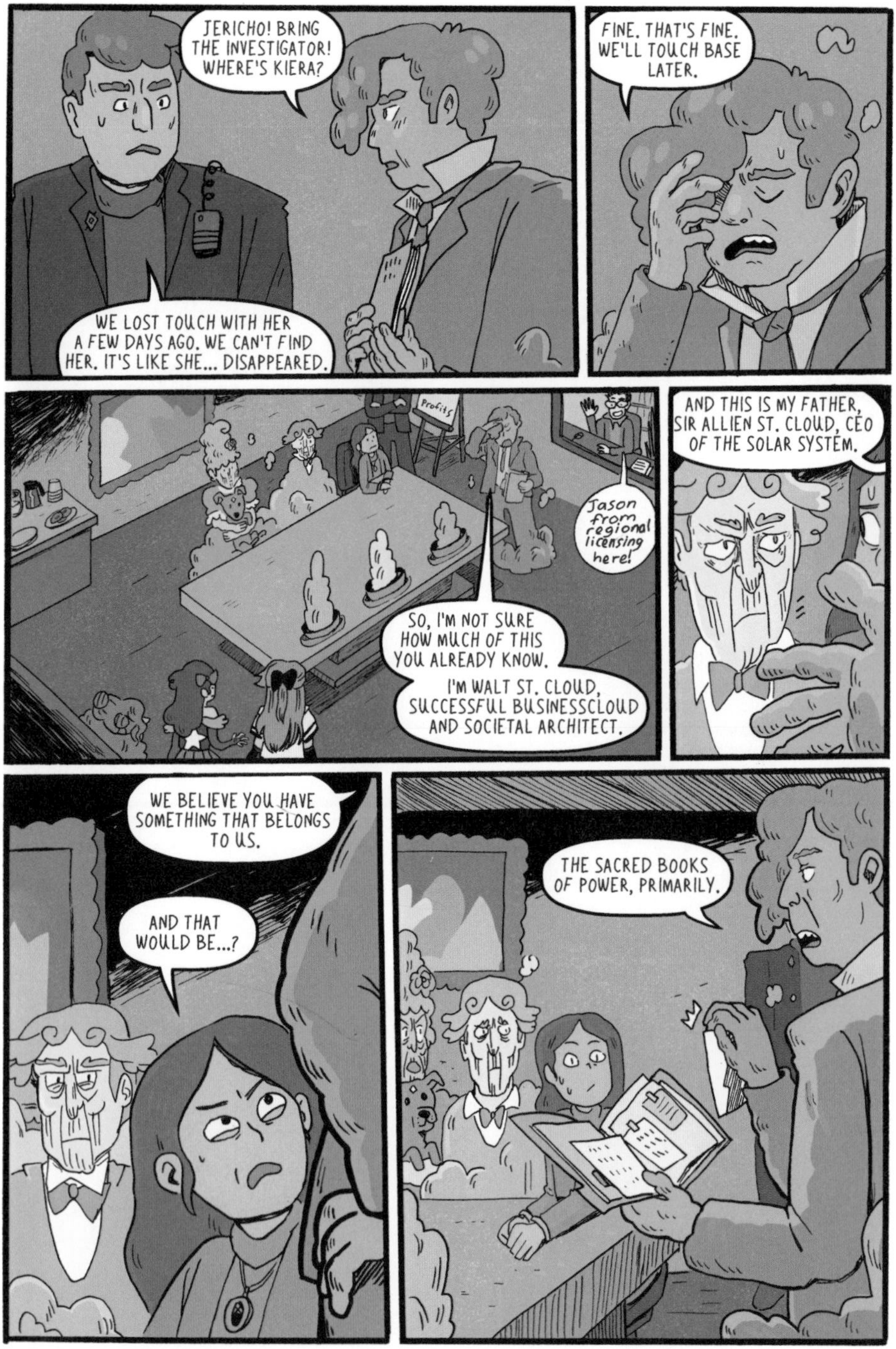
JERICHO! BRING THE INVESTIGATOR! WHERE'S KIERA?
WE LOST TOUCH WITH HER A FEW DAYS AGO. WE CAN'T FIND HER. IT'S LIKE SHE... DISAPPEARED.
FINE. THAT'S FINE. WE'LL TOUCH BASE LATER.
Profits
Jason from regional licensing here!
SO, I'M NOT SURE HOW MUCH OF THIS YOU ALREADY KNOW.
I'M WALT ST. CLOUD, SUCCESSFUL BUSINESSCLOUD AND SOCIETAL ARCHITECT.
AND THIS IS MY FATHER, SIR ALLIEN ST. CLOUD, CEO OF THE SOLAR SYSTEM.
WE BELIEVE YOU HAVE SOMETHING THAT BELONGS TO US.
AND THAT WOULD BE...?
THE SACRED BOOKS OF POWER, PRIMARILY.

I DON'T KNOW WHAT YOU'RE TALKING ABOUT. LET MY KIDS GO, AND THEN WE CAN TALK.

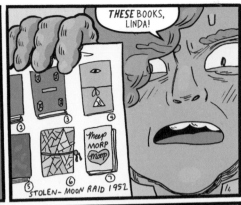

THESE BOOKS, LINDA!

STOLEN- MOON RAID 1952

WE'RE KEEPING THINGS CIVIL HERE. WE DON'T STRICTLY HAVE TO.

NOW, WHERE DID YOU HAPPEN TO ACQUIRE THESE SACRED BOOKS OF POWER?

LOOM

CHOOSE YOUR WORDS WISELY, EARTH WOMAN. THE SURVIVAL OF YOUR PLANET, AND OTHERS, HANGS IN THE BALANCE.

MY AUNT ELMA DIED EARLIER THIS YEAR. I INHERITED HER BELONGINGS, INCLUDING SOME ITEMS THAT TURNED OUT TO BE MAGICAL. BUT MY KIDS AND THEIR *FRIENDS...* THEY HAVE NOTHING TO DO WITH IT.

gasp!

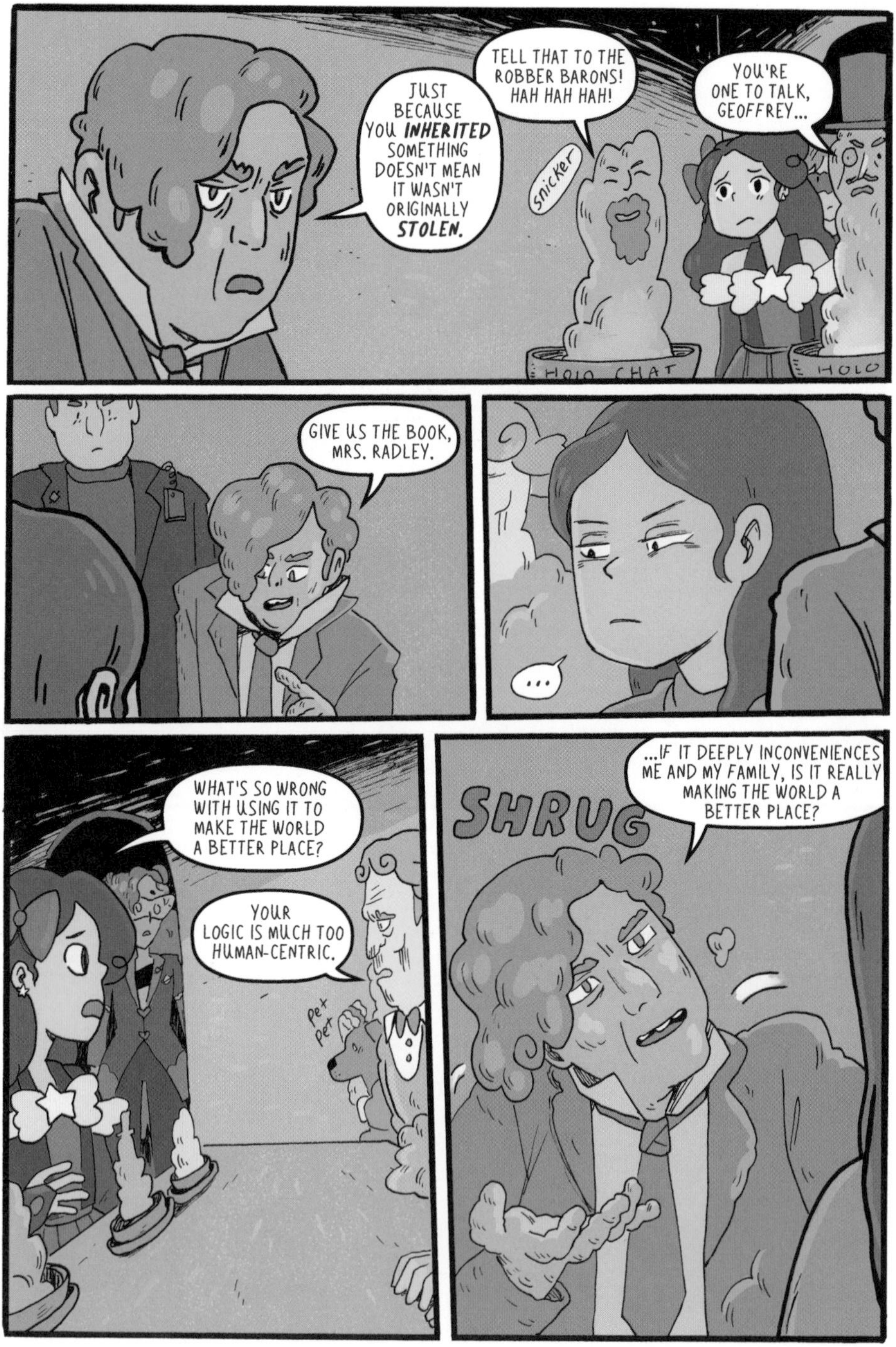
JUST BECAUSE YOU **INHERITED** SOMETHING DOESN'T MEAN IT WASN'T ORIGINALLY **STOLEN.**
TELL THAT TO THE ROBBER BARONS! HAH HAH HAH!
snicker
YOU'RE ONE TO TALK, GEOFFREY...
HOLO CHAT
HOLO
GIVE US THE BOOK, MRS. RADLEY.
...
WHAT'S SO WRONG WITH USING IT TO MAKE THE WORLD A BETTER PLACE?
YOUR LOGIC IS MUCH TOO HUMAN-CENTRIC.
pet pet
SHRUG
...IF IT DEEPLY INCONVENIENCES ME AND MY FAMILY, IS IT REALLY MAKING THE WORLD A BETTER PLACE?

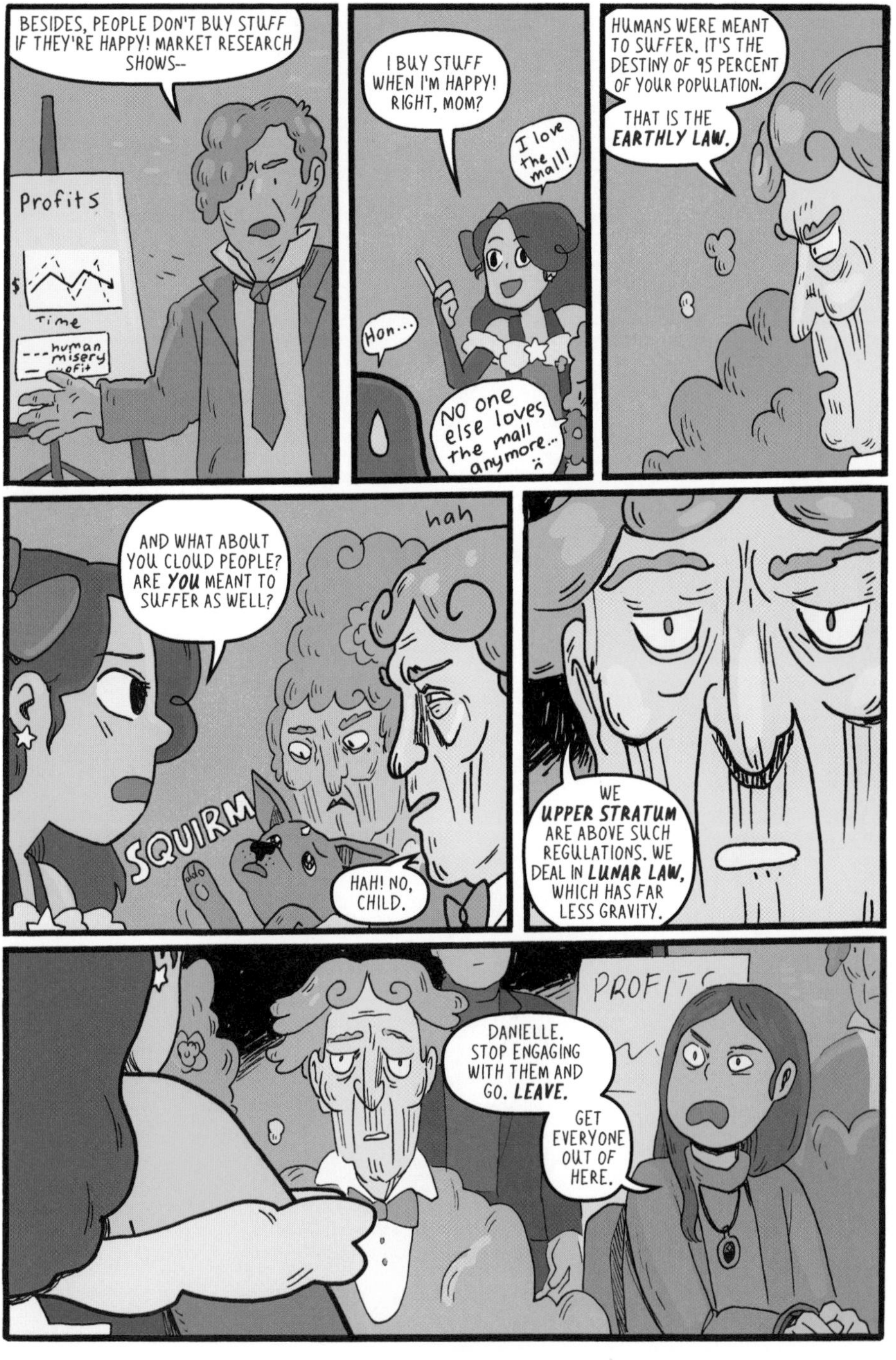
BESIDES, PEOPLE DON'T BUY STUFF IF THEY'RE HAPPY! MARKET RESEARCH SHOWS--
Profits
$
Time
human misery
profit
I BUY STUFF WHEN I'M HAPPY! RIGHT, MOM?
I love the mall!
Hon...
No one else loves the mall anymore...
HUMANS WERE MEANT TO SUFFER. IT'S THE DESTINY OF 95 PERCENT OF YOUR POPULATION.
THAT IS THE **EARTHLY LAW.**
hah
AND WHAT ABOUT YOU CLOUD PEOPLE? ARE **YOU** MEANT TO SUFFER AS WELL?
SQUIRM
HAH! NO, CHILD.
WE **UPPER STRATUM** ARE ABOVE SUCH REGULATIONS. WE DEAL IN **LUNAR LAW,** WHICH HAS FAR LESS GRAVITY.
PROFITS
DANIELLE. STOP ENGAGING WITH THEM AND GO. **LEAVE.**
GET EVERYONE OUT OF HERE.

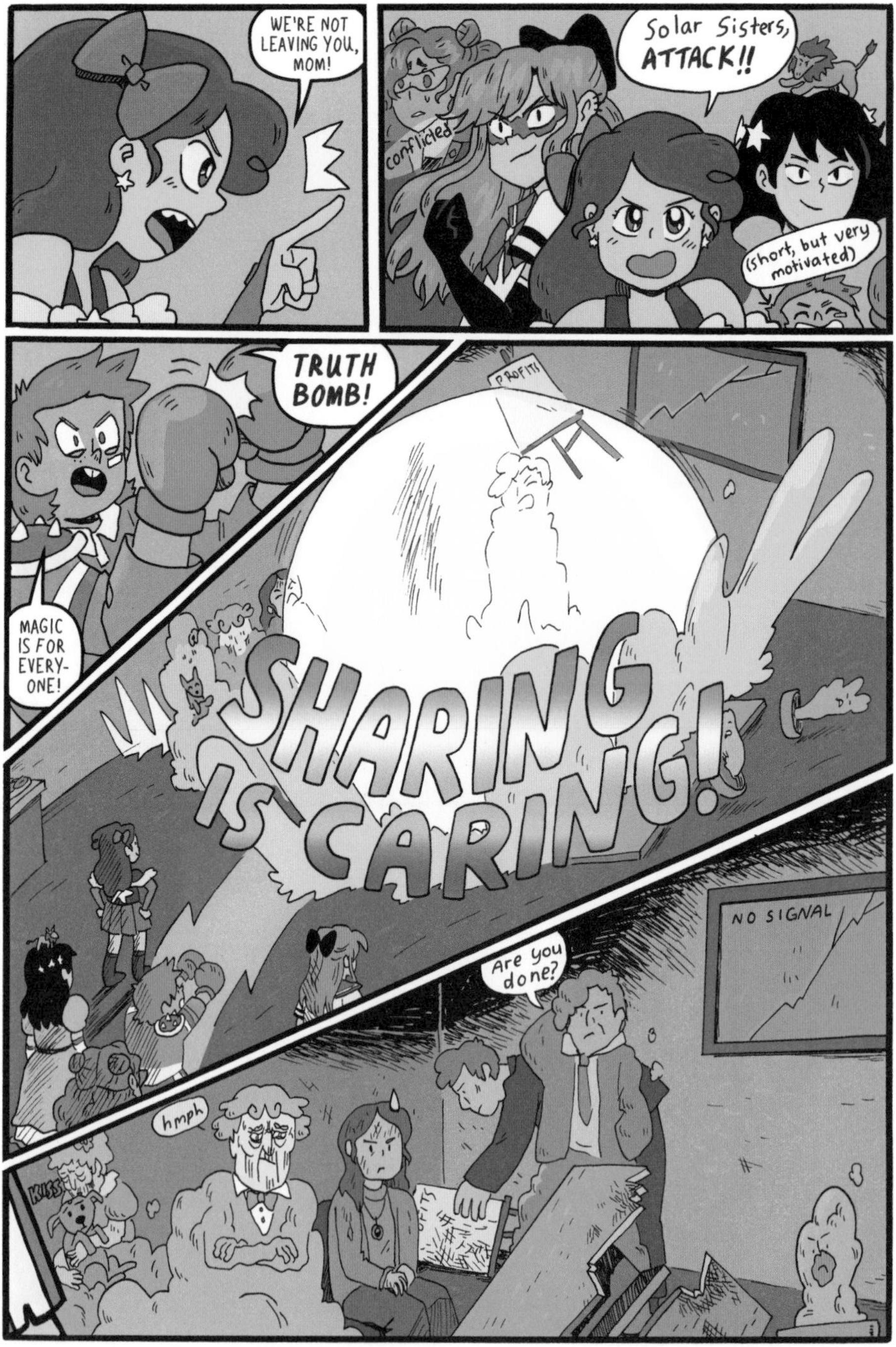
WE'RE NOT LEAVING YOU, MOM!
Solar Sisters, ATTACK!!
conflicted
(short, but very motivated)
TRUTH BOMB!
MAGIC IS FOR EVERY-ONE!
PROFITS
SHARING IS CARING!
NO SIGNAL
Are you done?
hmph
KISS

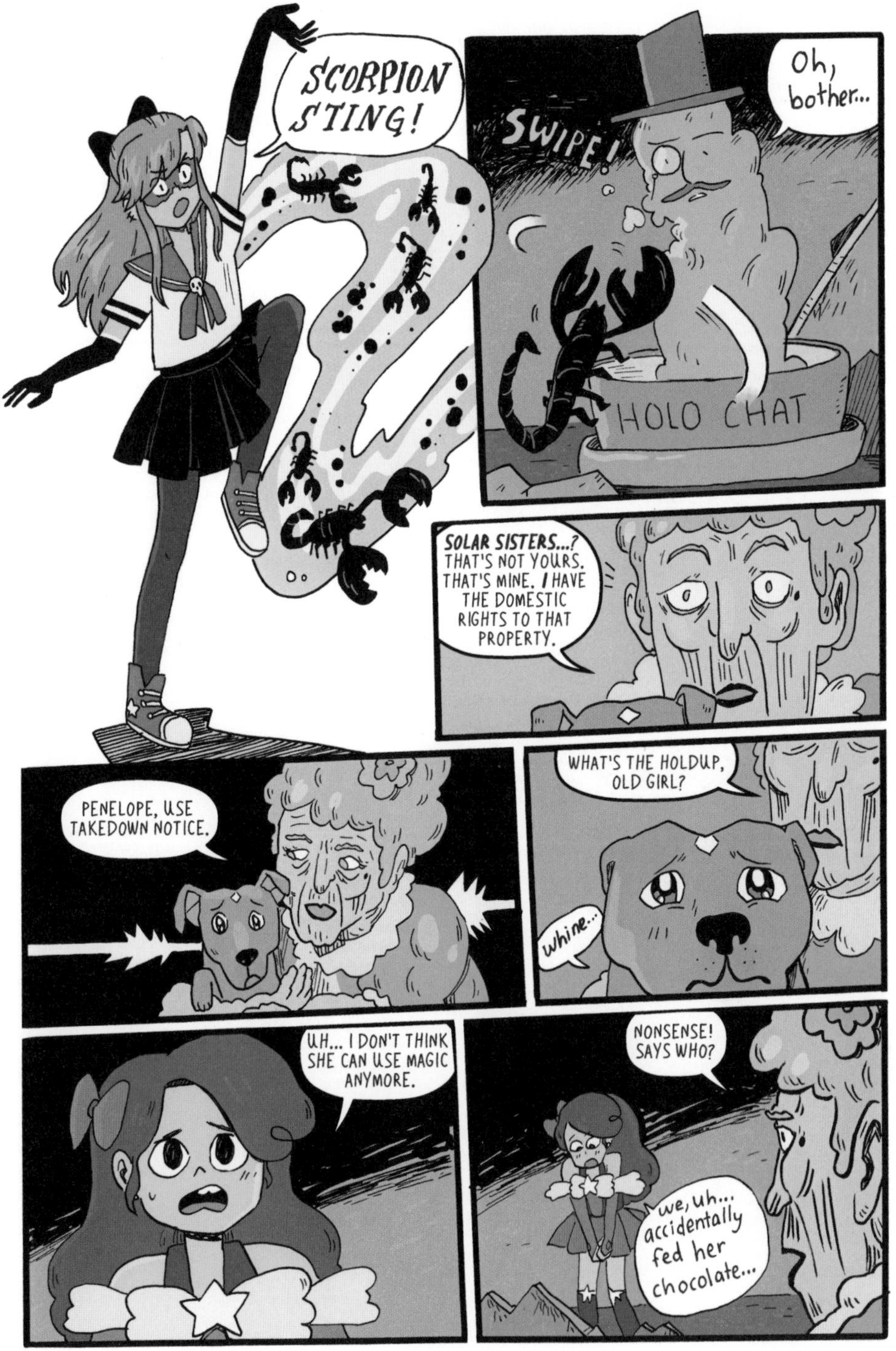
SCORPION STING!
SWIPE!
Oh, bother...
HOLO CHAT
SOLAR SISTERS...? THAT'S NOT YOURS. THAT'S MINE. I HAVE THE DOMESTIC RIGHTS TO THAT PROPERTY.
PENELOPE, USE TAKEDOWN NOTICE.
WHAT'S THE HOLDUP, OLD GIRL?
whine...
UH... I DON'T THINK SHE CAN USE MAGIC ANYMORE.
NONSENSE! SAYS WHO?
we, uh... accidentally fed her chocolate...

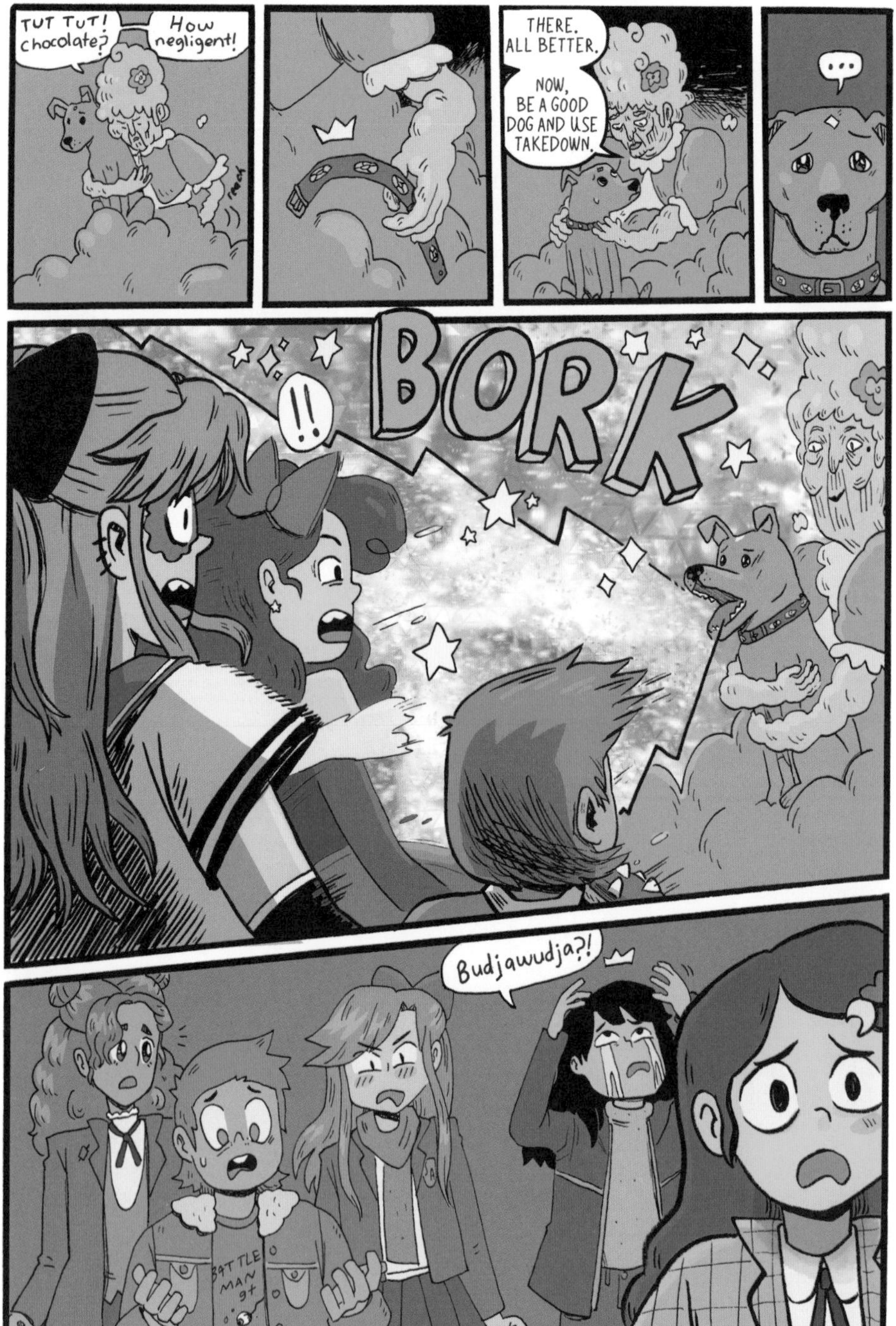
TUT TUT! chocolate?
How negligent!
THERE. ALL BETTER.
NOW, BE A GOOD DOG AND USE TAKEDOWN.
...
BORK
!!
Budjawudja?!
BATTLE MAN 9+

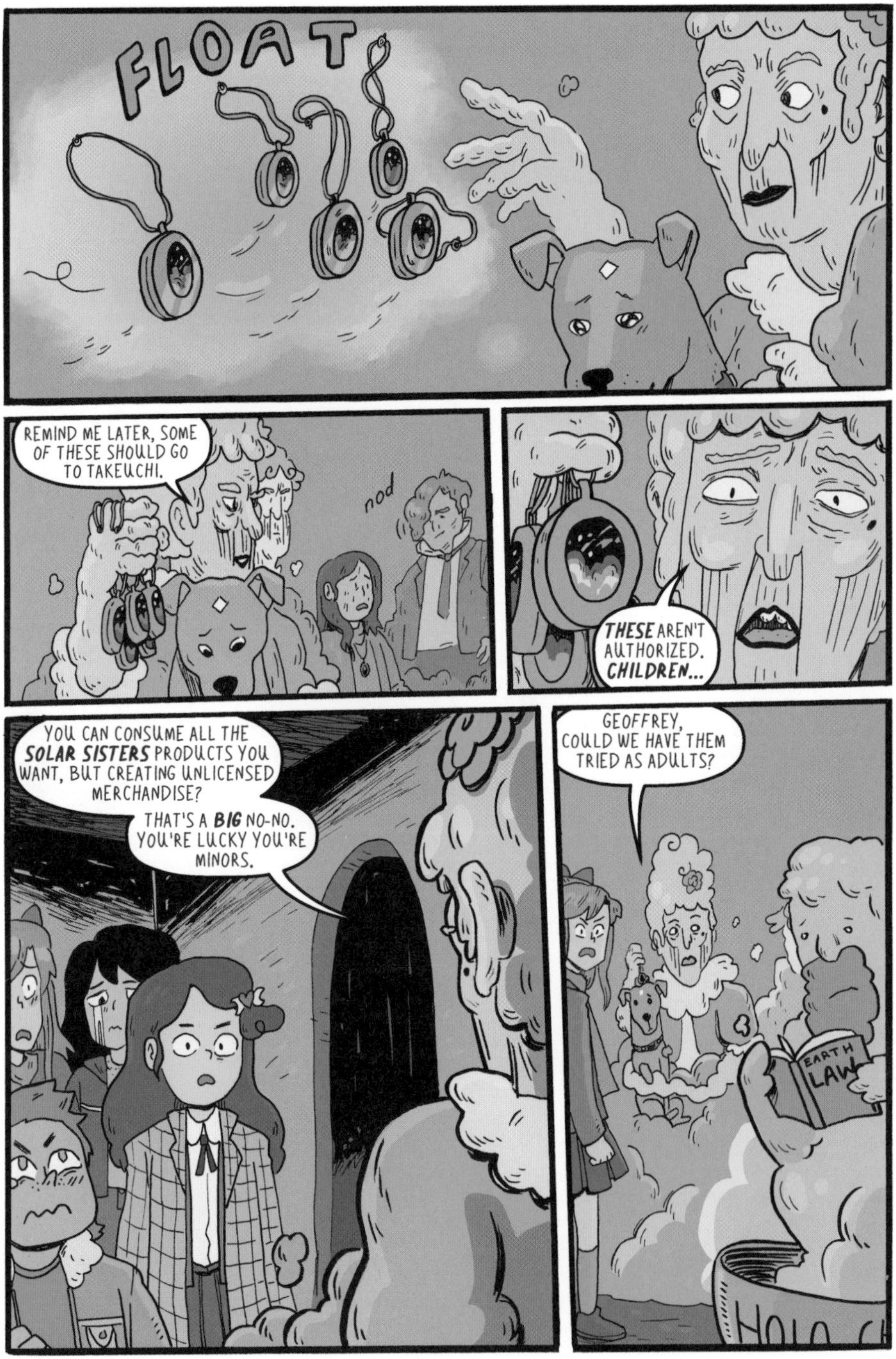
FLOAT
REMIND ME LATER, SOME OF THESE SHOULD GO TO TAKEUCHI.
nod
THESE AREN'T AUTHORIZED. CHILDREN...
YOU CAN CONSUME ALL THE SOLAR SISTERS PRODUCTS YOU WANT, BUT CREATING UNLICENSED MERCHANDISE?
THAT'S A BIG NO-NO. YOU'RE LUCKY YOU'RE MINORS.
GEOFFREY, COULD WE HAVE THEM TRIED AS ADULTS?
EARTH LAW

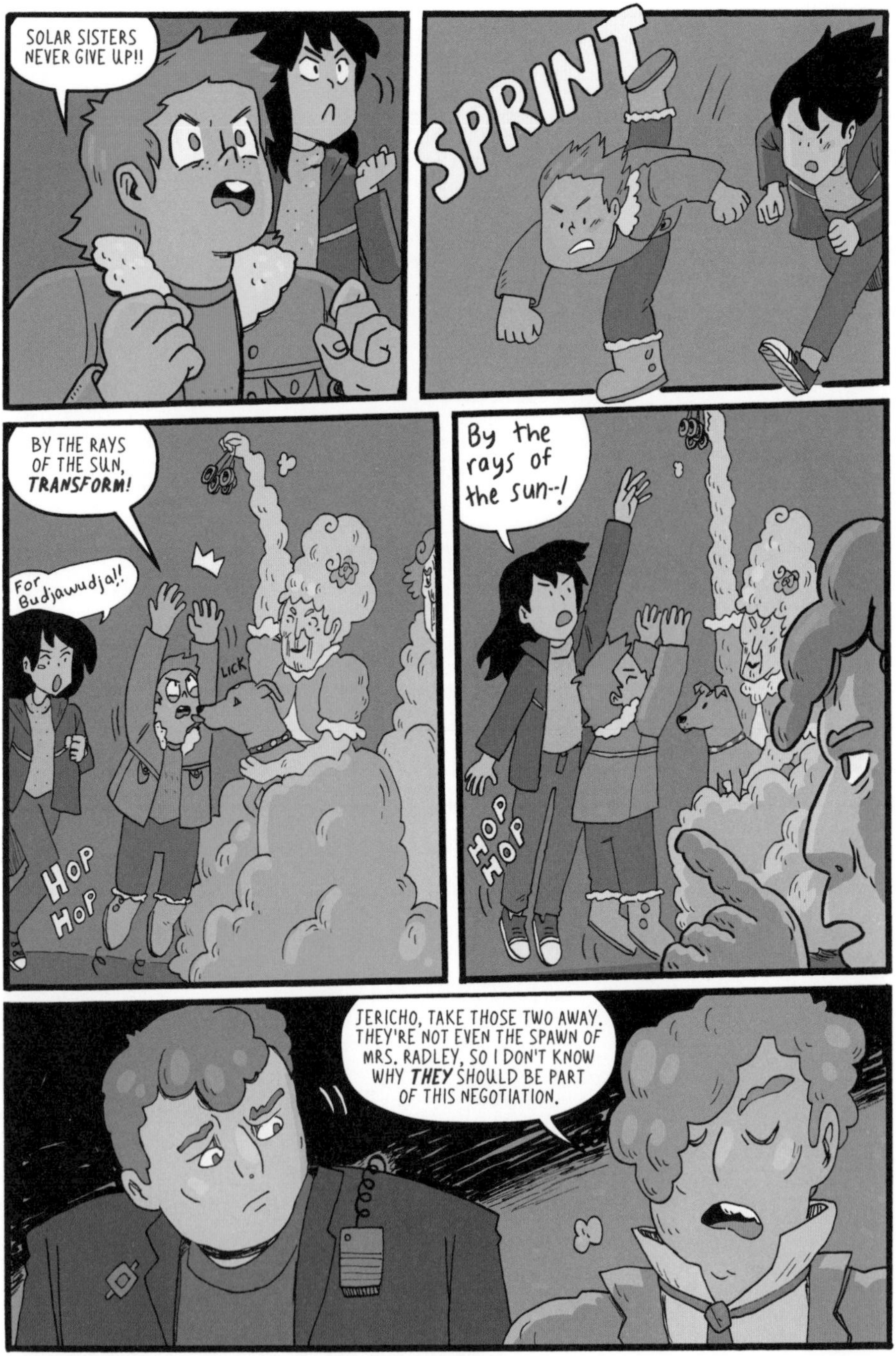
SOLAR SISTERS NEVER GIVE UP!!
SPRINT
BY THE RAYS OF THE SUN, TRANSFORM!
For Budjawudja!!
LICK
HOP HOP
By the rays of the sun--!
HOP HOP
JERICHO, TAKE THOSE TWO AWAY. THEY'RE NOT EVEN THE SPAWN OF MRS. RADLEY, SO I DON'T KNOW WHY THEY SHOULD BE PART OF THIS NEGOTIATION.

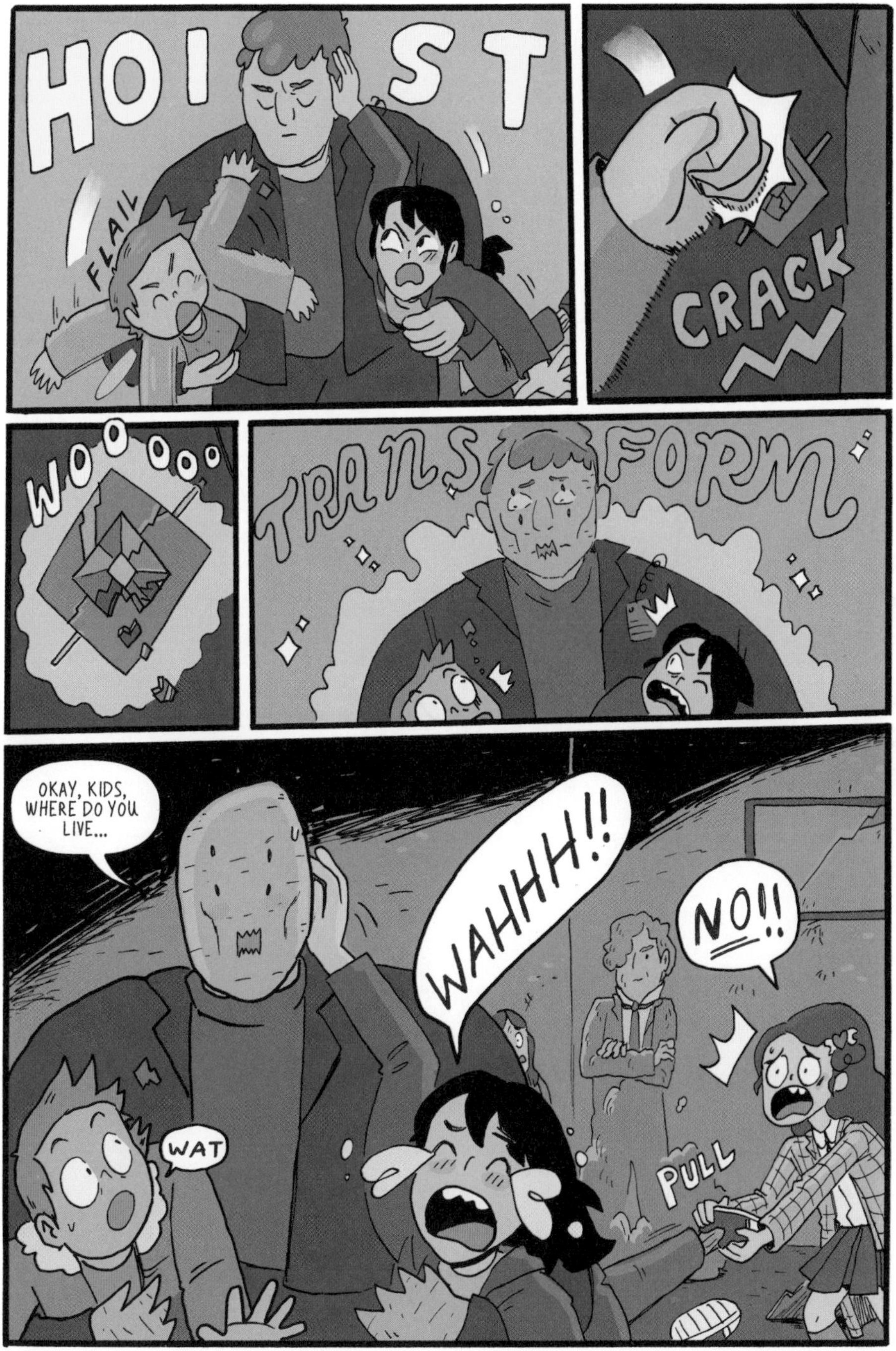
HOIST
FLAIL
CRACK
WOOOOO
TRANSFORM
OKAY, KIDS, WHERE DO YOU LIVE...
WAHHH!!
NO!!
WAT
PULL

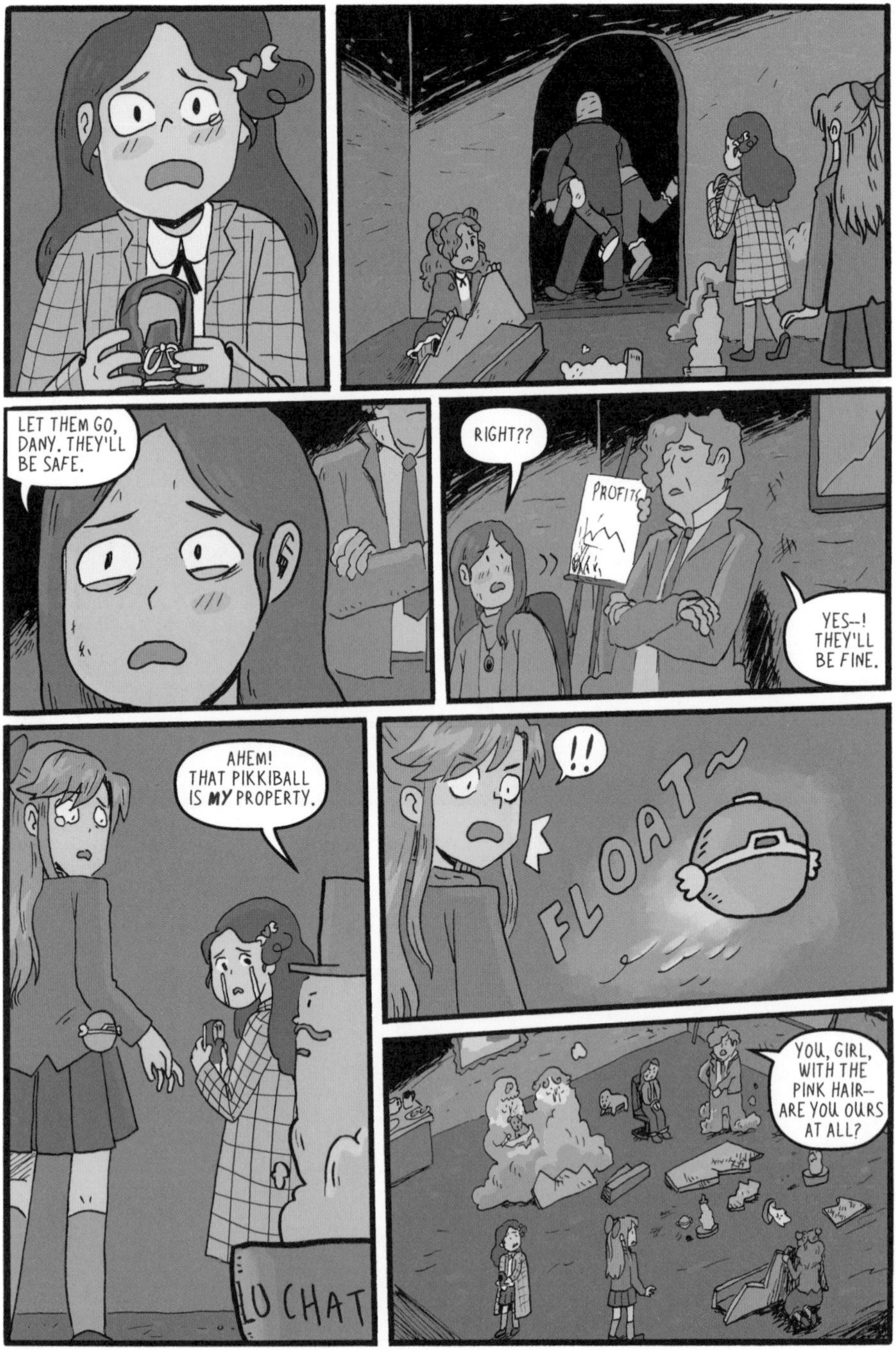
LET THEM GO, DANY. THEY'LL BE SAFE.
RIGHT??
PROFITS
YES--! THEY'LL BE FINE.
AHEM! THAT PIKKIBALL IS **MY** PROPERTY.
!!
FLOAT~
YOU, GIRL, WITH THE PINK HAIR-- ARE YOU OURS AT ALL?
LU CHAT

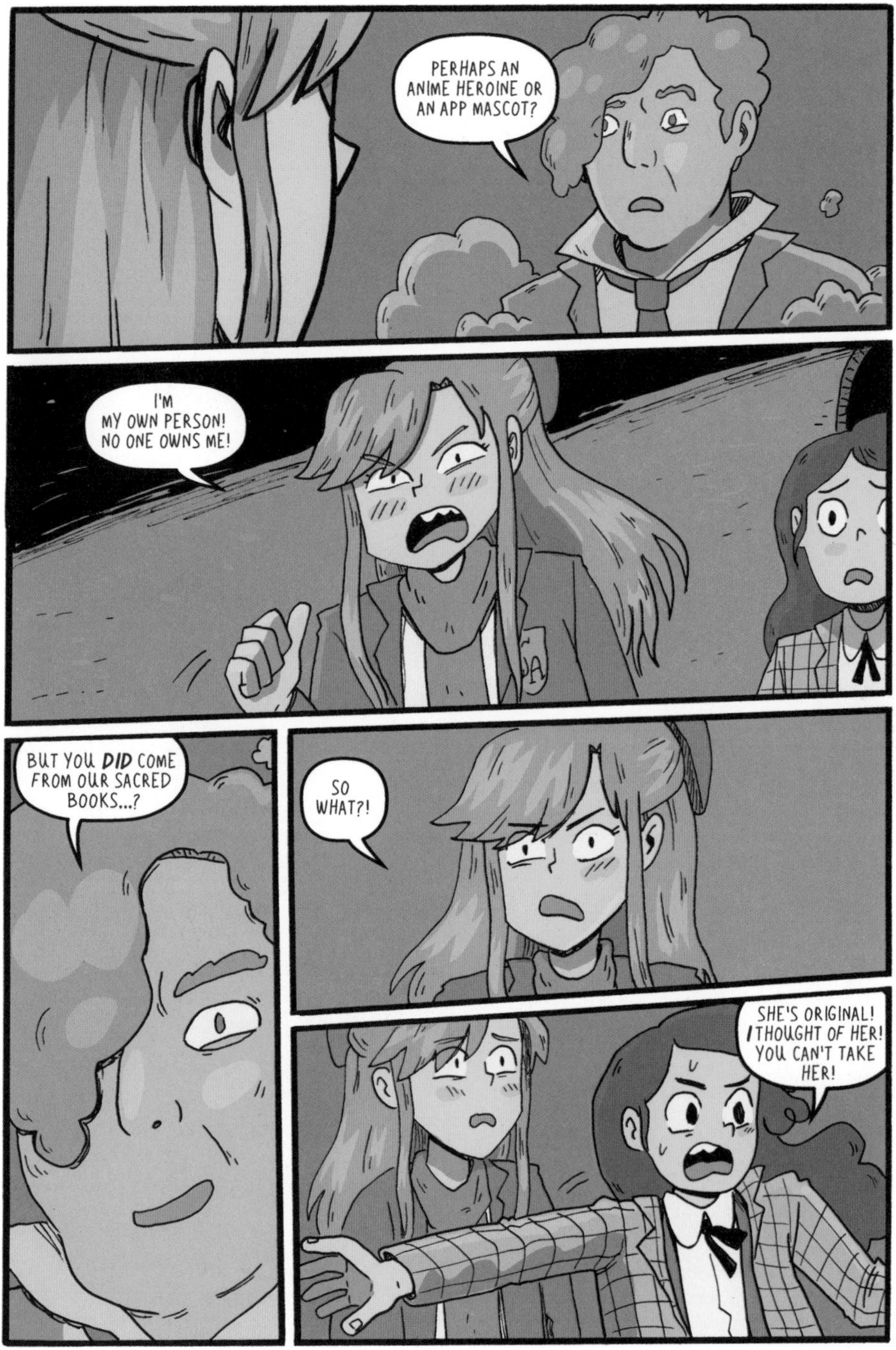
PERHAPS AN ANIME HEROINE OR AN APP MASCOT?
I'M MY OWN PERSON! NO ONE OWNS ME!
BUT YOU **DID** COME FROM OUR SACRED BOOKS...?
SO WHAT?!
SHE'S ORIGINAL! **I** THOUGHT OF HER! YOU CAN'T TAKE HER!

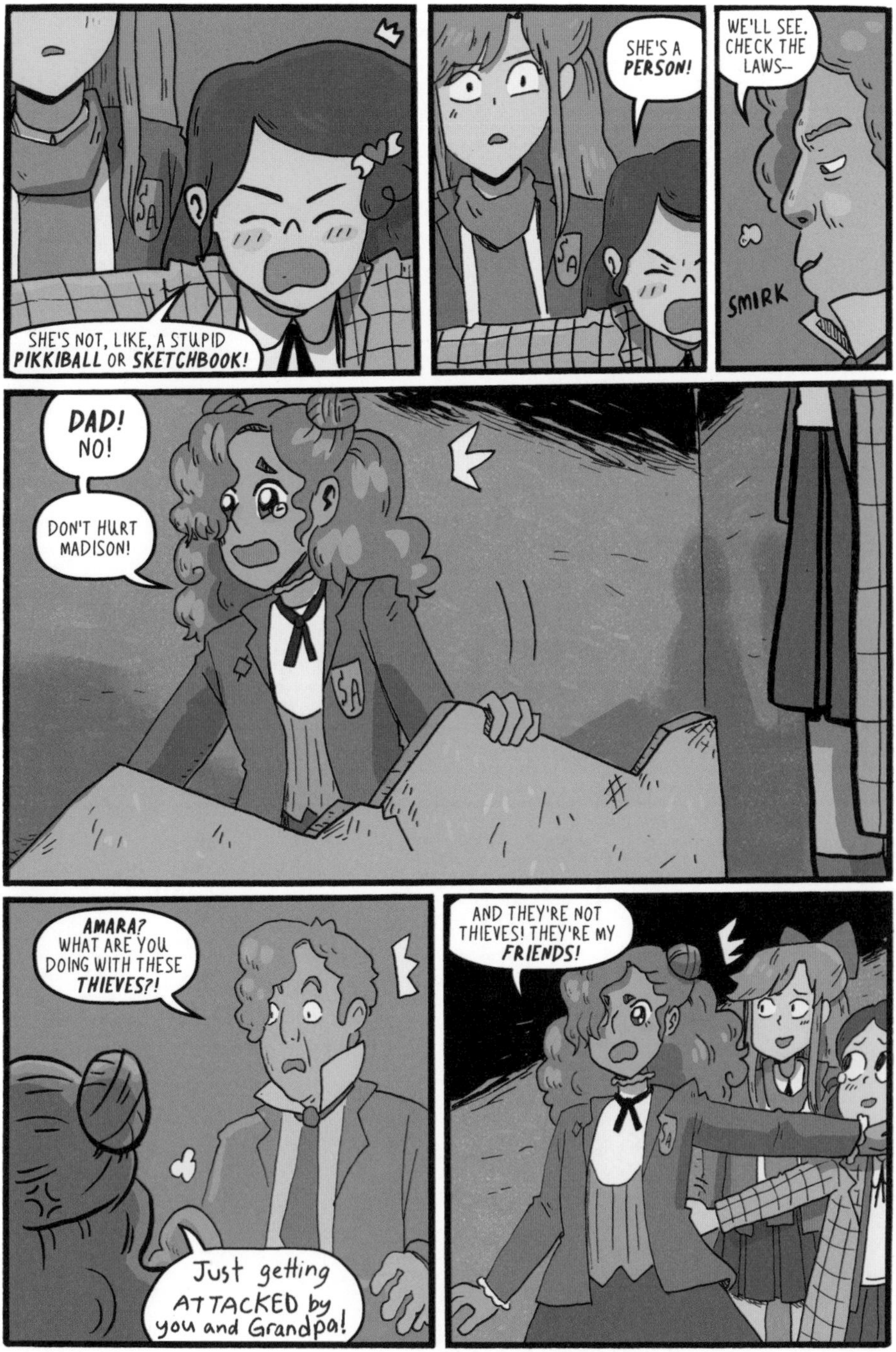
SHE'S NOT, LIKE, A STUPID PIKKIBALL OR SKETCHBOOK!
SHE'S A PERSON!
WE'LL SEE. CHECK THE LAWS--
SMIRK
DAD! NO!
DON'T HURT MADISON!
AMARA? WHAT ARE YOU DOING WITH THESE THIEVES?!
Just getting ATTACKED by you and Grandpa!
AND THEY'RE NOT THIEVES! THEY'RE MY FRIENDS!

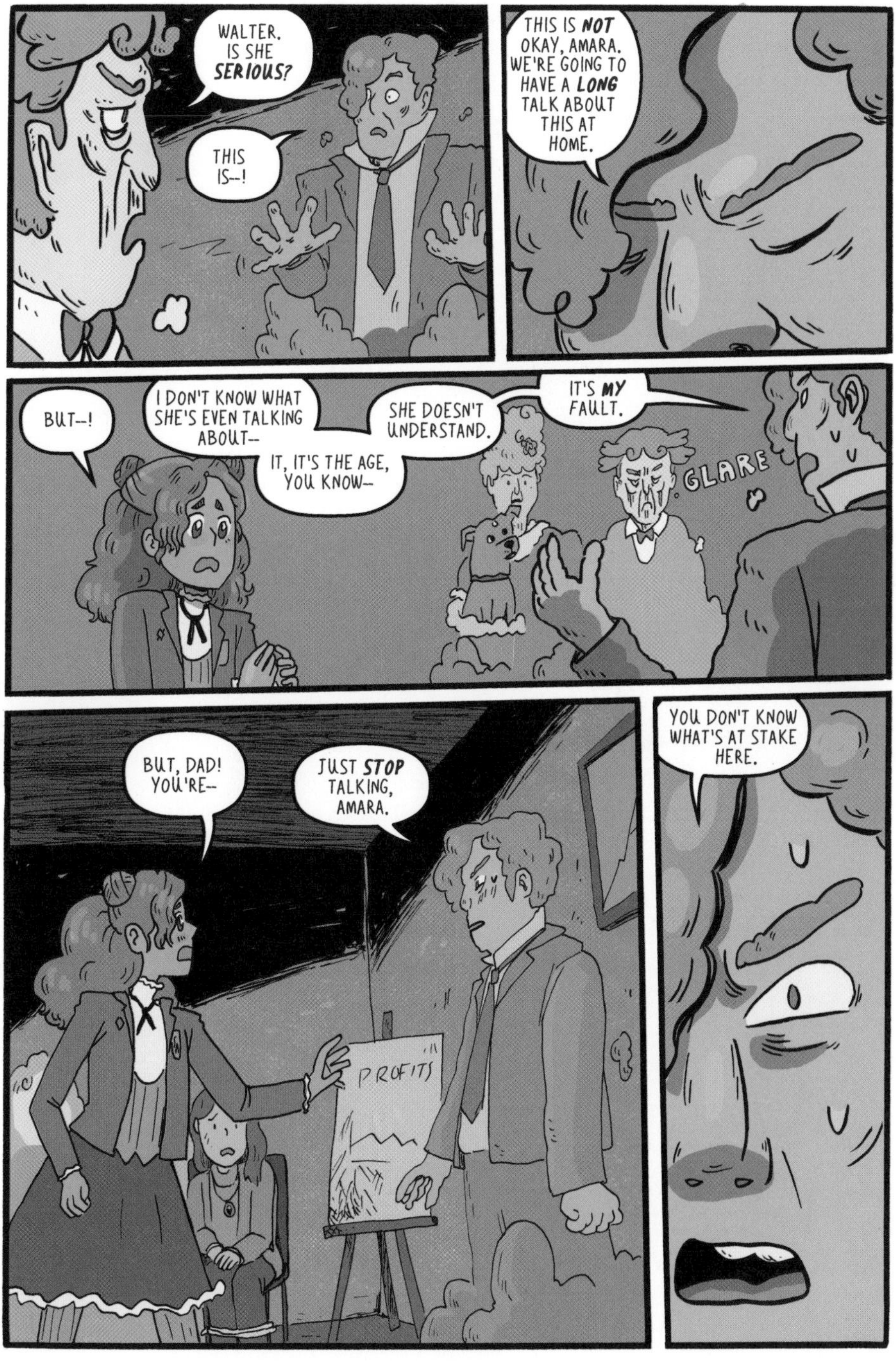
WALTER. IS SHE **SERIOUS?**
THIS IS--!
THIS IS **NOT** OKAY, AMARA. WE'RE GOING TO HAVE A **LONG** TALK ABOUT THIS AT HOME.
BUT--!
I DON'T KNOW WHAT SHE'S EVEN TALKING ABOUT--
IT, IT'S THE AGE, YOU KNOW--
SHE DOESN'T UNDERSTAND.
IT'S **MY** FAULT.
GLARE
BUT, DAD! YOU'RE--
JUST **STOP** TALKING, AMARA.
PROFITS
YOU DON'T KNOW WHAT'S AT STAKE HERE.

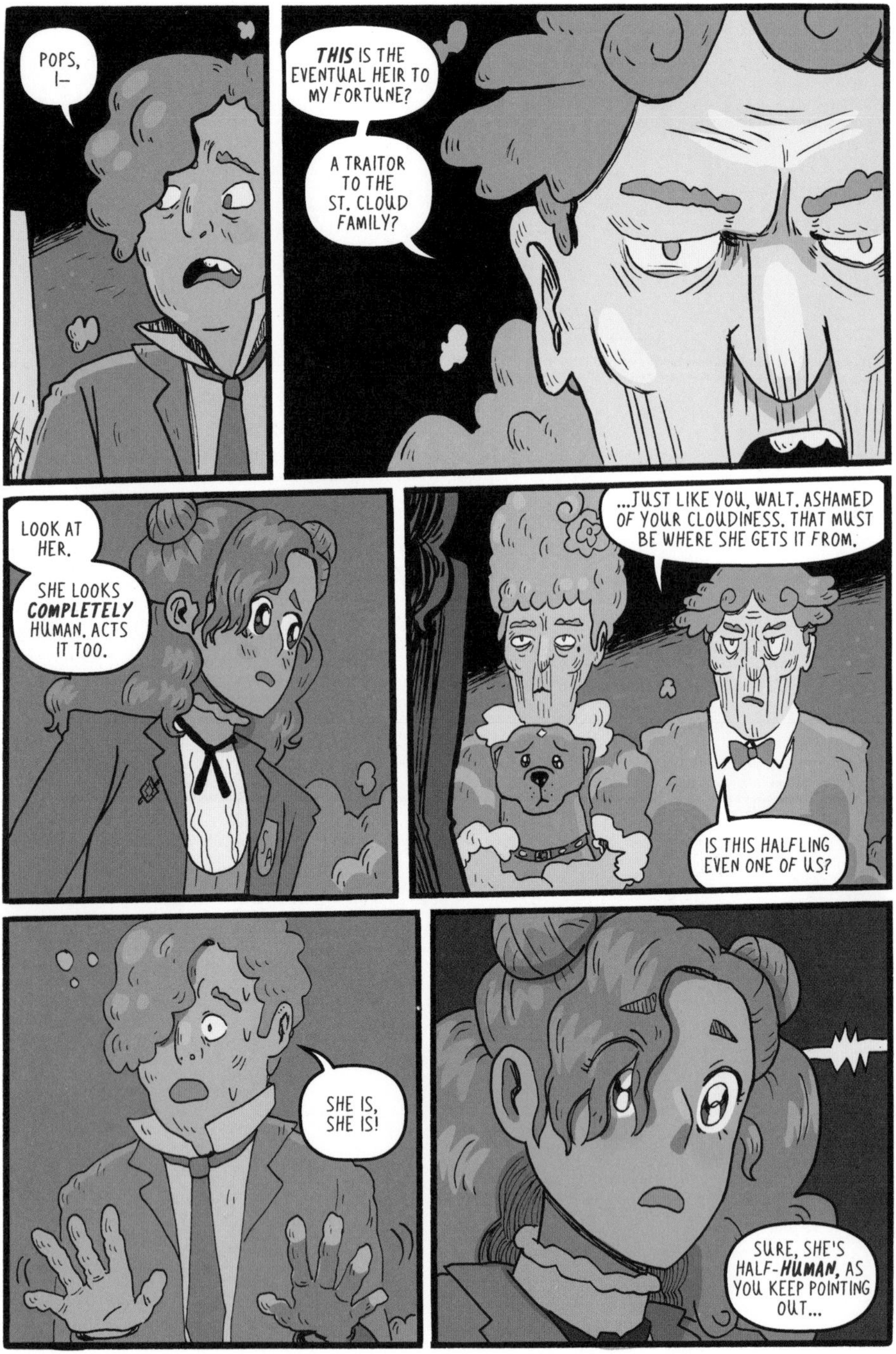
POPS, I—
THIS IS THE EVENTUAL HEIR TO MY FORTUNE?
A TRAITOR TO THE ST. CLOUD FAMILY?
LOOK AT HER.
SHE LOOKS COMPLETELY HUMAN. ACTS IT TOO.
...JUST LIKE YOU, WALT. ASHAMED OF YOUR CLOUDINESS. THAT MUST BE WHERE SHE GETS IT FROM.
IS THIS HALFLING EVEN ONE OF US?
SHE IS, SHE IS!
SURE, SHE'S HALF-HUMAN, AS YOU KEEP POINTING OUT...

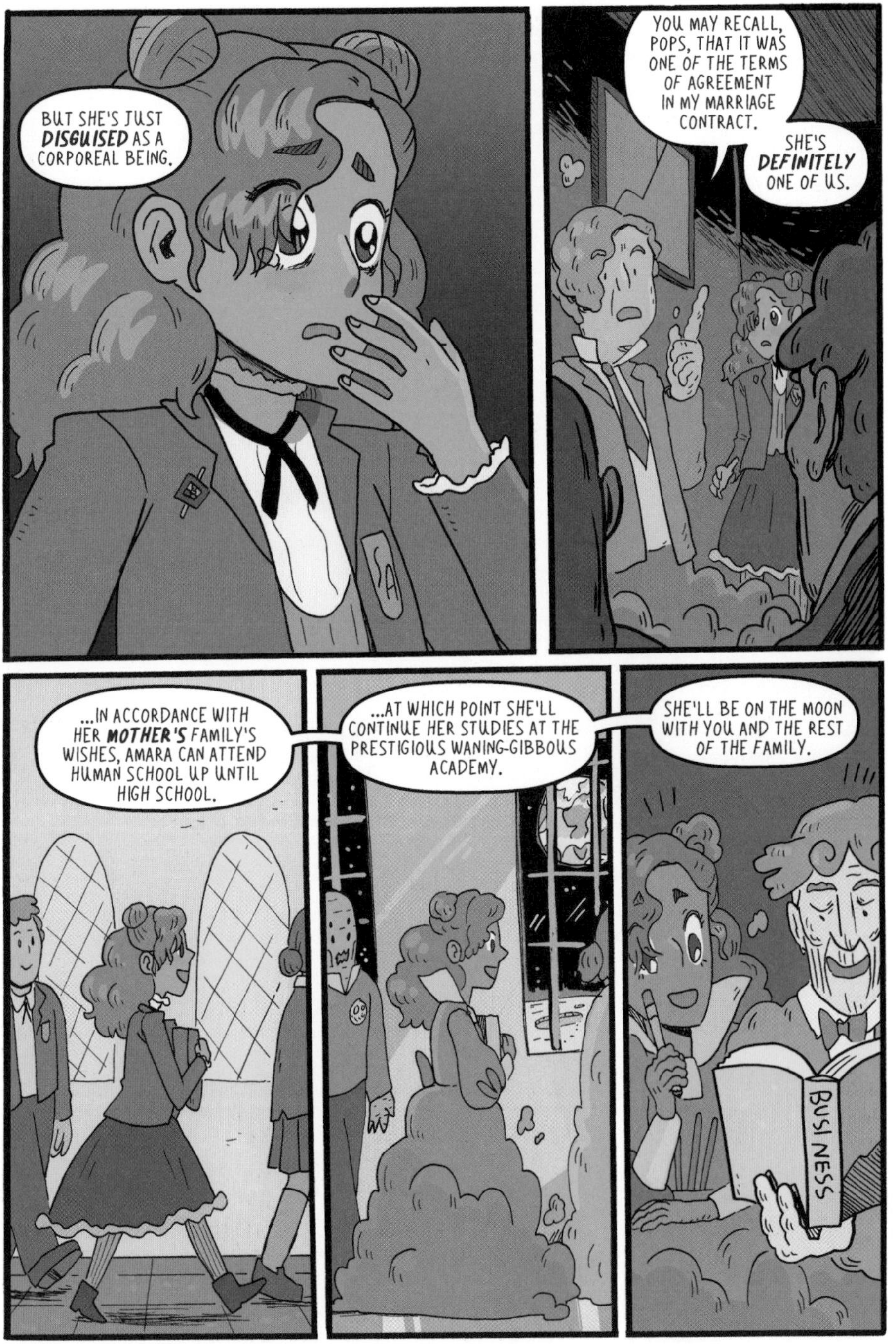
BUT SHE'S JUST **DISGUISED** AS A CORPOREAL BEING.
YOU MAY RECALL, POPS, THAT IT WAS ONE OF THE TERMS OF AGREEMENT IN MY MARRIAGE CONTRACT.
SHE'S **DEFINITELY** ONE OF US.
...IN ACCORDANCE WITH HER **MOTHER'S** FAMILY'S WISHES, AMARA CAN ATTEND HUMAN SCHOOL UP UNTIL HIGH SCHOOL.
...AT WHICH POINT SHE'LL CONTINUE HER STUDIES AT THE PRESTIGIOUS WANING-GIBBOUS ACADEMY.
SHE'LL BE ON THE MOON WITH YOU AND THE REST OF THE FAMILY.
BUSINESS

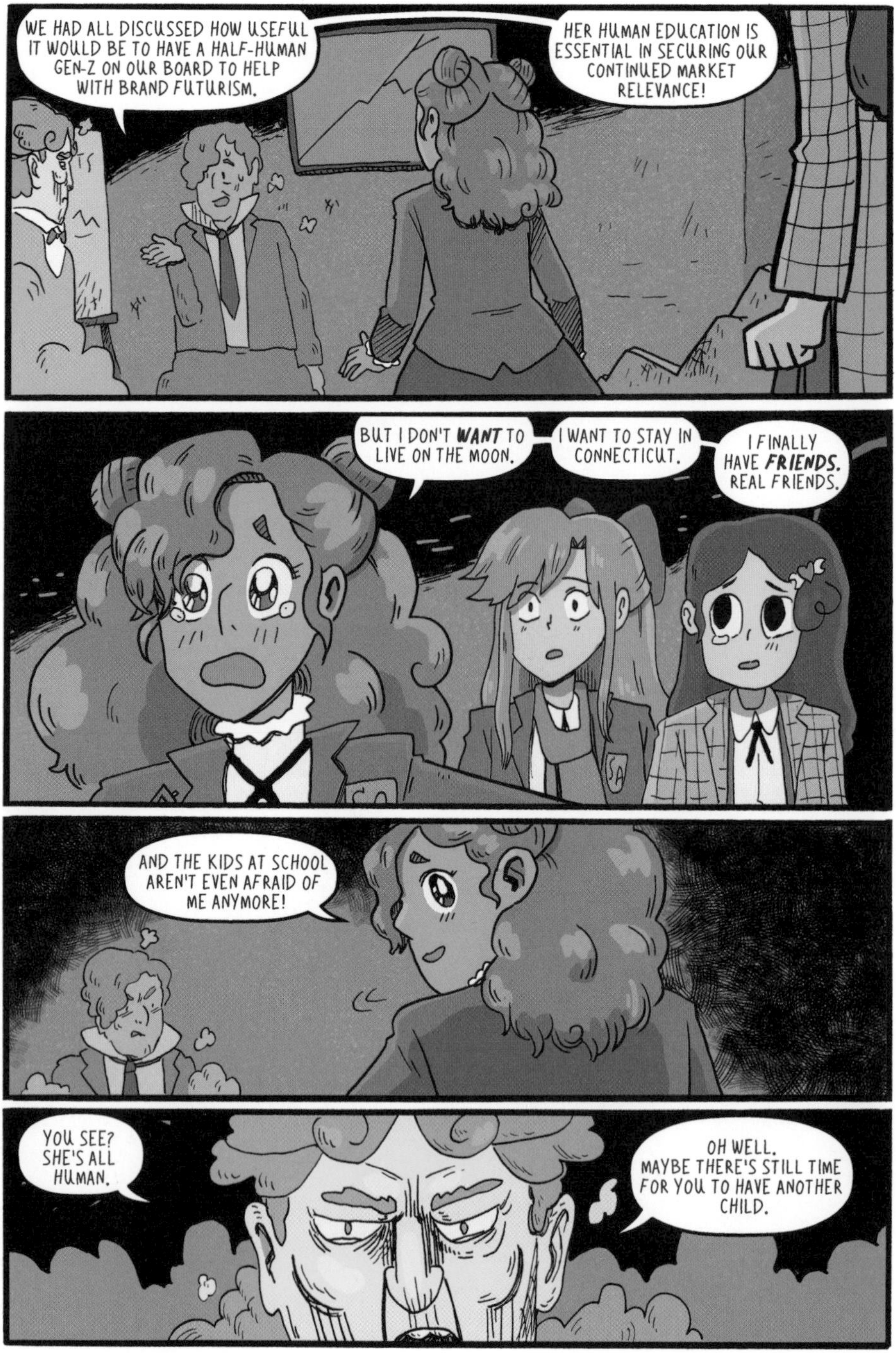
WE HAD ALL DISCUSSED HOW USEFUL IT WOULD BE TO HAVE A HALF-HUMAN GEN-Z ON OUR BOARD TO HELP WITH BRAND FUTURISM.
HER HUMAN EDUCATION IS ESSENTIAL IN SECURING OUR CONTINUED MARKET RELEVANCE!
BUT I DON'T **WANT** TO LIVE ON THE MOON.
I WANT TO STAY IN CONNECTICUT.
I FINALLY HAVE **FRIENDS.** REAL FRIENDS.
AND THE KIDS AT SCHOOL AREN'T EVEN AFRAID OF ME ANYMORE!
YOU SEE? SHE'S ALL HUMAN.
OH WELL. MAYBE THERE'S STILL TIME FOR YOU TO HAVE ANOTHER CHILD.

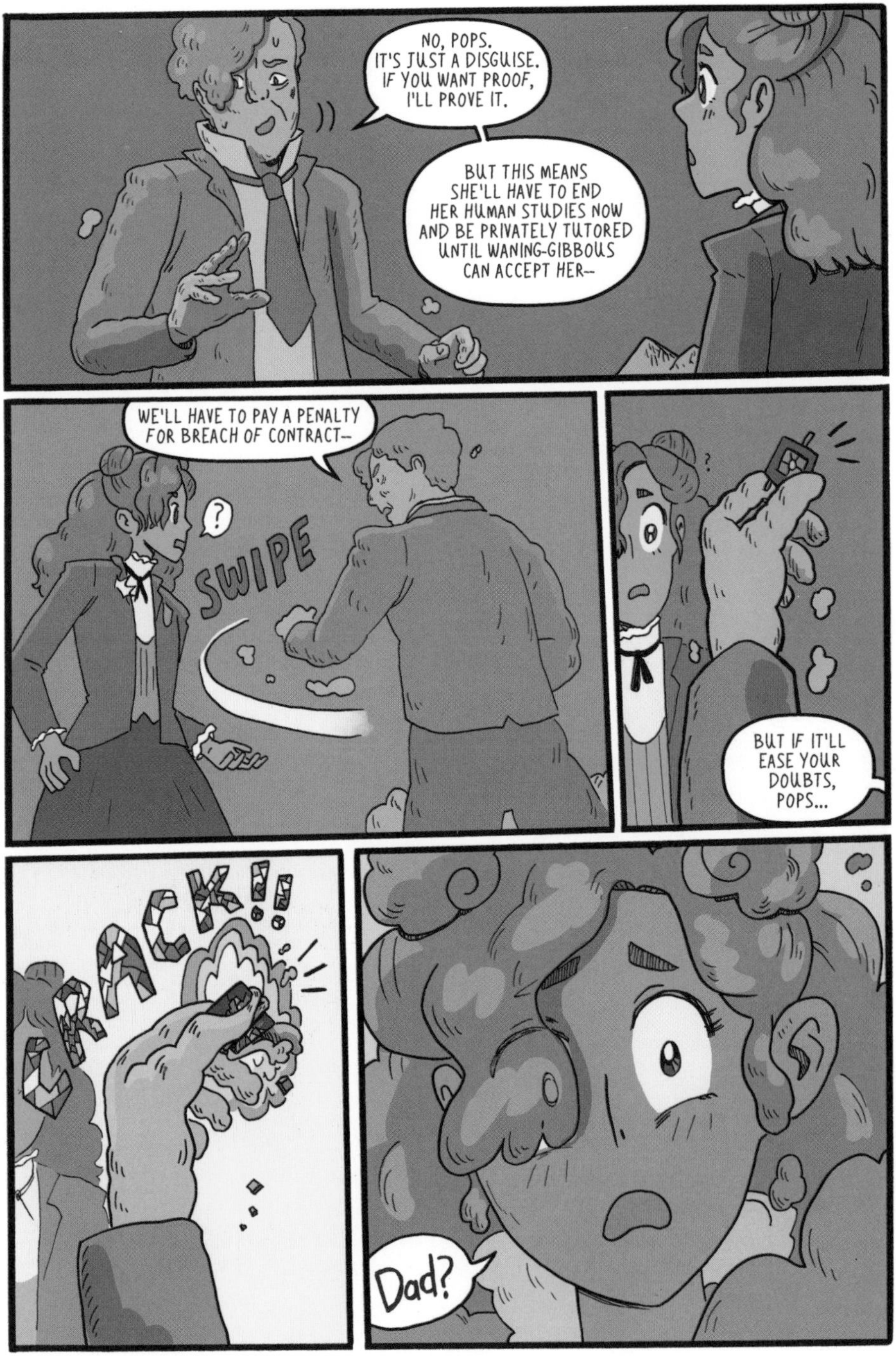
NO, POPS. IT'S JUST A DISGUISE. IF YOU WANT PROOF, I'LL PROVE IT.
BUT THIS MEANS SHE'LL HAVE TO END HER HUMAN STUDIES NOW AND BE PRIVATELY TUTORED UNTIL WANING-GIBBOUS CAN ACCEPT HER--
WE'LL HAVE TO PAY A PENALTY FOR BREACH OF CONTRACT--
?
SWIPE
?
BUT IF IT'LL EASE YOUR DOUBTS, POPS...
CRACK!!
Dad?

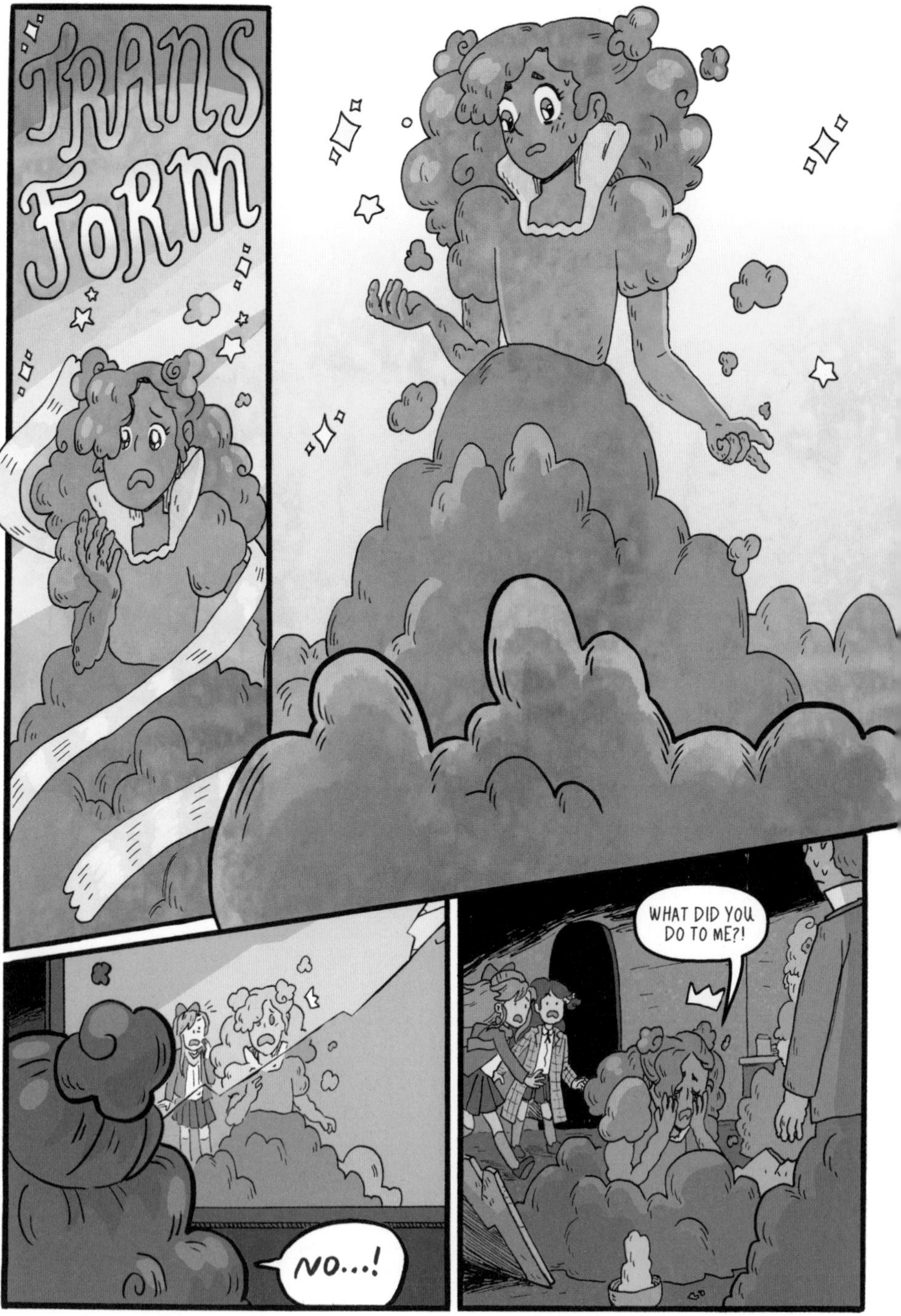
TRANS FORM
NO...!
WHAT DID YOU DO TO ME?!

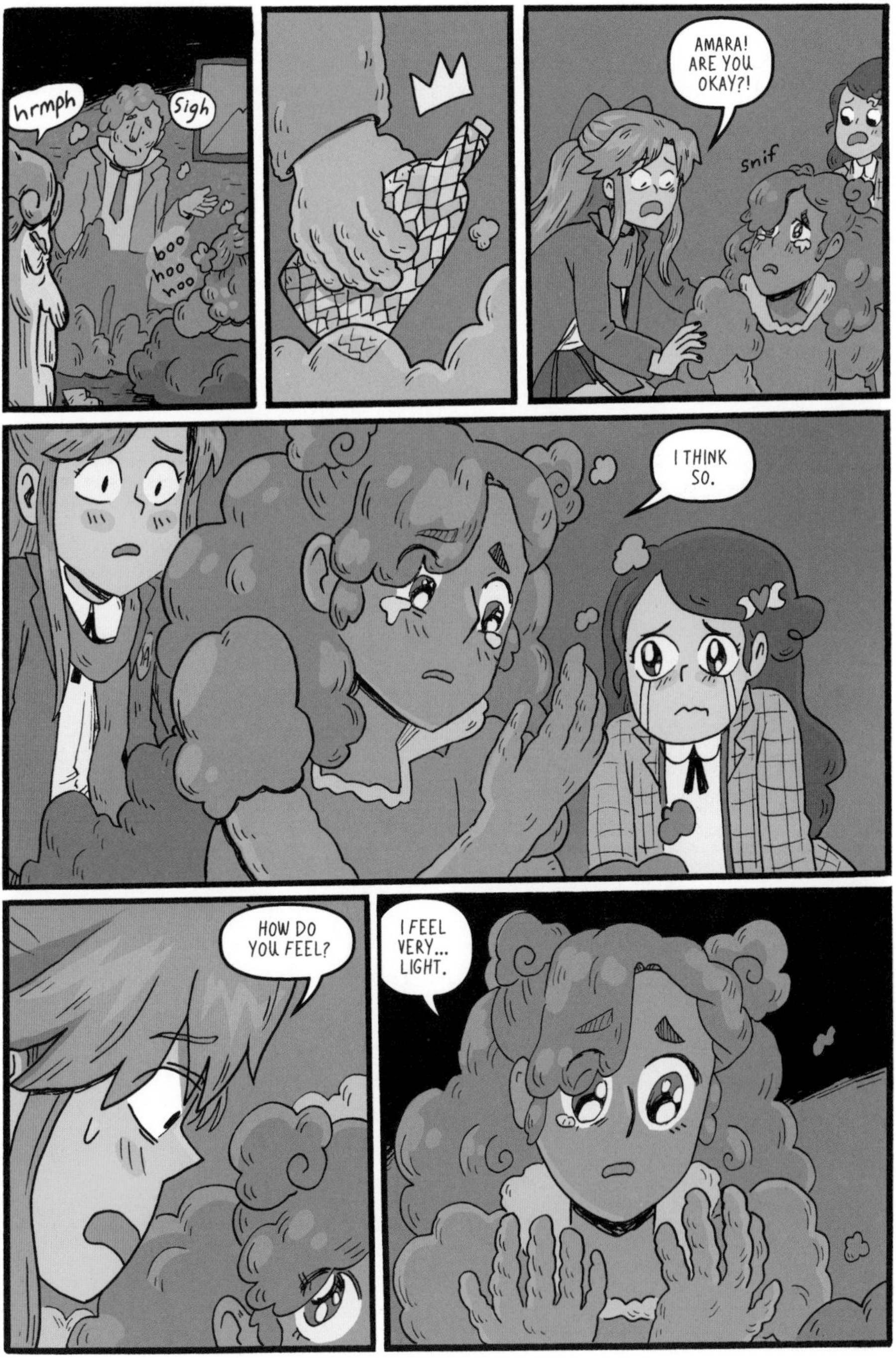
hrmph
Sigh
boo hoo hoo
AMARA! ARE YOU OKAY?!
snif
I THINK SO.
HOW DO YOU FEEL?
I FEEL VERY... LIGHT.

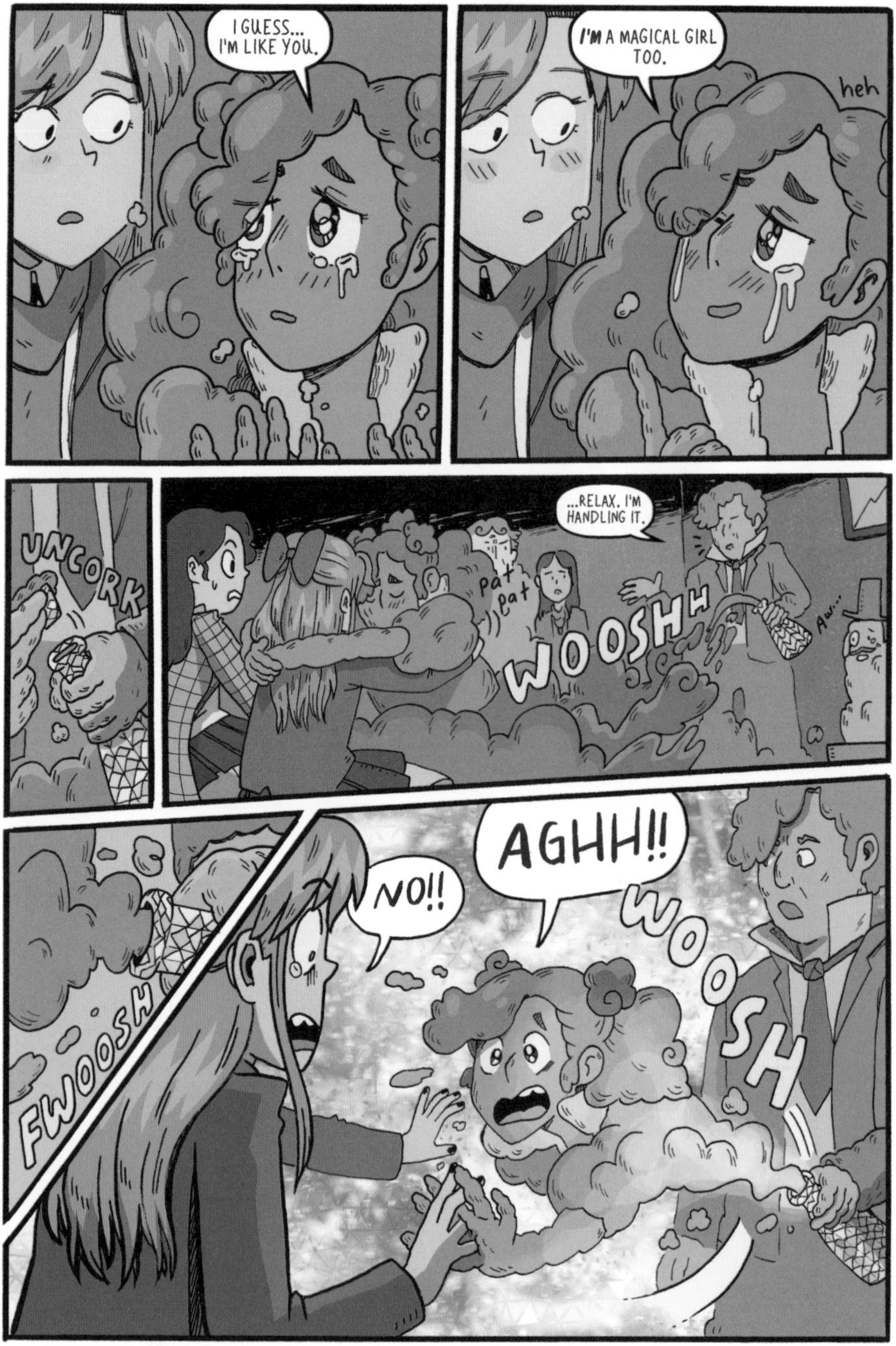
I GUESS... I'M LIKE YOU.
I'M A MAGICAL GIRL TOO.
heh
UNCORK
...RELAX. I'M HANDLING IT.
pat pat
WOOSHH
Aw...
FWOOSH
NO!!
AGHH!!
WOOOSH

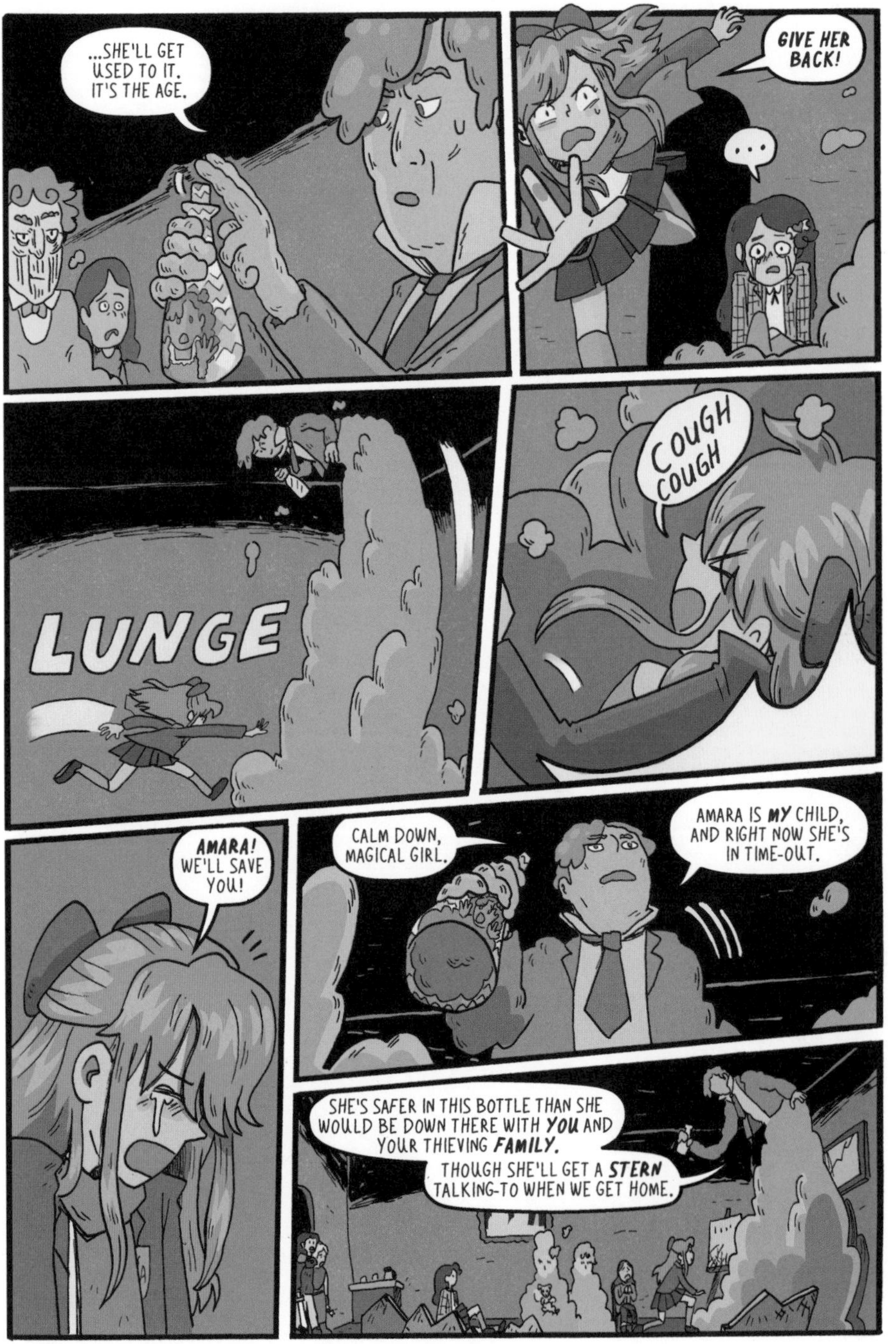
...SHE'LL GET USED TO IT. IT'S THE AGE.
GIVE HER BACK!
...
LUNGE
COUGH COUGH
AMARA! WE'LL SAVE YOU!
CALM DOWN, MAGICAL GIRL.
AMARA IS MY CHILD, AND RIGHT NOW SHE'S IN TIME-OUT.
SHE'S SAFER IN THIS BOTTLE THAN SHE WOULD BE DOWN THERE WITH YOU AND YOUR THIEVING FAMILY.
THOUGH SHE'LL GET A STERN TALKING-TO WHEN WE GET HOME.

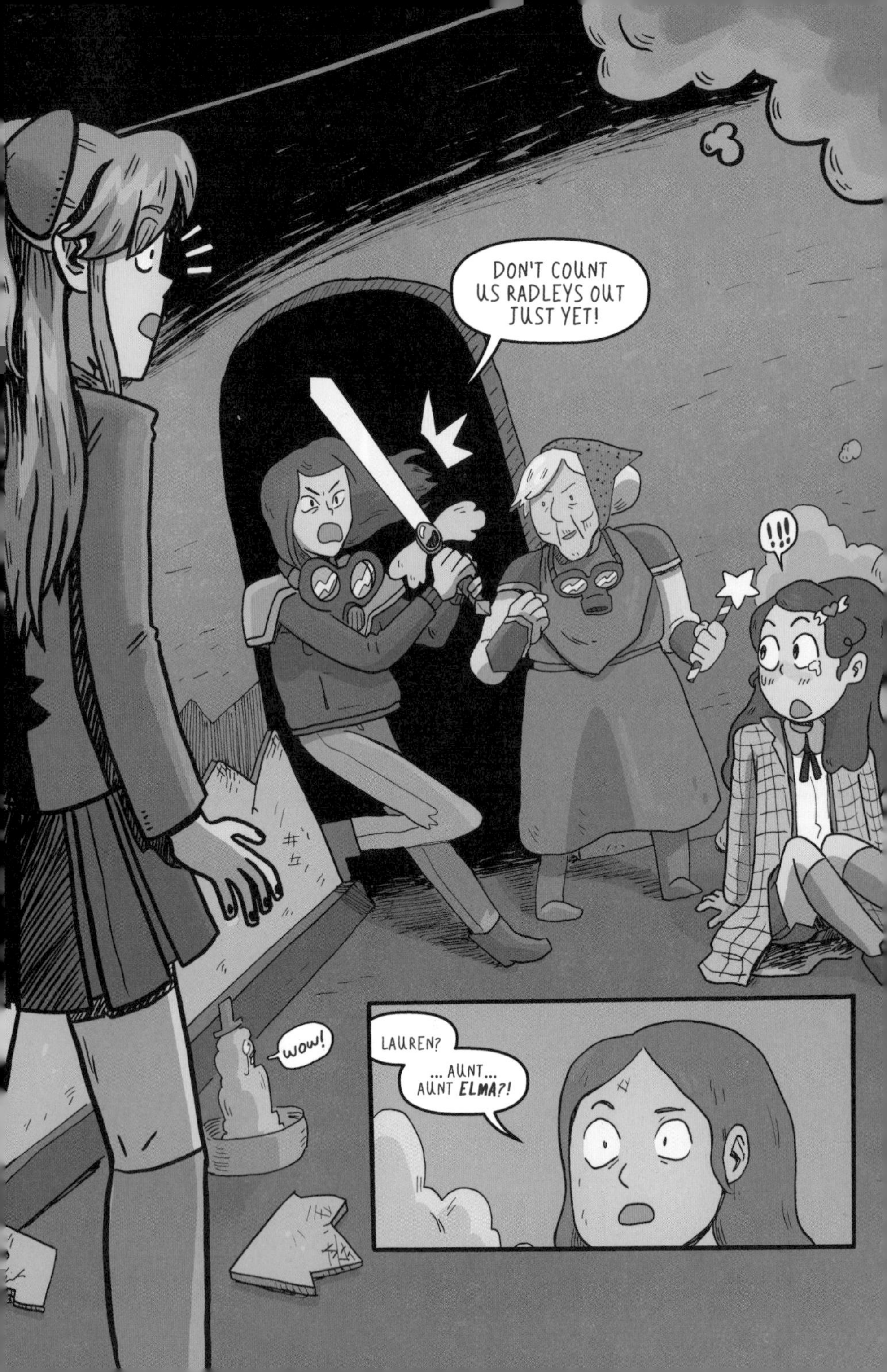
DON'T COUNT US RADLEYS OUT JUST YET!
!!!
WOW!
LAUREN?
... AUNT... AUNT ELMA?!

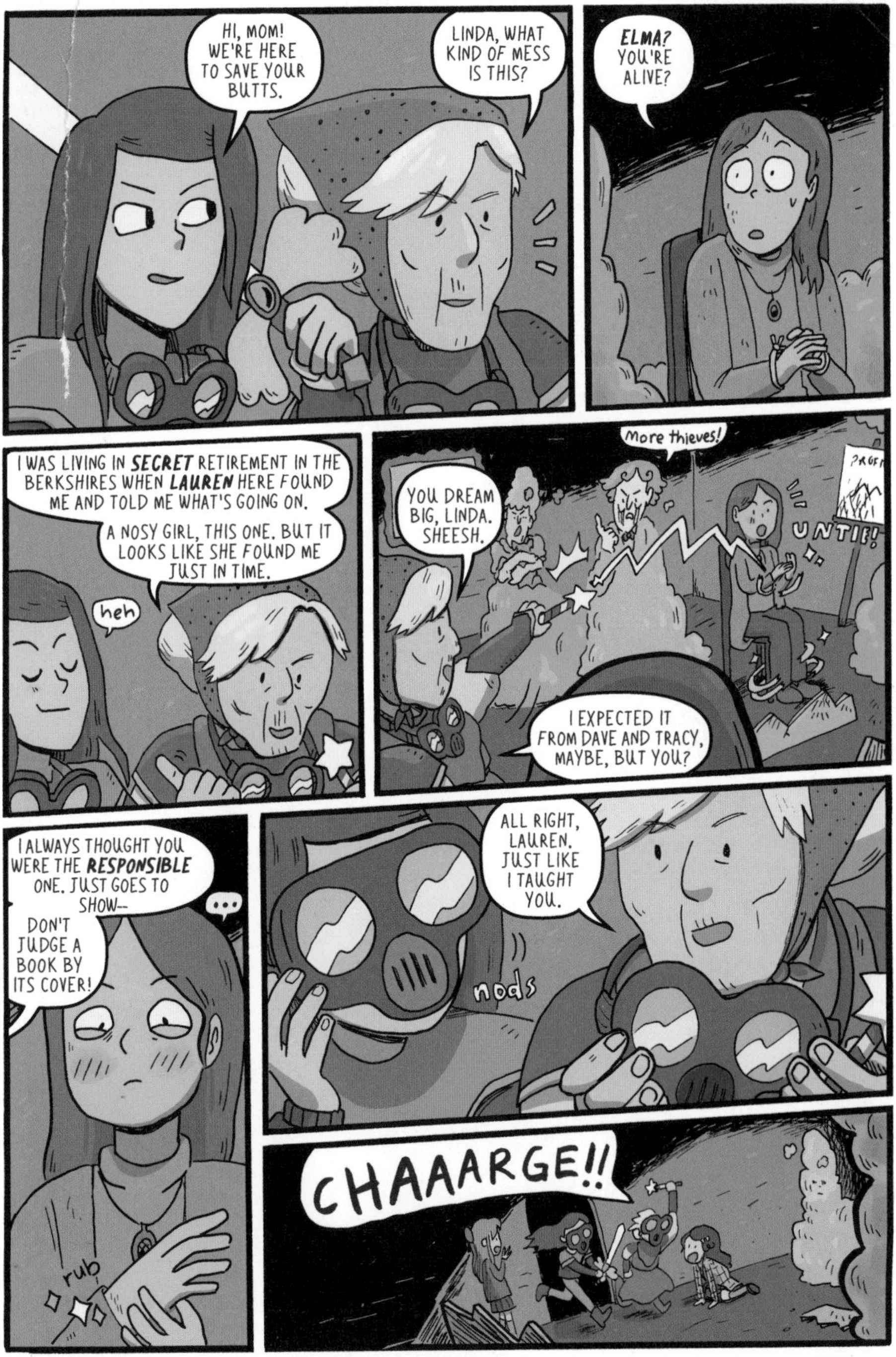
HI, MOM! WE'RE HERE TO SAVE YOUR BUTTS.
LINDA, WHAT KIND OF MESS IS THIS?
ELMA? YOU'RE ALIVE?
I WAS LIVING IN SECRET RETIREMENT IN THE BERKSHIRES WHEN LAUREN HERE FOUND ME AND TOLD ME WHAT'S GOING ON.
A NOSY GIRL, THIS ONE. BUT IT LOOKS LIKE SHE FOUND ME JUST IN TIME.
heh
More thieves!
YOU DREAM BIG, LINDA. SHEESH.
UNTIE!
I EXPECTED IT FROM DAVE AND TRACY, MAYBE, BUT YOU?
I ALWAYS THOUGHT YOU WERE THE RESPONSIBLE ONE. JUST GOES TO SHOW--
DON'T JUDGE A BOOK BY ITS COVER!
...
rub
ALL RIGHT, LAUREN. JUST LIKE I TAUGHT YOU.
nods
CHAAARGE!!

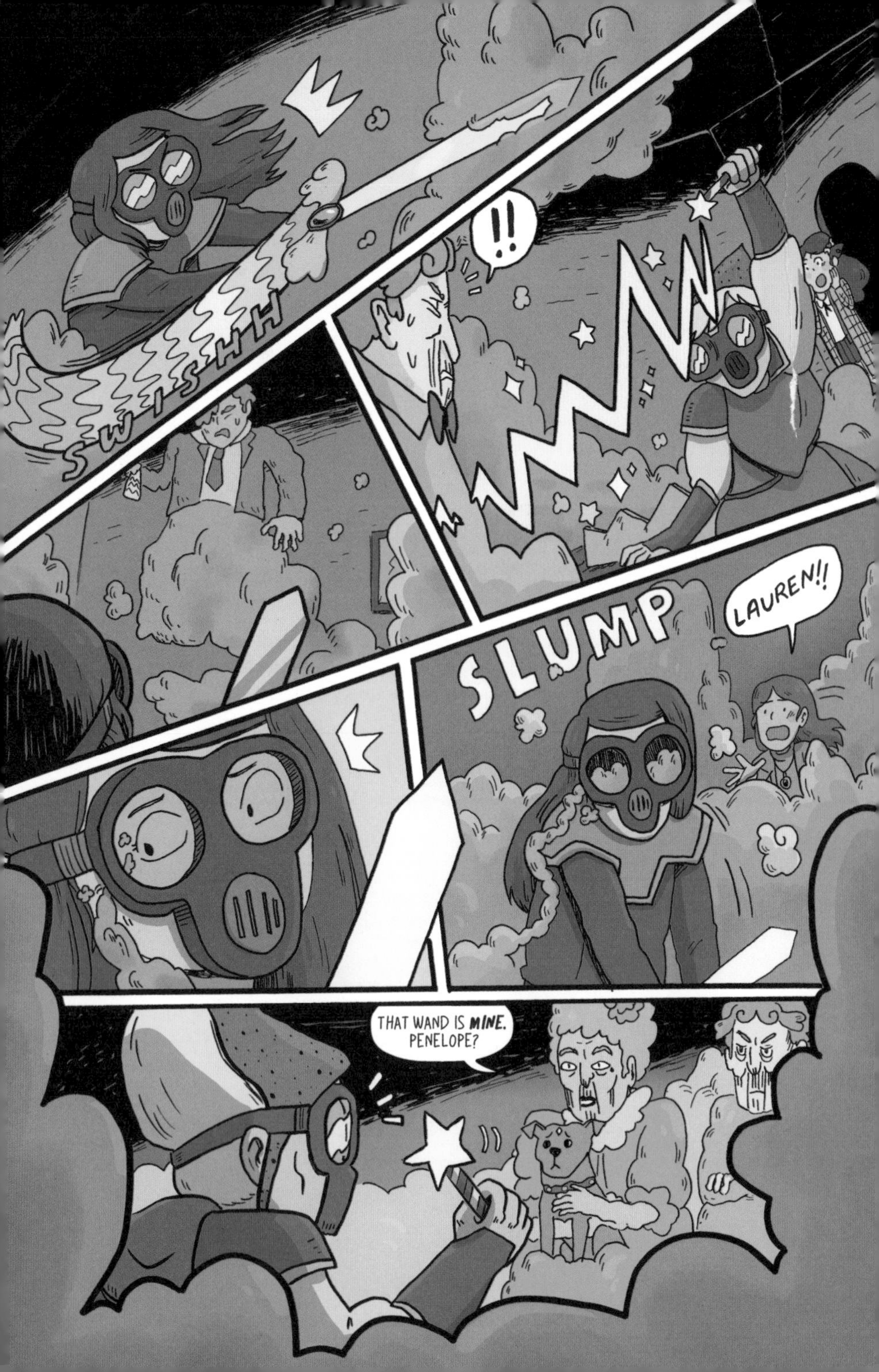
SWISHH
!!
SLUMP
LAUREN!!
THAT WAND IS MINE.
PENELOPE?

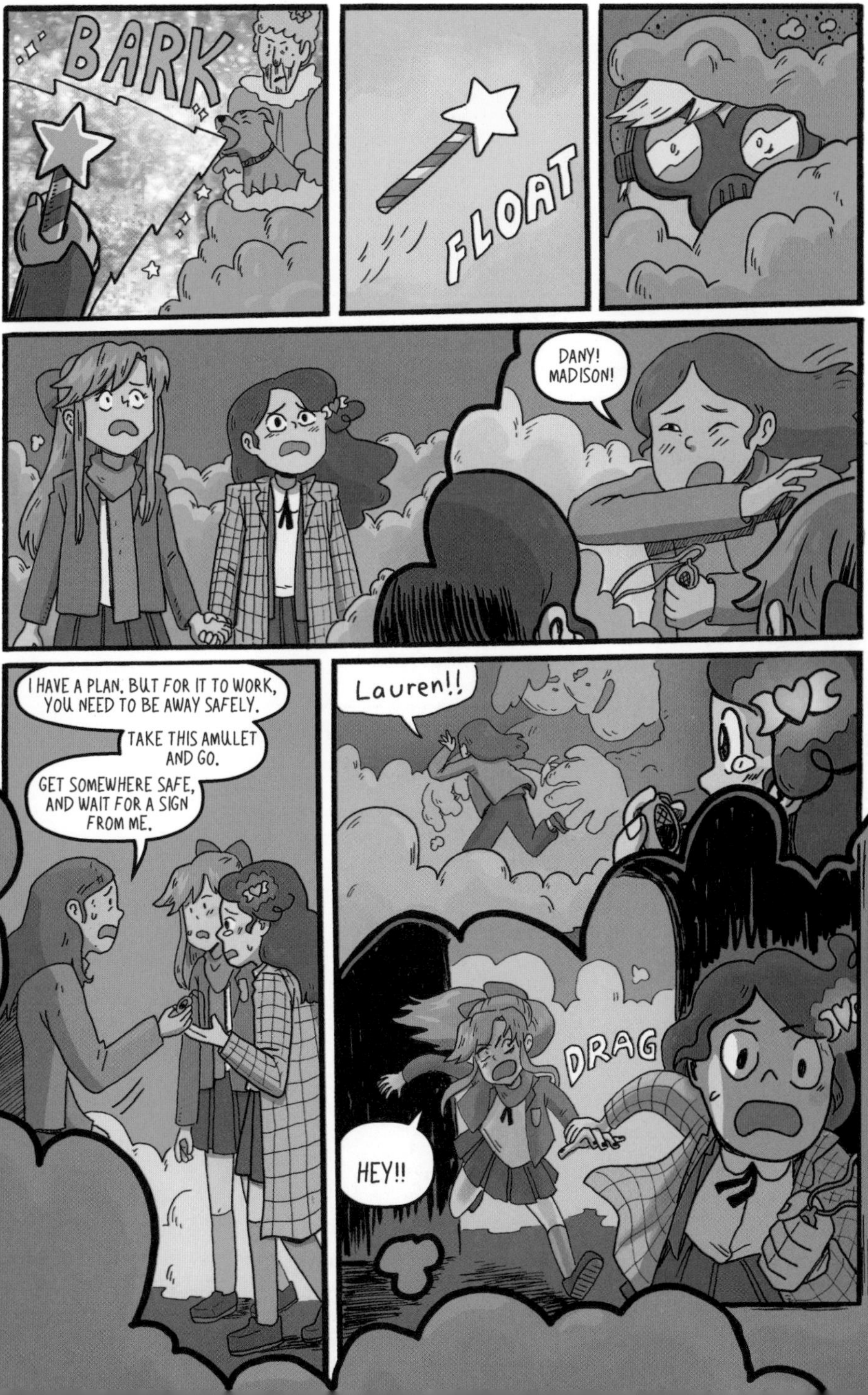
BARK
FLOAT
DANY! MADISON!
I HAVE A PLAN. BUT FOR IT TO WORK, YOU NEED TO BE AWAY SAFELY.
TAKE THIS AMULET AND GO.
GET SOMEWHERE SAFE, AND WAIT FOR A SIGN FROM ME.
Lauren!!
DRAG
HEY!!

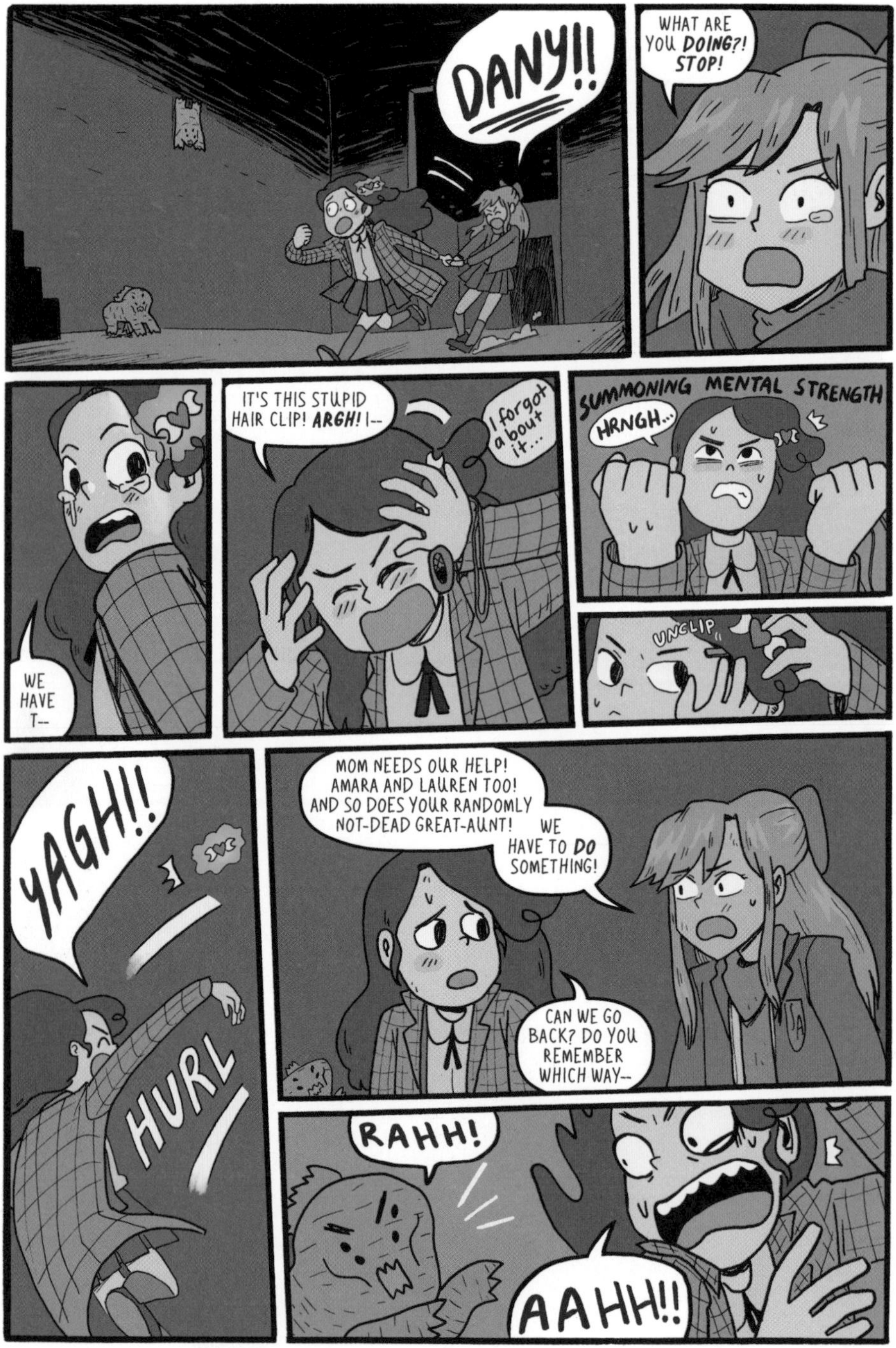
DANY!!
WHAT ARE YOU DOING?! STOP!
WE HAVE T--
IT'S THIS STUPID HAIR CLIP! ARGH! I--
I forgot about it...
SUMMONING MENTAL STRENGTH
HRNGH...
UNCLIP
YAGH!!
HURL
MOM NEEDS OUR HELP! AMARA AND LAUREN TOO! AND SO DOES YOUR RANDOMLY NOT-DEAD GREAT-AUNT!
WE HAVE TO DO SOMETHING!
CAN WE GO BACK? DO YOU REMEMBER WHICH WAY--
RAHH!
AAHH!!

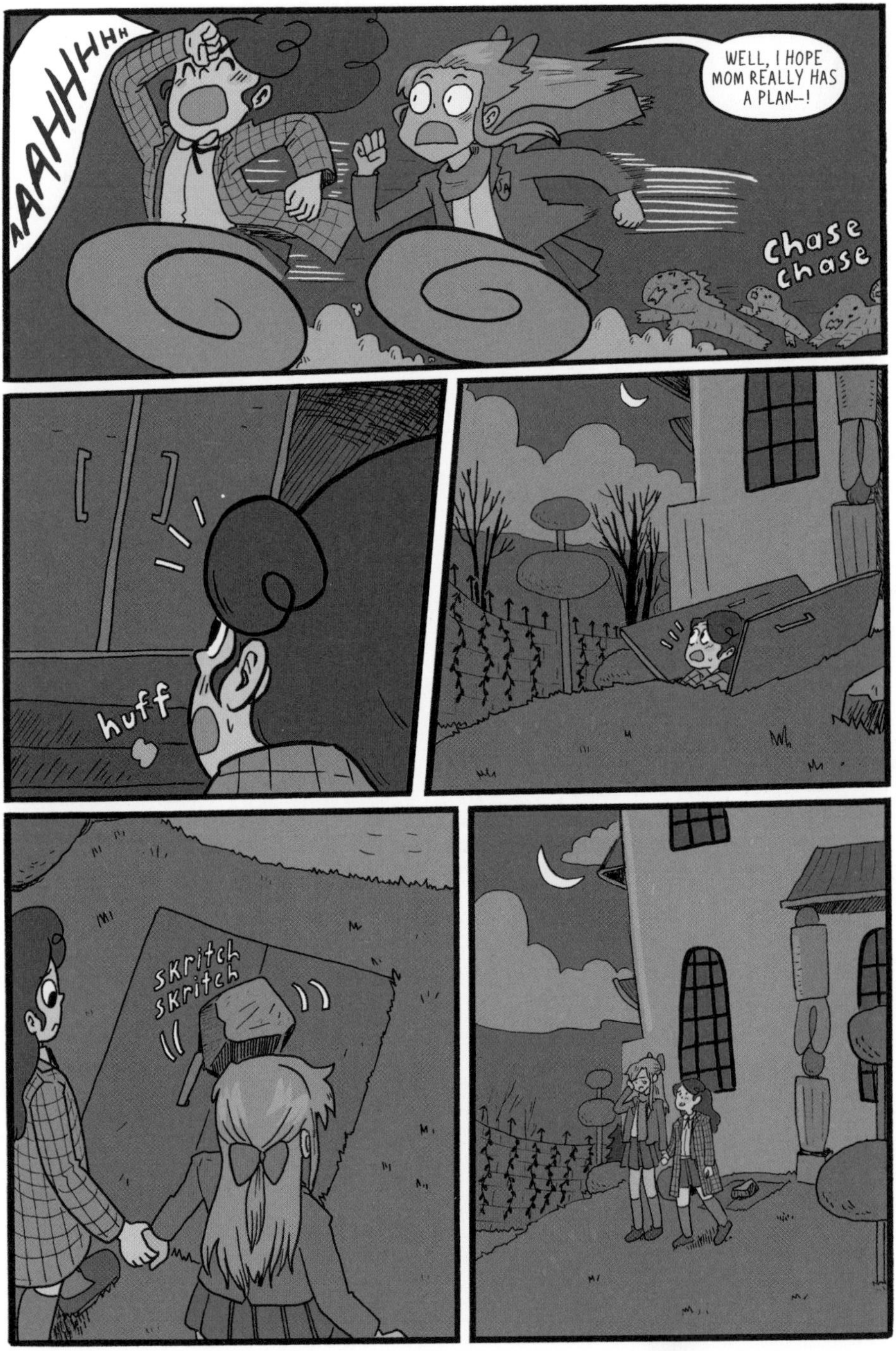
AAAHHHHHH
WELL, I HOPE MOM REALLY HAS A PLAN--!
chase chase
huff
skritch skritch

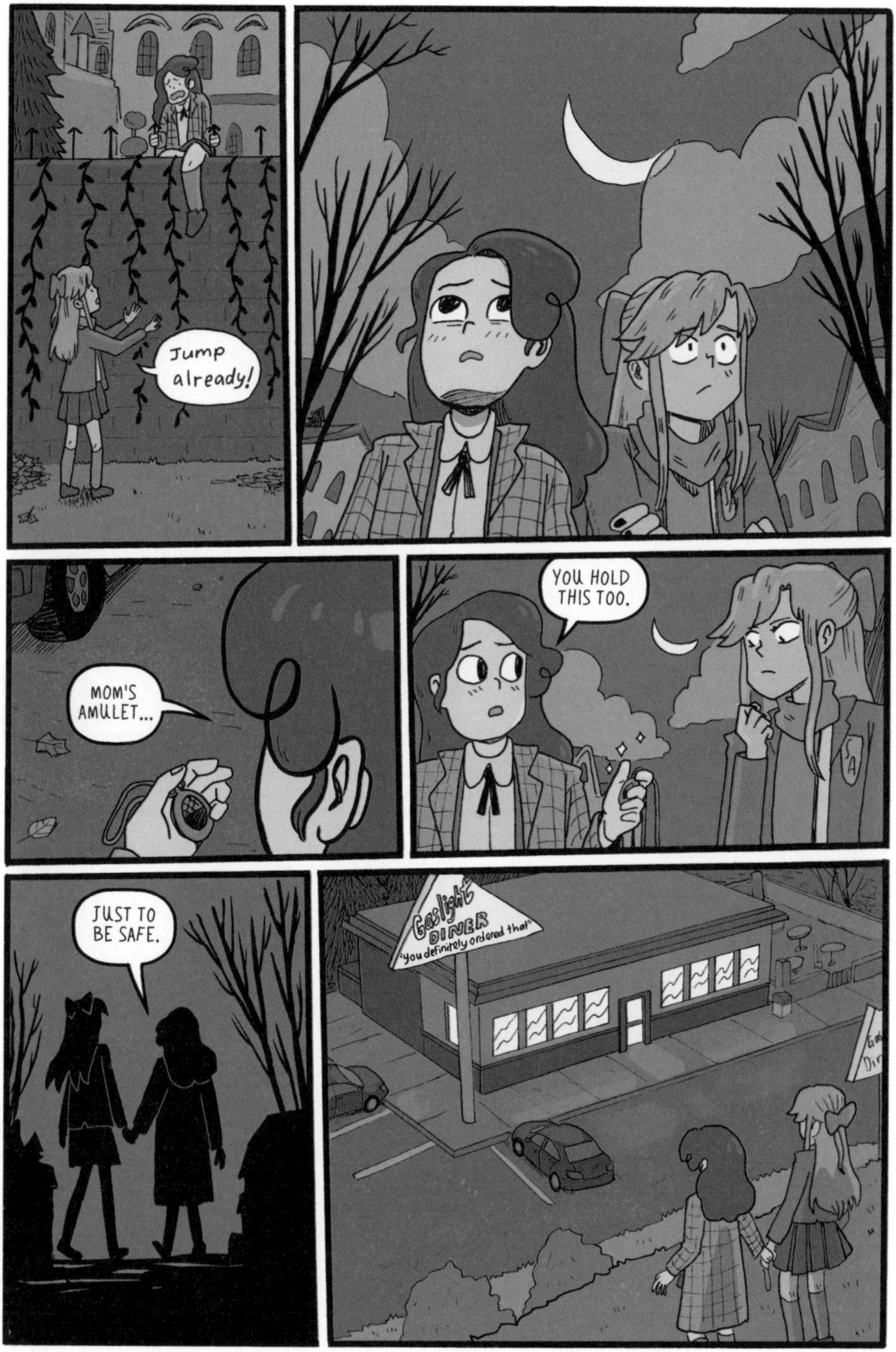
Jump already!
MOM'S AMULET...
YOU HOLD THIS TOO.
JUST TO BE SAFE.
Gaslight DINER
"you definitely ordered that"

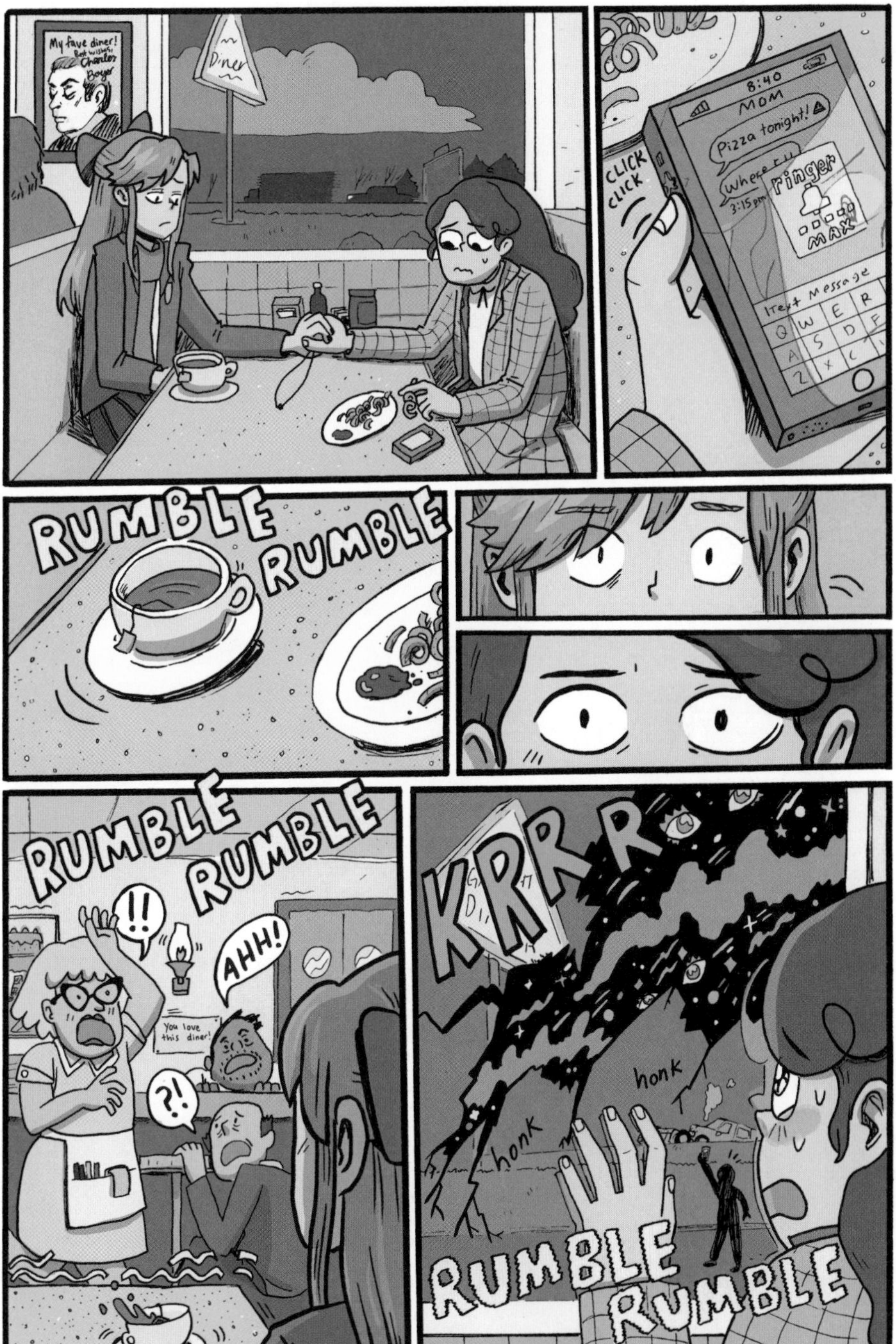
My fave diner! Best wishes, Charles Boyer
Diner
8:40
MOM
Pizza tonight!
3:15 pm
ringer
MAX
Text Message
CLICK
CLICK
RUMBLE
RUMBLE
RUMBLE
RUMBLE
!!
AHH!
You love this diner!
?!
KRRR
honk
honk
RUMBLE
RUMBLE

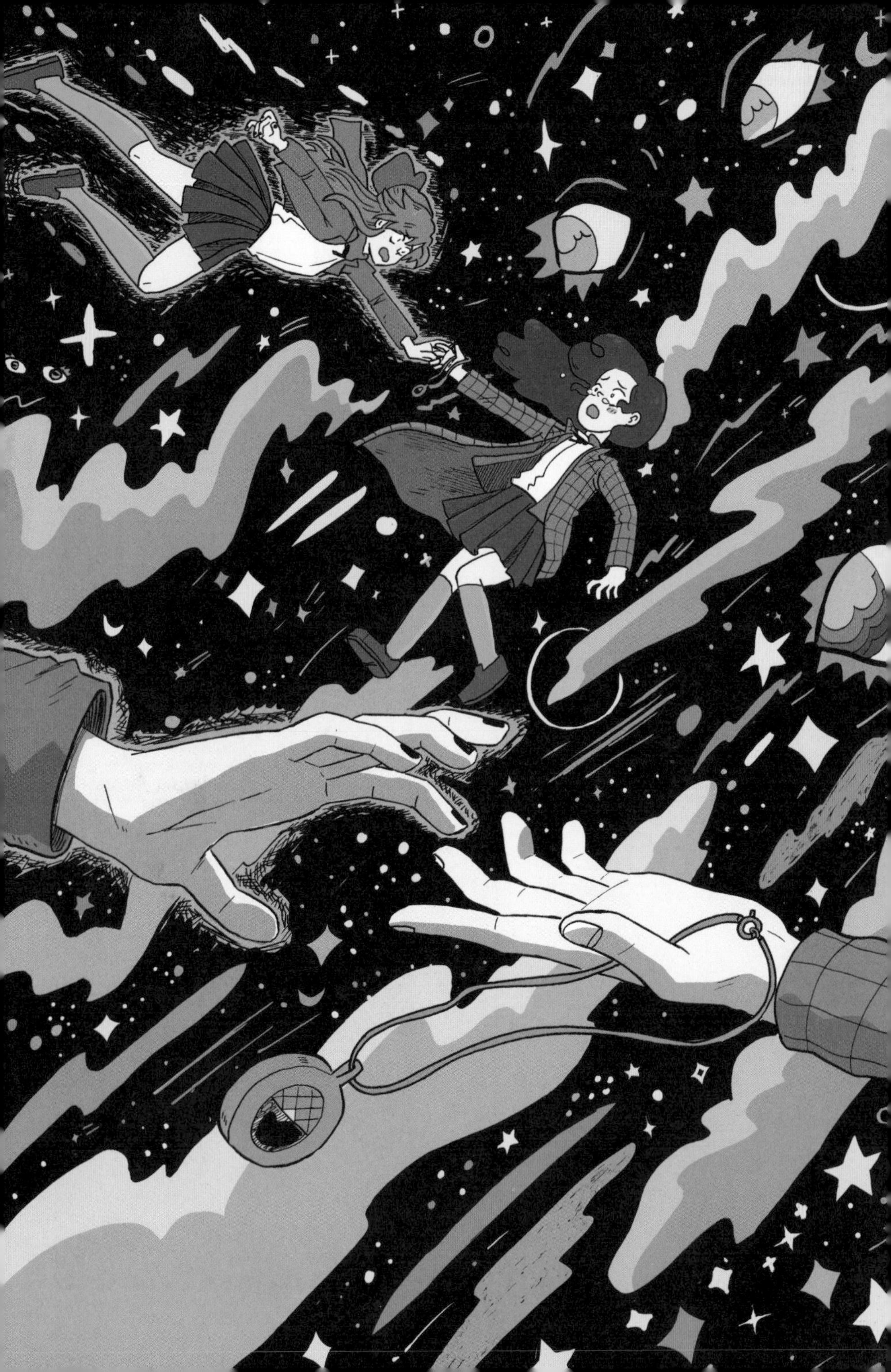

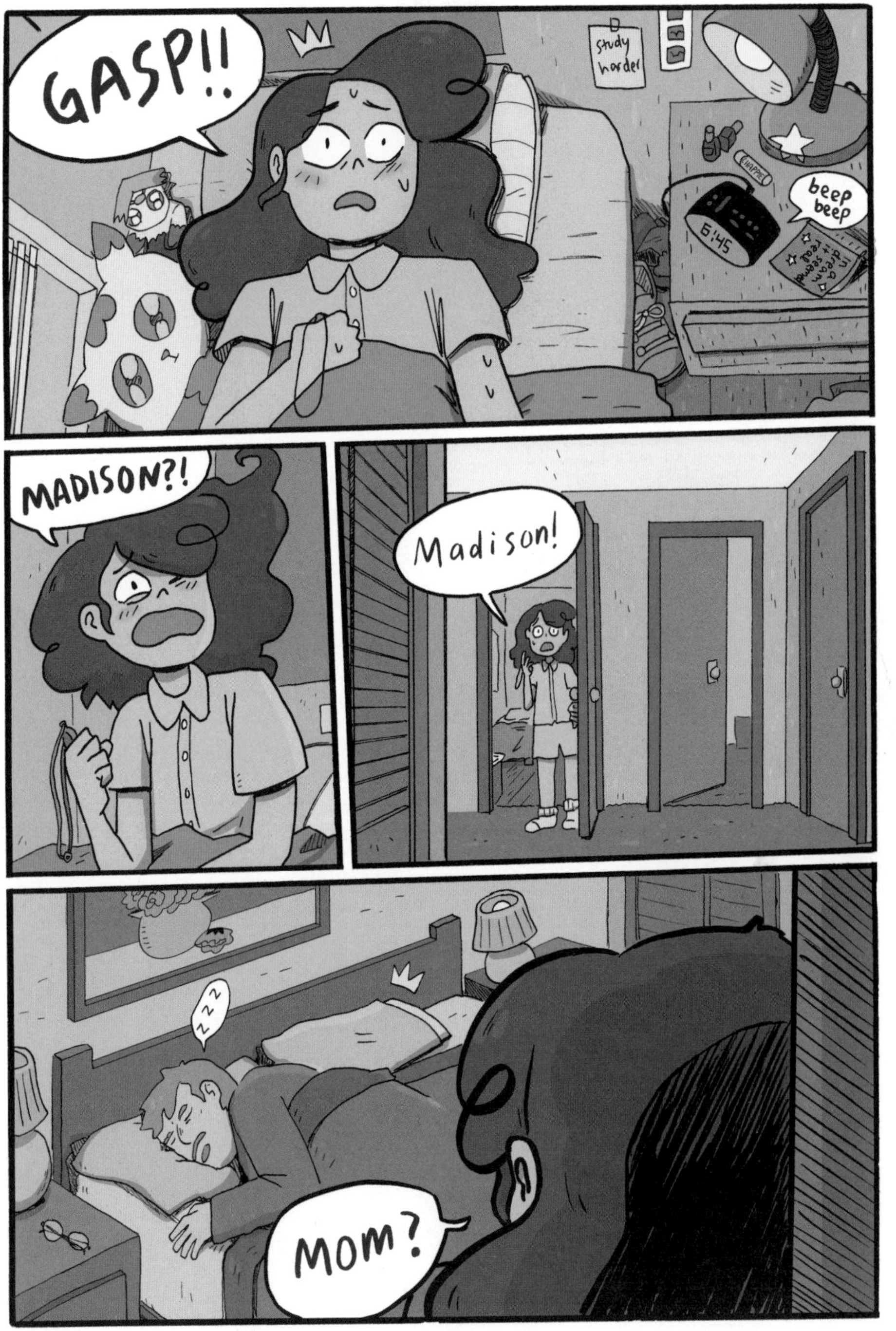
GASP!!
study harder
beep beep
6:45
MADISON?!
Madison!
zzz
MOM?

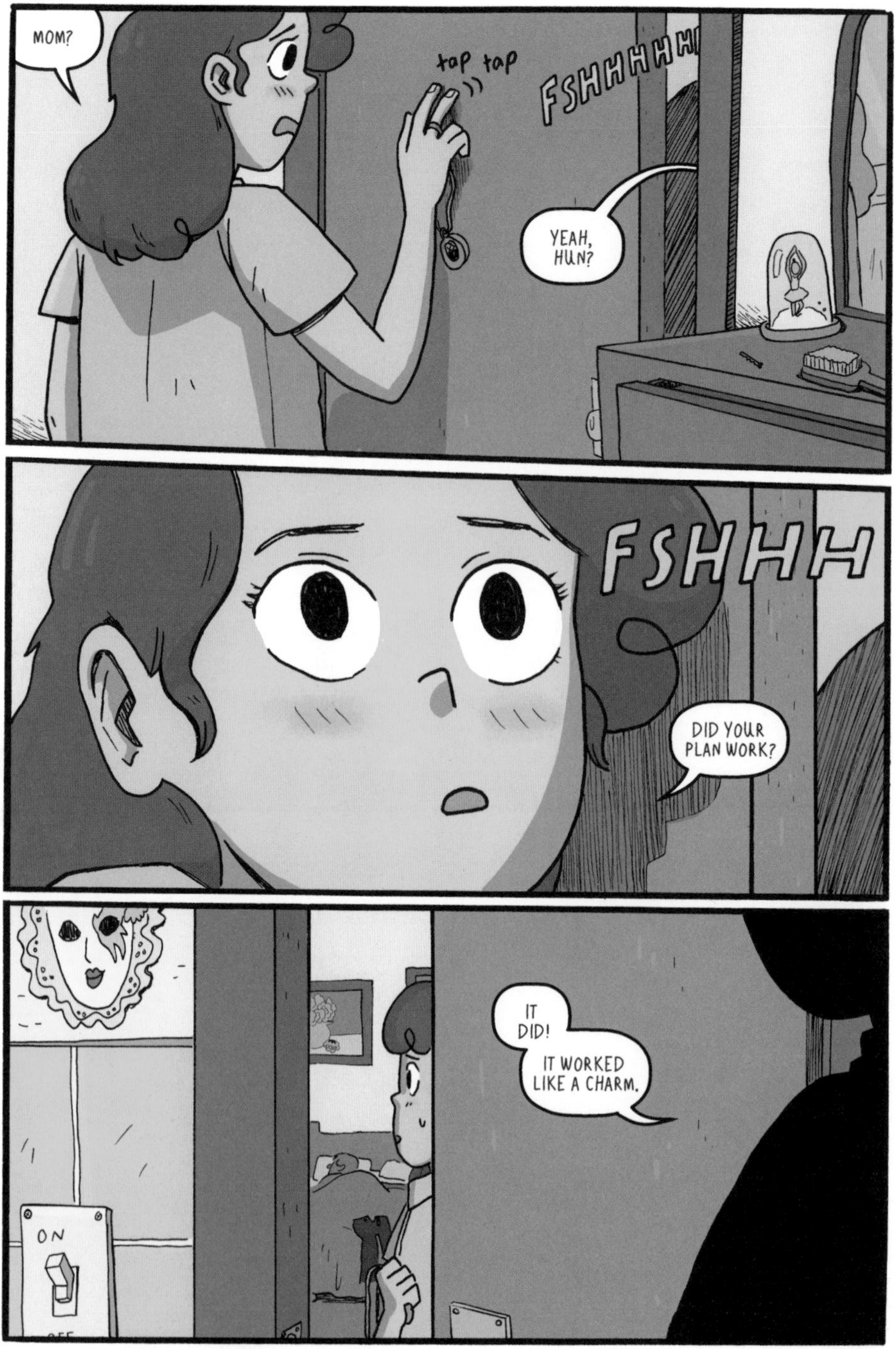
MOM?
tap tap
FSHHHHHH
YEAH, HUN?
FSHHH
DID YOUR PLAN WORK?
IT DID!
IT WORKED LIKE A CHARM.
ON

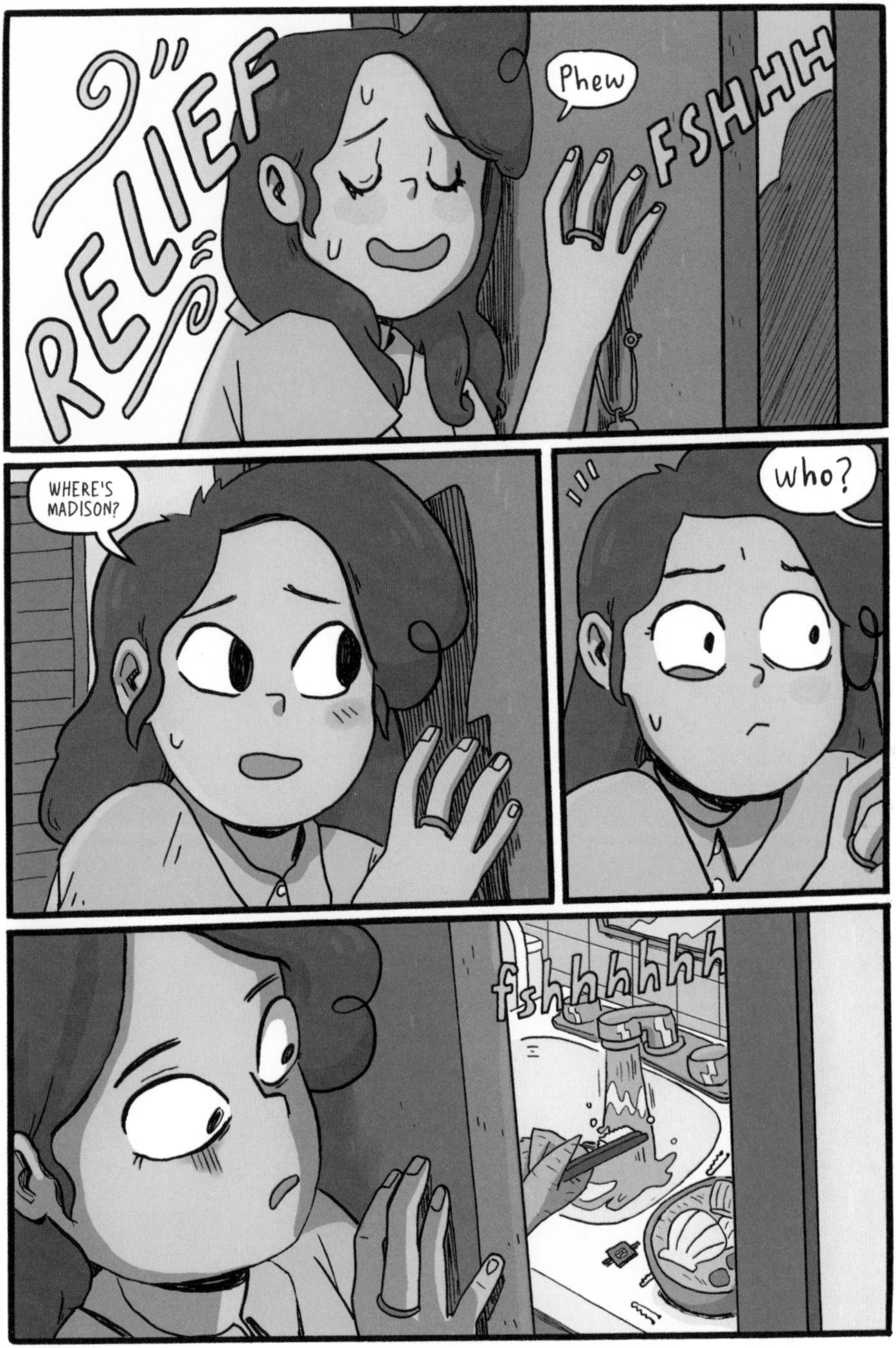
RELIEF
Phew
FSHHH
WHERE'S MADISON?
who?
fshhhhhh

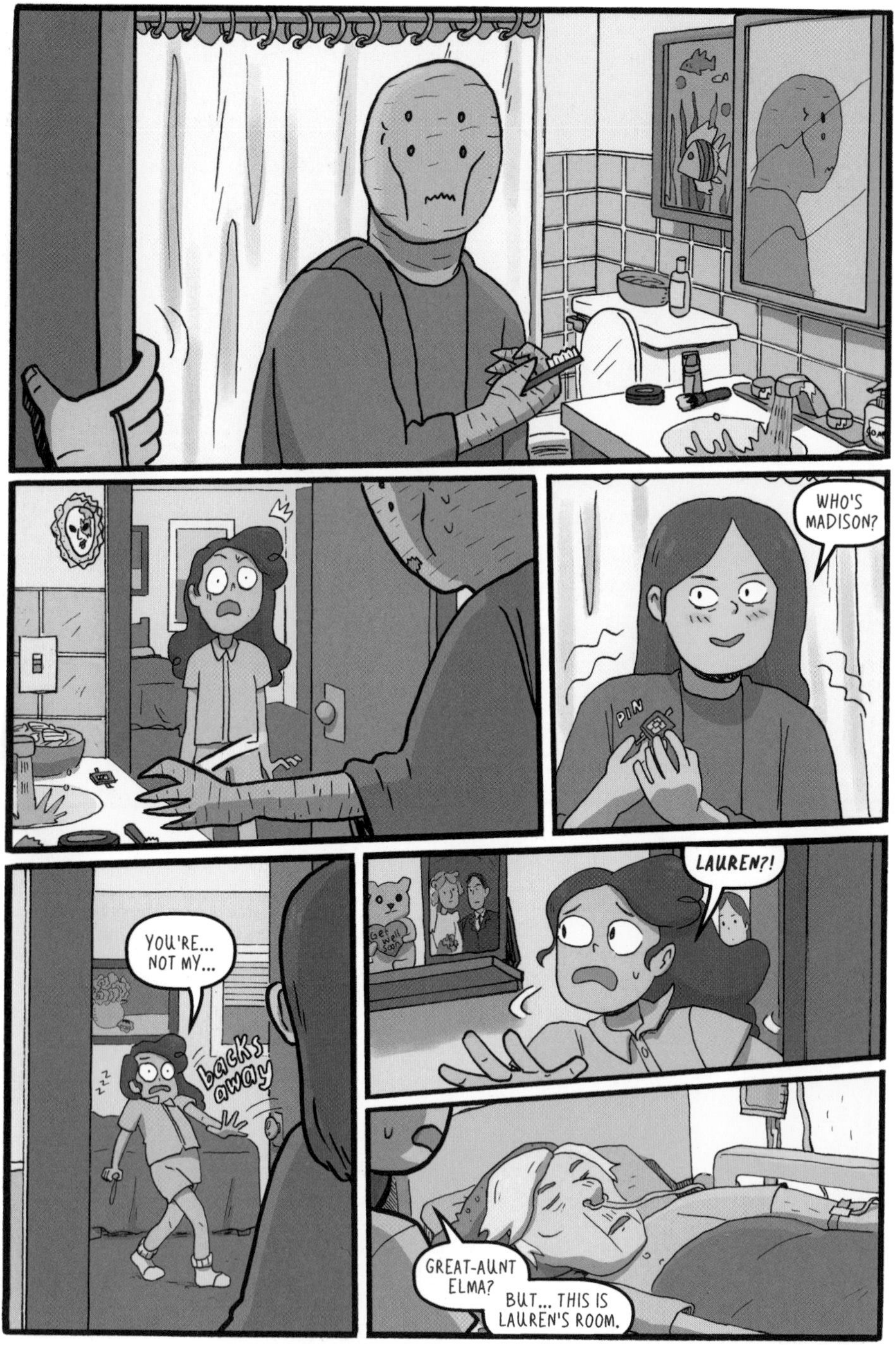
WHO'S MADISON?
YOU'RE... NOT MY...
backs away
LAUREN?!
GREAT-AUNT ELMA?
BUT... THIS IS LAUREN'S ROOM.

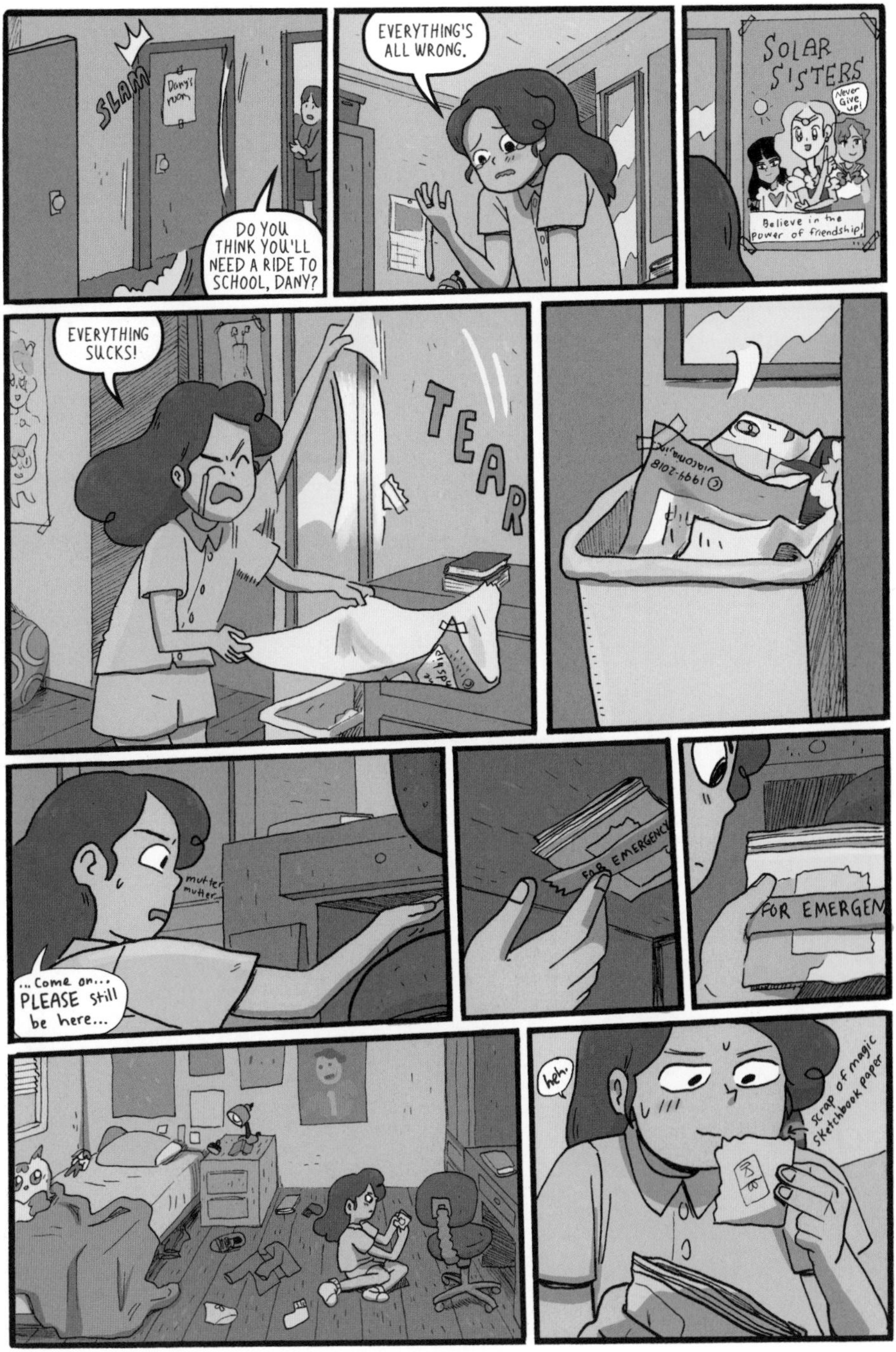
SLAM
Dany's room
DO YOU THINK YOU'LL NEED A RIDE TO SCHOOL, DANY?
EVERYTHING'S ALL WRONG.
SOLAR SISTERS
Never Give up!
Believe in the power of friendship!
EVERYTHING SUCKS!
TEAR
© 1994-2018 viacom...
mutter mutter
...Come on... PLEASE still be here...
FOR EMERGENCY
FOR EMERGEN
heh.
scrap of magic sketchbook paper

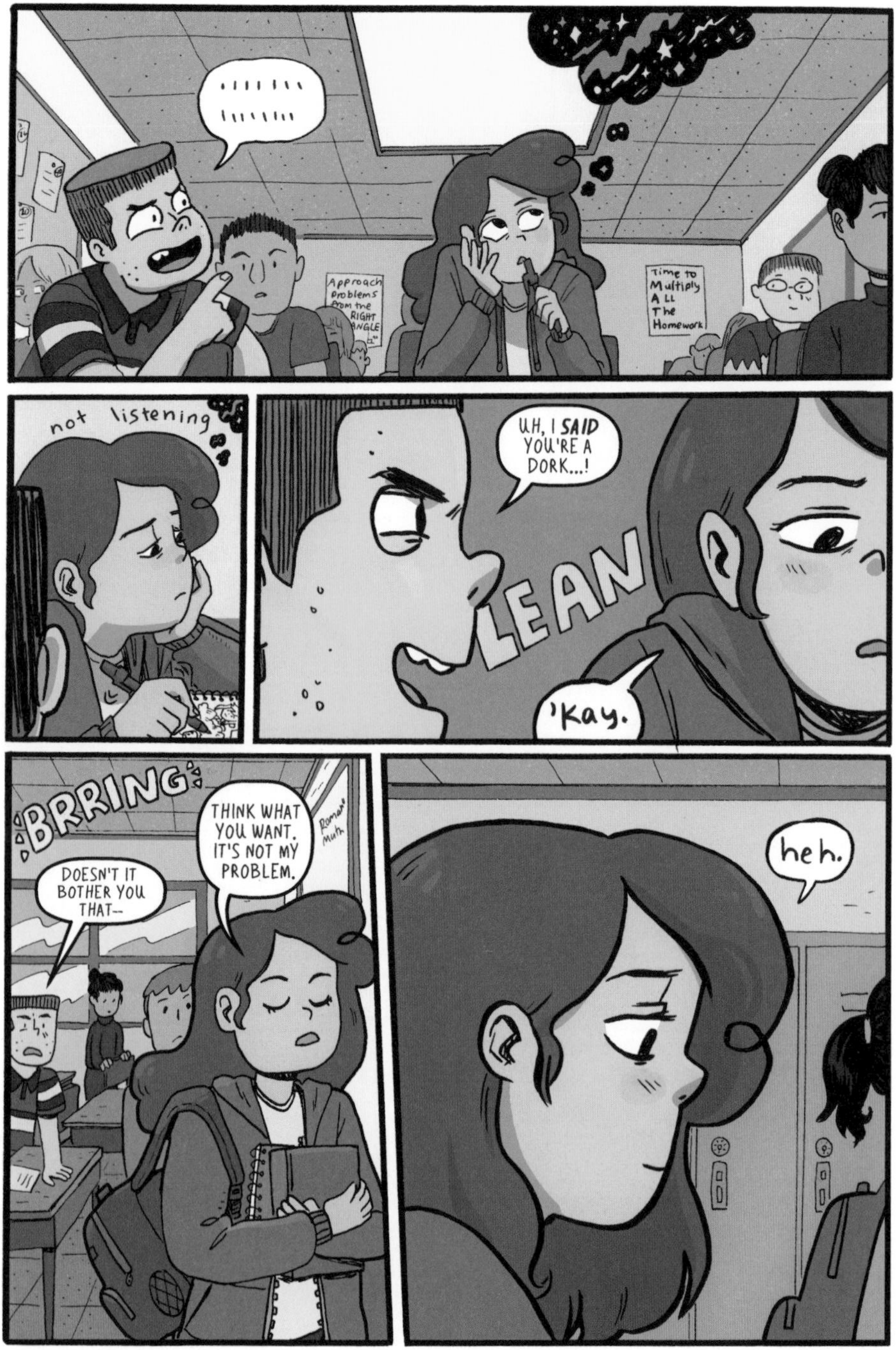
Approach problems from the RIGHT ANGLE
Time to Multiply ALL The Homework
not listening
UH, I SAID YOU'RE A DORK...!
LEAN
'Kay.
BRRING
Roman Math
DOESN'T IT BOTHER YOU THAT--
THINK WHAT YOU WANT. IT'S NOT MY PROBLEM.
heh.

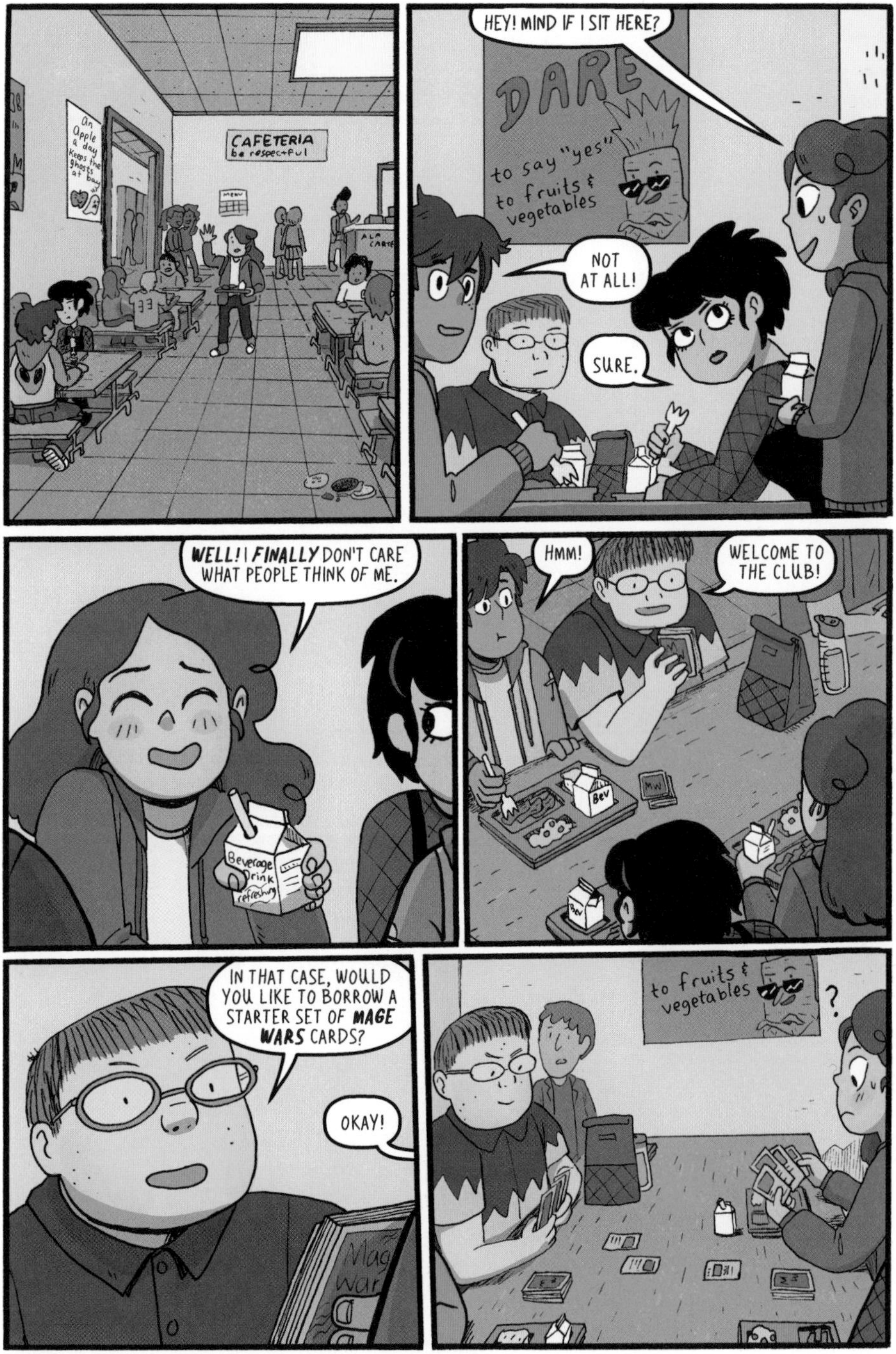
An Apple a day Keeps the ghosts at bay
CAFETERIA
be respectful
HEY! MIND IF I SIT HERE?
DARE
to say "yes" to fruits & vegetables
NOT AT ALL!
SURE.
WELL! I FINALLY DON'T CARE WHAT PEOPLE THINK OF ME.
Beverage Drink refreshing
HMM!
WELCOME TO THE CLUB!
Bev
MW
IN THAT CASE, WOULD YOU LIKE TO BORROW A STARTER SET OF MAGE WARS CARDS?
OKAY!
to fruits & vegetables
?

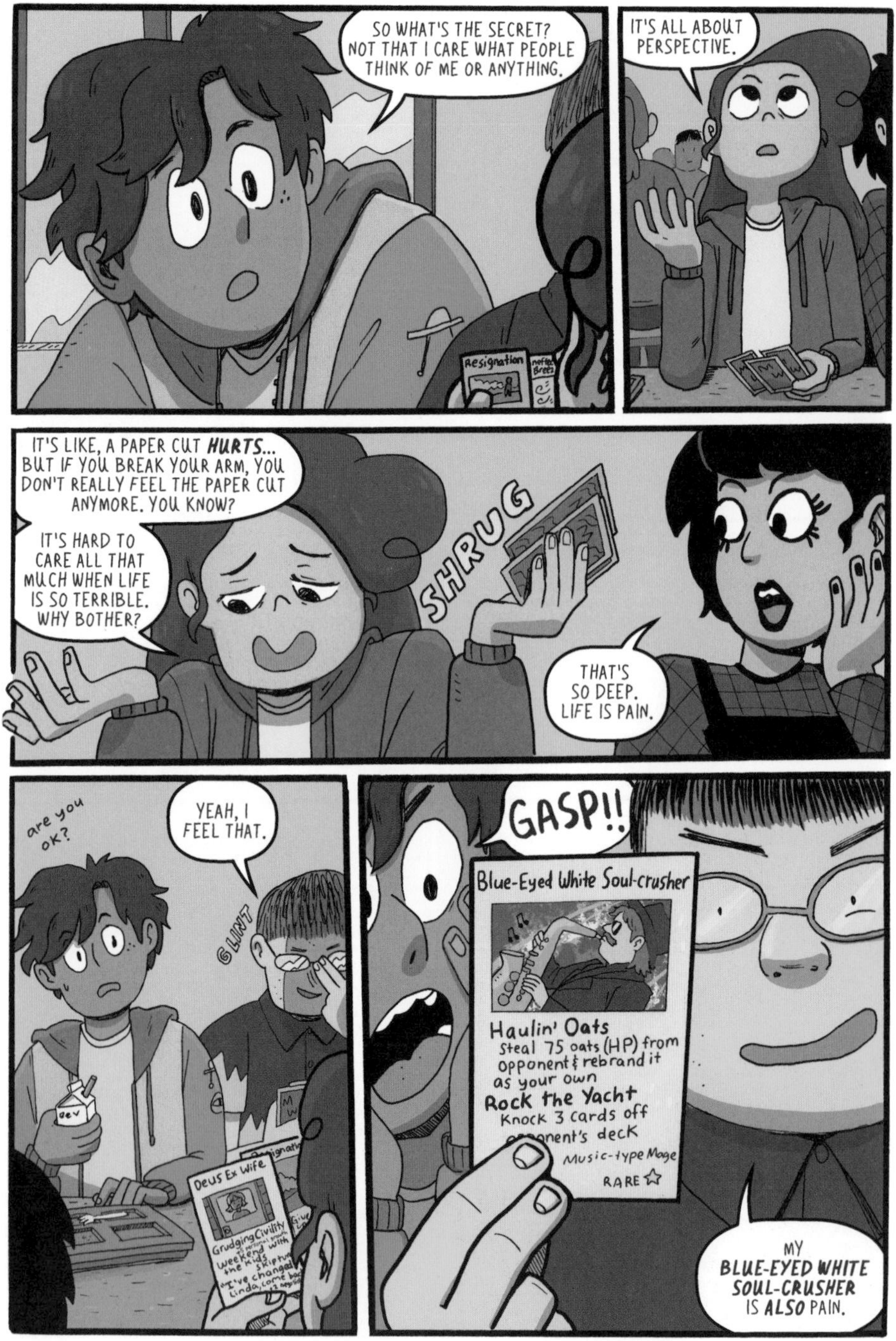
SO WHAT'S THE SECRET? NOT THAT I CARE WHAT PEOPLE THINK OF ME OR ANYTHING.
Resignation
IT'S ALL ABOUT PERSPECTIVE.
IT'S LIKE, A PAPER CUT **HURTS**... BUT IF YOU BREAK YOUR ARM, YOU DON'T REALLY FEEL THE PAPER CUT ANYMORE. YOU KNOW?
IT'S HARD TO CARE ALL THAT MUCH WHEN LIFE IS SO TERRIBLE. WHY BOTHER?
SHRUG
THAT'S SO DEEP. LIFE IS PAIN.
are you ok?
YEAH, I FEEL THAT.
GLINT
Deus Ex Wife
Grudging Civility
GASP!!
Blue-Eyed White Soul-crusher
Haulin' Oats
Steal 75 oats (HP) from opponent & rebrand it as your own
Rock the Yacht
Knock 3 cards off opponent's deck
Music-type Mage
RARE ☆
MY **BLUE-EYED WHITE SOUL-CRUSHER** IS **ALSO** PAIN.

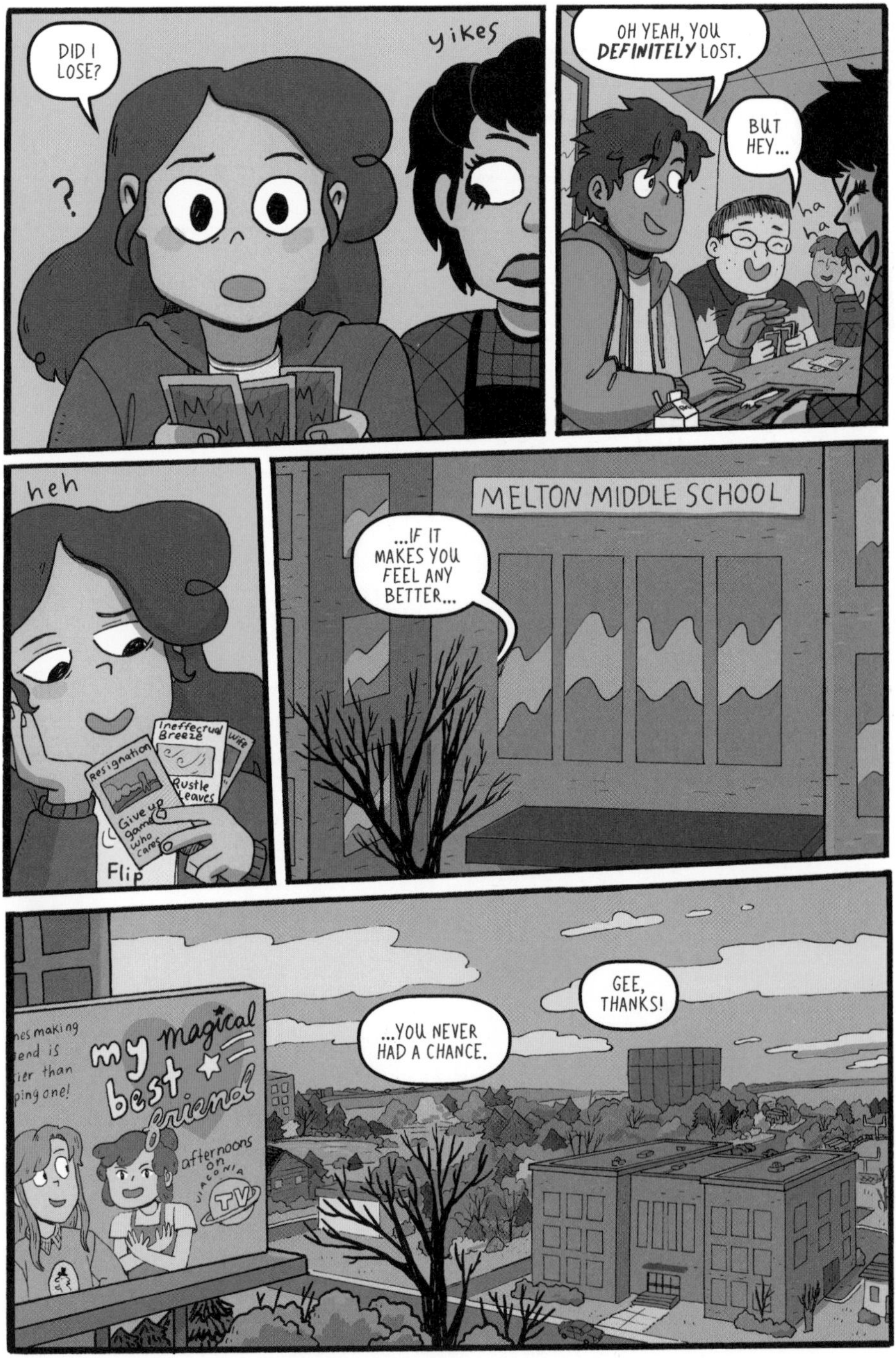
DID I LOSE?
?
yikes
OH YEAH, YOU **DEFINITELY** LOST.
BUT HEY...
ha ha
heh
Resignation
Ineffectual Breeze
Wife
Rustle Leaves
Give up game who cares
Flip
MELTON MIDDLE SCHOOL
...IF IT MAKES YOU FEEL ANY BETTER...
...YOU NEVER HAD A CHANCE.
GEE, THANKS!
my magical best friend
afternoons on VIACONIA
TV

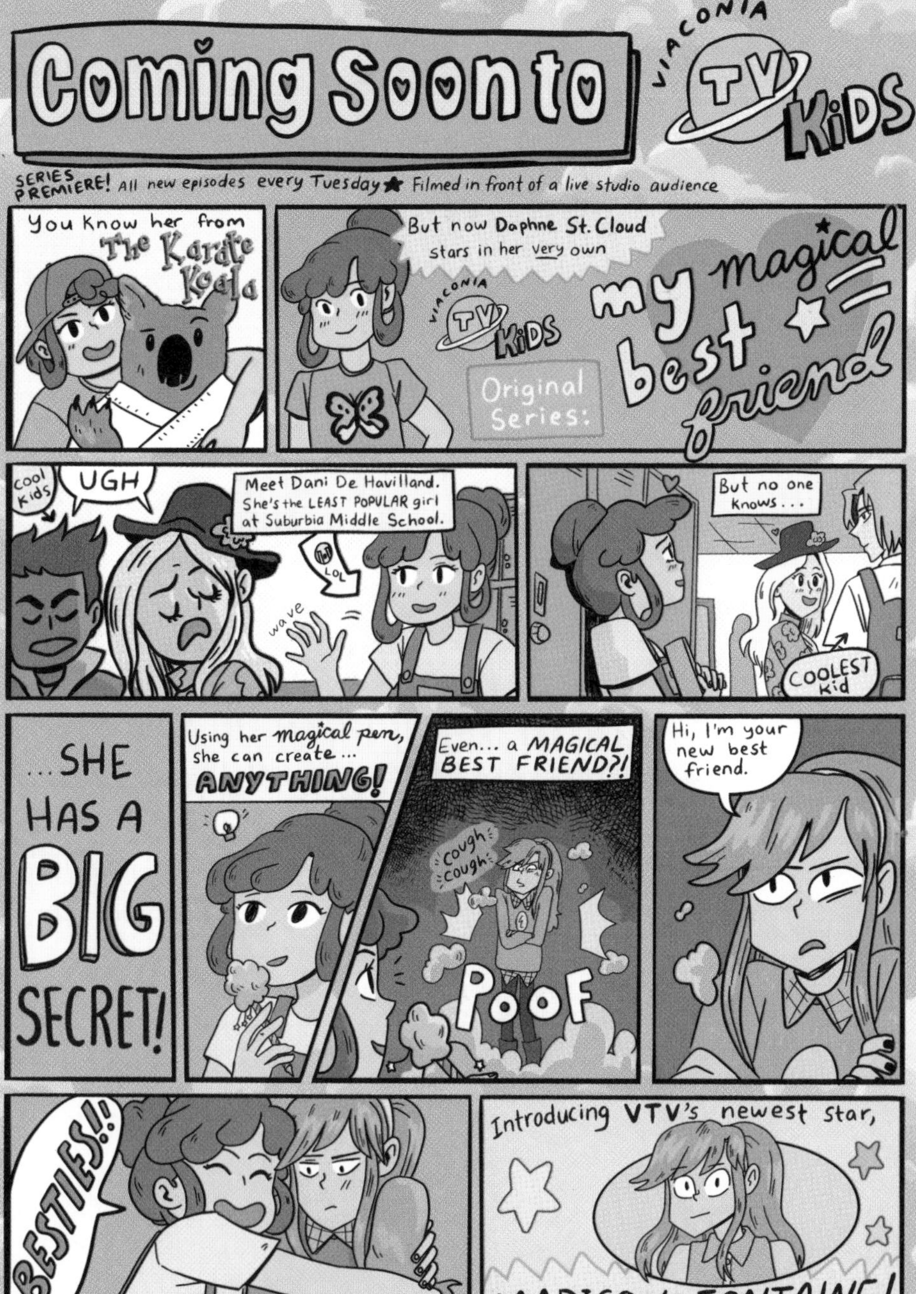
Coming Soon to
VIACONIA TV KiDS
SERIES PREMIERE! All new episodes every Tuesday ★ Filmed in front of a live studio audience
You know her from
The Karate Koala
But now Daphne St. Cloud stars in her very own
VIACONIA TV KiDS
Original Series:
my magical best friend
cool kids
UGH
Meet Dani De Havilland. She's the LEAST POPULAR girl at Suburbia Middle School.
LOL
wave
But no one knows . . .
COOLEST kid
. . . SHE HAS A BIG SECRET!
Using her magical pen, she can create . . . ANYTHING!
Even . . . a MAGICAL BEST FRIEND?!
cough cough
POOF
Hi, I'm your new best friend.
BESTIES!!
Introducing VTV's newest star,
MADISON FONTAINE!

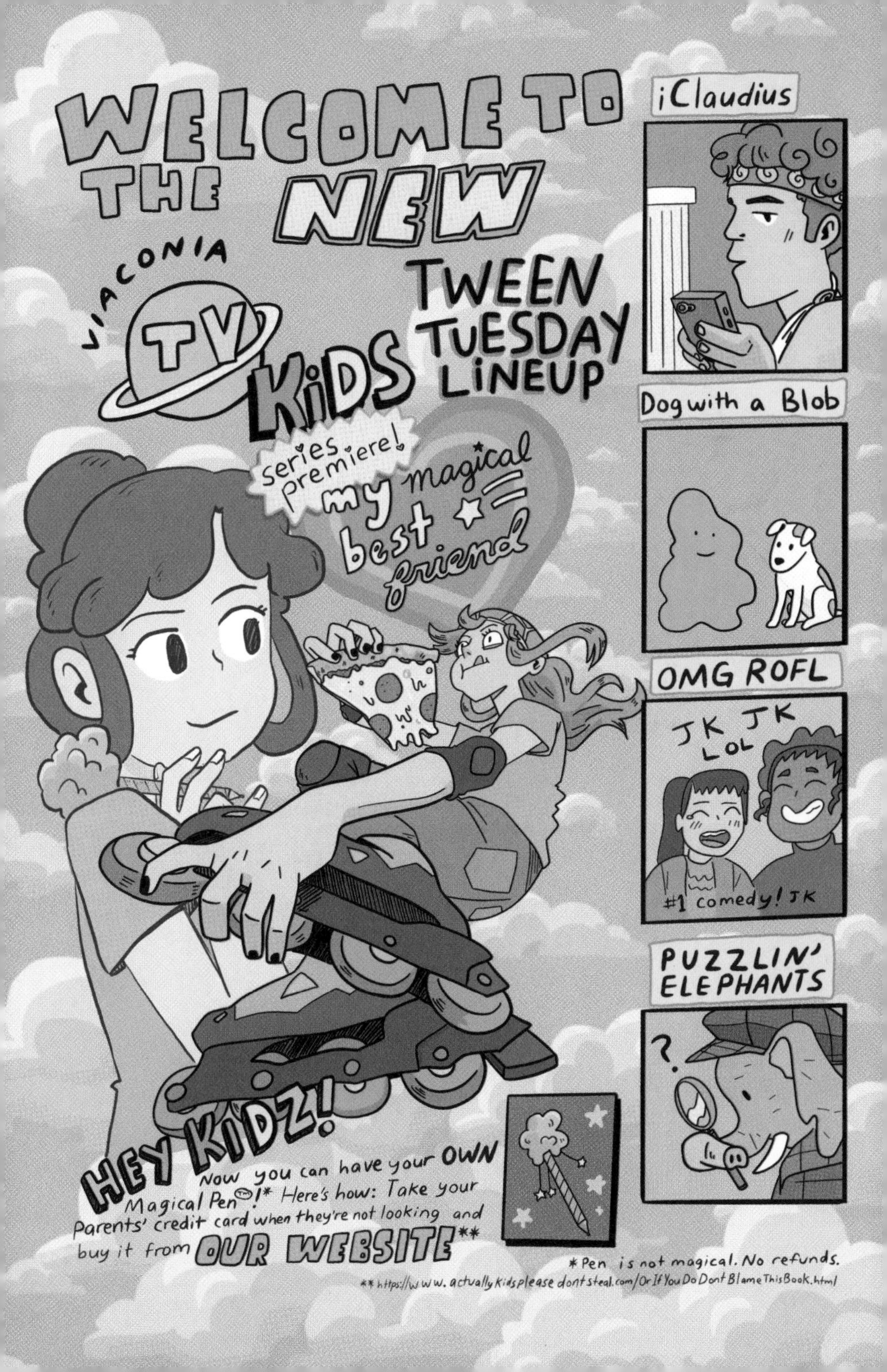
WELCOME TO THE NEW
VIACONIA TV KIDS
TWEEN TUESDAY LINEUP
series premiere!
my magical best friend
iClaudius
Dog with a Blob
OMG ROFL
JK JK LOL
#1 comedy! JK
PUZZLIN' ELEPHANTS
?
HEY KIDZ!
Now you can have your OWN Magical Pen™!* Here's how: Take your parents' credit card when they're not looking and buy it from OUR WEBSITE**
*Pen is not magical. No refunds.
**https://www.actuallykidspleasedontsteal.com/OrIfYouDoDontBlameThisBook.html

KRISTEN GUDSNUK

is the creator of MAKING FRIENDS, an IndieBound bestseller and YALSA Great Graphic Novels for Teens selection. The sequel, MAKING FRIENDS: BACK TO THE DRAWING BOARD, was included in the 2020 ILA Children's Choices reading list. She's also the writer and artist of the Minecraft comic series Wither Without You, and her Henchgirl comic series is being developed into a TV series for Freeform. Kristen was born in suburbia, didn't go to art school, and now lives in Queens, New York. Learn more about Kristen and her comics at kristengudsnuk.com.